MW01030593

REAPERS

BREAKERS, BOOK FOUR

~

EDWARD W. ROBERTSON

Cover art by Stephanie Mooney

ISBN: 1492184756
ISBN-13: 978-1492184751

To Geoff, who works like a crazy person to help me make these books better than I could ever do on my own.

I:

STRANGERS

1

Ever since Lucy had been born with her cord around her neck, her mother had told her she was living on borrowed time. Lucy thought her mom would change her tune when, at six years old, Lucy had got run over by a Cadillac in front of the house on Pine Street and stood up with nothing worse than a bloody knee, but it turned out Lucy just didn't know her mom. The old woman laughed and told her this was further proof the Reaper was eager to collect.

Same thing with the staph infection that hit her when she was twelve and the doctors had to plunk her in a tub of ice to keep her brain from boiling in her skull. Most of that week was a black hole, but as soon as her fever simmered down enough for Lucy to form memories again, the first thing she saw was her mother's crooked grin.

"Can you smell him?" The gaunt woman leaned forward, nosing at the air. All Lucy could smell was rubbing alcohol and antiseptic. Her mom sniffed theatrically. "He missed you again. Think he's teasing you?"

The tables turned when the Panhandler virus hit. Then it was Lucy's chance to watch from a chair while her mother burned up in bed. Lucy opened all the windows, but the spring breeze wasn't enough to chase out the stink of sick and blood. By the third day, her mom no longer spoke except to ask for water or to let Lucy know her spit cup was full.

"What do you think, Momma?" She meant to make it mocking, but she heard it come out scared. "Think he'll get me this time?"

Her mom's eyes were scratchy and opaque as the sand-worn

glass Lucy picked up on their yearly trips to Myrtle Beach. The woman made a stuttering, choking noise. Laughing.

"He got sick of trying to hunt you down," she groaned. "So he took the whole world instead."

She died a day later. Lucy never even got the sniffles. Since then, six years had trickled past and the world had gone pretty quiet, but the ghost in the black cassock still hadn't come her way. If she was living on borrowed time, she intended to default on the debt.

Where the man with the scythe had failed, however, the heat might just succeed. It was fall, but nobody had told southern Georgia that. She was biking up I-95 and the coastal humidity felt like God had declared a hangover on the whole damn world. Sweat beaded in the small of her back and soaked through the backs of her jeans. It made her mad, but that made her bike harder, thighs flexing as she climbed the grade, the straps of her bag digging into her tank-topped shoulders.

At least Florida was done. Just nine hundred-odd miles to go.

Bugs of all kinds whined from the thickets. Cars rusted on the shoulders of the highway, dust caked on the windows thicker than the sun-peeled paint. You wouldn't think a car would make for much of a planter, but that didn't stop the grass from sprouting where dirt collected in the creases of the hood and trunk. More than a few old wrecks had vines creeping up the side mirrors and antennas. Wouldn't be much longer till they were nothing more than vague shapes beneath the crawling green curtain.

She didn't bother checking them. No doubt plenty had keys—skeletons lolled over the wheels and slumped against the doors—but cars weren't immortal. By now, they were just as dead as their owners. Batteries failed like senile minds. Gas rotted in the tank. Aluminum bones, nothing more.

Before rolling out of Daytona, she had given serious thought to stealing Lloyd Dobson's pickup or Beau's little Honda, but Lloyd had seen to her after she'd broken her foot last year, and Beau was so crazy for his wimped-out little hybrid he would have tailed her all the way up the coast. Could have coaxed either to give her a ride, but that would have been to invite them into her business. Lloyd and Beau were good for certain things, but cunning wasn't one of them. Anyway, they'd just muck things up with Tilly.

So she'd taken her bike. Not a big deal. Might mean the ride took her two weeks instead of two days, but Lucy was in no great hurry. Most likely, Tilly was already dead.

In the meantime, it felt good to be propelled by leg power. Except for this hair-frizzing, patience-melting, underwear-soaking heat.

Around noon, she swerved into a truck stop to take some shade and water. The lot smelled like sun on leaves and it was hardly any cooler out of the sun than in it. She ate some pecans and drank from a scuffed plastic canteen. She'd kept the bottle deep inside her bag so it wouldn't go blood-warm, and the lukewarm water helped soothe the sweaty itchiness crawling over her body. She gazed into the woods with half a mind to find a creek. Still had half a gallon in her bag, but she was sweating hard and would run through it fast. Rinsing off would feel fine, too.

She got up to have a poke around, but before she'd taken two steps, a far-off hum swelled above the din of crickets. A car was coming.

She hefted her bag, shouldered her umbrella, and jogged out to the road, leaving her bike leaned against a gas pump. On the faded white line of the shoulder, she thrust out her thumb.

The car roared in from the south. Green sedan, engine growling like an affronted bear. Didn't take a genius to guess there'd be a man behind the wheel of a car like that. Lucy cocked her hip.

As it whooshed past, she got a look at its true colors. Camouflage. Its wind swept her hair past her face. She breathed out the start of a swear. The car braked hard, squealing like a stepped-on dog, smoked rubber billowing from its tires. It rocked to a stop in the middle of the road and sat there, idling.

Lucy waited three seconds to see if it would back up, then walked down the highway, letting her hips roll a bit. The smell of burnt tires boiled across the asphalt. It was a Charger and it might have been brand new when they stole it off the lot, but nobody had been manufacturing new cars since the plague. The trunk and back left wheel well had been bashed in and inexpertly hammered out, which explained the sloppy camo paint-over. A crack hairlined the rear window. But it moved plenty well.

A man in his mid-twenties sat behind the wheel, grinning, shirtless, sweat tracking through the black hairs on his sternum.

Lucy bent in for a closer look, getting a whiff of the AC, which had the smell of laundry left undried. It would soon fail.

The man in the passenger seat had a shaved head and wore a plain black tee that wouldn't show the sweat. In back, a third dude swept long black hair from his eyes and gnawed the nail of his ring finger, smiling past the seats. Same age as his friends, but clearly a boy.

"What's your name?" the driver said.

"Lucy," she said. After the virus, she'd thought about changing it completely—if the reaper were out looking for the girl with the cord around her throat, he'd walk right past her—but she didn't think he was so easily fooled. That, and Tilly wouldn't quit calling her by her given name.

To hedge her bets, she'd changed her last name instead. Anyway, it felt right. The old world died and a new one was born in its place. Anyone who'd made it through had been reborn, too. The first Lucy, Lucy One, she was long gone. In her place was Lucy Two.

"Jeremy." He stuck his hand out the window. His palm was damp and callused. "Where you headed, Lucy?"

"New York City."

"You're in luck, girl. We're headed to Philly. You lookin' for a ride?"

"Nah, I was just giving my thumb a stretch."

He snorted and narrowed his eyes. "We can't let any old body in the car. So we got an entrance exam. Just one question."

She knew what was coming. "What's that?"

"Grass, gas, or ass?" He grinned. The boy in the back giggled. The man with the shaved head made no sound at all.

"I'm sorry?" she smiled. Not that she didn't understand. She had gotten the message clear enough the first time she heard it when she was thirteen and hitching away from home. And more, she'd seen the message behind it: a threat, a crushing boot, a way to make her feel about the contents of her jeans the same way she felt about a sign advertising $2.98 per gallon. A commodity, and not a particularly expensive one.

People used words to put a pretty face on an ugly want. She liked to make them restate a thing to watch the mask slip. This was fun, which would have been enough, but more vital, it got you a crystal look at the person behind it.

"No such thing as a free ride," Jeremy said. "Question is, how do you want to pay?"

False-aggressive. The projection of confidence. But here he was dancing around the question. The fact he had to hide behind such an old cliche of the road spoke enough. And he was the driver.

She eyed him, mock-reproachful, then grinned and patted her shoulder-slung bag. "Might got some weed in here. Tobacco, too, if you prefer."

"That'll do," said the man with the shaved head.

Jeremy's grin went hard. "I prefer to taste it first. But if it's no good, we got other options."

The boy in the back kept biting his nail. Exhaust drifted from the idling car. Jeremy popped the trunk latch and stepped into the sunlight. "Let's get your bags there."

"No need," Lucy said. "I travel light."

He gazed at the umbrella angled on her shoulder. "Expecting rain?"

"Sooner or later."

"Suit yourself."

He walked around to the rear passenger door and held it open. The inside of the car smelled like male sweat, towels at the bottom of a hamper, and stale body spray. She set her bags on the floorboard and climbed in. When she looked up, Jeremy was gazing at her chest. He smirked and closed the door.

He accelerated hard. The musty AC didn't reach the back seats. The man with the shaved head handed her a handkerchief. She dabbed her temples and collarbone.

"Where you from, Lucy?" Jeremy called from up front.

"St. Augustine," she said, which was a lie. "You know it?"

"I had a cousin there," said the boy beside her. His name was Tommy. The man with the shaved head was named Wilson and he did nothing but stare out the window at the wall of trees and vines.

"The Big Apple," Jeremy said after a couple seconds. "What's a girl want with a place like that?"

He was watching her from the rearview. Lucy met his gaze. "Meeting a friend."

"What's his name?"

"Tilly."

"Tilly?" Jeremy chuckled. "That's a thousand-mile walk from Florida. Figured it had to be a man at the end of the line."

"The world's full of surprises," Lucy said. "Where are you from?"

"Here and there." There was nothing witty about it, but Tommy burst out laughing. Jeremy sniffed and rubbed his mouth. "So how about a smoke?"

She smiled crookedly. Some people liked to barter with gold necklaces and platinum rings. Some carried heavy sacks of yams to swap. Others used bullets or shotgun shells, which was smart because often the people you wanted things from most treated ammo like cash, and you had to be a real wizard to cook that stuff up on your own. Even Beau couldn't get the gunpowder recipe right. Had cost him half a finger. Lots of work.

So Lucy traded in drugs. None of the hard shit; that too was heavy with effort. Much easier to loot a pharmacy and swap hydros, Tylenol, and Percocet for anything she needed. Funny thing, almost right away, people started asking her for caffeine, too. At first she'd dealt it in pills, but she soon found out they accepted coffee just as readily, including the freeze dried kind that would stay good from now until dinosaurs once more roamed the earth.

The problem with all these pills and powders was they ran out. She wasn't the only looter out there. Around the third year after the Panhandler virus had mown down everyone employed in producing new pills and powders, her supplies ran dry. Could maybe scrounge more going door to door from sunup to sundown, but again, that was an awful lot of work. And the thinking was very short-term.

Before running completely dry, she transitioned her business to a sustainable, Earth-friendly model: products that literally grew themselves and didn't need more prep than a bit of curing. Marijuana and tobacco. Properly dried, they hardly weighed a thing. The market thrived, too. Something about the apocalypse had flipped on the libertine switch in people. Just about everyone enjoyed the occasional puff of one or the other or both. These days, there weren't too many other ways to relax.

In the car, she carried baggies of both, Ziplocked to cut down on the smell of earth, pine, skunk, and raisins, which could get overwhelming when in quantity. She had pre-rolled joints, too. She fetched one from her bag, lit it, and passed it to Jeremy.

He sniffed it, gaze flicking between the smoke and the road, then inhaled.

"How is it, man?" Tommy said.

"Give me a second," Jeremy said, whiffs of smoke escaping with each word. He blew out a big blue cloud and laughed. "Picking you up was the best idea I ever had, Lucy."

He handed it to Wilson, who took his turn and passed it to Lucy. Tommy watched her without complaining that he was to be last. It was his place and he knew it.

They finished up and Jeremy rolled down the windows to clear the car, which now smelled like a pine forest had been wadded up and stuffed in the bottom of a sleeping bag and forgotten about for three or four months. Trees flashed by the window. For a while, each of them went as quiet as Wilson, except to laugh stutteringly or point out crows hopping alongside the road. The sun hid down behind the trees but it was still humid and no matter which way Lucy positioned her limbs they wound up sticky with sweat.

Jeremy cruised past Savannah. They stopped at the turnoff to Charleston to eat. Lucy still had food of her own, but Wilson handed her a twist of dried meat. It was chewy and stringy and gamey.

"Rabbit?" she asked.

He shrugged. "Mostly."

They got back on the road. Lucy produced another joint. She would have known where to stop for water in Florence, they had a nice little river there socked in among the trees, but the car was fully loaded and Jeremy didn't pull over until it was dark and the headlights played across the brick homes of Richmond. He pulled up in front of a house with plenty of space between it and the neighbors. Crickets sang from the woods, troubling Lucy with a memory she couldn't place. Wilson got out a pistol and chambered a round and walked up to the porch. He opened the door and slipped inside.

A couple minutes later, he walked out and crunched down the drive to the car, tucking the pistol into the back of his jeans. He leaned into the open window. "Nothing."

Jeremy nodded. "See you around back."

Tommy touched Lucy's arm and smiled wincingly. She grabbed her pack and umbrella. Tommy and Wilson shouldered gear from the car and walked through the weeds to the back. Jeremy swung off the drive into the grass, lights off, and took the car to the back yard where you couldn't see it from the street. Lucy sucked on her teeth. Could have more brains than she'd given them credit for.

Except the first thing Jeremy did after he parked was to light a fire in the yard. They had dry food and the night was as hot as an armpit, but some people just got to have a fire. While he poked at the logs, Lucy helped Wilson set up the tent.

"You know why we stopped using tents?" she said. "Because we invented roofs."

Wilson threaded a spindly pole through the tent's eyelets and moved to the next corner. "There ain't always roofs."

"There's one tonight."

"And when there aren't, best to be used to it."

Waste of time, but she helped anyway. The tent was roomy and smelled like old grass and staticky plastic. She wasn't the least concerned about sharing it with them and was beginning to believe she had misread Wilson.

They sat around the fire and passed around dried meat and unleavened bread. At Jeremy's prompting, she lit a third joint. As she prepared to hand it over, he sat beside her and took it from her, fingers brushing.

"Bet you were scared to get in the car," he said. "But we're not so bad, are we?"

She squinted against the campfire smoke. "So far."

He laughed. A quarter of the way around the fire, Tommy watched them, sweeping his hair from his eyes. Later, when they were proper destroyed, Jeremy rested his hand on her thigh. She picked it up and returned it to his lap and drew her feet close to her body. He smiled hard, eyes shining in the light of the fire.

"I'm beat." Wilson stood, arching his back. He raised his brows at her. "You beat?"

"Does stoned count?" she said, and they all laughed, even Jeremy. She went to the tent and brushed her teeth with water. Inside, she lay down under her thinnest sheet, but even that was too hot. Someone crawled through the flap and she reached for her umbrella.

"Just me," Wilson said.

He retired to his sleeping bag and soon snored in the darkness. Lucy lay with her eyes open. Two pairs of feet shushed through the grass, fading into the distance. Fifteen minutes later, the steps returned and Jeremy and Tommy climbed inside. She pretended to sleep until both of them snored as well.

The heat woke her before the sun could slash into the tent. Her clothes were getting grimy, so she headed into the house, a creaking and dusty old place, and found a t-shirt that was a pretty good fit. She stripped off her sweat-crusted tank top and pitched it into a corner. She had no use for it anymore.

The boys got up and they ate and got on their way. No one had much interest in talk and she gazed out the window for signs of human life. Trees stared back. Jeremy stopped the car just past Baltimore to grab a bite and stretch his legs. Lucy went for a walk into the woods. She didn't go far and the men's voices drifted on the damp air. When she climbed back on the shoulder, they stopped chatting and waited for her to get in the car.

This far north, the day cooled down a bit, but humidity clung to the horizons in a white haze, softening the sprawl of cities and townships. The highway jogged through Delaware and then into Jersey, the sunken lanes buffered by tall corrugated walls.

Jeremy didn't wait until they got to Philadelphia. With the road still nestled below the sound-dampening barrier walls, he let the camo Charger coast to a stop and cut the engine.

He twisted in his seat. "You got a cigarette in that bag of yours?"

"Hope unfiltered isn't too strong for you," she said.

He rolled his eyes. She reached into her bag and got out two hand-rolled and hand-grown twists of shredded tobacco. Jeremy lit up, inhaled, and drew back his head, holding the white cigarette away from his face.

"Tastes funny."

"That's because it's real."

He brought it to his lips and took a drag and let the smoke trickle from his nose like some sort of gangster. "Three of us had a talk, Lucy."

She cocked her head. "What about, Jeremy?"

"New York is dangerous. We don't want you to go there by your lonesome. You should come with us."

"That's mighty generous, but I need to find my friend."

He nodded, gazing across the highway at the rusted-out cars, blowing smoke from the corner of his mouth. "We can't let you leave, Lucy. For your own good."

She raised her brows at Wilson. "You agree with him?"

Wilson glanced at Jeremy and for just a second she thought he might buck orders. And if he bucked, that was the end of it; he followed because of his daddy issues or because Jeremy owned the car or what have you, but if Wilson ever stood up for himself, he'd discover he was the real authority here.

But an angry look came into his eye and he wouldn't quite meet her gaze. "It don't have to be like that. We can be partners."

Lucy set her umbrella across her lap and tucked her knees together. "And if I don't want to be partners? If I get out and walk?"

Jeremy reached into the gap between the driver's seat and the gear shift and withdrew a chrome .45. "There's bad men out there, Lucy. You wouldn't last a day."

Lucy couldn't say she was surprised. When a man saw a woman on the road, he saw a trip that could only end in rape or death. Something about that sight in their mind's eye made too many of them plenty happy to take on the role for themselves and ensure it came to pass.

She had to admit she got a kick out of teaching them to expand their minds.

She jerked her head at Tommy. "You really that tired of fucking him? He looks pretty cute to me."

The three of them gaped. Jeremy's hand moved on the pistol. She spat her cigarette in his face, swung up her umbrella, and pulled the custom trigger of the pistol-grip shotgun that composed the umbrella's handle and shaft. The bang was loud enough to blind a man. The top of Jeremy's head vanished. The driver side window shattered. A hail of safety glass bounced across the road.

Wilson grabbed for the umbrella's closed spokes. Lucy swung down from his grasp and shot him in the solar plexus. He banged into the door and collapsed over the gear shift. She turned, tucking her shoulder against her head in case Tommy had a mind to sock her one, but he'd flung open the door and scrambled onto the asphalt.

She scooted out into the afternoon sunlight and whistled. "Stop right there, boy."

Tommy's shoes skidded in the overgrown grass of the median. He turned with great reluctance, as if fearing she'd shoot as soon as she saw the whites of his eyes.

She aimed the umbrella at his chest. "I want that car, Tommy."

"Take it!"

"I would, but someone has made a terrible mess of it. Mind running a rag around it for me?"

He dry-heaved. "You'll shoot me after."

"Could be. I will certainly shoot you if you don't."

Blinking back tears, he walked toward her. "All our blankets and such are in the trunk."

"I seen your rifles in there, too. So don't try to get smart with me."

Keeping the gun on him, she opened the driver's door. Jeremy spilled onto the pavement. Gunk sopped from the bowl of his skull. She kicked him out of the way, took his pistol, and knelt to pull the trunk release at the base of the door frame. Finished, she circled around Tommy, keeping the umbrella pointed square at his chest. He extracted an armful of blankets from the trunk.

"And get those pants off you, for God's sake," Lucy said. "I do not want you leaking piss in my brand new car."

Miserably, he wiggled out of his jeans and peeled away his soaking briefs. His balls were shriveled against his body. He opened Wilson's door and lowered the body to the pavement. Inside the car, he tried to swab up the mess with the blankets, but much of it was heavy and thick and he had to scoop it out with his bare hands. He began to cry, retching between sobs.

"Don't you feel sorry for them," Lucy said. "All I wanted was a ride. Your friends were the ones who decided to get violent."

Tommy didn't reply, but he stopped crying, indicating there was a hint of steel in his spine after all. She wasn't worried. If Jeremy and Wilson had been sharks, Tommy was a remora, there to remind the sharks they were big, grateful to snatch up the scraps that tumbled from their toothful mouths.

He went to the trunk for a fresh blanket and pressed it into the puddled blood. Once it was sodden, he faced her, hands stained red. He wore a dark t-shirt and his thighs were bright white and squiggly with long black hairs.

"I can't get any more," he said. "I need some water or something."

"It's okay, Tommy. You done just fine."

The anger he'd built up swabbing the hot, bloody car fled from his face. "I did what you wanted. I cleaned it best I could."

"I know." She let the tip of the umbrella droop. "Now git."

He glanced down the highway. "I ain't got no pants."

"And I got a gun in my hand and a yearning to use it."

Tommy let out a shuddery breath, then bolted down the black asphalt. She watched him go, then consulted her map, turned on the Charger, and drove north. With the late afternoon light bouncing from Manhattan's distant towers, she pulled into the Knickerbocker Country Club, which was the funniest thing she'd seen all day, and stashed the car. The boys had a lot of goods in their trunk and it was close enough to retreat to should the city prove a challenge.

Before walking to the bridge into Manhattan, she made sure to oil and clean her umbrella. Based on Tilly's letter, she was all but certain her friend was dead. And that meant she had a lot more killing to do.

2

When her one and only daughter announced she was getting married, Ellie's first response was not her proudest one.

"Who?"

"Who?" Dee honked with laughter. "The drifter who slept behind the Masons' barn last winter. I'm pregnant, but despite the fact he's a toothless hobo, he wants to do the right thing."

Ellie gazed across the sunlit kitchen and thought unparental thoughts about the girl she'd rescued from New York when the plague's shadow fell over the world. "Tell me you're not actually pregnant."

Dee raised a brow. "Would you kick me out?"

"Of course not. But I might kick Quinn Tolbert's balls into the lake."

"You're supposed to be happy."

"For the sake of clarity—and Quinn's balls—will you answer the question?"

Dee sighed and stared at the light on the lake past the window. "Not that I know of. So you can stop strangling that rolling pin."

Ellie glanced down at her hands, which were whitened with flour and her death-knuckle grip on the pin she'd been using to roll out the week's bread. She went frozen with a sudden case of Split.

She'd first heard the word in town and understood its meaning at once: the disconnect that came when your brain, focused on its daily tasks, remembered how different your life used to be before the two apocalypses. She, for instance, had once been incapable of cooking anything more complex than macaroni. Instead, she'd ordered takeout four times a week and nuked leftovers on the days in between. Between college, post-grad, and the DAA, she'd never had time to cook, let alone to learn how to do it.

But first and foremost, cooking was women's work. While the DAA had been progressive in hiring, in general attitude, it was positively caveman. Half its agents thought of themselves as the techno-analyst version of James Bond while the other half saw themselves as the techno-analyst Jason Bourne. In that environment, the women had to out-man the men. So hell no she didn't know how to cook. Cooking was for housewives.

Then the plague taught her how few meals could be eaten completely raw. Particularly when you lived in a seasonal place like the Adirondack mountains, where frost and snow meant edible plants were only available in quantity for half the year at best.

So she had learned, bit by bit, to cook. Starting with boiled pasta and rice, with chicken and veggies stir-fried in a pan atop the wood stove. And after a few months, when she hadn't yet burned down the house, and learned that as long as you were paying attention, it was hard to utterly destroy food, she discovered cooking wasn't all that hard. In fact, the power of deduction told her that people had probably been doing it for thousands of years.

After an enthusiastic couple years of experiments and kitchen enhancements, she'd settled down, favoring methods that produced the most food for the least effort. With the exception of harvest season, for the last four years, she'd spent every Wednesday baking bread in the brick oven in the yard. And she thought nothing of it. In fact, she looked forward to it.

The end of the world was a hell of a thing.

She set down the pin and dusted flour from her palms and took a deep breath. "If you're happy, I'm happy."

Dee glanced over her shoulder, as if sharing a look with someone who wasn't there, and laughed. "No you're not."

"If you're happy, then I will make minimal criticism of your rash and foolish decisions involving people of questionable character."

"You think Quinn is questionable?"

"I haven't decided. His dad sure is."

"Well, we're getting married in the spring." Dee lifted the lid from the block of white cheese Ellie kept on the counter and inspected it for mold. "So you've got plenty of time to decide whether you like the people who will soon be part of your life forever."

"The spring?" Ellie said. "Why so long?"

Her nonbiological child gaped in affront. "Invitations? The food? The dress? We'll be lucky to be ready by next fall."

She knifed a wedge of cheese from the block and walked outside, shaking her head. The screen door banged. Beyond the window, Dee wandered to the dock and stood at the edge, munching the cheese, watching the yellow mountain light shimmer on the waves of the lake.

Ellie closed her eyes. Sometimes she didn't understand her daughter at all.

She didn't see much of Dee for the next week. Not that there was anything wrong between them. As far as she knew, anyway, although she'd grown old enough to recognize her habit of assuming everything was fine unless someone explicitly said otherwise. Which, in practice, proved to be one more example of a rational stance spoiled by irrational humans.

But in this case, she felt reasonably confident Dee's physical distance had less to do with ill will toward Ellie and more to do with her love for the Tolbert kid—or her love for their looming nuptials. With sudden horror, Ellie knew Dee would ask her to bake the cake.

It was October, however, and this new doomsday was slated for April. Or possibly May. In fact, all the details remained scant. Instead, their talk seemed to be geared toward preparing for the preparations themselves.

Ellie didn't understand it in the slightest. Weddings were one of the few things the Panhandler virus had made better. If Dee and Quinn wanted, they could row out to the island and be married this afternoon. Dee could throw a bouquet picked from the shore. Do you love each other? Then quit worrying about the color of the napkins and go start your lives together.

She punched her dough and flipped it on the floured counter. As it thumped, someone knocked at the front door. Ellie's shoulders jumped. She sighed and rinsed her hands in the bucket of lake water, thumbing clumps of flour off her fingers. Out front, George Tolbert stood on the porch, a smile slanting his lips, backlit by the yellow October light.

"Mizz Colson," he said.

She didn't bother to inform him that she was technically a miss. "Hello, George."

"May I step inside the abode?"

A sudden imp tempted her to say no. George Tolbert smiled too much. He paid more attention to the cleanliness of his clothes than his fields. And that drawl of his. It added up to a charming and not uneducated Southern man of the land, a fellow who could get along with Appalachian dirt farmers just as readily as Upper West Side professors.

And that was exactly why Ellie disliked him.

"Yeah," she said. "Kitchen's a mess."

"Mess is nothing more than a welcome sign of honest labor." He stepped over the threshold. His aphorisms sounded as old as the colonies, maybe even the Greeks, but as far as Ellie knew, they were original. Drove her batty.

She offered him a seat in the shade of the back porch. "Care for some tea?"

His elegant little eyebrows crawled up his forehead. "You have tea?"

"Brewed from the finest weeds I can find."

If he was disappointed, he hid it well. "Splendid."

She nodded and excused herself. She kept a red cooler in the shallows under the dock where the mountain-fed waters of the Lower Saranac kept her tea a few degrees from chilly. She opened the cooler and fetched the metal jug out of the water inside. It dripped all the way back to the porch.

"Take sugar?" she said.

George smiled. "Any chance I get."

She was hoping he'd say no—she had a couple hundred pounds of the stuff tubbed in the cellar, but once it was gone, it was gone for good—but gave him two spoonfuls anyway. Resentment spiked through her gut. Based on her and Dee's usage, she knew exactly how long that sugar should last. Visits like this threw that figure off. Meanwhile, she had dough waiting on the counter.

George sipped his tea and smacked his lips, though she suspected that was to hide an involuntary wrinkle of his nose. "Reminds me of the old days. You do well for yourself, Ellie. Commendable blend of the old and the new. Or should that be the old and the medieval?"

"Thanks," she said, ignoring his philosophizing. She sprawled in a chair and drank her tea, which she'd intended to cool down with after a long afternoon working the oven. "What brings you across the lake?"

"Nothing less than the blessed union of our two children." He smiled wryly, eyes crinkling. "Though to speak in confidence, I cannot wait for the day it's over."

"Tell me about it."

"The list of wants they've compiled—why, we might have to hire help from town."

Ellie shrugged. "If they want bells and whistles, I better see less talking and more working. These fields won't harvest themselves."

George laughed. "Maybe they would if we had a few more kids."

Despite herself, she laughed too. "Why hire help when you can give birth to it?"

George grinned, rolling his glass of tea between his hands. Condensation slipped to the patio. He nodded for several seconds, smile fading. "Since we've broached the subject that brought me here, I'll dare to crash brazenly forward. Fact is, we are about to incur certain expenses. Not just in raw materials, but in time. Something I have precious little of this time of year."

Ellie glanced toward the yellow wheat swaying beside the lake. "I'm right there with you."

"Well, I face an additional wrinkle. I'm having problems with my tractor, Ellie."

She chuckled. "There are days it feels like I spend more time keeping them running than I save by using them."

"Indeed. I believe I have worked mine to death at the moment I need it most." He bit his lip and lowered his eyes. "I'm not too proud to confess I'm in trouble. Any other year, I'd muddle on through, but with those two kids at my house, eating up my larder when I ought to be filling it for winter, not to mention the coming celebration..."

"Yes?"

"I was searching for the right words to a delicate question. Having failed to find them, I will employ these instead. Forgive me for noticing you've got a spare machine."

She stopped herself from sighing. "With something this vital, I like to have insurance."

"Does it run?"

"What do you think?"

He worried his lip and gazed across the lake. "Then I wonder if, for the sake of our two families—which I suppose are about to become one—I could use it."

"Yeah, you can borrow it," she said, although she was stingy by nature and the very thought of watching him drive off on the backup she had spent so many hours maintaining caused her skin to constrict. "I shouldn't need it this harvest."

"I appreciate that. I'll have to come begging again for the spring planting, though. Given that we might soon have hungry new mouths to feed, I wonder if I might simply have it."

"Have it," Ellie repeated. "Hold on. Are you talking about a dowry?"

George Tolbert cocked his head, eyes snapping to hers. "I'm asking for help guaranteeing this family's future. I'm about to absorb considerable expense."

"I'm not?"

"I'll level with you. Quinn doesn't know it, but I'm struggling to put food on the table. These days my cellar stores more air than grain. As you stand more able to withstand the coming tax on our resources, and have a spare machine where I have none, I thought it made sense to ask."

"For a dowry." Ellie set down her tea with a clink of glass on glass. "Sooner or later my John Deere is going to wheeze its last, George. When that happens, I'll need a replacement. That's why I made sure to find the time to get one running. You can borrow it this fall. Then I suggest you spend the winter finding one for yourself."

His eyes went hooded. "Working machines are few and far between."

"George, why do I believe your conversion to communism was sudden and recent? Find one that's broken and fix it."

George set his tea on the patio table, glaring at the bits of weeds floating in the bottom of the glass. "I hope it's that simple, Ellie, but lives are like words: the plainest ones are the hardest earned. I'll send Quinn around for the tractor. I appreciate its use."

She saw him to the door and watched him walk down the path

through the trees. For now the path was clear, but in a few weeks it would lie under a crunching carpet of orange and yellow leaves. With Dee occupied at the Tolberts', Ellie would have to rake them for herself. There was always too much work and too few hands.

Resentment welled in her chest. She had brought Dee to the Saranacs for the specific purpose of getting away from every last human being. To avoid the plague, but also to avoid the chaos that would come after. At first, they'd been alone here, but in the intervening years, settlers had trickled in, drawn to the lakes' fresh water, fish, and isolation. Hardly five miles away, an actual village cropped up in Lake Placid. For the last couple years, Ellie had toyed with the idea of relocating, plunging deeper into the mountains, perhaps even to Canada, but it was too late. Dee was entangled. There would be no tearing her away from the bonds tying her to Quinn.

And thus to George. Who couldn't be bothered to find himself a new god damn tractor. This was the problem with planning ahead. Rarely did it benefit you. Instead, it benefited those who didn't, and who had no shame in asking you for what you'd worked to build for yourself. Same old ant and grasshopper bullshit.

George, at least, would go no further than wheedling to try to get his hands on what she'd built. High-end, utterly shameless wheedling, sure—if she hadn't agreed to lend him the tractor, she was certain he would have sent Quinn to ask again, banking that the boy's doe-like good nature and connection to Dee would do the trick—but that's where it would end.

She couldn't say the same for the people in Lake Placid. Especially those who lived just outside town. If their farms failed, and they had no one to turn to, they wouldn't throw up their hands and agreeably starve. They'd come for people like Ellie. She didn't know most of them. She'd be nothing more than an exploitable resource. A couple of the business-owners liked to call Lake Placid a "community," but it was no such thing. All they had in common was they knew where Ellie lived, and that she had food.

Wind gushed through the turning leaves. It was chilly and smelled like the clean water of the lake. A strange fear took her. She walked briskly toward the lake until she could see her fields along its shore. The heavy-headed wheat bobbed in the wind, yellow and ready. She'd put together a few acres. It saw her and Dee through the long winter and inconstant spring, with enough left over to barter grain and bread in Lake Placid.

When the wind had flowed through the leaves a moment ago, she had been momentarily convinced her fields had disappeared, stolen or dead overnight. The sight of the golden blanket calmed her heart. Made her feel foolish. It was something about George Tolbert. His life in this new world was so careless, so clearly precarious it made her fearful for her own.

Her crankiness returned. Typically, she had no interest in anyone's business but her own, but George was right. They were about to become family.

Time for some field work.

She went home to bake bread, smoke roiling from the outdoor brick oven and filtering through the slits she'd cut in the canopy. She worked in a sleeveless shirt but the heat of the bricks was relentless. Shuttling dough in and loaves out, she quickly sweated through her clothes. The sun died behind the mountains, casting the lake into shadow. Ellie shivered and brought the last of the loaves inside.

She lit candles and sat in the chair by the bay windows overlooking the lake and wished for the thousandth time for caffeine. She used to run on the stuff. Thick espresso, which cut back on bathroom breaks and allowed her to drink it in shots that jumpstarted her mornings. She hadn't tasted fresh beans in three years—June 14, to be precise—when a man with a Caribbean accent had rolled into Lake Placid with a sack full of the stuff. The streets filled with the caramel-soot smell of the roast. She bought two pounds at a dear price and prayed the man would return. Three years later, she was still waiting.

Meanwhile, forty pounds of freeze dried crystals sat in the cellar in their proud red tubs, but it wasn't the same. And unless she had a fire going, she'd have to bank the stove and boil water, all for a thin brownish liquid that just made her wish for the real thing.

But she was nodding off, sapped by the day of baking and dealing with George. And she had nothing better to do. She headed downstairs for a tub of instant coffee and built up the fire in the indoor hearth and boiled a kettle. Twenty minutes later, she had her brew, wincing at the weak and stale taste.

She read a Terry Pratchett novel and watched the moon move on the waves. She didn't expect Dee back that night, but she waited to dress until ten o'clock—she had no clock, but she'd learned to read the stars well enough—and then donned black from head to toe, including a cap over her dark hair. She brought binoculars and a heavy pistol. The community hadn't weathered any raiders for close to three years, but you never know when you might run into wild dogs.

The night was cool and smelled of the lake. A low breeze rattled the leaves, the first of which began to fall in fluttering silhouettes. She had a five-mile walk ahead of her, but that was fine. Would ensure the Tolbert home was fast asleep. These days, people tended to go to bed not long after the sun.

The lake washed calmly at the shore. Perch and bass broke the surface with silent ripples. She followed the path, avoiding crunching leaves. An owl screeched from the hills. After a few minutes of brisk walking, she warmed inside her clothes.

She kept one eye out for lights and one ear out for voices, but encountered no sign of human life until she circled the lake and crested the short ridge above George Tolbert's fields. A quarter mile away, his house sat on the north shore, perfectly dark.

Even before she got out her binoculars, she could tell there was something wrong with his fields.

They were patchy. Scraggly. Several portions were blank brown dirt. As if his irrigation lines had failed, which made no sense, given that she knew he had a hand pump in case the solar system went awry. She scanned the moonlit fields through her binoculars, ensuring she was alone, then left the safety of the sweet-smelling maples and minty pines and walked to the edge of George's wheat. She knelt beside the breeze-tousled stalks, plucked one of the long-tailed heads, and rolled it between her palms, popping the kernels from the dry sheaths. She raised them to her face and sniffed. Typical faint smell of grain. Looked fine, like opaque brown rice. No obvious sign of bugs or rot; hesitantly, she popped the wheat in her mouth and chewed. The kernels were hard, but broke down soon enough, tasting like unleavened bread and pasty gluten.

She pulled another couple heads and put them in her pocket to take a closer look back at the house. As she walked back to the treeline, leaves crackled uphill.

She shrank against a pine bole and peered into the darkness. Moonlight tried and failed to penetrate the canopy. Leaves crunched again, furtive, but with the particular rasp of a big animal trying to hide its noise.

She wasn't alone.

3

Lucy brought only the essentials. Water, food, first aid kit, couple knives, several baggies. Her umbrella and a box of shells. With luck, she'd be in and out of Manhattan within a couple days. Without luck, or anyway the wrong kind of it, and she could barter buds or leaves for anything she wound up needing.

The bridge to the island was a tall steel suspension job with latticed towers and a whole lot of cables. She was halfway across before she saw the soldiers.

The Hudson River flowed far below, muddy green in the morning light. They had erected a barricade behind the suspension tower at the other end of the bridge and she thought about finding another, but if they had this bridge staked out, no doubt they'd claimed the others, too. She sighed. At least she'd had the foresight to stuff her shells inside a tub of oatmeal with a false bottom. She strolled up to the concrete blocks set across the lanes. Two men stood behind them in gray-white modern urban camo, black rifles slung across their chests.

"Hey, beautiful morning, ma'am." The soldier had one of those braying city accents that sounded like he'd been cheering the Yankees too long. He looked her up and down and stepped around the concrete barricade. "Here for a Broadway show?"

She let her umbrella hang beside her leg. "You still have those?"

"Nah, just like to see if people believe me." He got out a clipboard and clicked a pen. "Name, citizenship, and business in the city?"

"Lucy Two. Like the number. Last I checked, I was American. And my business is wondering why you got to know mine."

The other soldier waved a fly off his shoulder. The first man finished scribbling and glanced up from his clipboard. "This is the sovereign nation of Manhattan, ma'am. We let anyone in, and we'd be running a zoo instead."

"I'm here to find a friend."

"Uh huh." He returned to his paperwork. "Where do you intend to stay during your visit?"

"Well, I don't right know. With her, I suppose."

"And her name and address?"

Lucy stuck out her lower lip. "You mean to tell me you got the name and address of everyone in town?"

He smiled. His teeth were getting yellowed and he was missing his upper left eyetooth. "What kind of a government doesn't?"

"Then maybe you can tell me where I'm staying. My friend's name is Tilly Loman. She in your records?"

"Our records?" He glanced at the other soldier and honked laughter. "We kept those here, we'd be operating out of Shea Stadium, not this little shack. Try City Hall. Are you armed, Ms. Two?"

She smiled teasingly. "I got here, didn't I?"

"Unregistered firearms aren't allowed inside Manhattan. You got anything goes boom, you need to leave it with us. File advance notice at least 48 hours prior to your intended departure and we'll see it's ready for you on your way out."

Lucy looked dubious. "I don't know if I should do that. I heard New York was mighty dangerous."

He laughed again. "Not since Giuliani, ma'am. And these days we keep it even cleaner."

"Well, all right." She knelt and unstrapped the .22 pistol from her ankle, then dug into her bag for her spare clip and little green box of ammo.

The second soldier took these from her, examined the pistol's serial number, and opened the slide. "This a .22?"

"That's right," Lucy said. "Hits hard enough if you know where to aim it."

He handed it back. "These are fine. But nothing higher caliber. Understand?"

"Fair enough."

The first man leaned over her bag and sniffed. "You got anything else we need to know about?"

"Oh, I wouldn't think so."

"Marijuana is a controlled substance, ma'am."

"Is it?" She widened her eyes. "I just use it to trade for food."

"Nah, I'm just fucking with you!" He brayed at his own joke and glanced at his friend, who chuckled for the first time. The first soldier winked at her. He was handsome enough, in an Italian way. "You're our first visitor in three days. Got to do something to pass the time, know what I mean?"

"I think I take your meaning." A joint materialized in her fingers. "Would you care to test it? Make sure I'm not bringing anything too nasty 'cross your borders?"

"I'd only stop you if it weren't nasty enough."

Lucy lit up and passed it over. He nodded appreciatively, smoke tumbling from his mouth, and handed it to his coworker, who accepted it without looking, still writing details on his clipboard.

"Tell you what, Lucy." The first soldier blinked at the hazy white sky, as if seeing it for the first time. He frowned and squinted at her. "Normally I'd say, hey, this girl she sounds kind of iffy, but I get the feeling you know your way around. So I got a deal for you."

"What's that, sir?"

"We got special housing for tourists, visitors, and immigrants. If you go straight to City Hall and let them know you'd like a room, I can let you inside."

"And I can ask for my friend, too."

He tapped the side of his nose. "Exactly, Lucy. Exactly. And then I'll know where to find you and see if you want to go out for a drink, you know?"

She grinned lopsidedly. She'd expected these boys to be puffed up on their own authority, but she liked this garrulous little asshole. "Are all New Yorkers like you?"

"Oh no, ma'am. I'm one of a kind."

His name was Phil and he gave her a laminated passport and opened the waist-high aluminum gate through the barrier. As she entered, he swept his arms to the towering skyline.

"Welcome to New York, Lucy Two. I hope your stay is a good one."

She touched his shoulder lightly as she stepped past the fence. Two steps beyond, she cocked her umbrella on her shoulder at a rakish angle and turned back to him with a smile.

"It's sure off to a fine start. Y'all have a good day, won't you?"

"Y'all too," Phil said, making the worst pass at a Southern accent Lucy had ever suffered to hear. She laughed and shook her head and walked down the warm pavement sloping toward the city.

And holy shit, what a city. A strip of green fronted the Hudson, but beyond that it was wall-to-wall apartments standing so close you'd hardly have room to take a deep breath. Way south on the lower third of the island, the Empire State Building stood as proud as a stiff prick, its spire piercing the underside of the sky. Dozens of other towers loomed hundreds of feet into the air. She'd seen her fair share of big cities, but this was something else. Like God's own vision of how a city ought to be.

Phil had warned her it was a hell of a walk down to City Hall, but helpful young man that he was, he'd directed her to a place where a girl might get a bicycle. She exited the freeway at Broadway, just like he'd told her, and walked south, counting down the streets to 168th. There, at a stamp-sized park forested with dinky trees, a fat man sprawled in a lawn chair, shirt off, catching the warm fall sun on every inch of his round gut. As Lucy neared, he blinked at her through his aviator shades.

He gestured to the lot across from him, which was filled with four tidy rows of bicycles. "Let me guess, you're here for one of our fine fleet."

"Sure am."

"Passport?" He held out his hand and she gave him her laminated card. He inspected it, mouth half open. He had a husky accent that was downright unfriendly to its R's and she associated it with the TV shows about city firefighters. "Okay, here's the deal, little lady. You want a bike, you got it. No questions, no fees, no problem."

"Sounds like a heck of a deal."

"A government's got to provide for its people, don't it? All you got to do in return is bring it back when you're done. You can do that here or at any of our other stations, which I have helpfully marked on this map." He handed her a tourist map marked with a half dozen bright red X's. "You think you can do that for me?"

"No doubt." She met his sunglass-visored gaze. "I got to say, you boys run a tighter ship than I expected."

"If you don't do right by your people, how you expect them to do right by you?" He waddled over to the bikes, unlocked one, and scribbled her information on a clipboard. "And I wish you a good day."

She saddled up and pedaled down the street, turning to give the man an airy wave. She was beginning to wonder if she might not have use for her umbrella after all.

She whisked down the streets. Downtown, the smoke from a couple fires mingled with the haze, but she didn't see much sign of life along the brown project housing that spoked from Broadway. Half the shop windows were smashed but there was no glass in the street. She didn't smell much beside the humidity and her own fresh sweat. Why, if they had working sewers and running water, she might not ever leave.

Broadway turned into St. Nicholas. She biked easy, pacing herself for the long ride. After a couple-three miles, the towers clambered higher and higher, gothic white stone and classy glass and steel. A block to her left, apartments overlooked an unbroken stretch of green.

She cut left and rode along Central Park. It smelled like leaves and dew and manure. Some of the grass had gone to seed, but most had been converted to crops, neat sections fenced off with wire. A cow lowed from the trees. Lucy pedaled slowly, watching a man and a woman hack at the weeds with hoes.

She was so taken aback by these signs of civilization she crashed into the back of a dusty yellow cab.

The collision was low speed and she came out of it with nothing worse than a scraped palm and a bruised rib. After that, she kept at least one eye on the road, which was clear of traffic and as wide as you could want. At the south end of the park, she crossed paths with another biker, who saluted with two fingers and sped away, knees pumping. She coasted through block after block of glossy office towers, but didn't stop until she was two blocks up from the terraced heights of the Empire State Building. There, she drank water and took a good long breather.

The rest was good for her. She'd been goggling like a country yokel. All right, so they had some vestige of a proper city. A government. Big deal. The world used to be lousy with such things.

Perspective restored, she continued downtown past clothing stores and pharmacies locked behind metal grilles and brownstone apartments humble enough that they likely didn't rate an elevator. Way downtown, the buildings climbed again. She followed a slanting street all the way to City Hall, a regal place that looked like the shameless offspring of a ritzy hotel and a German castle. A soldier stood out front, assault rifle hung across his chest. A block away, Lucy stopped and got out her little mirror and combed her hair, which had gone frizzy from the humidity.

She walked her bike up to the soldier, who inspected her passport and nodded her inside.

"You'll keep an eye on my bike?" she said.

"If you come back and it's not here, I'll carry you home myself."

She snorted and went inside. Austere stone led to a rich walnut reception desk complete with receptionist, but Lucy stopped cold. Something was wrong. The world had gone the wrong hue, like when you been out in the dazzling sun and you go into a shady room and your eyes can't seem to make it out.

The lights. They were white. And steady. They had electricity.

Well, la dee da. She strode up to the woman at the desk and smiled and handed over her passport. "I was told you had a place for me to stay?"

"You mean our guest housing," the woman said. She was young and pretty and had the generic northern accent. "Is this your first visit to Manhattan?"

"And the way y'all are treating me, it won't be my last."

"We're so happy to hear that. Please sign in here and I'll be back with your key."

The woman went into a back room. Lucy entered her name and a fake address on another clipboard. The woman clicked back to the desk, passed her a map, and set down a key with a sharp metal clink.

"Room 707," she said. "Very pleasant neighborhood."

"That's just great," Lucy said. "Listen, I'm here to visit a friend, but the silly goose didn't give me her address. Suppose you could look it up for me?"

"Information retrieval?" The young woman tipped back her nose. "There's just a small filing fee."

Lucy laughed. She'd been wondering when they'd start to sink their teeth into her. "Don't suppose you take dollars."

The receptionist smiled regretfully. "We prefer hard goods."

"You accept tobacco?" she said.

"Tobacco?"

"You know, Joe Camel. Cowboy's breakfast." She reached for her bag and retrieved one of her smallest baggies.

The receptionist took it hesitantly, as if it might be alive. She pried open the plastic zipper, inhaled, and poked at the ragged shreds. "Did you grow this yourself?"

"Sure did."

A sharp look entered the woman's eye. "Just so you know, all businesses on the isle of Manhattan must be registered with the Office of Commerce. Third floor."

Lucy's fingers played over the handle of her umbrella. "I'm just here to find my friend."

"And we wish you all the best. But during your stay, you may find that Manhattan has more opportunities than you're used to elsewhere. Should your goals expand, please be sure to register with the appropriate office."

"Will do. Until then, you got an address for me?"

The woman smiled brightly and palmed the baggie. "Let me find those files."

She disappeared into the back room again. She was gone long enough for Lucy to have a good look around, but other than the electric lights, there wasn't much to see. Once, footsteps echoed further inside the building. The receptionist brought back a handwritten address.

Lucy thanked her and walked into the October light, which had the nostalgic yellow color of an old movie. She smiled at the soldier watching over her bike. A strange feeling settled on her shoulders. At this rate, she'd find Tilly and be on her way by sunset. And somehow, that was disappointing.

She squished the feeling down and biked uptown, threading west. At Tilly's street, Lucy slowed, owling at the addresses. Ten minutes after leaving City Hall, she stopped in front of a brick walkup and leaned her bike across a brass pole supporting a battered canvas strung over the stoop. The glass in the front door was greasy and the door behind it was protected by a buzzer but when Lucy tried the handle it opened without resistance.

She braced her umbrella across the crook of her arm and gazed up the winding staircase. It was perfectly silent and smelled like water that can't quite dry up. The stairs bent under her feet with creaks that wouldn't quit no matter how lightly she stepped.

At the fifth landing, she stepped onto the grimy carpet and headed for 511, rapping her knuckles against the door in a jaunty little beat.

Several seconds went by. She knocked again. "Hey, Tilly! Guess who!"

She tried a third time, pounding the door with the meat of her fist. Across the open space of the stairwell, a door squealed open. Lucy whirled, finger on the trigger of her umbrella.

A Hispanic woman stared across the dim space; skylights let some sunlight down the stairwell, giving everything a twilight cast. "Who are you?"

"Friend of Tilly's," Lucy called. "She out chasing boys again?"

The woman gazed blankly, then shook her head. "She doesn't live here any more."

"Yeah? City Hall says different."

"I haven't seen her since the spring."

Lucy frowned, umbrella sagging. "Don't suppose she left a forwarding address."

The woman shrugged. "I didn't hear nothing. One day she wasn't here."

"Funny, that was my last experience with ol' Tilly, too."

She left the woman with her address in case Tilly came back, then clumped down the stairs to the street, shoulders swaying. She supposed she ought to be upset. Ten minutes ago, it was looking like a done deal. Now she was alone in a strange city without a whole lot of food and with a six-month gap since anyone had seen hide or hair of Tilly.

But the weight was gone from her shoulders. She felt good. Back on the hunt.

She headed for her government-assigned home, pedaling past a whole slew of coffee shops and bars and tattoo parlors and Chinese restaurants. The roads were clear except at one intersection where an apartment building had burned down and collapsed in the street like a drunken old fool. She circled around and found her new home on the corner of Third Avenue. It was fifteen floors high and built of modern windows and clean concrete. Lucy liked it.

She was less impressed that the locks on the front doors were busted, but at least she had to use her key to get into her room on the seventh floor. Light speared through the blinds, outlining a bed and a desk and an itty bitty kitchen. None of the lights worked. Neither did the stove. She threw open the blinds and cracked the window to flush out the must, then sat at the desk and got out Tilly's letter.

The envelope it had arrived in was as battered as an old mutt. The organized postal service had collapsed during the same two-week span as everything else. These days, letters got passed along via a complicated system of trades resembling a pyramid scheme. Inhabited towns and and major crossroads (inhabited or not) often had a secure box set up on the outskirts—a mailbox, a safe, a fridge. Anything that would keep the weather off the papers inside. Which weren't letters, but job listings for letter carriage: "Letter for delivery to Savannah," say. When people passed through town, or prepared to leave it for a trip, they checked the box's listings, and if their trip would take them closer to the intended recipient, they'd claim the listing, which would include a note about how to get in touch with the sender, a process which, to protect the sender's safety, resembled the directions of a treasure map: go to the church, walk fifty paces east, and fire your gun three times into the air. Or light a fire in the trash can by the McDonald's. That sort of thing.

Anything that would alert the sender to the fact he had a carrier. The two would then meet and haggle out a price, which varied depending on how far the carrier was taking it, the urgency of the letter, whether the two parties knew each other, and so on. If the carrier wasn't intending to bring it all the way to the recipient, he would arrange to bear it as far as he could, then either sell it to a speculator (who would expect to be paid more on delivery) or just leave it in a box, where another carrier would eventually find it and continue its journey.

Fraud was a problem, naturally, and the entire system was so belabored people rarely bothered with letters at all. But that meant the few they did send were so important that the carrier could expect to receive a handsome reward from the recipient as well. Combine that with the professional mailmen who'd cropped up—survivalist nomads who'd discovered they could make a tidy income in luxuries just by adding a few detours to their constant travels—and the process more or less worked.

But that explained why it had taken Tilly's letter five months to wend the thousand miles between New York and Daytona, and why it had been brought to Lucy smudged with half a dozen different sets of fingerprints, its corners blunted from travel. On seeing the return address, Lucy's heart had pounded, but she'd kept her cool so as not to excite the carrier's greed and paid him off with a thick sheaf of tobacco.

Inside the dirty envelope, the pages were crisply folded and Lucy imagined she could catch a whiff of Tilly's strawberry perfume on them. The letter was seven double-sided pages long, and judging by the ring-shaped stains on the fifth and sixth pages, Tilly had needed a cup of coffee to complete it, but through a modern-day miracle, the girl had managed to compose several thousand words without letting slip one god damn detail Lucy might use to track her down. Most of it was dedicated to rehashing the fun they'd had as kids. Tilly also made three different attempts to apologize for her abrupt departure and ensure Lucy that everything was fine and there was no need to worry. In the end, there was a single useful tidbit:

"I am in New York now & it is not nearly as dirty as they say & I have met many wonderful people."

In her new apartment, Lucy gritted her teeth, finished rereading Tilly's concluding platitudes and looping signature, then folded up the letter and stared out at the empty street.

Well, she was a long ways from beat. She'd already made a friend. She biked back down to City Hall, saluted the guard, and jogged inside.

"I'm back," she told the receptionist. "I wonder if perhaps you pulled the wrong file? My friend appears to have moved."

The woman behind the walnut desk gave her a skeptical look and took Tilly's address from Lucy's hands. "Let me check."

Five minutes later, she returned with her professionally regretful smile and a shake of the head. "I'm sorry, this is our most recent record."

"I see." Lucy leaned her elbows on the desk. "Listen, you know a soldier named Phil? Hangs out on the bridge way up north?"

"Phil Abruzzi?" Her face darkened in a way that made Lucy smile inside; the two of them had done the deed, perhaps even shared a full-on relationship. She tucked that factoid away for later use. The receptionist flipped her hair over her shoulder. "I know him."

"Mind if I leave him a note?" She thickened her Southern Belle accent to the consistency of cold honey and was rewarded with a knife-sharp glare that made her want to laugh out loud. "He was right nice to me this morning and I could sure use his help."

The receptionist was a professional, however, and accepted Lucy's note with a curt nod. Lucy smiled and walked out.

To get a feel for the island, and to scout for a market or some such where she might barter for food, Lucy looped east all the way to the river before heading back toward her building. Neighborhoods changed in a flash, trendy little gentrifications one second, heroin addicts' havens the next. Pre-plague, anyway. These days, they were probably just empty.

A highway fronted the river. On the other side of the road, an Asian fellow with an accent as husky as the bicycle-man's stood behind a stall dickering with a white lady. Behind him, a mess of fishing lines trailed into the gray water. Once the woman left, he happily traded Lucy four fish as long as her hand for a couple of rolled cigarettes. When Lucy's stomach growled, he offered to cook them free of charge. She flopped in the grass. The smell of fried fish mingled with the heavy scent of the river. After a few, he called her over for chow. It was delicious.

She attached no particular significance to her makeshift meal, but it turned out to be fate. Full-bellied, she biked west at a more than leisurely pace. As she crossed First Avenue, moving so slowly her bike wobbled side to side, the sinking sun playing peek-a-boo behind the downtown towers, Lucy caught the scent of roasting coffee.

She braked, tires skidding on the asphalt. You didn't see much in the way of coffee these days. Except she had, hardly an hour earlier, stained onto the pages of Tilly's letter.

4

Ellie thumbed the latch on her holster, wide-eyed in the darkness, and drew her pistol. Inside the treeline, leaves crackled again.

She'd lived in this place long enough to know animals always sounded bigger at night. You'd swear you had a black bear thrashing around your yard and a minute later a raccoon would pad into the open and make you feel like an idiot. But to her ear, the footsteps in the woods didn't sound like a raccoon. They sounded human.

More than likely, it was Dee and Quinn, quiet and raptly breathless after an energetic—paddle in the canoe, she forced herself to conclude. The steps neared. She pulled closer to the trunk of the pine, smelling its earthy bark and sugary sap. Sixty yards down the treeline, a silhouette slipped into the open field.

Too dark to see much. Male shape. Too tall to be Quinn and too straight-spined to be George. Ellie breathed shallowly, maneuvering more of the tree between herself and the stranger. Crickets peeped in the night. The figure strode to the piebald wheat field, plucked a single head of grain, and gazed toward the dark farmhouse.

It wasn't Ellie's nature to confront. Not right away. It was in her nature to collect data, then act. So she watched in perfect stillness, unwilling to risk the glint of light on the lenses of her binoculars. After a moment, the man turned and retreated into the woods. She got out her binoculars and spotted his shadow among the black boles of the pines but it was too dark to make out more than she had already seen.

She waited there for a long while, crouched in the cool dirt between the trees and the field, binocs in one hand, pistol resting lightly on her thigh. Her legs grew stiff. The screech owl sounded up from the hill again. Finally, she stood, brushed off her jeans, worked the feeling back into her feet, and walked home. By the time she locked the door behind her, it was past one in the morning.

A knock woke her from a late sleep. She jolted up, scrabbling for the pistol on the nightstand. The knock sounded a second time as she tugged on her jeans. She jogged to the door, gun in hand, and cracked it open.

"Mrs. Colson," Quinn grinned from the porch.

She leaned to the right, putting the pistol out of sight behind the jamb. "What's up, Quinn?"

"My dad said you'd let us use your spare tractor?"

She wasn't too sure about the kid's psychoemotional status, but she couldn't question Quinn's physical health. He wasn't overly tall, but his shoulders were wide and sturdy enough to cut wood on. Annoyingly, she felt suddenly bedraggled and frumpy.

"I'll grab the keys."

She shut the door on him and put the pistol away and dragged a comb through her hair. Feeling halfway civilized, she found the keys, got on her shoes, and rejoined Quinn outside. They crossed the weedy lawn toward the barn.

"You two still making wedding plans?" she said.

"Oh yeah. I never knew how much work it was."

"So where are you building the Taj Mahal?"

"Taj Ma-what?"

"Nevermind."

"But yeah, it's going really well," he forged ahead. "Yesterday Dee went into town to get measured for her dress."

"Wonderful." Ellie unlocked the barn, batting at the cobwebs that materialized each morning. Rays of late morning light beamed through the chinks in the walls, blazing on the dust motes like heatless yellow flame. She pulled aside a dirty tarp, revealing a red AGCO with uncompromising tires that reached above her waist. "Do you ever wonder if simpler might be better?"

Quinn tried on a thoughtful look. "You think?"

She wadded up the tarp, raising her voice over the crinkling plastic. "Weddings used to cost more than most wars and require more coordination than a North Korean halftime show. Does $20,000 in bills sound like a good way to start a marriage?"

He blinked, wary, and she was reminded that despite the fullness of his body, his brain was still a teen's. More importantly, a teen who wanted to impress his girlfriend's mom. It was possible some dogs were more pathetic, eager to please, and easy to cow than a young man in his situation, but if so, she hadn't met one.

She laughed and shelved the tarp. "Do what you want, Quinn. It's your wedding. I certainly hope it's your only one."

"Well yeah," he said. He frowned, then spit it out. "That's why I want it to be perfect. Isn't that what she wants?"

"Have you asked her?"

"What girl doesn't want a perfect wedding?"

Ellie leapt into the seat, suspension bouncing. "I've only known Dee since she was thirteen. It could be she has a hidden reservoir of girliness waiting to be tapped by a deep-drilling event like a wedding. But in my observation, she would choose blood red over pink ten times out of ten."

She turned the key and the blattering engine drowned out whatever Quinn said next. She let it idle until she was satisfied it was in fine shape. Not that she was overly concerned about handing it over in less than tip-top condition. She just wanted to gauge where it was at so if George returned it worse for wear she could nail his ass to the wall.

The tang of burnt ethanol filled the barn; years back, she'd tried producing biodiesel for a different tractor, but that was wizardry compared to ethanol fermentation. This was an age of simplicity. The first generation to remember how to manufacture cars could worry about homebrewing their own diesel.

She shut off the engine and lobbed the keys at Quinn. He was so deep in thought they bounced off his face. He jerked back, staggering in the dirt and old straw.

"Sorry," he said, as if it were his fault, and stooped to search out the keys.

Ellie regarded him for several seconds. "Last night, there was a stranger in your fields."

Quinn glanced up. "What do you mean?"

"I mean a man was outside watching your house."

"What? Who?"

"I don't know," Ellie said with evaporating patience. "He was strange to me."

"That's weird." A sly look crossed his face. "What were you doing there?"

"I was out for a walk."

He smiled at the ground. "Were you trying to watch us?"

"If I want to watch you, I can just pull up the security camera in your room." She walked across the grit and plucked up the keys and handed them to him.

Confusion rippled over his eyes and mouth. Eventually, deciding she must be kidding, if only because they had no electricity, he pulled back his shoulders and put on a face like a new recruit.

"I'm sorry, Mrs. Colson, that was an inappropriate joke. While Dee's under my roof, it's my responsibility to see that everyone's safe. I'll put the dogs out at night and let my dad know to keep sharp."

She tipped back her head, giving him a second look. "Call me Ellie."

He climbed into the tractor and started it up and drove out of the barn. Back at the house, the door hung halfway open. Ellie's blood froze. She grabbed the shovel by the porch and knifed inside.

"Mom?" Dee called from the kitchen.

Ellie rolled her eyes and pitched the shovel off the porch with a clang. "Did you come over with Quinn?"

Dee padded out to the living room, shaking her head. "I just got back from town. Quinn has me getting fitted for the most ridiculous dress you've ever seen."

Ellie laughed until she cried.

She figured Dee was just back to do laundry and grab a bath in the cover-heated tub, but to her surprise, her daughter was back for the harvest. Ellie hadn't intended to begin for another couple days, but she wasn't about to turn down free labor. Dee donned gloves and helped her rig the combine mount to the tractor. Ellie pinched in her ear plugs and settled a surgical mask over her mouth and drove into the fields.

The engine roared across the sky. The header scythed into the golden stalks, spewing dust and pulverized fiber behind the trundling machine. Despite the late start, Ellie cleared the whole field that day, returning once so Dee could empty the grain from the shoe while Ellie went in for a drink of water and a short rest. After she got back from the second trip, she saw Dee had swept the barn, too. One of these days, the machines would go dark for the last time and they'd have to take the fields by hand, but for the moment, it was incredible that a day's labor from two people was sufficient to bring in enough grain to keep them in bread and pasta for the rest of the year.

Not that the work was entirely done. Ellie had very particular ways of tubbing the grain to keep it free from rot and mice and she didn't like leaving all that straw out where it could light up like Las Vegas the first time lightning struck or a passing bum dumped his pipe embers in the field. Cleanup was hard, sweaty, limb-deadening work. Along with the storage process, it chewed up four more days.

It was a good thing Dee had come home when she did. The night they finished, as Ellie sat on the back porch with a hot mug of instant coffee, she smelled frost in the air.

"You know why I went to college?" Ellie said, tipping some rum into her drink. "So I'd never have to work this hard."

Dee laughed. "Too bad about the aliens. What did you do, anyway? Before?"

"You know that."

"I know you worked for the government. Shady spy sh—stuff."

"I wasn't a spy."

"Whatever," Dee said. "What did you call it? 'The nerd CIA'?"

Ellie had forgotten that. Funny what kids remembered. "My job was to travel to the most exotic lands in the world and make sense of the most boring numbers they had available."

"If you were just poring over numbers, why'd you have to travel at all?"

"We always wondered why the bosses never reached that same conclusion."

"I wish I'd grown up in that world instead of this one."

Ellie nodded, then stared at Dee. Ironically, it was moments like this when she missed Chip the most. He was the one who knew how to comfort people. For all her talent at plucking wisdom from inscrutable spreadsheets, or her new life running a post-industrial farm, situations like this tripped her on her face. She recognized the emotions that needed to be expressed, but somehow she could never search out the words that could make them manifest.

"He saved your life, you know."

Steam wafted from Dee's mug. "I know."

"I wish we'd had a life together," Ellie tried. "But I'm glad you got to know him for the years you did."

"Me too." Dee pulled her blanket so high around her shoulders Ellie could barely see her hair sticking out the top.

That morning, she woke to frost.

When Dee got up, she accepted the eggs Ellie had brought in from the coop an hour before, then let Ellie know she was going back to Quinn's. Ellie didn't complain. To her surprise, it had turned out she enjoyed parenting, but she still appreciated time to herself.

She watched Dee pack, waved as the girl walked down the trail around the lake, then proceeded to do nothing the rest of the day. The following afternoon, she was still doing nothing—in the specific form of sitting on the back porch reading Philip K. Dick and thinking about working up the motivation to throw a bobber into the water—when a voice called from out front.

"Ellie?" Quinn called. "Mrs. Colson?"

She wiggled into her sandals and headed around the house. "How's your harvest?"

Quinn started, windmilling his arms to keep from toppling off the porch. "It's all right. Thanks to you."

"It was nothing." Crickets chirped from the mown fields. "Dee need some clean socks?"

He worked his mouth, then nodded. "Yeah, come to think of it."

Ellie nodded. "You better not have come here to tell me I'm a grandma."

"It's not that bad," Quinn laughed nervously. "I hope."

"Well?"

"This morning, I was out for a walk. I like to take one as soon as I get up. Helps me wake up. And when I was out in the woods, I found Ringer. My dog." His brown face paled. "He was stabbed."

Ellie glanced across the shimmering lake. "Have you told your dad?"

"I didn't want to scare him."

"Maybe he ought to be scared." She sighed through her teeth.

"Better let me take a look."

She went inside for her pistol and proper shoes and a jacket and binoculars and latex gloves. She walked beside Quinn in silence. She could tell the quiet made him uncomfortable, but at the moment, she didn't care. She had thinking to do.

On the trail, the leaves fell in earnest, yellow and red pages spinning to the forest floor. Ellie expected they had at least a couple clear weeks ahead of them, but the first snows could come at any time.

The walk to the house took a full hour. Quinn veered deeper into the woods, keeping a thick screen of trees between them and his father's home. At a rocky upthrust northeast of the property, he stopped to glance at the stands of maples and pines and the boulders mapped with red and gray-green lichen. He beckoned her to a small fold in the land.

A dog lay at the bottom. Its fur was black and white and blue-gray and the hair on its side was matted with blood.

"Did you move him?" Ellie said.

"I found him right here. I touched him and petted him. Did I mess things up?"

"It's fine." She climbed down the embankment, one arm out for balance, and knelt beside the body. Its eyes were open and blank. She tugged on her latex gloves and brushed back its fur. There was a lot of blood and it took her a minute to find the first wound, a narrow, inch-long puncture between its ribs. Two more were spaced higher up its brisket. She squatted on her heels and stared into the trees. "When was the last time you saw him?"

"Last night," Quinn said thickly. "I been setting them out every night since you saw the stranger."

"Does your dad have any enemies, Quinn?"

"Enemies?"

"You've been here four years. Has he made anyone mad?"

The boy wrinkled his brow, blinking at the moisture in his eyes. "He and Bill Noesi in Lake Placid have never got along. Not since Dad bought that cow from him that died the next month. But I don't think they've seen each other since last year."

Ellie edged around the dog and brushed a wide brown maple leaf from a depression in the soil. "Anyone else?"

"He and Mr. Franklin ain't big fans of each other, but I wouldn't say they're mortal foes." He shook his head. "Who would kill a dog?"

"What about you? Pissed anyone off?"

"Me?" Quinn looked surprised to the point of affront, then his eyebrows banged together. "Sam Chase. He always had a thing for Dee."

"Who just announced her intention to get married." Ellie placed her foot beside the print next to the dog. Her shoe was a little shorter. "Let me see your foot."

He gave her a puzzled look, lining his shoe up next to the print. It was identical in size. His face cracked. "I'm real sorry. I went and mucked up your scene, didn't I?"

She shook her head. "It wasn't cold enough to frost last night, but the ground was moist. It's dried since. Print's shrunk. What size do you wear?"

"Nine? Nine and a half."

She petted the dog's thick fur, moving her hand to its back legs and giving a little tug. They were so stiff the whole body moved with them. "Was he this stiff when you found him?"

"Yeah. I knew the second I touched him."

"Okay." She rose, still sore from gathering up the last of the wheat straw the day before. "Well, let's find some shovels."

They trudged across George's fields. The wheat stood tall under the brittle sunlight. Unharvested. She was about to comment when she saw the potent green combine parked beside the barn.

"Is that new?"

"Dad picked it up in town," Quinn said.

"How'd he swing that?"

"Think he promised part of the crop."

"For a new combine? Let me know that guy's name. Maybe he'll trade me a jet for the peanuts in my cellar."

"Dad's gonna owe for a lot more than one year. But he didn't have much choice."

Quinn creaked open the tool shed and grabbed shovels and two pairs of leather gloves. They returned to the dog and buried him in the woods, sweating in the weak autumn sun. After, Quinn crouched and patted the coffee-colored soil.

"Should have played more fetch with you, Ringer, but you never wanted to quit and after a while I got mad. But I guess that was just your way of saying you wanted to spend time with me. I'm — "

He sobbed, tears dripping to the grave. Ellie bent down and put a hand on his shoulder.

They walked back to the house. Ellie tapped the rivets on the back of her jeans. "Maybe you should keep the dogs in at night. I'll ask around town. Don't tell your dad yet."

"Why not?"

"Why did you come to me and not him?"

Quinn tipped his head to the side, examining that question for the first time. Ellie waved and walked along the cool shore toward the Chases, who lived just down the lake. They'd moved in two years ago, much to Ellie's resentment. For the most part, the Lower Saranac was unpopulated, but a few dozen people trickled into Lake Placid each year. Sooner or later, they'd start spilling west. And in the meantime, she was just getting older. Another ten or fifteen years, and she'd start slowing down just as she most need to be on her guard.

The Chases had moved into a vacation home built to look like a log cabin. The moss over the front stoop might even have been real. A manual saw rasped from the back, but in the interest of politeness, she knocked on the front door. When there was no answer, she walked to the back yard. A shirtless twenty-year-old man bent over a post, sawing through one end.

"Sam?" she said. "I'm Ellie Colson. Dee's mom."

Sweat trickled down his thick shoulders. "I know who you are."

"Last night, Quinn Tolbert thought he saw someone outside his place. Where were you?"

"In bed. The sun knows best. No sense being up when you can't see what you're doing."

"What about last Wednesday night?"

"Ask my pillow."

She walked halfway around the sawhorse. "What size shoe do you wear, Sam?"

"Whatever fits."

"Have you ever seen George Tolbert's dogs around?"

He set down the saw and turned to face her, not bothering to hide the annoyance in his brown eyes. "Sure. Mutts are always diggin' around our yard. Somebody ought to paste their fuzzy asses with some rock salt."

"Curious," she said. "Last night, someone stabbed Ringer. Australian shepherd. That wasn't you, was it, Sam?"

He snorted and brushed at the sawdust clinging to the damp hairs on his forearm. "What kind of man stabs a dog?"

"A man who's just heard that the woman he wants is engaged to someone else."

"You think I'm hot for Dee?" He laughed and bent back to his saw. "Not hardly, ma'am. Her tits aren't big enough."

A cold tingle flowed through Ellie's hands. Her pistol was in her waistband and she could feel its steel weight against her back. "If I see you around their place, you'll wake up in a box."

His saw rasped. She walked away before her temper got the best of her. She followed the dirt lane up to Forest Home Road and walked so briskly to the dead town of Saranac Lake that she had to strip off her jacket from the sweat. There, she swerved off the highway to grab a bike from the makeshift depository the locals had set up in the parking lot of the Blue Moon, then pedaled to Lake Placid. The trip smelled of cold mountain air and leaves that have fallen but have yet to decay.

Confusingly, the town of Lake Placid was situated on the south shores of several interconnected lakes, one of which shared the same name as the town. She biked to the general store Millie Perkins had set up inside the old resort on Mirror Lake, meaning to ask after Bill Noesi. Millie tucked her hands in her apron, quirked her mouth, and told her Noesi lived in the house at McLenathan Bay a couple miles north.

After two miles of a whole lot of nothing, she reached a Cape Cod cottage at the wrong address, backtracked to another wrong address, this one too far the other way, then crept back toward the Cape Cod, scowling into the trees. A cow lowed to the north. She stopped the bike and stared. Bill Noesi had dragged brush and brambles across the turnoff to his house.

"Mr. Noesi?" she called. "Bill?"

She tried again and got no answer. She found a branch and knotted the arm of her jacket around its tip. As she walked through the woods to the house, she held the branch over her head, the lining of her jacket bright white. She wasn't certain how this custom had sprung up, but generally speaking, the locals understood the person thus approaching their house was a fellow lake-dweller who didn't need to be shot.

Generally speaking.

She deliberately crunched through the leaves on the trail to his front door. He had painted his house a dull green to match the trees. Deer antlers littered the yard. As she climbed up the front steps, a bearded man materialized from the side of the house.

With the branch in her right hand, Ellie went for her gun with her left. "Mr. Noesi?"

"Who asks?" the man rumbled.

She lowered the branch and took her hand from the pistol. "My name's Ellie Colson. I live on the Lower Saranac. Have you seen or spoken to George Tolbert recently?"

The man didn't hesitate. "That animal was perfectly healthy when I sold it to him. It picked up something on his farm or he doesn't know how to treat a beast."

"So you remember him," she said dryly.

"We had words. And then a heck of a lot more words. If you're looking to buy, you come see them for yourself. Talk to anyone in town. Then decide for yourself whether those winds of doubt are just a bunch of hot air."

"Were any of those words recent?"

Noesi shook his shaggy head. "Haven't seen him since last Christmas. I was in town to find a present for a lady friend. George seized the opportunity to slander me."

"Last night, someone killed one of his dogs."

Anger flared in the man's deep-set eyes. "I'm a friend of everything on four legs. You accuse me of killing a dog again and we'll see how I feel about those on two."

"I'm not accusing anyone," she said levelly. "I'm narrowing things down. Thank you for your time, Mr. Noesi."

He watched her go. When she glanced back down the path, he was gone.

She dropped the bike off at the Blue Moon and walked back to the Tolberts'. Shrieks carried over the lake. She broke into a run, then saw Quinn leap off the dock and cannonball into the frigid water.

Dee laughed and high-stepped out of the water, hugging herself, water dripping from her bikini. Ellie slowed to a walk and waved. Quinn got a funny little smile and wrapped a towel around his waist. He said something to Dee and then approached Ellie by himself.

"It wasn't Bill Noesi," she told him. "Jury's out on Sam Chase."

"I didn't want to tell you this," Quinn said, "but this summer when we were swimming, I went inside for a drink and when I came back out, he was in the water with her." He lowered his voice further. "He propositioned her."

"Maybe he's just a fan of the free market. I'm going to spend the night out here, Quinn. Don't get trigger happy."

"You sure you trust me?" he grinned. "I'm not sure the law would arrest a man for shooting his mother-in-law."

She snorted and went home to grab a nap. At twilight, she walked to the woods beyond the Tolberts' home with her camping gear and set up for the night. She kept watch until the early morning, then returned home to sleep. Not long after, an engine grumbled through the open window. She flopped over and went back to sleep.

A rolling crackle woke her a few hours later. She lay in bed, thick-headed, but then it repeated twice more. From dead north across the lake. She tore out of bed and sprinted up the trail to the Tolberts'.

5

Lucy waited astride her bike in the shadow of the towers, oblivious to the cold bay wind channeling down the avenue, and tasted the air. This wasn't some Folgers shit she was smelling. These were fresh beans.

Down the block, a man emerged onto a sidewalk overhung with scaffolding and headed across the intersection. Caught in the full beam of the fall sunlight, a brushed steel thermos winked under his arm.

She flung aside her bike with a metal rattle, grabbed her umbrella, and strolled to the doorway the man had vacated. Through the dim windows, she took in something she hadn't seen since the prior age: a coffee shop.

She entered, jangling the bell mounted on the door. A row of candles burned behind the counter and the rich, sickly smell of tallow mingled beneath the scorched caramel smell of the beans. The man behind the counter looked less like a barista and more like the bartender at an Old West saloon: prolific sideburns, heavy jaw, a mustache whose handlebars were as sturdy as the ones on her bike. Two young men turned from their booth to give her the eye. By the window, a conversation between two middle-aged men and an older woman continued uninterrupted.

The saloon-looking dude scanned her up and down. "All you can drink for ten minutes in the back room."

"That's not a very profitable way to run a business." Lucy slid onto a round padded stool. "What do you charge people you don't want to stick your wick in?"

"Couldn't say." He kept a straight face as he lifted a carafe and poured a steaming mug and slid it over the counter. "First one's free. Cream or sugar is extra. I accept gold, silver, and anything else that tickles my fancy."

She smiled at him and had a sip. It was good. Fresh roast all right. She drank at it while the man went down the counter and used one of the candles to light a few more. The room brightened slightly. He came back and rested his elbows on the bar.

"New in town?"

Lucy ran her finger around the lip of her mug. "How'd you guess?"

"What brings you to Manhattan?"

"Looking for a girl."

"Join the club."

She smiled tightly and withdrew a dog-eared photo from her shirt pocket. "You got to age her six or seven years. Recognize her?"

He made a thinking noise. "Should I?"

"Well, she's in town and she likes coffee."

"Are you suggesting there's a person who doesn't?"

Lucy took back the photo. "She was drinking it last time I heard from her."

He ran his thumbnail across his brow. "You know she was drinking coffee but you don't know where she lives?"

"This new world don't make a whole lot of sense, does it? You seen her or not?"

The man pulled back from the counter. She swore at her temper. Her mother always told her the man with the scythe could smell anger the way a bear smells blood on the wind. You think it's coincidence so many furious men wind up dead, Lucy? You got wrath, you keep it to yourself. Otherwise there will be no hiding from what you owe.

"I'm sorry," she said. "I'm just real worried for my friend. I don't think she's as suited to the city as she likes to think."

The man paused a blink, glanced over her shoulder, then smiled in return, mustache twitching. "We've still got coffee shops. How bad can it be here?"

He walked to the back of the room, opened an oven door, and banked on more logs. Lucy swirled her coffee to stop herself from smashing the mug against the floor. Someone moved beside her. She jerked up her cup to ram it into the man's temple. As he showed no further sign of aggression, Lucy stopped her strike halfway through and swerved her coffee toward her mouth instead.

The man gazed straight forward at the mirror behind the bar. He had a lot of stubble and a dirty face that made him look years older. "What would be in it for a guy who's seen your friend?"

"Dope," she said. "The green kind, not the white."

"Dope's a lot easier to find than a lost friend. Stuff grows like a weed."

"If you don't care about the quality. How about premium Charleston tobacco leaf? Get a lot of that up here?"

The man met her eyes for the first time. "You for real?"

"Smell for yourself," she said, full of conviction, because for all she knew her homegrown shreds did trace their lineage back to South Carolina. She produced a hand-rolled and held it under his nose. He dug into his pocket and got out a lighter. She grabbed his wrist. "I said smell, not taste."

His eyes flicked between hers, as if seeking permission, then he leaned his nose over the cigarette and inhaled. "I want a pack."

She laughed out loud. Here they were in a coffee house lit by tallow candles where the barista had to percolate his product over a wood stove and this joker was still thinking in packs. The world had moved on but people's heads were in the same old place.

It was the sort of thing an unscrupulous person might take advantage of.

"Let's go on outside and enjoy the evening," she said.

The man narrowed his eyes. "What happens if I spill my guts and you try to skip out on the bill?"

"Then you beat me up and take whatever you like."

She pushed off the stool and was out the door while the grimy man was still processing what he had just heard. The sun was hidden behind the western skyline and a chilly wind blew in from the bay. Lucy lit up and passed it to the man as he stepped out the door.

"This is good," he said.

"Great," she said. "Now talk before I get sore about you spying over my shoulder in there."

He glared at her through a cloud of white smoke, then greed got the best of him and he let his annoyance dissipate down the empty avenue. "She's got an accent like yours, right? Like honey on a biscuit?"

"If you say."

"I seen her around." He took another drag. "She works with Distro."

"Who's Distro?"

"The Distribution."

"Sounds scary," Lucy said. "They on record at City Hall?"

The man chortled and side-eyed her. "You're new in town, aren't you?"

"And getting mighty sick of being asked that. How about we skip the part where you act like anyone who's not from this island is a retard? Who's Distro and how I find them?"

The man dug grit from the corner of his eye and flicked it away and grinned. "You would have made a great New Yorker."

"That's because I am a girl of the world." She got out a baggie of tobacco and dangled it from two fingers. "Care to guide me through your corner of it?"

He took and pocketed the bag. "The first thing you need to get through your head is the Feds and Distro aren't exactly friends. The government likes to think they can tell everyone on the island what to do. That doesn't jibe with Distro's business."

"Which is?"

"Business. Export, import, you name it. Where you think the coffee comes from? You want it, Distro wants to sell it to you."

"And the Feds want their cut."

He grinned, showing a dead upper molar. "So you go to City Hall with a sack of questions about how to get in with Distro, maybe you wind up on a list. Best case you walk out with the answers the Feds want you to have."

Lucy nodded, taking it in. "So where would I go to speak to the source?"

"You go down to the Chelsea Piers right now, you're gonna find them hauling stuff off the boats. But I don't know if they got a public office."

"Good enough. When you saw my friend, what was she doing for them?"

"Driving the wagon."

"Figures," Lucy laughed. "That girl is horse-crazy. When was the last time you saw her?"

He didn't hesitate. "Two, three months."

"You sure it was her?"

"You don't forget that accent," he said. "Or that face. I would have made a run at her if not for her dude."

"She only had one?"

The man laughed and licked his fingers and pinched out the cherry of his cigarette. He pulled apart the roach and sprinkled the remaining tobacco into his new baggie.

"My coffee's getting cold. Name's Reese. You need anything else, leave a note with the mustache in there."

She walked to the intersection and got out one of her government-issue tourist maps. The Chelsea Piers were only a couple miles away on the other side of the island, but she was beat. Long day. She fetched her bike from the sidewalk and rode the few blocks to her apartment on Third and 9th. At the bottom of the stairwell, she thought she heard feet rasping above. She tipped back her head to the darkness and listened. Wind whistled through the street.

The stairs were pitch black. She lit a candle and ascended to her room. Inside, she locked the door and opened the shades and blew out the candle. No sense wasting it when you had moonlight to work with.

She was still full from the fried fish, so she spread her blankets on the bed and brushed her teeth with water and spat out the window. As she withdrew her head from the frame, a gunshot popped from far to the north, the report echoing down the towers. She didn't hear a second.

She lay in bed but couldn't sleep. It was quite the piece of luck to have picked up the trail again. She supposed there weren't so many people here. A girl like Tilly stood out. She looked like bottled sunshine with a pair of breasts. She'd smile for anyone, even Lucy, who none of the other kids had spoken to except to tease her about her mother or when the boys circled her on their bikes and squawked like crows protecting the nest.

Tilly didn't take no for an answer, either. They had first met in the lot beside the irrigation ditch where Lucy liked to explore. Lucy was throwing a knife at a tree and getting madder and madder that she couldn't cause it to stick. Feet crunched through the brush. Figuring to face one of the bicycle boys, Lucy picked up her knife.

A girl walked out and tipped her head to the side. "What are you doing?"

Lucy lowered the knife, then whirled and slung it at the tree. It clanked away. "Baking cupcakes. Want one?"

The girl had big eyes and an expressive mouth and she used both to display her confusion. She looked to be nine or so, Lucy's age, but you could tell she was going to be real pretty when she grew up.

"But that's a knife."

"You're smart." Lucy picked up the knife and clenched her teeth. She couldn't get the dang blade to stick and now this pretty little thing was watching her fail. "This tree's too tough. Think you'd make a better target?"

The girl laughed and pinched the skin of her tan, spindly arm. "I hardly got any bark at all."

Lucy drew back the knife. "Why don't we find out?"

"Can I try?" The girl entwined her fingers in front of her stomach and tried out a small smile. "Maybe we can figure it out together."

Bugs droned from the grass. Water trickled in the ditch. It smelled like wet green leaves and the girl seemed oblivious to the heaviness of the air between them. Lucy lowered her elbow and walked over and held out the knife point-first so the girl had to take the blade without cutting herself.

"You got to throw it hard," Lucy said. "Otherwise it won't stick."

The girl pursed her mouth and glared at the tree. She wound back her arm and flung the knife. It fluttered wide of the tree and plopped straight into the ditch.

The girl burst out laughing. "Did you see that?"

"You lost my knife!"

"I throw just like a girl!" She laughed some more, folding in on herself, hands on her knees. Lucy could only stare. The girl composed herself and managed to look sheepish. "I'm sorry about your knife. Let me fetch it out for you."

Lucy had seen water moccasins down in the ditch, but the girl strolled down the bank and squatted by the stream and plunged her arm into the water, groping carefully. Her eyes lit up and she brought out the gleaming steel blade.

"Your turn." She used both hands to present Lucy with the knife. "Can you show me how you throw so good?"

Lucy was so disarmed that all she could do was nod. "When you throw, it's like watching a busted spring. You got to use your whole arm like a whip."

That was Tilly. She seemed to float along in a world of her own, one completely free from bicycle boys and pit vipers and little girls who might decide you make a more tempting target than a tree. For the first time in her life, Lucy had a friend. Someone to share time with beside her mom, whose wicked eyes and sour words told Lucy she was born to die, and that mothers weren't there to care for their daughters, but to scorn and resent them.

Wind gusted against the window. Lucy lay in bed and listened for the breathing of the man with the scythe, but he was elsewhere that night. She slept.

Her window faced west and the dawn was slow to come. For whatever airs the Feds put on, there was no water in the faucet or the toilet. She went down to the courtyard meaning to use a planter and found that someone had dug an outhouse.

Her mother had been a bitch but her taunts had taught Lucy to be free with her money. She wasn't one to sit on her riches like a suspicious old dragon. Dragons lived forever. When it came to people, you were lucky if you got a blink; if you had it, spend it.

So she biked to the coffee house, which was manned this bright yellow morning by a right ogre of an old woman, and parted with a bit of her stash in exchange for eggs, biscuits, gravy made from bacon grease, and all the coffee she could drink. Feeling good, she saddled up her bike and rode toward the Chelsea Piers.

Leaves tumbled down the streets. To get a feel for the place, she zigzagged northwest through the city's grid. A tall white clock tower watched over 14th Street. As if it were keeping out the shabby apartments south of it, the digs improved notably from there, twenty-story towers with proper balconies and snazzy stone corners. Glass-fronted clothing stores took up the bottom two or three floors.

She coasted down 21st. The green-gray river winked a couple blocks ahead. Shouted orders and the clatter of labor drifted on the chilly marine air. To her right, a horse whickered from somewhere behind a building.

A horse. Lucy braked hard and leaned her bike against a brownstone. She jogged through its front door and tried the rear apartments until she found an open door. The back windows overlooked a courtyard shaded by thick trees that had just begun to shed their leaves. As the foliage shifted in the wind, beads of sunlight danced across the unkempt grass.

Eight mounted men gathered in a loose circle. Each bore an assault rifle and a sidearm. A couple of them were smoking. The window was closed and she couldn't hear their words but one of the men pointed dead west and made a series of sweeping gestures.

Lucy sank down until she could no longer see the riders, then crawled from the room, jogged outside, got on her bike, and pedaled straight to the piers.

Just as Reese had promised, men worked in the thin morning light, offloading crates and barrels from a sailboat tethered to the broad docks. While stevedores wheeled hand carts through the open doors of a former seafood restaurant, a man in a pinstriped suit and mirrored shades reclined in a deck chair atop a dais, propping himself on one elbow to bark orders at his men.

No one paid Lucy any mind. She swung out her kickstand and walked to the dais.

"Hola," she said to the man in the suit. "I wonder if you might be interested in swapping information?"

The man jerked, spilling a mug of brown liquid. He glanced from side to side, as if searching for someone to whip for this breach of security, then sighed and set down his cup.

"Get off my dock. I got traffic to direct."

"Surely your staff is competent enough to handle its own affairs for sixty seconds without burning down the pier."

"Spoken like someone who's never been in management."

She cast a baleful gaze at his high platform. "Unless you want to manage their funerals, you better get down and talk to me."

"Is that a threat?" He twisted to face her, lowering his shades like that goofus from the cop show.

"No sir. It's a warning." She smiled and ducked her chin. "Unless the caballeros with the machine guns are friends of yours."

He glanced down the dock, then at her, then back to the men lugging sacks and boxes off the barge. He stuck his pronged fingers in his mouth and whistled.

Too late. Hooves racketed into the street. Lucy made a face, spat, and ducked behind a barrel.

6

She ran flat-out, shoes slipping in the pine needles and damp leaves. She was conditioned by farm labor but had to slow after the first mile. Hard autumn light sliced through the branches. Mist whirled from her mouth.

She hadn't heard any more shots. It was possible she was winding herself for nothing. Locals hunted deer and rabbits. Took warning shots at bears and dogs. People were conservative with ammo these days, but gunfire wasn't that uncommon in the lakes and mountains.

But this felt different.

It was half an hour before she cleared the trees and caught sight of the house. The fields were empty. Yellow light played on the patchy wheat and weedy yard. She slowed to a jog, gasping for breath. Dee came out to the front stoop while Ellie was halfway across the field.

"I heard shots," Ellie panted.

Dee gazed to her left. "That would be me."

"You?" She climbed the step and grabbed Dee's shoulder. "Did you hurt someone?"

"I wish. I was just getting their attention."

"Sit down. Tell me exactly what happened."

"Did you run the whole way?" Dee smirked. "Want a glass of water, Mama Bear?"

She ducked inside. Ellie paced across the stoop. When she'd mentioned the shots, her daughter had glanced leftward. Toward their neighbors. Dee came back with a cool glass of water and sat beside her on the steps.

Ellie drank half in one go. "Did Sam Chase come by?"

"You're spooky," Dee laughed without much humor. "He showed up hollering for Quinn. He was drunk."

"How do you know that?"

"When he tipped back his Jack, he got more on his chest than down his throat."

"What was he saying?"

"I don't know, I don't speak Shitfaced. He wanted Quinn to stay away." She pointed to a patch of grass ten yards from the stoop. It was as trampled and divoted as the day after Augusta. "Quinn went to tell him to go away. They just started fighting. Like a couple of bobcats."

Ellie nodded. "And the gun?"

"I was afraid they were going to hurt each other. I fired into the air to make them quit." Dee stared at the torn-up grass. "Sam wasn't armed. He wasn't even wearing shoes."

"I take it everyone's all right."

"Quinn's got a black eye, but I think they hurt the grass more than each other." Dee scowled through the trees toward the Chase house. "What the hell's his problem?"

"I'm afraid it's me." Ellie drank the rest of her water and pulled herself to her feet. "Is George inside?"

"He's with Quinn."

"I'm going to ask a few questions. If Sam comes back, stay inside the house."

Dee nodded and followed her inside and locked the door. Ellie left her glass beside the sink and headed down the hall to Quinn's room. The door was half open but she tapped it with her knuckles.

"Knock knock."

Father and son swung up their heads. They were seated on the edge of the bed and Quinn had his shirt off. Welts reddened his chest. His left eyesocket was swollen and the color of an underripe plum.

"Yeah, but should I see the other guy?" Ellie said.

Quinn cocked his head. "Huh?"

"What happened out there?"

George planted his palms on his knees. "That trash who lives beside us was spoiling for a fight."

"I'm asking Quinn."

The boy shook his head. "Sam came over drunk and shouting. Next thing I know he's throwing punches."

"Rest assured I'll be speaking to the sheriff," George said.

Ellie didn't know whether to laugh or sigh. "Let's go out back, George."

He touched Quinn's shoulder and smiled paternally, then followed her to the back porch. The air was brisk and now that Ellie's pulse had slowed her sweat felt cold on her skin.

"The way that Chase boy carried on, you'd think I stole his favorite dolly." George shook his head. "The youth are crazy these days."

Ellie made a noncommittal noise. "This wasn't the first incident."

"Oh, I know they have a history. Chase seems to think Dee is a prize to be won."

"Last week, I saw someone lurking around your yard. Yesterday morning, Quinn found Ringer in the woods. He'd been stabbed."

George's jaw dropped. "Sam Chase did that?"

"He has an unhealthy fixation on Dee."

"And when were you intending to tell me?"

"Once I had hard facts."

The man slowed his voice like an idling car. "A man has the right to know when his family is being terrorized."

She met his eyes. "That's a little dramatic."

"My dog has been stabbed. I can think of few things more dramatic." He tugged down the hem of his coat. "I am off to see Sheriff Hobson."

"Why?"

He thrust his finger in the direction of the Chase house. "That fool assaulted my boy! He belongs in jail."

"Last I checked, we don't have one of those," Ellie said. "And the esteemed Sheriff Hobson is both self-appointed and a civilian. I checked up on him. He taught literature in Buffalo. Big fan of Chandler and Arthur Conan Doyle."

George laughed harshly. "I know what this is about. As usual, you think the most qualified man in the room so happens to be yourself."

"I used to work for the government."

"Doing what, exactly?"

"That's classified." She gestured at the scraggly wheat fields. "Why don't you bring in the grain already? The mice are getting at it."

His brows met in a peevish glower. "I had intended to. Now my assistant's hurt."

"Quinn will be fine." Ellie cleared her throat; the run had worked up some phlegm. "See to your fields while I do some poking around. Once you finish, if you're not satisfied with my results, then take the issue to Sheriff Hobson."

"Why don't I head straight there?"

"Because we're family. I like to keep our business our own."

George nodded slowly. "You have three days. After that, I go to the sheriff."

"Deal." She folded her arms. "Mind if I sleep here tonight? I'd feel safer knowing we were all under the same roof."

"Of course. You can have my room."

That was hardly necessary, but now wasn't the time to argue. Not when George was trying to reassert control of his homestead. Ellie checked in with Dee and Quinn, who were talking softly in his bedroom, then walked back to her house at a rather more leisurely pace than she had left it. She spent most of the walk thinking about the "sheriff." With his goatee and his prissy little bowler. She'd never had a run-in with him, but it troubled her that George took him seriously. That was the other problem with the growing population. Once a place got big enough, people started to believe that it needed a select few to run it. And it was a truism that the people most interested in power and authority were those least qualified to exercise them. If Hobson had his way, he'd probably decree all the residents of the lakelands were henceforth required to wear full-body bathing suits before stepping foot in the waters.

Back home, she fed the chickens, checked their water, grabbed her one-day bag from the front closet, locked the doors, and walked back to the Tolberts'. The western mountains dragged the sun down to their cold lips. Breezes circled through the woods, carrying the brown sugar smell of maple and the promise of cold.

Twilight neared as she returned to her soon-to-be in-laws' farm.

Tinkering filtered from the barn. Ellie poked her head inside. George crouched over a tarp spread with tools, his spine curved like a rod that's hooked a four-pound bass, readying the tractor and combine for tomorrow's work.

The house was hot and smelled like woodsmoke. Dee and Quinn curled on the couch in a mess of blankets and arms. Dee was reading aloud and stopped as Ellie stepped into the living room.

"Hey Mom."

"Hey kids. I expect Sam is busy sleeping it off, but if you hear or see anything funny tonight, wake me up first thing, okay?"

Quinn grinned. "You're so ready, Ellie. I hope our first son is just like you."

She stared him down. "If you ever say that again, I will render you incapable of having a son."

His smile went saggy. Feeling meanly pleased with herself, Ellie retired to George's room. He had set beeswax candles for her on both nightstands. She checked her pistol—loaded, safety on—and set it on the stand to the right of the bed.

George returned to the house after dark. While he scrubbed the grease from his hands, Ellie started dinner. Quinn lent a hand. They ate and washed the dishes and retired to their rooms; George set up blankets for himself on the couch.

Way back in high school, Ellie had learned that the night before tests, she tended to blip in and out of sleep like a stone skipping over a calm lake. This trait worsened in college—freshman year, many of her essay responses had come back marked with a single red "?"—but she learned to manage it. By the time she entered the DAA, she had turned it to her advantage. Near the front lines of a foreign country, she cat-napped through the night, ready to move at a moment's notice, letting her dreaming mind draw strange connections between the problems she had been sent to solve. More than two or three nights of this reduced her to a buzzing ball of nerves, but a single night was no problem at all.

That night, she woke every thirty to sixty minutes to gaze at the moonlit fields. At the deepest part of the night, her mind relaxed enough to let her sleep the final three hours straight through.

At dawn, engines roared from the barn. George drove the combine while Quinn paralleled him with the tractor. Ellie made sure Dee knew where George's rifle was, then walked home to clean up and see to the chickens. She had dressed, but her hair was still stuck to her neck in dark damp strands when Sheriff Hobson strolled up to her front door.

"Good morning, Ms. Colson." He produced a pocket watch, sprung it open, and examined the hands. "Or should I say good afternoon?"

"Whatever it is, I doubt it's 'good,'" she said. "Or you'd have no reason to be here."

The man grinned. "Very good. So have you likewise deduced the nature of my visit?"

He carried a cane and wore a wool suit well-tailored to his elfin frame. He had just begun the particular male transition from middle age to senior citizen and his hair remained mostly brown but the skin of his neck and under his eyes had a shiny, slack paleness to it, like egg whites brushed over dough. He was mostly harmless, but that was exactly what bothered her.

"Sure," she said. "I forgot to file a permit for my new shed, didn't I?"

Hobson chuckled and tucked his cane under his armpit like a lost safari guide. "If only it were that quotidian. I'm afraid there's been a complaint."

"About the shots? That was nothing."

He shook his head, face gone grave. "From Sam Chase."

That looped her. "What's his beef?"

"He is unappreciative of Quinn Tolbert's ongoing campaign of harassment."

"Is he? Then maybe he should stop skulking around the Tolberts' farm and leering at my daughter."

"Charges he denies. Lacking physical evidence, I can't say one way or the other. But I did bear witness to the letter Quinn left at the Chase household. It was...incendiary."

Ellie glared across the lake. "This is ridiculous."

"Nevertheless, if it continues, there will be consequences."

"Such as?"

"Consequential actions." Hobson took on a look of pained patience. "I have talked young Sam out of pursuing charges. I believe it's in the interests of both parties to keep their respective distances. Wouldn't you agree?"

"Completely. Thanks for letting me know how things stand, sheriff."

He tipped his cap, checked his pocket watch, and strode down the trail, impaling stray leaves with his cane. As soon as he was gone, Ellie got in the canoe and paddled across the lake to the muddy beach just down the shore from the Chases.

Sam's dad answered the door, gray hair awhirl around his ears. "He's in bed."

"Hangover's that bad? He'll want to talk to me."

"See about that."

The man closed the door in her face. Two minutes later, Sam opened it back up. His eyes were bloodshot and his hair stuck up from the side of his head. As always, he was shirtless.

"The hell do you want?"

"What was in the letter Quinn sent you?" Ellie said.

Sam flushed. "Bunch of horseshit, that's what."

"Did he tell you to stay away from Dee?"

"Like I told him, I was never there. The way you crows keep circling, I'm starting to think she's got a thing for me."

Ellie examined him a long moment. Those who found themselves at the center of a perpetual storm tended to think of themselves as the victim, the target of malicious persecution—that was how they justified striking back, which they always did—but she didn't see it in Sam's face. Maybe it was the hangover, but he looked tired. Ready to be done with it.

"I'll keep Quinn away," she said. "If you have a problem, you come to me. And for god's sake, put a shirt on first."

She walked down the shore to her canoe, shoes squelching in the mud. Back toward the Tolberts', motors droned. Good thing they'd finally got to work. The day was overcast, gray. Might rain later.

"I don't think we'll have any more trouble with Sam Chase," she announced when the men came back in from the harvest.

Quinn crossed his arms. "I'll believe that when I see it."

"Then no more letters."

Dee blinked. "Letters?"

"It's nothing," Quinn said through the redness of his face. "I'm just looking out for my family."

Ellie didn't press. What she'd already said seemed to do the trick. Quinn and George went on with the harvest. Dee cleaned the spent straw from the fields. Lacking better purpose, Ellie joined her, and once the men finished with the grain, they pitched in on cleanup too. Ellie neither saw nor heard from Sam Chase. George cursed the boy a couple times, but didn't pursue it with the sheriff. Maybe he was too busy with work, but Ellie suspected he'd got wind that Sam had gone to Sheriff Hobson for himself, and had no desire to stir the pot further.

The rain held off until the day they expected to finish raking up the straw. That morning, it fell steadily and froze when it landed, cementing the leaves to the ground. It thawed by midday, but the straw was sodden and heavy. With no chance of fire, George decided to leave it until it dried.

Lost in the rhythm of work, Ellie's anxiety relaxed its hold on her chest. But it never left completely. If Sam Chase were guilty, that meant her daughter was staying just down the shore from a man who stabbed dogs and left them in the woods to die.

And if it weren't Sam, that meant she had no suspect or motive at all.

But each day the threat felt that much further away. And Ellie had work of her own to do. Dragging in wood and splitting it for the winter. Cleaning the machines and getting them locked up until next spring. Checking the windows and walls and attics for chinks that would bleed heat. She hadn't done so the first winter and soon discovered the house shed warmth like a sick dog. She'd underestimated the amount of wood they'd needed, too. February and March had been miserable: slogging through the snow for cracked branches and fallen logs, dragging them back to the garage to dry them out as best she could. She and Dee had been reduced to sleeping in the same bed bundled in coats and three pairs of socks.

She put together sacks of grain and loaves of bread and hitched the trailer to her bike. In Lake Placid, she bartered for supplies she hadn't learned to make or grow for herself—soap, candles, black pepper and sea salt for the fish they'd catch throughout the winter. A northern wind chilled the streets and the handful of vendors set up around the downtown plaza wore mittens.

She enjoyed bartering. There was some game theory behind it

and some psychology, too, which varied depending on who was doing the selling. Timothy Yao, the former chemist who now made soaps and toothpaste, liked to yammer on about the special processes involved in compounding each of his goods. The experiments that had failed before he perfected each batch.

It was a way of displaying his expertise, without which Ellie would be scrubbing herself with water and sand. She nodded along and matched him with talk of the composted fertilizer she'd fiddled with this summer. The homebrewed pesticide that saved her from an unexpected grasshopper hatch. Not to mention the new yeast she'd found to give her latest batches that tangy, sour taste. Timothy smiled slyly and allowed that there might be more to farming and baking than he knew.

Mrs. Stoltz, on the other hand, was no-nonsense. She got salt and rarer seasonings shipped in from the coast and wasn't shy about letting Ellie know precisely what she'd paid and how much she needed in return to make it worth her while. Ellie counted with a hand-drawn spreadsheet of her estimated harvest minus what she and Dee would eat over the year and thus the (conservatively estimated) surplus she had leftover for "minor niceties" like salt.

Mrs. Stoltz leaned over the figures and muttered and eyeballed her own ledgers. She made quick calculations on her abacus, beads clacking, then arrived at a figure, take it or leave it. Ellie took it.

If she wanted, she might find a wagon and borrow a horse and drive it to Ottawa or Syracuse to scavenge instead of dealing with all this trade. She had no doubts the cities would yield something interesting. After six years of being picked over by other scavengers, however, there were no guarantees she'd find the specific something she was looking for. Guns and ammunition, for instance. These days firearms outnumbered living people a hundred to one, but good luck finding them. Most had been hoarded, first during the plague, then again during the invasion. If you tracked down some prepper's secret compound, you might be set for life, but in the meantime, it was usually easier to trade with someone who had a spare.

It was the same with everything. Much had been lost to hoarders who were now dead. More had been destroyed by fires and looting. Most had simply spoiled or rusted. In practice, scavenging was a crapshoot.

Add in the time and hassle of travel, not to mention the danger in picking around a foreign city, and for Ellie's money, it was easier to stay at home, grow and hunt your own food, and figure out how to make things for yourself—or learn how to go without. She wasn't alone in this thinking. She didn't have an exact head count, but at least two hundred people had gathered in and around Lake Placid, pursuing their crafts and trading the excess for anything they couldn't produce on their own.

To date, they'd lived in relative peace. A few fights, no murders. Low-key enough that either the sheriff or the people themselves had been able to settle disputes. But Ellie had the feeling the dog-killer was about to push them into territory they weren't ready to explore. Trials. Punishment. Retribution.

By the time she emptied her trailer of wheat and bread and refilled it with candles and knit socks and fresh blankets and her one splurge item, a bow and arrow set she'd always intended to learn how to use, the daylight was spent as well. As she rode the last leg of trail to her house, candles flickered in the windows. Maybe Dee would have dinner waiting for her.

Dee was inside, but the only smell in the front room was fear.

"Where have you been?" Dee said.

Ellie set down an armload of blankets. "In town. What's the matter with you?"

"It's not me, it's George," Dee said. "Half his grain's been stolen."

7

The men galloped onto the pier, shouting, firing short bursts from their assault rifles. Dock workers yelped and scattered. One dropped in a skid of blood, clutching his guts. Men dived off the docks into the cold, gray-green waters.

The man on the dais crouched around the back side. "What the fuck?"

Lucy hunkered behind a barrel, umbrella on her knees. Men screamed while the invaders laughed. Hooves struck the piers with hard thumps. Gunfire answered the raiders and was met with a full-on, ear-shredding, five-second burst of multiple fully automatic weapons converging on the same offender. In the silence after, the shots rolled across the river and echoed back from the New Jersey towers. It smelled like smoke and horse.

A gift shop blocked Lucy's view of the battle. That was just fine with her. Nails groaned and wood splintered. The raiders barked orders and positions. Lucy lowered herself to the dusty green ground and peeked around the corner of the building. Next to the barge, the raiders bashed apart a crate and divvied up heavy fabric bags. The raiders saddled up and raced from the docks, firing over their shoulders. Caught flat-footed, the Distro workers had no time to mount a counter.

Hoofbeats faded into the distance. Lucy got up and brushed off her clothes. "Bold leadership, Attila."

Atop the dais, the man in the pinstriped suit had lost his sunglasses and his eyes were alive with fury. A pistol appeared in his hand. He pointed it at Lucy's right eye.

"I got one!" he shouted to his people. "Get your sorry asses out here!"

A couple pairs of feet shuffled from the other side of the buildings. Lucy drew back her chin. "What in the world are you pointing that at me for?"

"Don't play dumb, you runty bitch."

She laughed. "You think I'm scouting for them?"

"You stroll in and two minutes later we're hit with a fucking raid? What was the signal?"

A man sprinted around the gift shop, rifle in hand. Lucy gritted her teeth. "I assure you, sir, my arrival was nothing more than unfortunate coincidence."

The man laughed. He had a thick City Yankee accent that made Lucy want to ram a poker down his throat and wiggle it around until he learned to talk right.

"You dumb whore." He stepped down from the platform, keeping the gun on her. "Your friends forgot you, didn't they?"

She cursed herself for not slipping away during the raid. Ought to have seen this one coming. She'd been looking forward to seeing a few people get shot and she'd wound up bagged herself. She only had two shots in the umbrella and her .22 pistol was all the way down at her ankle. As she considered this, a woman ran to join the others, chrome pistol held aloft like the torch of the green lady on the island in the bay.

Lucy sighed and leaned on her umbrella. "You got a manager I can talk to?"

The man in the pinstripes laughed. "I got a manager all right."

She swore he was about to grab his crotch, but instead he disarmed her and took her pack and umbrella and marched her down the docks to a gutted French restaurant. Inside, they climbed a spiral staircase to a rotunda with a sweeping view of the pier, the river, and the skyline.

The dining tables had been converted to desks thick with paperwork and toy-like square objects rigged with wires and beads. At the windows overlooking the docks, a man with slick black hair spoke very softly to a pudgy man with a rifle who looked ready to shit his pants.

"Bossman looks busy," Lucy said. "Why don't we— "

Her captor clamped her wrist until the bones ground. Lucy bit her teeth together, partly from pain, partly to stop herself from sinking them into his steroidal neck. After a moment, the pudgy man across the room nodded repeatedly and ran for the stairs.

The pinstriped man marched her toward the windows. "Sir?"

The dark-haired man gazed at Lucy in a way that made her skin itch worse than Georgia humidity. "Yes?"

"We got a prisoner. A scout for the raiders."

"Then shoot her."

"Hold your horses," Lucy said. "This is slander. You'll be hearing from my lawyers."

The man holding her wrist laughed. "If you weren't working with them, how'd you know they were coming, smart guy?"

"Because my eyes happen to be connected to my brain. I saw the riders in a park across the street and figured I'd do the neighborly thing and warn you."

"Nuh uh. No way. They went straight for the greenies. How'd they know to do that?"

Lucy glanced over her shoulder. "What the hell's a greenie?"

The man glowered and crushed her wrist some more. "I told you not to play dumb. The green beans. The coffee. Fresh off the boat."

"In that case," she said, real slow, "I would say you got a mole."

The man in the suit scrunched up his face. "I would say you're full of shit."

"Yeah?" With her free hand, she gestured dock-wards. "Are all those people your brothers and sisters? Or are they some dumb humps you pay in dried corn? How much can you trust them?"

"More than I trust some skank looking to save her own skin."

She turned to the man with the slick hair. "Then I guess you ought to shoot me. It'll feel good, won't it? Right up until the next time your enemies run off with the one thing you covet most."

The man gazed back at her. "Go downstairs, Jimmy."

The pinstriped foreman beetled his brows. "Sir, she showed up not two minutes before the cavalry struck."

"Incidentally, who allowed that to happen?"

Jimmy paled. "We never been hit like this before."

The other man tipped his head ten degrees to the side. "That doesn't answer my question."

"I did, sir. And I'll see that it never happens again."

He watched his boss the way an unarmed man watches a trigger. The other man opened and closed his palm, rings clicking. Finally, he gestured toward the stairs.

"Times are changing. If you can't change faster, I'll find someone who can."

Jimmy smiled in relief and hurried down the spiral stairs. A door closed below. Shouts filtered through the windows.

Lucy jerked her thumb past her shoulder. "Not exactly the kind you're eager to promote, is he?"

The man with the slick hair examined her eyes. "What do you mean?"

"Decisive enough, but no imagination. Great sergeant, but you wouldn't want him to wind up leading the platoon, if you know what I mean."

"Who are you?"

"My name is Lucy Two," she said. "I came from Florida, but that's not where I'm from."

"They call me Nerve," he said, and for a moment she thought she was off the hook. "You're a smart girl, aren't you, Lucy?"

"I never got the chance to find out."

He almost laughed. "You have three days to find the mole."

She squinted at him. "Or you decide it's me."

"Very smart."

"What happens when I do?"

"I reconsider our situation."

"Well, that ain't much of a deal, but I guess that's why you're the businessman and I'm the girl with the not-so-metaphorical gun to her head." She gestured toward the piers. "Who were the raiders?"

Nerve shrugged. "Figure it out."

He glanced toward the bar at the side of the rotunda. The man there was much too large to have hidden so long yet it was the first Lucy had taken note of him. His head was shaved to the scalp and there was such violence concealed in his walk that it made you want to run away.

"Where is she allowed?" the man said.

"For this?" Nerve said. "Anywhere she wants."

"Can I have my umbrella?" Lucy said. "My skin's real sensitive to the sun."

"When I inspect it, I'll find a sword, won't I?" Nerve said.

"Shotgun," Lucy said, feeling sheepish for the first time since she'd brought back Beau's Honda with a dent in the back fender.

"Get to work."

The large man took hold of her arm and led her to the stairs. He descended in perfect silence. Lucy made a quick assessment of the circumstances. When she'd walked up to Jimmy, it hadn't been her plan to get saddled with a life or death challenge before she'd discovered whether Tilly still worked for Distro, but when you get thrown a curveball, you don't watch it go by, then argue it wasn't a strike. You won't change his mind and all you'll get is ejected from the game. Anyway, she had two and a half days before she'd have to do anything crazy.

She smelled opportunity, too. She got the vibe Nerve had rare judgment and the good sense to trust it. Put yourself in front of a person like that, and you can rise in a hurry.

"Anyone call in sick today?" Lucy said to the man of quiet menace.

"Sick?"

"No sick days? Real union-busters, huh? I need a list of everyone who didn't show up today. If you know armed horsemen are about to bust into the office, you might be inclined to take the day off."

"I don't have access to that," the man said.

Lucy glanced up at him as they exited the converted restaurant into the sunny morning. "Nerve said to give me anything I want. I want attendance records."

The man laughed like shifting rocks. "He's going to love you or kill you."

"More likely he'll order you to."

She headed toward the road. Some blood had splashed on the green surface of the docks but nothing indicative of a massacre. Men had already resumed unloading the barge. Others stood watch with guns in hand. Lucy crossed the street and strolled to the apartment where she'd first seen the raiders plotting in the courtyard. The big man accompanied her without a word. Through the grimy window, the courtyard was silent and shadowed. She shoved at the window, but it stuck fast.

"Give me a hand, Hulk," she said.

The man gazed down at her. "My name is Kerry."

"How about you put those big muscles to use, Kerry?"

He gazed at the window as if contemplating smashing it, then bent into the frame and heaved. His shoulders bunched like swelling waves. It held for two seconds and lurched up with a pained screech. Lucy ducked through and dropped into the courtyard. With considerable difficulty, Kerry squeezed through.

The grass was torn up like it had been punished. Horse turds lay in fibrous brown pellets. She moved methodically through the grounds. A cigarette butt had been caught in the thick green blades and when she picked it up it looked new but the butt was damp and the grass was not.

She held it up to her eye. A tiny golden crown had been stamped on the filter. "These must be stale as shit. You recognize the brand?"

Kerry shook his head. "I don't smoke."

"Good. They'll kill you, you know."

She tucked the butt into her pocket and continued to pick through the grass, finding two more butts of the same brand with just a bit of dirt on them. Recent. Satisfied there was nothing else to find, she headed back to the piers.

"I need that list," she said.

He nodded and moved toward the restaurant. She peeled off to approach the dock workers.

Kerry stopped and shook his head. "With me. All times."

"I don't have time for this."

"Then work without your list."

"Jesus H." She rolled her eyes but followed him to the restaurant. Inside the back door, a woman sat at a desk, hunched over a report the way felons guard their food.

"Today's attendance," Kerry said. "Do you have it?"

The woman glanced up, just noticing them. "Today's files."

Kerry moved to a stack of plastic shelves at one side of her desk. He withdrew a sheaf of papers, leafed through them, and handed a list to Lucy.

"That's my original," the woman said slowly. "If you want the records, make a copy."

"Mr. Nerve said I have access to whatever I want," Lucy said.

The woman gazed at her over her glasses. "You want my original? Leave your left hand as collateral. If that's too steep, then make a fucking copy."

"Don't strain your back celebrating when Nerve executes me." Lucy gestured around. "Pen and paper."

The woman pursed her mouth and retrieved both. Lucy set to work. Still scribbling, she glanced up at Kerry. "Listen, beefcake, you got any idea who did this?"

He didn't hesitate. "The Kono."

"The Kono being?"

"Fans of violence."

"You disapprove? Isn't violence your job?"

He shrugged mildly. "Most people don't like their jobs."

Lucy finished up and walked out, taking the pen and extra paper with her. The list was comprised of 33 names. Two of the dockworkers had not been present for morning attendance, but there had been a revision since then. A man named Woody Sloan had shown up just after the attack.

She tapped her notes. "Take me to Woody."

Kerry led her toward the barge tied at the pier, where he exchanged words with a gnarled woman overseeing the stevedores. She swore and climbed up in the boat. A seagull cawed from the roof of the neighboring pier. It smelled like cold fresh water and a drop of salt. A stevedore rattled by with a hand cart. Lucy smelled something she hadn't smelled in a long time: cinnamon.

The woman came back leading a short thin man with muscles as taut and tough as the ropes mooring the barge to the dock. A mess of cross-hatched scars covered the socket where his right eye should be.

"Mighty rude not to cover that thing, Woody." Lucy flapped her paper at him. "You were late to work today."

"I was given leave," he said.

"Not according to what I've got."

"Just ask Miss Tibbs." His sweat smelled like cumin and beef. "I got switched to the afternoon shipment."

Lucy looked up from her papers. "Then what brought you in early?"

"I heard the shots."

"You live nearby?"

He pointed across the street to a narrow tower overlooking the piers. His index finger crooked at the last knuckle where it had once been broken. "I'm not much for commutes."

Lucy frowned. "You like tobacco, Woody?"

"When I can get it."

"Filtered or unfiltered?"

He squinted at her with his good eye. "If I like it, why would I stick a filter on it?"

"Perhaps you intend to make it to your sunset years." She repressed a sigh. "That will be all, Woody."

As long as she was there, she took the chance to interview every stevedore hopping in and out of the boat. Most resisted her inquiries until Kerry shook his head, a gesture that somehow promised they could either move their mouths or lose their teeth. After that, the workers answered with grudging brevity. Lucy avoided insinuations and accusations, sticking to questions about what they had been doing when the raiders swooped in, who they thought the raiders may have been, and whether they'd seen anyone acting funny, whether that morning or within the last couple weeks.

Most didn't know jack shit, but several were happy to cast shade on their fellow employees. She wrapped up the first round of interviews with four names to attack with a second round of questions. Along with the man who still hadn't come in to work, that gave her five leads.

Kerry announced it was time for dinner. They ate at a picnic bench beside a netted driving range aimed out at the water. She finished fast and plunged into her second interviews, starting with a weatherbeaten man named Rolando Quiroz.

She tapped her notes. "Rumor has it you went to the bathroom right before the riders arrived, Rolando. Why is that?"

"Rumor has it I had to shit." He took such a big bite of oatmeal he had to chew for ten seconds before answering her next question.

The next name on her list was Zoe Goodwin, a round-faced woman who kept her iron-gray hair clipped an inch from the skin. She ate at a round glass bistro table.

Lucy straddled the chair across from her. "When the raiders rode in, I hear you laughed. Something funny about your friends getting shot?"

The woman picked her teeth with a fish bone. "I was relieved."

"Relieved?"

"That I was about to be freed from this hell."

Lucy smiled and got out her bag, which Kerry had allowed her to grab out of storage (though he'd refused her the umbrella). In the waning sunlight at Zoe's table, Lucy got out a baggie of shredded leaf and jogged it up and down.

"You like to smoke?"

Zoe moved her hand beneath the table. "Got any cigars?"

"Seems a bit greedy, Zoe."

She poked at Zoe's apparent lack of satisfaction with her job, but the woman provided bland non-answers about long days, a stiff back, and a limp husband.

Sunset painted the towers red and gold. When night took the island, Kerry locked Lucy in a windowless pantry off the restaurant kitchen. His footsteps receded on the linoleum, then returned. Fabric shuffled. Ten minutes later, his snores cut through the door. He was sleeping right in front of it.

Lucy wadded her blanket under her back and swore. Nerve's challenge had felt like a lock. She'd accepted it with the steel-firm certainty she could outwit these trunk-headed stevedores, gain Nerve's trust, and use his knowledge of the Distro organization to track down Tilly. But as the limits of her investigation clarified like islands in the mist, Lucy saw just how little she had to work with. These piers were just one wing of the Distro organization. What if the mole worked at another dock? Or their headquarters?

Even if there were a mole, and he was here at Chelsea, all he had to do was lie to her. She didn't know these men. She didn't have the chance to bide her time and trip them in a contradiction. Would Nerve allow her to torture them? Unlikely. Not that he seemed squeamish about the ol' ultraviolence. But if he really thought that would get results, he'd skip this game with her and unleash Kerry on the dock workers instead.

Nope. Lying in the darkness, it became very clear. Nerve had nothing to lose in sending her on this fool's quest. He didn't care if she failed and he had to kill her. She'd been the walking dead from the moment Jimmy marched her up to the rotunda.

She hadn't found a mole, but she'd found an answer of another kind. The game was rigged. In 48 hours, she would lose it and her life.

8

Ellie eyeballed her daughter. "How do you know it was stolen?"

"Because two of George's bins have been replaced with empty spaces," Dee said. "It could be that one of us is a sleep-eater. But if nobody here passes a five-hundred-pound bolus of grain, there's only one other answer."

She sighed and set the blankets by the door. "We'd better get over there before Quinn murders Sam Chase."

Dee helped transfer the contents of the bicycle trailer inside. Ellie locked up and they jogged down the trail together. She had spent hours contemplating a way to strengthen or even pave the trail, but between the leaves, the pine needles, the mud, the washouts, and constant freezing and thawing of the ice, anything she was capable of building was unlikely to last longer than the average pair of shoes.

And until the last couple weeks, Ellie had never had much need to sprint across the woods. There had been no major accidents or mysterious gunshots or unmotivated acts of violence. A few raiders, years ago, but that had been settled. Ever since, the lakes had been lulled to sleep.

She jogged on, listening for shots. She could smell the coming frost. The sun vanished. The air in the woods was perfectly still and their breath hung behind them like judgmental ghosts.

"When did this happen?" Ellie asked.

"George just noticed," Dee said.

"Was it there yesterday?"

"I dunno. We were in town."

"We've got to work on your powers of observation."

They ran in silence from there, feet swishing through the damp leaves. The limbs were growing bare and Ellie was growing sick of all this rushing back and forth. It had reached the point where it made sense to invite George and Quinn to live with her and Dee. At least that way, when trouble came calling, Ellie wouldn't have to put on her shoes.

"What's so funny?" Dee said.

"Family."

The run took as long as always. As they jogged toward the Tolbert house, two silhouettes emerged onto the front porch, guns glinting in the moonlight of the cloud-patched sky.

"It's us," Ellie called.

"Hell." George lowered his gun. "I thought the bandits were back for the rest."

"Wasn't bandits," Quinn muttered. "It was Sam Chase."

Ellie stopped in front of the stoop, pressing her hand to the stitch in her side. "You didn't confront him, did you?"

"Dee wouldn't let me."

"That's because I raised her to use her brain. Sam isn't stupid enough to steal two bins of wheat from his own neighbor."

Quinn laughed harshly. "Sam is stupid enough to eat the plate when he runs out of dinner."

"We'll see who's right in the morning. When men are 85% less likely to answer a knock with a shotgun blast." Ellie climbed the first step and leaned on her knee. "Now how about you two Southern gentlemen get out of the way so I can get a drink of water?"

The Tolbert men shot up their eyebrows and fell over each other to vacate the stairs and bring her some water. George had a fire going in the living room, and after the five-mile run, the home felt stiflingly warm. Ellie glugged down a full glass of water, refilled it herself, and went out back to cool down. The others followed, settling into the lawn chairs.

"Have you seen anyone around here lately?" she said.

George shook his head. "Just your midnight skulker."

"When was the last time you saw the wheat?"

"Yesterday. Morning." He leaned forward with a frown. "Do you mean to lead this investigation?"

"Do you have a problem with that?"

"It's my farm. My business."

Ellie took a long drink to stop herself from saying something stupid. "No offense, George, but you and your son keep running into trouble. I think a third party is the best chance to put a stop to it."

"Just like you did with the Chase boy?"

"Has there been another incident? Then don't question my work."

She'd spoken with more vehemence than she'd meant to and for a moment the night was so quiet they could hear the lake lapping the dark shore.

"I'll go with her, Dad," Quinn said.

Ellie raised a brow. "Not to see Sam."

"If it isn't him, I mean."

George rubbed his jaw. He normally kept it clean shaven but white bristles showed in the candlelight. "It would be nice to have a Tolbert represented in the field."

"You're kind of young, aren't you?" Ellie said.

Quinn laughed in a careless way that did not bode well for a long and happy life. "I'm nineteen. In the old days, nineteen-year-olds were sent to war."

"The old days? You mean like 2007?"

"Before the plague. When everything was safe and kids had to be sealed away from anything that could hurt them."

Ellie glared into her water glass. "The army knew it's best to train killers from an early age."

"It's a new world," George declared. "Time for my boy to learn how to navigate it. Think you're the best person for the job, Ellie? Then you're the best one to show Quinn the ropes."

Ellie bristled, but she forced herself to take a mental step back. Quinn meant to marry her daughter. Some day—a day that would come much sooner than Ellie had grown up to expect—she wouldn't be there for them. Maybe it was time to introduce them to the darker shades of adult life.

"George, I want a list of everyone you talked to in town yesterday," she said. "At first light I'll take a look at the barn and talk to Sam." She raised her eyebrows at Quinn. "I want you ready by the time I get back."

"Yes ma'am," he said. "Suppose we ought to sleep in shifts?"

She doubted the thieves would come back tonight, but it couldn't hurt. She took one of the middle shifts. While the others slept, she gazed through the front window at the dark fields. The dew had frozen to the shorn stalks and the frost gleamed in the moonshine like lost treasure.

It hadn't melted at dawn when she walked to the barn. She unlocked the padlock. The hinges squeaked. The dust and straw had been stirred every which way. She was mostly interested in the stray grains of wheat that had been crushed into a homogenous powder. And the pair of ruts leading northeast from the barn toward the road to town.

She closed up the barn and walked down the shore to the Chase's. After the third time she knocked, she heard the old man bellowing.

Sam's eyes were red, his face creased and swollen from insufficient sleep. "Man, I am so sick of your face."

"I hope this is the last you have to see it."

"Great. What would you like to accuse me of now?"

She felt herself flush. "Night before last, some of George's grain went missing."

Sam gritted his teeth and hooked his finger in his cheek like a snagged fish. "Want to check my pouches?"

"I don't think you did it," Ellie said. "But if I can check your sheds, we can stave off the drama before it starts."

He sighed and bladed his hand against the dawn to peer at the trees separating his home from the Tolberts'. "Let me grab a shirt. For you, I'll even put on shoes."

The attached garage housed two Mustangs, a powder blue '65 and a late model as bright as first blood. Ellie walked past, confirming there were no tubs of wheat concealed at the back of the garage.

"These things run?"

"You looking to buy?" Sam said.

"Just want to know what to steal if the zombies roll in."

He snorted and led her to two sheds: one filled with tools, the other stacked with wood. As he opened the door to the second, a black widow scrambled up its shredded webbing. Sam cursed and yanked off his shoe and smashed the widow into yellow goo.

Last, he took her to the little boathouse. The only thing that smelled fishy was the air.

"Sorry to wake you, Sam," she said. "I owe you one."

"This early in the morning, the price goes up to three."

He closed the door on her. She walked through the pines to George's. The others sat in the kitchen eating eggs and bread toasted in the skillet on the wood stove.

"It wasn't Sam," Ellie said. "Not unless he's working with someone else."

"How do you figure?" Quinn said.

"Wagon ruts outside the barn. Anyway, he's more tired of us than he is mad." She grabbed a slice of toast from the plate and beckoned at George. "Where are my names?"

He handed her a sheet of paper. It included fourteen people, mostly by name, though there were a couple vague descriptors like "man in the black hat." She scanned it twice, then tapped one of the names, letting her memory do its work.

"Mort Franklin. Quinn, you said he'd had trouble with your dad."

"Sure enough," Quinn said.

"Who is he?"

"A religious nutbag is who he is."

"Quinn," George reproached.

"Well, ain't he?" Quinn said through a mouthful of eggs cooked in saved fat. "He's got like three wives and ten kids."

"Mormon?" Ellie said.

George shook his head. "The gentleman is simply taking advantage of the lax enforcement of polygamy laws. We really ought to have requirements for citizenship. We can't go on allowing freaks and madmen to attach themselves to our town."

"Why's he mad at you?"

George shrugged. Quinn rolled his eyes. "Because Dad sold him a fake piano."

George pitched up his voice. "It's got 'Steinway' printed right on it. He inspected it himself."

Ellie glanced between the men. "You knew him before the plague?"

"Heavens no. Last year."

"We're digging latrines and watching the skies for a second wave and Mort Franklin is up in arms over a fraudulent piano?"

"Nutbag," Quinn muttered.

"Sounds promising," Ellie said. "Now take that pistol off your hip and let's go."

He glanced at the bulge on the side of his untucked shirt but did as he was told.

"He's a crazy person," Dee said, "and that makes you think it's a good idea to confront him?"

"Enemies are like family," Ellie said. "You don't get to choose them. And you can only avoid them for so long."

Quinn had wheeled the bikes out of the garage while she was at Sam's. Dee and George watched from the porch as Ellie and Quinn walked them across the field toward the road north of the property.

"Were you some kind of detective?" Quinn said.

"Of patterns. Predictions. I never ran investigations like this."

"Then how come you're so good at it?"

"We'll see what the results have to say," she said. "Actually, that's dead wrong. In evaluating success, we don't care about the results. We care about the process."

Quinn gave her a dubious look. "I care about results. But I'm one of those weirdos who prefers not to starve to death."

"When things are in flux, you can't guarantee a good outcome." She frowned vaguely. "If you do things the right way, and things turn out wrong, that's not failure. That's bad luck."

"What if you keep doing things right but things keep turning out wrong?"

"Then you question whether the process is right in the first place."

They crossed the churned-up dirt to the road and biked through Saranac Lake en route to Lake Placid. The wind was frigid, numbing Ellie's ears and nose. In Saranac Lake, a flagpole chain clanked senselessly. Neither of them spoke until they were on the other side of town and the pines enclosed the road.

"So what is our process?" Quinn said, as if the silence had lasted ten seconds instead of ten minutes.

"Ask Mort Franklin what happened."

"Thieves don't lie?"

"People with something to hide don't react well to direct

questions," Ellie said. "Most aren't professional liars. Their emotions get the best of them."

Quinn glanced at her from under her brow. "Does Dee know all this stuff?"

"Are you asking me whether you can get away with lying to your wife?"

"Well no, I was just wondering if you'd trained her. Like if someone tried to swindle us."

Ellie chuckled. "See?"

Quinn pushed his brows together, then flushed. Mountains framed the town of Lake Placid. The trees had gone red and orange like living flame. Ellie biked past the quaint downtown to Millie Perkins' lakeside general store. It was early in the morning but the old woman had already opened shop, a fire crackling in the proud hearth of the converted resort.

"Mort Franklin," Ellie said. "Know where he lives?"

Millie pulled her hand from her apron pocket and gestured east. "Thereabouts."

"Perfect. See you next year." Ellie bit her tongue. "You deliver. I thought you knew the address of everyone upstate and half of Vermont."

"Franklins always pick it up themselves."

Ellie began to curse and halted mid-syllable. Like many of the locals, Millie swore with homespun euphemisms that felt pickled and preserved from the 1820s. In the face of real obscenity, she got curt in a way that implied you'd best be on your way.

She tried again. "Know anyone who might know where they live?"

"Well." Millie leaned over the counter and planted her chin in her palm. "They tried to run services a few years back. Dan Beavers might have thought to attend."

"The guy who makes the shoes? Thanks, Millie." Ellie led Quinn into the cold autumn street. Brick shops and stolid New England homes stared them down. "Beavers is an honest-to-god cobbler. I don't get it. Every closet in town has a dozen pairs of shoes in it."

Quinn glanced at the clouds moving in from the mountains. "People do a lot more walking these days. There's something to be said for getting fit for a pair made just for you."

Dan Beavers tanned his own leather and had been considerate enough to locate his business upshore and generally downwind from town. Ellie headed up the road through the trees to his home, another faux log cabin with bay windows and a separate multi-car garage Beavers had converted into a workshop. The doors were open and he sat inside bent over a bench, hands full of leather and an oversized needle.

"Dan?" Ellie called from a polite distance. "My name's Ellie Colson. I'm looking for the Franklin home. Millie thought you might know it."

The man straightened from his work and threw back his head for a good look at her. "Mort Franklin? Lives on Holcomb Pond. What do you want with him?"

"Just a few questions."

Beavers had wild white hair and a gnomish face. He poked his tongue in his cheek. "Unless they're the burning variety, you might want to skip the trip."

Ellie stepped inside. It smelled like fresh leather and honest sweat. "Why's that?"

"Few years back, he began a revival. Don't have much in the way of church these days. Thought I'd drop by. But if he's quoting scripture, the man's got a different Bible than I do."

"Oh?"

"He's one of those 'dangling by a spiderweb over the pits of Hell' types." Dan cracked a smile. "Haven't heard words like those since my grandpa took me to see the Finneys."

Ellie smiled helplessly. "I appreciate the warning, but I don't have much choice."

"Take Riverside south from 86. Trail's about a mile in, left-hand side."

Ellie thanked him and turned to go, but her curiosity got the best of her. "Dan, why do you make shoes? Not that they're not good..."

"But anyone can loot as many as they need?" He smiled and gazed across his workshop. "It won't be like that forever. Best we start preparing for that day. Anyway, people like to get things made special just for them. Things they know will last. Not everyone wants to be a cobbler, you know? There's something fine about not having to do everything for yourself."

She returned to the road. Soon, all signs of civilization disappeared besides the pavement, swallowed by a forest that suddenly felt pre-Columbian. Wind sifted through the pines. Birds twirped to each other, disinterested in the pair of cyclists hissing along the road.

She turned south on Riverside. A mile later, the eastern trail was nearly as well-hidden as Bill Noesi's; it was Quinn who spotted the unmarked dirt path. Ellie sometimes suspected the young had the advantage on that front. She'd been spoiled by GPS, cell phones, Google maps.

The trail wound through the pines. When it grew too muddy and leaf-clogged, they dismounted to walk their bikes.

Quinn pointed ahead. "Suppose that's it?"

Past the thinning trees, a meadow lay in the overcast morning. Three fresh-hewn log cabins had been arranged on the banks of a modest pond, its wind-driven riffles glinting dully.

"Let me do the talking," Ellie said.

The voice came from nowhere. "You the law?"

Ellie whipped her gaze both directions and reached for her pistol.

"I wouldn't." The voice was accented with harsh vowels that lingered like the call of a predatory bird. On a bough to the side of the trail, a young man leered down at them, shoeless feet black on the soles. A rifle canted across his lap. "This is private property. So I say again: are you the law?"

"I'm here to see Mort Franklin," Ellie said.

"And he isn't here to see you," the young man said. Ellie stepped forward. The boy snapped the rifle to his hip and stared down steadily. "If you was to disappear right now, do you suppose anyone would know it?"

She grimaced. "We'll be back."

"Look forward to it," he smirked. She turned and walked her bike back up the trail. The voice followed them through the trees. "I know you, Quinn Tolbert!"

"Well, that wasn't cool," Quinn said to her. "What's the next step of our process?"

Ellie shrugged. "We bring the law."

The clouds hid the sun's true position, but by the time she rode to the rustic cabin on the point north of Paradox Bay, it was noon or later. In the day's first stroke of luck, Sheriff Hobson answered the door bearing a briar pipe and a look of eager curiosity.

"Ms. Colson!" he declared. "And young Quinn Tolbert. I hope there hasn't been another incident?"

Ellie couldn't force herself to maintain eye contact. "We need your help. Legal matter."

"Aha. And what would be the exact nature of these matters?"

"Theft."

"If I have to keep pulling your figurative teeth, I'll have to arrest myself for theft."

She let out a long breath through her nose. "A significant portion of George Tolbert's wheat crop has been stolen. I've ruled out Sam Chase. Now, signs point to Mort Franklin."

Hobson's gray brow rose with intrigue. He sucked on his pipe, enfolding himself in prodigious blue smoke. "The man of God forgets the Eighth Commandment, eh? What inclines you to read his name in the signs?"

Ellie wanted to vanish through the porch. "A while back, George sold him a piano. Franklin believed it was a Steinway. It wasn't."

The arch look crumpled from Hobson's face, replaced by bafflement. "A counterfeit piano? Why wasn't I notified?"

"Was a couple years back," Quinn said. "One of those 'he said, he said' deals."

Hobson withdrew his pipe from his mouth and examined the stem. "And you believe the chickens are now coming home to roost."

"Franklin is a Great Awakening-style doomsdayer," Ellie said. "The type to hold a grudge. After running into one of his brood this morning, I think I know who's been harassing the Tolberts."

"Your evidence seems..." He rolled his hand in the air.

"Shitty? That's because the Franklin boys ran us off their compound before we'd asked question one. He insisted we come back with the law or not at all—and he knew Quinn by name."

"Hardly a crime in itself," Hobson muttered. "However, the lakelands are blessedly quiet today. One might even call them 'placid.'" His eyes glittered as he waited for laughter. When none came, he dashed his palm against the bowl of his pipe, scattering dottle to the cold wind. "And duty is duty. I'll fetch my steed."

He disappeared inside, then came back with his bicycle. Given his Victorian affectations, Ellie was surprised its front wheel wasn't six feet tall.

The three rode back through town to the highway. Hobson peppered her with questions regarding the "case." She answered best she could, but it only highlighted how little she had to work with.

"My most significant question is why now?" Hobson's bowler fluttered in the wind. He tugged the brim to snug it over his long, graying hair. "Revenge is elementary, but delaying for so long is highly unusual."

"Unless you're a Klingon," Ellie said.

"Mort Franklin isn't normal," Quinn said. "If you expect his mind to act like yours, you're gonna be left holding your dick in your hand."

"Quinn," Ellie said, if only to hide her grin.

"A touch vivid," Hobson said, "but I shall bear it in mind."

This time, Ellie spotted the trail herself. At its head, Hobson moved in front and parked his bike. "I'll take it from here."

Ellie swung her jaw to the side. "This is my investigation."

He gazed at her, eyebrows raised. "If you were a homicide detective, would you take the victim's family with you to question your suspects?"

"Don't be ridiculous."

"You came to me because you've hit a block. If you'd like to move past it, kindly let me do my job."

"Damn it." Ellie folded her arms. "Get them to speak with me. And don't get shot."

"Thank you for the professional advice." He touched the brim of his bowler and picked his way down the path.

Quinn tried to make some talk, but Ellie just grunted. She had half a mind to follow the puffed-up duffer down the trail, but just before she'd made up her mind, a shot cracked across the forest. She bolted forward. Quinn's feet splashed mud behind her. A minute later, Hobson appeared on the trail walking back their way.

"What happened?" Ellie said.

He tilted his face at the muddy ground, brow creased with equal parts annoyance and embarrassment. "I was shot at."

"What?" Ellie said. "Are you okay?"

"I believe it was just a bluff." The sheriff looked over his shoulder.

Weak light dribbled through the dwindling leaves. "But it was a crucial mistake. I am the official representative of lakeland law. With shots fired, they have elevated my power to act."

"Really? I'd say they called your bluff."

"We shall see. I'll try again—tomorrow. When a pot is boiling, one must let it cool before touching it again."

"Let me know how that turns out," Ellie said. "And what you'd like on your epitaph."

"'A man passed, yet his convictions stand immortal,'" Hobson intoned with zero hesitation. "You're too cynical, Miss Colson. If the Franklins reject the law, then they have confessed that the old world is lost forever."

Hobson was an idiot, but Ellie didn't have the breath to argue. It had been a long day and shots fired in her vicinity tended to make her cranky. Birds twittered back and forth, oblivious to the threat of violence hanging in the air more cloyingly than the earthen, maple scent of newly rotting leaves. At the highway, they biked back toward town. The overcast light dimmed, northern mountains going blue. Ellie's sweaty shirt was clammy on her skin.

They stopped at the edge of the quiet mountain town. Ellie's throat was so dry it took her two tries to speak. "Do you really intend to go back there?"

"They shot at me, Miss Colson," Hobson said. "It's my duty. If I refuse, everything I've built falls apart."

She nodded vaguely. "Still think our evidence is weak?"

"It's certainly been given a shot in the arm. No pun intended."

They parted ways, Sheriff Hobson heading downtown, Ellie and Quinn heading west for the Tolberts' farm.

"What happens if they drive the sheriff off again?" Quinn said once they were on the road. "We need that wheat to get us through the winter."

Ellie shook her head. "Can't go in guns blazing unless we know they stole it."

"Why else would they shoot at the sheriff? Do you think he grew a pair of antlers?"

"Check your assumptions. Mort Franklin is a religious extremist. Paranoid. He doesn't let anyone make deliveries to his home. It could be standing policy to shoot at anyone who comes close."

"They did it," he said. "I'm sure of it."

She saved her arguments, wagering she'd have to make them all over again to George. She was right. When they returned to the farm and broke the news, George went nuclear. Stamping around the house. Pulling open drawers. Dee sat on the couch, eyes frightened.

"What are you doing, George?" Ellie said.

He yanked open a drawer and shook pencils and paperclips onto the floor. "Finding my ammunition."

"You don't know where you keep it?"

"I intend to use a lot of it."

"Why don't you sit down and have a drink?" Ellie said. "In fact, that's not a question." She fetched a bottle of bourbon from the Tolberts' pantry and poured a glass and cut it with water. "God, I miss ice."

George wandered in and gazed at the brown bottle. "I had to sell the combine back, Ellie. If I don't retrieve my crop, I doubt we'll make it through the winter."

"We won't let that happen." She poured a second drink and led him to the coffee table. His couch smelled welcomingly of dogs. "Sheriff Hobson's going back tomorrow."

George got out two coasters from the drawer and slid one under her glass. "I doubt whether my respect for his office is shared by the Franklins."

"It's not."

"Wonderful. My chances of getting back what is mine depends on a charade."

"We may need the support of the town," Ellie said. "They'll want to know we exhausted our legal means first."

"Which consist of a trumped-up geriatric who looks like he was shaken from the pages of a Sherlock Holmes novel." George laughed, sputtering. He rolled his eyes at the ceiling and drank. "Then what? Beseech the good people of Lake Placid to write the Franklins a stern letter?"

"This is uncharted territory. Until now, people have worked it out for themselves, or let the sheriff act as mediator. If that won't work, what do we do instead?"

"Waco springs to mind."

Ellie laughed, caught off guard. She'd been expecting a lot more self-pity. There was a new spark in George. Something feral. "We could try sanctions."

He gave her a look. "They aren't Cuba."

"They won't be happy about losing trade with town."

"How long will it be before they care? Where does that leave me this winter?"

Ellie reached for her glass. She was supposed to be trained to produce unconventional solutions to murky problems, but she didn't have the first idea what to do. "I don't want to confront them on their compound."

Quinn walked in from the kitchen bearing a glass of his own. He was underage, and Ellie glanced at George, expecting him to say something, and then she understood he didn't give a shit and neither did she.

"So we don't go back," Quinn said. "Mort sends his boys into town to pick up supplies. Kids got big eyes and bigger mouths. We scoop one of them up, I bet he'll spill the beans."

"Sounds like kidnapping."

"Then let them be napped!" George blurted. "We don't have to pull out their toenails. Just put a scare into them."

"That's not a bad idea," Ellie said, although it carried a definite risk of escalation. "Call it Plan B. With any luck, Sheriff Hobson will save us the trouble."

But luck was not on her side. Sheriff Hobson arrived on a new bicycle late the following morning. He wore a fresh suit and an aggrieved scowl.

"The Franklins were not amenable to my approach," he explained.

"Get shot at again?" Quinn said.

"Not quite. But given the thicket of rifles brandished at me, it's sheer fortune that none of them went off."

"We're going to pick up one of the Franklin boys," Ellie said.

Hobson raised his graying brows. "I assume you will ensure you have his consent."

"We're just going to ask a few questions. I considered keeping you in the dark, but I thought you had the right to know."

He closed his eyes and massaged his forehead. "Don't do anything you wouldn't tell your grandchildren about."

As Ellie watched him go, she noticed the first snows had dressed the peaks of the mountains beyond the lake. She and Quinn rode out to stake out the road leading past the Franklins' trail. Across and just south of the trailhead, they pitched a tent in the pines. While Quinn kept an eye on the road, Ellie covered the tent with a screen of pine branches, as much for insulation as for camouflage. She lay the bikes on their side and covered them with a tarp and old leaves.

Millie had told her the Franklins didn't visit on a regular schedule —could be days, could be weeks—but Ellie didn't have much else to occupy her. Her farm was in maintenance mode. As long as Dee kept the chickens fed, the land wouldn't miss her.

She didn't talk much. Quinn blathered some about the wedding; they had resolved to go low-key with it after all, family and a few friends. He asked her about her previous life with the government. She hadn't thought much about it since the plague and revisiting the memories of travel and intrigue gave her a killer case of Split. She had been a globetrotter, shuttling from one country to the next. Over a matter of years, her world had shrunk to a couple of valleys and lakes in an isolated corner of New York State.

That night, with the cold creeping down from the mountains and each stir of an animal in the brush crackling like the step of a bear, Ellie felt a restlessness she hadn't dealt with in years.

She was concerned a snowstorm would drive them out before they snared their quarry, but as it turned out, they only had to wait two days before a teen boy and his younger brother swung onto the road, laughing and cussing, and pedaled toward the highway.

She swept the tarps off the bikes and hit the road, lagging so they were never in direct line of sight. In town, the two boys enter Millie's general store. Ellie backtracked a mile down the highway to a spot where an old accident blocked one of the lanes, then dragged a bumper across the open lane and crouched behind the smashed-up cars.

"We're here to scare them," Ellie said. "To get them to talk. If any guns go off, that's a failed mission."

"Roger," Quinn said. He double-checked the safety on his pistol, which Ellie had allowed him to take.

Sunshine fought with the clouds for control of the sky. The insects had died in the frosts and there was no sound except the chirp of birds and the rustle of wind. An hour later, the voices of two boys carried down the highway.

Ellie got out her gun. Quinn did the same.

Bike tires squeaked as the boys swerved to an abrupt stop in front of the bumper marring the road. "Who the hell put that there?"

"Oops." Ellie swung from behind the cars, gun in hand, and faced a scruffy-haired twelve-year-old and the older boy who'd menaced them from the trees. "Hello, boys."

The older boy laughed. "Why don't you put that thing down before I stuff it up your— "

She fired a round past his shoulder. He flinched, tripping on his bike and skinning his palms on the pavement. The report of the shot echoed from the hills.

"Your father has taught you certain things about the world," Ellie said. "There's just one problem: he's a fucking moron."

"He'll kill you," the older boy said from the ground, but the smug light in his eyes had been replaced with anger and fear. "He'll skin you and feed you to the trout."

Quinn brandished his pistol. "Shut up."

Ellie lowered her gun but kept it by her hip. "I doubt your dad would just throw the meat away, kid. Given that he's such a bad farmer he has to steal another man's grain."

"Nuh uh!" The younger brother pushed greasy hair from his eyes. "He didn't take it 'cause he had to. He took it 'cause— "

The other boy kicked his brother in the back of the knee, bucking him. "Shut up!"

Ellie laughed. "Go home, boys."

The older kid stood, sucking on his bleeding palm and glaring into Ellie's eyes. "He will kill you. You and your whole family."

"Then enjoy watching him get lynched."

The boy spat on the asphalt between them and picked up his bike, shoulders hunched high. Ellie waited until they swung around the bend before she holstered her pistol.

"I can't believe we pulled guns on a couple of kids," Quinn said.

"It was a good plan. Nice work." She gazed in the direction of the Franklins' pond. "Better get back to the farm. I don't entirely trust Mort Franklin to not try to burn the place down."

On their way through Lake Placid, she detoured to the sheriff's, but he wasn't in. She scribbled a note and slid it under his door and rode back to George's.

He met them on the porch, bare forearms goosebumped in the frigid air. "Well?"

"They took it all right," Quinn said. "Ellie tricked them into confessing."

"Are you okay?" Dee said from the doorway.

"We're fine," Ellie said. "But we might have kicked a hornet's nest."

"What else are we to do?" George said, drawling the last word. "A civilized society can not abide rogues. Without enforcement, how can there be law?"

"We'll see what Sheriff Hobson has to say. It's make-or-break."

The next few hours passed in quiet tension. Quinn helped Dee with the wash while Ellie watched out the front window and George took the dogs on a long walk around the fields. With daylight to spare, Sheriff Hobson rode down the path to the front door, propped up his bike, and doffed his cap.

"I received your missive," he told Ellie. "Shall we talk?"

George invited him inside. The kids came in from the wash room. George offered Hobson a nip of bourbon and hot water to warm him up, which the sheriff accepted gratefully.

"I've been asking around town." He placed his mug on the coaster and passed his palm over the steam. "There is no love lost for the Franklins in Lake Placid."

"Meaning?" Ellie said.

"I won't dance daintily around the truth. I can demand Mr. Franklin allow me to search his grounds, but a letter is only as strong as the hand that delivers it."

George planted his elbows on his knees and leaned forward. "I am driven by more than principle. I have a hard need for that grain. Can you get it back?"

"That," Hobson said, lifting his index finger to the air, "is the question. The lakelands stand at a critical juncture. I can't force the Franklins to acquiesce by myself. Here and now, we choose to admit that injustice is the way of the brave new world—or decide we need a central authority stronger than those who'd oppose it."

"Less talk, more details," Ellie said.

"A posse comitatus."

"A posse?"

"Deputies, militia, whatever you'd like to call it." Hobson waved his hand. "The Franklins are despised. It will be no trouble to gather good people to our cause. A forward-thinking lawman might even seize the opportunity to establish a permanent authority."

Ellie tipped her head. She didn't like where this was headed. Sounded a lot like mob rule. This time, it might work in her favor, but if the sheriff were able to summon a posse whenever he pleased, sooner or later there would be a mistake. An accident. Or the posse might depose their fussy figurehead and start taking whatever they liked.

"You're not thinking of pulling a coup, are you, sheriff?"

"High heavens, no. But we can either accept a future of Hatfields and McCoys, or establish a neutral institution to adjudicate disputes."

"The only future I care about is this winter," George said. "Gather your men. Me and my boy will march with you."

Hobson didn't stay to chat. That night, George piled blankets in the kennel and left the dogs outside. He locked the doors. During Ellie's watch, one of the dogs whuffed. A silhouette moved on the fringe of the fields. She reached for her binoculars, but by the time she sighted in on the darkened woods, the figure had gone.

In the morning, she found no tracks. Hobson returned that afternoon. "Tomorrow at Millie's. Ten AM."

"I'll be there," George said.

Over dinner, they agreed George and Quinn would join the posse while Ellie and Dee remained at home. A part of Ellie wanted to go with them—while Sheriff Hobson looked like less of a boob than she'd thought, she didn't trust him or anyone else to handle this right—but it was George's justice to be won, not hers. And she didn't want to leave Dee by herself. Not until this feud had been resolved for good.

George banked up the fire. Dee had first watch. Ellie forced herself to sleep. She woke to the cold, an hour past the start of her shift. She poked her head through Quinn's door. The kids snored under the down comforter. She rolled her eyes and sat in the chair by the window and watched the moon on the fields.

She'd gotten a late start, so she didn't bother to wake George to take last watch. He strolled from his room at dawn, hair askew, eyes puffy, and helped himself to a mug of instant coffee with hot water from the stove. As Ellie was starting to think about boiling some oats, Dee emerged and plunked herself at the table.

"Don't tell me he's still asleep," Ellie said.

Dee looked up, dull-eyed. "Quinn?"

"There better not be anyone else in that bed."

She cast around the room. "How long have you been out here?"

"Since about three in the morning. Quinn missed his shift, but he'll need more sleep today than I will."

"He's not asleep." Dee stood up so fast she knocked her chair to the ground. "He's gone."

9

The lock rattled on the closet door. Lucy sat up, blinking against the light knifing under the frame. She had a line all ready for Kerry, but when the door opened, Nerve gazed back at her.

"Couldn't wait two days to see my pretty face?" she said.

He ignored her. "What do you know?"

"The Earth is round, the sun sets in the west, and Manhattan is much nicer than I was led to believe."

"I take it you have nothing."

"When Michelangelo was halfway through carving that man's thing, would you have said he had 'nothing'?"

He tapped his fingernails on the doorframe. "Did I make a mistake?"

Before she could answer, he closed and locked the door. Lucy sat on the floor and thought through what she'd turned up the day before, which didn't take long. She had just lain down in her blanket-nest to catch a few more winks when the lock scrabbled again. She shielded her face against the morning light, most of which got blocked by Kerry's hulking frame.

"There you are." She reached up and pinched his cheek. "I was afraid a crew of whalers had tied off at the pier and harpooned you by mistake."

He didn't move. "Mighty cheery for someone two days from death."

"I been ducking the Reaper my whole life, man. Either he's blind or he thinks he already got me." She sat down to pull on her shoes. "The last of yesterday's no-shows come in today?"

Kerry nodded. "He's not your man."

"I'll be the judge of that. Like you say, it's my life on the line."

They walked out the back door to the docks. Kerry strode to the barge, which was now being loaded for departure, and returned with a longhaired dude in his twenties. Lucy's heart sank.

He walked up to her with a limp, right foot swaddled in a colossal bandage. "You rang?"

"Where were you yesterday?" Lucy said.

He lifted his bandaged foot off the dock. "Nursing my hangover. Surgery's a bitch."

"Don't suppose you got a doctor's note."

The man looked at Kerry. "You think I had this chopped off for fun?"

Kerry folded his arms. "Bear with us."

Lucy wrinkled her nose. "Pretend I'm real dumb and lost your records. What exactly caused you to miss the shipment yesterday?"

The man sighed. "Mind if I sit down?"

"Be my guest."

He lowered himself to a nearby barrel, wincing. "Couple weeks ago, I get a box of pig iron dropped on my foot. Splits a couple of my nails. No big deal. Until they turn green and fall off. Doc says unless I want the rest of me to turn the same color, he's got to take off my toes. Fine by me, at least they're the little ones. Two days ago, snip snip, all better. Yesterday, I was sleeping off the anesthetic."

"Sound right?" she said to Kerry.

The man laughed roughly. "Don't tell me you expected me in yesterday. Crazy enough I'm here today."

"You're fine," Kerry said. He raised his eyebrows at Lucy. "Unless you'd like to see the wound."

He was needling her, but it wasn't his neck on the block. "Doc around?" she said. "How about I confirm with him?"

Kerry jerked his chin at the waiting barge. "You're free to go."

The longhaired man smiled sarcastic-like and hobbled back to work. The doctor's office was housed two piers down. He sat in front his office watching the stevedores hump goods into the barge. He confirmed the longhair's story.

Lucy wandered down the pier to watch the river. Could rule out Eight-Toe Jones over there. As for Woody Sloan, the man who'd shown up after he heard the shots, his alibi wasn't airtight, but he didn't give off a guilty vibe. She couldn't say the same for Zoe Goodwin. Something off about the woman. Hard to say what, but it was her gut doing the twitching, and her gut was rarely wrong.

Motion drew her eye to the upper floors of the glass towers across from the piers. Someone dangled a white sheet from the window and waved it back and forth, as if surrendering to life.

"Woody Sloan lives right across the street," Lucy said. "How about the rest of your crew?"

"I don't know," Kerry said. "Close enough to get here every day."

"You don't keep them under wraps somewhere?"

"We don't keep slaves. Everyone who works here wants to."

"Except me," she said. "You got a car, big boy?"

Kerry stood there. "You're not filling that sharp little head with ideas, are you, Lucy?"

"I intend to put the Feds' bureaucracy to my advantage. You got a problem with that?"

"You sure you aren't more interested in the guards they post out front?"

Lucy rolled her eyes. "For Pete's sake. I got the impression the Feds aren't eager to tangle with Distro. If I try to bug out on you, shoot me in the head and tell the soldiers whatever damn lie you like."

He bent to put his gaze level with hers. "I will, Lucy. Play it straight or you win a permanent swim in the East River."

"My heavens, you'd kill me two days sooner than planned? What a terrifying threat."

He didn't have a car, but he allowed her to take her bike. He rode back and to her left with a pistol holstered on his right hip. She thought about rabbiting just to spite him, but she had the impression he know how to use his gun. Besides, if she ran out on Distro now, she was going to have a hell of a time using them to get to Tilly.

The sky grew overcast, spitting itty-bitty drops of rain on her face. She wove downtown, passing a pedestrian or another cyclist every few blocks, but after the bustle at the piers, it felt downright ghostly.

Outside the building that couldn't decide if it were a hotel or a Swiss castle, a soldier stopped them and tried to confiscate Kerry's weapons. Kerry produced three different registrations. The man read them, mumbled to himself, then entered City Hall, locking the door behind him. Five minutes later, he came back with a second soldier.

"You're cleared." He gave Kerry a lopsided smile. "Corporal Ruiz will be behind you at all times."

Kerry returned his registration to his wallet. "Safety first."

It was a small moment, the Fed-Distro rivalry playing out in front of her. Easy to miss. It would change everything.

But that was ahead of her. There and then, she strolled through the echoing lobby, shadowed by her entourage of Kerry and Corporal Ruiz, and leaned her elbows on the receptionist's desk.

"Don't you ever take a break?"

The same woman as always smiled back. "What can I say, I love my job. Are you enjoying your visit to Manhattan?"

"Lovin' it to death," Lucy grinned. "I'm looking for information on a group called the Kono. You know of 'em?"

"I've heard of them, yes."

"Would you happen to have records of which of your citizens might be involved with them?"

The woman drew back a fraction of an inch. "As any such records would be part of an ongoing investigation, they would be unavailable for public inspection."

Lucy sucked her front teeth. "How about criminal records? Ain't those public?"

"There would be a processing and copying fee for each file."

"Put it on Distribution's tab." Kerry fished in his pocket and withdrew a few documents.

The woman leaned over them. "And the records you'd like copied?"

Lucy slid her the list of employees she'd copied the day before. "Have fun."

"Excellent. We'll have these ready for you in five to eight business days."

"Won't cut it. I need them today."

The receptionist shook her head. "There must be fifty names on this list. I can expedite them, but you're still looking two, three days."

Quick as a cobra, Lucy slipped her hand behind the woman's head, lanced her fingers into her bunned hair, and twisted her wrist. The receptionist's head yanked back. She shrieked.

"Most of these people won't be in your system," Lucy said. "It doesn't take three fucking days to copy five or six pages."

Corporal Ruiz moved sideways, crab-like, to aim his rifle at Lucy. "Let her go!"

Before the soldier was done with his command, Kerry snapped a long-barrel revolver from his holster and drew down on him. "Lower your weapon, soldier."

Instead, Ruiz recentered it on Kerry's chest. "You are threatening agents of the sovereign nation of Manhattan. Drop your weapon and get down on the ground."

Kerry sighed and let his barrel lower a couple inches. "Let the poor woman go, Lucy."

Lucy clenched her fingers, drawing tears from the receptionist, then withdrew her hand.

Slowly, Kerry holstered his revolver. "I call a mulligan."

Ruiz stared at him for a long second, then puffed his cheeks with nervous laughter. He took his hands off his machine gun, letting it rest from the sling around his neck.

"Mulligan granted." The soldier glanced between Kerry and Lucy. "You won't get a second one."

"I'm sorry for bugging out on you," Lucy said. "Due to some goddamn ridiculous circumstances, I don't got two or three days. If I don't have those records tonight, it could cost the lives of Manhattan citizens."

The receptionist untied her bun, finger-combed her hair, and ignored Lucy in favor of Kerry. "Will you vouch for this?"

"Consider it vouched," he said.

Without turning, she pointed to the grandfather clock ticking away in the corner. "Our office closes at 5 PM. I will have your records ready at 4:45 PM. If you are late, you may pick them up tomorrow."

"It's a date," Lucy said.

Ruiz straightened. "I'll see you out."

"Don't do that again," Kerry murmured to her once they were outside and crossing the street.

Lucy's temper flared. "Right. Much more important to be polite than to save my fucking life."

They biked back to the piers. To give herself longer to cool down, Lucy returned to the apartment courtyard to have a second look around, but the only thing that had changed was the firmness of the horse manure. When they returned to the piers, the barge had departed and so had nearly all the stevedores.

"What the hell?" Lucy said. "How'm I supposed to run down your mole when I can't talk to your people?"

Kerry sniffed. The day had never warmed and the chill wind had caused his nose to run. "Figure that out and Nerve will be right to spare you."

She tried to work it out, but mostly wasted a couple hours stomping up and down the docks and seething. As the afternoon waned, they biked back to City Hall and she retrieved the requested records.

She leafed through the files over a dinner of fish and potatoes. Not much to them. Lillian Wurtz had been busted for petty theft from a food stall. Victor Villareal had been hauled in for assault on the bouncer of a moonshine joint. Dude by name of Flynn Hortag liked to smack his wife. If the zero hour rolled around and she still didn't have her mole, Lucy might shank Flynn just to bring some justice to the world before Nerve's injustice was done upon her. Beyond that, the criminal files did not look promising.

Night fell. Before locking her closet, Kerry let her know there would be another boat tomorrow. She wasn't particularly tired and she spent a couple hours rolling cigarettes and thinking on what questions she'd ask come morning.

With dawn peeping through the sill of the door, Nerve arrived. He looked as well-rested and implacable as ever, but his presence belied his interest.

"What do you have for me?"

"Genius takes time," Lucy said.

"You have 24 hours, genius."

He closed the door. Kerry reopened it a few minutes later and gestured her into the light.

"Good luck," he said.

She wasn't in the mood to banter. She headed straight to the docks, where men and women gathered to await the incoming ship, chattering and eating bowls of mashed corn. Some eyed her. Word had gotten around. Or maybe they'd just noticed Kerry the enforcer dogging her every step, compared notes, and concluded she wasn't to be trusted. Whatever the case, it wasn't going to be Lucy's easiest day on Earth.

She got Kerry to ID Victor Villareal and pull him from the crowd. He was in his early thirties and had a shiny scar under his left eye.

"Let's talk about the assault," Lucy said.

He wiped his nose. "Which one?"

"I get to choose? The bouncer at the Trough. Last spring."

"He was staring at me."

"So you busted his arm?"

"And two of his ribs." Victor shrugged. "He shouldn't have stared at me."

Lucy gritted her teeth. "You're a real asset to the company, aren't you?"

"I do my job. What now?"

"We'll send your medal in the mail. Get back in line." She watched him join the others at the pier. Kerry stood behind her, quiet as ever. She scuffed at the green fabric lining the ground. "How do y'all feel about torture?"

"The desperate refuge of someone who isn't smart enough to uncover the truth."

She had him pull Flynn Hortag, but he was a wife-beater, plain and simple. Lillian Wurtz fed her a sob story about feeding her three children. Gene Goldschmidt was about sixty years old and insisted his assault charge had been self-defense.

Lucy sent him on his way. Nothing but dead ends. Nothing remotely organized, gang-related, or connected to the Kono. As she diverted Mikaela Davids from the crowd, a barge hove up the river with a blast of its air horn.

Lucy waited for the horn to fade, then held up Mikaela's rap sheet and tapped the handwritten account. "You like to take things that aren't yours, Mikaela?"

The woman's face and body were tough-worn with work and weather, but her expression crumpled immediately. "They said that was purged."

"Nerve likes his workers clean. Maybe you can explain it to me. Help me understand."

"I needed money. I was living in a Fed place and the winter got so bad I couldn't afford the oil." She glanced toward the stevedores waiting on the incoming barge. "It wasn't my idea."

"I'm sure Nerve will take that into account. Who put you up to it?"

The men and women were strung down the dock and she glanced back to the same spot as before. "Don't make me say. She'll hurt me."

Lucy smiled comfortingly and touched the woman's arm. "Who else was Zoe working with?"

She lowered her voice, but couldn't quash her swelling panic. "Who said it was Zoe?"

"You're not in any trouble. Not if you give me a name."

"I don't know. I didn't want to know."

The imp in her wanted to drag Michaela into the restaurant kitchen and see if a meat mallet to the head jogged her memory, but she had already broken the woman. Either that or Michaela was a sidewinder. But a snake that sneaky would take more time to pin than Lucy had to spare.

She sent the woman back to the docks. The river flowed along, a gray to match the skies. "It was Zoe Goodwin."

Kerry gazed at the workers swarming aboard the barge. "Bet your life on that?"

"Real funny. She acted weird the first time we talked. Hid her hand from me. You know what they were stealing? Solar chargers for car batteries. You see a lot of cars around here? Who was she fencing to?"

"Could be anyone."

"We'll let Nerve be the judge of that." She tucked her thumbs in her pockets. Kerry was always quiet, but his new silence was that of a dam holding back cold torrents of truth. "What?"

He said nothing. When Lucy was about to give up on him, he folded his arms. "I like you. You do your own thing. I'll be straight with you: this won't be enough to convince him."

"Well shit, I think it's pretty good for three days. If I had another week, I could set up a sting."

"Think of this as the game it is. If you can't prove you're the queen, then you're just another pawn."

"There is nothing more annoying than a chess metaphor." She shifted her pack on her shoulders and looked him in the eye. "He wants more? I'll get him more."

The barge pulled up and the stevedores tied it tight and piled aboard to haul away its goodies. Distro sure pulled a lot of cargo. Shipped enough back, too, though nobody but the bosses seemed to know where it was headed. But it gave her an idea. Wait for Kerry to turn his back, then slip into the water, swim under the boat, climb up the far side, and stow away to destinations unknown.

But that would take her away from Tilly. And long ago, when the shit was still being slung fresh from the fan, she had promised to keep Tilly safe.

A new idea stood up in her head. One that required Kerry's absence. She sat near the pier and bided her time jotting notes on the conversations she'd had with those with criminal records. She was scribbling gibberish by the time a man walked out of the converted restaurant and called Kerry's name.

"Stay put," Kerry told her.

Her heart thundered. He walked down to the restaurant and met the man who'd called him over. Lucy scanned the barge but couldn't find her mark. As she watched, Zoe trudged up from belowdecks bearing a cask, her face red with strain.

"Hey Zoe," Lucy called.

The round-faced woman glanced her way and continued down the plank to the dock.

Lucy beckoned. "Set that thing down and have a rest."

Zoe got down to the pier and set down the cask and pulled off her gloves. "What do you want?"

She fiddled out a filtered cigarette and lit it. "I need to follow up on yesterday's conversation. Won't take but a minute."

"I got work to do."

"Your back will thank you for it." She exhaled and held out the cigarette. "Take it. I got more."

Zoe examined it, the smoke twisting up from the cherry, then accepted. "If Kerry comes over here, you better let him know this is your idea."

"Don't worry about it. How is your back, Zoe?"

"Tight as a frog's asshole."

Lucy nodded and took a deep breath through her nose, as if she were enjoying the brisk morning air. "I gather you aren't too happy with your work here."

"Keeps food on the table and wood in the stove."

"It would be a hell of a thing to run a place like this, wouldn't it? Stand around watching while people like you and me do all the heavy lifting." She chuckled.

Zoe sucked on the cigarette and coughed and looked at it as if considering stamping it out. Way down the dock, Kerry continued his conversation.

Zoe eyeballed her. "You sound like you're planning a takeover."

"This is just a routine employee satisfaction survey." At the restaurant, Kerry took a step away from the man and nodded his head. Lucy raised a brow at Zoe. "You been moonlighting?"

"Moonlighting?"

"Your old back can't take this work forever." Heavy footsteps approached from down the dock. "Was that your retirement plan? Sell Distro out to the up-and-comers?"

The woman gave her a skeptical look, dropped the cigarette, and toed it out. "I don't know what you're talking about."

She turned her back and picked up the cask, grunting. Kerry came to a stop behind Lucy. As Zoe walked the cask over to a wagon waiting by the front curb, Lucy smiled at the ground, then bugged her eyes.

"Ho-lee shit," she said. "You see that?"

Kerry cocked his head. She crouched and spread out her arms as if warding people away from the scene.

"Kerry, you see me talking to Zoe Goodwin? She was having a smoke?"

"I saw. She just left."

Lucy sat back, withdrawing her body from its protective crouch. "What do you make of that?"

Kerry leaned over the crushed butt. "Looks smoked."

"Tall as you are, I know it's tough to see through the clouds, but use your damn eyes, man."

He glanced at her, then edged closer. His face went blank. "Oh."

"As in, 'Oh shit, we got our traitor.'"

Kerry picked up the spent cigarette and examined the tiny gold crown stamped on the filter. He whistled up the dock. "Zoe! Zoe Goodwin!"

Down the way, Zoe got an aggrieved look on her face like someone had spit in her soup. Then she saw it was Kerry and she clenched up like she had to use the bathroom.

She set down the cask and walked up to Kerry. "Yes, sir?"

He held up his hand in the okay sign, cigarette pinched between his thumb and forefinger. "You dropped something."

She looked over her shoulder at the barge wallowing beside the dock. "We bringing in ethanol or something?"

"Playing dumb again?" Lucy said. "You already know exactly what's on board, don't you? And so do the Kono."

"With all due respect, what the fuck is going on here?"

Lucy nodded at the little yellow stub in Kerry's hand. "Last time you met with them, you left your spoor, Zoe."

Zoe worked her mouth, then turned on her, face going purple. "You gave that to me!"

"Like hell!" She popped open her bag, jumbling the contents in Zoe's face. "You see any filters in there?"

"Save it," Kerry said. He jabbed a thick finger at the rotunda atop the converted restaurant. "Upstairs."

The lot of them marched up to the top floor. Nerve turned from the window, gaze ticking between them. "What am I looking at?"

"The gal who sold you out," Lucy said.

"Bullshit!" Zoe lunged at her. Kerry grabbed Zoe from behind and locked his elbow around her throat. She grabbed his thick forearm with both hands.

"After the attack, me and Kerry went to where I saw the Kono planning." Lucy paced the fancy hardwood floor, hands folded behind her back. "Found a few cigarette butts. Hadn't been there more than a few days. Now I find out Zoe Goodwin smokes the same brand."

Crushed in Kerry's sleeper hold, Zoe made a choked noise. Nerve made a small gesture and Kerry relaxed enough for the woman to catch her wind.

"These are lies and poison," Zoe coughed. "I don't know what the hell her problem is, but she's playing you for a fool."

"Check her house," Lucy said.

Nerve tipped his head to the side. "What will I find there?"

"Thirty pieces of silver." She watched Zoe's face. "Or is it solar?"

Zoe gaped, eyes receding. "That has nothing to do with this!"

"Pretty sweet deal. No need to pay for heat or juice. You might even be able to sell the extra to the Feds."

"Nerve," the woman said, voice gone fluttery. "How long have I worked for you?"

"I think we're all rats at heart," Nerve said. "You seen a rat when it's hungry? They'll chew off your lips in your sleep."

He made another gesture to Kerry. Zoe was a well-built woman, hefty-hipped and bulky in the shoulders from hauling crates, but Kerry lifted her clear of the ground, elbow crooked around her throat. Zoe choked and whaled her heels against his knees and shins. He didn't flinch. She drew her head forward, but he pressed the side of his head against hers before she could bash him. When she reached to claw his face, he gnawed her knuckles.

Zoe shuddered, arms flapping, heels jerking, and went limp. Kerry breathed out and held tight as her face crossed from bright red to hurt purple. He hung onto her for what felt like forever, forearm bulging, elbow projecting like the figurehead of a galleon. Zoe's gummy eyes bulged dumbly, bright red with popped vessels.

He let go. Her tongue flopped from her teeth. She thumped the hardwood, arm flopping straight at Lucy.

"Day of surprises." Nerve extended his hand. "Welcome to Distro."

10

They searched the house twice, including the closets and bathtubs and basement, then opened the barn doors and swept flashlights through the dark corners while Dee stood in the fields with the dogs and called Quinn's name. Ellie trusted logic and numbers, not her gut, but her gut was telling her they could yell Quinn's name for a year and not get an answer.

Because he'd been taken.

George reached the same conclusion. "It was Mort Franklin. They kidnapped him."

"In the middle of the night?" Ellie said.

Wind blew dead leaves across the cut stalks of wheat. "Sure. They come prowling around, make a bit of noise to lure Quinn outside, then sock him on the head and drag him off. No doubt they got wind of the sheriff's plans. Decided to preempt us with a hostage."

"Or he could be hurt somewhere. Broke his ankle in the woods and can't get back. Fell in the lake."

George turned to her, face twisted with anguish. "How can you say a thing like that?"

Her cheeks went hot. "I'm not trying to upset you. Just identifying other possibilities. Which means we shouldn't ride in guns blazing."

"The Franklins took him. Mark my words."

"Could be. So first thing we do is confirm that—or rule it out." She motioned toward the treeline, where Dee called into the woods, a golden retriever snuffling through the brush. "I don't want to leave her alone. I'm going to see the sheriff and find someone to stay with

Dee. Then we'll head to the Franklins'."

"What if they took him, Ellie?" George's face was pinched and his eyes were as bright as the lake under a July noon. "What if they hurt him?"

"They won't. Not if their goal is to use him as leverage." She put her hand on his shoulder. "Keep looking. I'll be back soon."

He smiled and sniffed and walked across the field, brittle wheat stalks crunching under his shoes. Ellie grabbed a bike and rode straight to Lake Placid. November had arrived and brought the cold with it. She knew it might not turn warm for a long time.

In town, she hit Main Street and prepared to swing north toward the sheriff's, but she spotted the wool-suited official speaking with a knot of people on the patio of what used to be Bozer's Grill. She squeaked to a stop and climbed off her bike and strode toward the sheriff.

"Quinn Tolbert's gone missing," she said. "George thinks it was the Franklins. If we don't act fast, he'll charge in by himself."

Hobson brushed his palms down the front of his suit and nodded to the four men and two women around him. "I was just gathering our deputies."

"Can you leave one at the Tolberts' with my daughter?"

"Wouldn't she best be overseen by George?"

"Sheriff, he thinks Mort Franklin has Quinn tied up in a dungeon. He's not going to sit on his rocking chair sipping lemonade while we go ask about his son."

"I would hope not, now that I think about it." Hobson stroked his mustache and considered his people. "Harold, you know Miss Colson? Could I impinge on you to stay with her daughter at the farm?"

Harold Dunston shrugged his bearish shoulders. "I dunno, sheriff. I might rather get my crown shot off at some fanatic's compound."

"What rustic wit," the sheriff said. "Miss Colson, as soon as you're ready, we're at your service."

Harold borrowed a bike and followed Ellie back to the lake, pedaling awkwardly, his heavy knees jutting to each side, bike squeaking rhythmically from the strain.

"Think there's gonna be a shootout?" he said.

"Considering the Franklins have already proven willing and able to open fire?" Ellie squinted against the eye-watering cold wind. "It's more likely than I'd prefer."

That satisfied Harold, who was one of those stolid farmer types who'd give the same nod of acknowledgment to anything that passed before his eyes, be it a casual acquaintance or a fire burning down his barn. Good man to leave with Dee. As they approached the farm, Dee and George's voices filtered from the woods. Ellie called them in.

"George tell you the plan?" she asked Dee.

Dee nodded and hugged her elbows in front of her body. "You won't get hurt, will you?"

"We'll have the law with us. A posse, too. Mort won't want to endanger his own family."

That seemed to console her, although Ellie didn't believe it herself. Fanatics wanted to be persecuted. To prove the rest of the world was as base and evil as their prophets claimed. Dee and Harold returned to the woods to search as Ellie and George departed for town. George had a rifle slung over his shoulder and a far-off look on his face.

"I think we should let the sheriff take the lead," Ellie said.

The highway whisked along beneath their bikes. "The sheriff is nothing but an empty suit."

"You were perfectly willing to defer to him when you thought Sam Chase was the villain."

"With a badge, even a fool can frighten a child. A true believer respects no law but God's."

Her rifle weighed on her shoulder. In Lake Placid, the sheriff was still on the patio of Bozer's, but he'd found another deputy to replace Harold. Sheriff Hobson approached and shook George's hand with both of his own.

"I respect your role as father," Hobson said. "At the Franklins', please respect my role as sheriff."

"What I respect most is results," George said.

Hobson frowned but said nothing. He turned to his deputies, who were mostly middle-aged and overweight, although in the way of farmers and tradesmen who have as much muscle under their skin as fat.

"For most of you, this will be your first time on the front lines of the law. I value you as volunteers but value your safety most of all. Don't draw weapons unless and until you intend to use them. With any luck, we shall effect a peaceful resolution."

They nodded their agreement. William Mooring had brought his horse-drawn wagon and most of the deputies rode in it, seated on the boards, rifles sticking up beside them. As they rode down the highway, Hobson asked George the usual questions about when he'd last seen Quinn and when the boy went missing, but drew nothing from George's answers.

The posse reached the path to the Franklins' by late morning. The deputies dismounted from the wagon, feet thudding into the gravel on the shoulder of the main road. The sheriff raised his eyebrows and led the way into the woods.

Ellie watched the trees. Songbirds trilled. Leaves crumpled underfoot. The posse was silent. And so, when they reached the clearing, was the compound on the edge of the pond. Halfway across the wild-grown grass, Hobson gestured the others to a stop, then continued toward the house.

"Mort Franklin!" the sheriff called. "My name is Sheriff Hobson. I serve the order of the lakes and surrounding lands. Step outside to speak with me, and I assure you as a gentlemen that words will be the only thing exchanged on this day."

Movement in the windows. Ellie's hand twitched. A crow cawed from the pines by the shore. The front door opened and Mort Franklin emerged into the overcast day. His hair grew like white kudzu. A shotgun dangled from the crook of his elbow.

"Quite a host you have gathered for this reckoning, sheriff. A distrustful man might think you aim to use it as a bludgeon."

"I can see you are a canny man, so I will confess it is a sad truth that the velvet glove of justice must be fitted around an iron fist." Hobson smiled, self-deprecating. "I won't waste words. George's boy Quinn has gone missing."

The old doomsayer narrowed his eyes, wrinkles spiderwebbing his skin. "Don't know a thing about that."

"The hell you don't!" George strode forward. Ellie cursed and followed. George stopped six feet from the Franklin patriarch and jabbed a finger toward the old man. "This crime has your stink all over it. You stole my wheat, and when I got ready to take it back, you stole my son to get me to back off."

Mort let his shotgun droop further. A deep frown etched his mouth. "Sir, I am a family man. I would no more hurt your son than I would my own."

"Your lordly morals didn't stop you from taking what's mine!"

"I sought compensation for the fraud you perpetrated against me. Took you long enough to come up with something worth taking." He swept a hand toward his home and fields. "I will grant the Lord blessed me with a bumper crop this season. But I don't have your son."

"Then you won't mind if I have a look around," Ellie said.

"This is private property."

Hobson stepped forward. "Then perhaps I, a disinterested third party, representative of the law, may do the looking."

Mort snorted. "You're no more 'disinterested' than I am the devil. But if you won't take my word, then have a look at whatever you want. Perhaps that will convince you my prayers for Quinn are sincere."

Hobson raised his eyebrows at George. "Agreed?"

George folded his arms. "We'll be right here."

Hobson nodded and strode after Mort Franklin. They disappeared inside the house. Upstairs, a curtain riffled.

Hobson's search was thorough. The house. The outbuildings. The fields and the boathouse. By the time he finished, more than one member of the posse was sitting in the grass. Behind the clouds, the sun marched to its peak. At last, the sheriff returned across the fields side by side with Mort.

"I didn't see any sign of captivity," Hobson said.

George's lips curled. He pointed at Mort. "So he's got him locked in a box! Or they saw us coming and took Quinn away. I want him arrested until his family gives up my boy!"

Mort stalked forward until his breastbone bumped into George's outstretched finger. The old man's blue eyes blazed like polished gems. "I did not take your son, sir. If I lie, may God burn the flesh from my bones."

"I looked everywhere," Hobson said. "Perhaps our efforts would be best spent combing the woods. Canvassing your neighbors."

Tears brimmed from George's eyelids. He took a ragged breath and stared down Mort, unashamed. "If I find you've hurt him, I'll come back for your head."

"And I would do the same." Mort bowed his head, climbed his steps, and closed the door.

"I believe him," Hobson said. "And that he purloined your wheat."

George shook his head vaguely. "All I want is to find Quinn safe and sound."

"I understand." He turned to the posse. "I consider your duties honorably discharged, but would welcome any further aid you'd like to give the search."

To Ellie's mild surprise, when they got back to Lake Placid, only one member of Hobson's ad hoc crew peeled off. Three said they'd ask around town while two others volunteered to help search the wilderness around George's farm. Ellie intended to ask around Lake Placid, but she wanted to break the news of their mission to Dee herself.

Back at the farm, Dee took one look at the arrivals and her face crumpled. "How could you leave without him? Who knows what that old son of a bitch— "

Ellie grabbed her arm. "Hey. I don't think the Franklins took him. Mort didn't try to use him. He even confessed to taking George's wheat. If Mort does have him, the game he's playing is so dark we'll wish we found him in the lake instead."

Dee's jaw hung open. "Mom!"

"I thought you were tough. That you'd rather swallow bitter medicine than sugary placebos. Was I wrong?"

The outrage faded from Dee's eyes. She stood straight. "What do we have to do to find him?"

Ellie smiled inwardly. "Do you remember anything more from last night? Anything unusual?"

"When my shift was over, I shook Quinn awake. He swatted at me like you do when you're so sleepy you'll hit anyone who tries to wake you. But he finally got up and I went to bed. That was the last time I saw him."

Ellie gestured at the woods and hills. "Try looking anywhere you two go together. Maybe he went there and got hurt and can't get back."

"Why would he run off to Mulehead Rock at one in the morning?"

"Why would he go missing at all? A search is the ruling out of possibilities, starting with the most likely." She gazed down the shore. "Speaking of, I've got other avenues to explore. I'll be back by dinner."

She was thirty feet toward the shore before she thought she should have hugged Dee. She considered turning back, but it was too late.

Pine needles brushed her jacket. She imagined the previous night. Quinn sitting by the window in the darkness with binoculars and a rifle. And then what? The bark of a dog? The shifting of a silhouette by the trees? Quinn was young, still had a lot of bad brains. He'd pick up the rifle and go outside. Verbally challenge whatever stranger had stepped onto his land. And then—

But that's where the story broke down. Did he take a shot at the figure? Get shot? No one had heard a gun go off. There had been no sign of blood spatter or dragging. It was as if he'd walked off. Followed someone. Vanished.

Been abducted by aliens.

A man stepped onto the trail ten feet away. Ellie hissed air through her teeth, lunging for her pistol. The man smiled and raised his hands to show they were empty.

She swore and folded her arms. "Hey Sam."

"Heard Quinn went missing," he said. "Thought I'd come see you and save you the trip."

She laughed wryly. "Just ruling out possibilities."

"Believe me, you've taught me how it is."

"So you won't be offended when I ask whether you had anything to do with this."

"Depends. If I don't yell at you, will that make me look guilty?"

"Did you see anything unusual last night? Hear any gunshots?"

"Last night? No." He spit in the grass. "But you might want to ask George about the men in the black fedoras."

Her eyebrows shot up. "Which men?"

"The ones who've been coming by the house. I got the sense he knew them. And they weren't friends."

She tipped her head. "Have you been watching the house?"

He drew back his shoulders. "Just since this started going down. To make sure Dee's safe. You want me to stop?"

"No." She sighed. "Thanks, Sam."

She strode back to the farm. Hobson's newly minted bodyguard Harold stood on the porch, watching the fields. He informed her George was up in the woods with the dogs. Ellie jogged across the cut wheat and entered the scraggly, bare-leafed branches. The forest stretched all the way into the mountains, but after a couple minutes she heard George calling Quinn's name. She homed in on him, letting the leaves crunch beneath her feet so she wouldn't take him by surprise.

"Who are the men in the black fedoras, George?"

He stopped cold. His golden retriever plunked its butt next to him and licked his hand. He ignored it. "What are you talking about?"

"The men you only bring to your house when I'm not around."

"That's just business."

"What kind of business?"

He met her eyes with a hard glare. "The kind I was reduced to when I needed a combine."

She planted her feet. "I let you borrow the tractor. Who are these people? What have you gotten yourself into?"

"Wait just a minute. They've got nothing to do with this."

"How did you pay for the combine?"

"The only things they were interested in taking are things I need to run the farm."

"You mortgaged the harvest. Which was patchy to begin with. And then it went missing."

"Hold on." George closed on her, glancing to the sides, as if afraid someone else might hear his shame. "They can't think I tried to hide it from them, to back out of the deal. That's crazy."

"Why is that?"

"Because those are the type of men..."

"Who would take your firstborn son if you screwed them over?" Ellie said. "Where can I find them?"

He swung his jaw to the side. "Ellie, I've had enough of you meddling in my affairs. He's my boy. This is my business."

"And your bone-deep investment in it means you're probably not the best choice to handle it. I used to be an agent for the federal government. I was the one they sent to the frontlines. Sometimes to regions no more civilized than what we live with now. That's why I've been throwing myself into this thing: I'm the best person for the job."

"Is that what you tell yourself? I think you miss the thrill."

She made a fist beside her hip. "How much longer would it have taken you to piece this together? If they lie to you, will you know it? Have you ever fired a gun at another person?"

"You have?"

"If you haven't, I wouldn't start now."

He pulled a red leaf from a branch and shredded it, casting the bits into the pile on the trail. "The big farm south of Lake Placid. You know it?"

"Off Bear Cub Road?"

"Kessler and Winston. Kessler's thin as a birch and Winston looks like a barrel of beer. Round black mole under his eye. Like you said, they wear black fedoras." George rubbed his mouth. "He's not my son, you know. Not biologically. But I promised to protect him as my own. What does it say about me that I have to send someone else in my place?"

"That you know the right tool for the job." Ellie touched her gun. "If I'm not back by sundown, tell the sheriff to bring the posse."

She jogged back toward the farm and got her bike and rode to town for the third time that day. The mountains hung to the north, blue-green and outlined with white snow. She cut past the cul-de-sacs on the developments on the south end of town, then turned down an up-and-down road through the pines.

A part of her screamed for more intel. You never go in blind. She was more than willing to let George believe she'd been some despot-sniping CIA ghost, but the truth of the matter was she'd worked for the DAA. Her job had been to study the situation on the ground, then recommend how others could impact it.

But there weren't a lot of people around these days. And the disappearance seemed to have caught George completely off guard. Under normal circumstances, men looking to recoup on George's debt would use the threat of harm first, and then, perhaps, take

Quinn to ransom. But they would make sure George knew about it. If he didn't, he wouldn't know to get his ass in gear and pay up.

So if the men in the black hats had taken him, that meant they valued Quinn for reasons beyond leverage against George.

The road fed into a broad farm. Most of the fields were tilled under, coffee-brown dirt mulched with dry yellow stalks. Two tall silos jutted from the fields. A farmhouse watched the entrance, surrounded by metal-roofed barns and outbuildings.

She knew of this farm, but if it was being run by post-apocalyptic loan sharks, that was news to her. The world may have shrunk, but its secrets had grown.

She stopped her bike on the long driveway to the farmhouse. While she was deciding which building to try first, a tall, thin man in a black fedora emerged from the nearest of the metal-roofed structures.

"Can I help you?"

"I heard you help people in trouble," Ellie said.

"We're humanitarians like that."

"Any day now, the ground will freeze. If I don't get my seed down before then, I'll miss the winter crop."

He pushed his hat up his head. "What are you looking to get?"

"I've been doing it by hand, but I ran out of time this year. I need a tractor. With a cultipacker."

"Step inside."

He held the door for her. The building was half stable, half office: the back half was blocked out with horse stalls, most empty, while the front half had been cleared for filing cabinets and two desks furnished with antique wooden chairs that had clearly been looted from one of the old Northeastern homes. A burly man sat with his boots up on one of the desks, careless for the dirt his soles had sprinkled on its surface. He had a round black mole under one eye.

"Tractor, cultipacker," the tall man said. He glanced at Ellie. "One-time lease, or rent-to-own?"

She stood beside the chair opposite the burly man. "Terms on rent-to-own?"

The man pulled his boots off his desk and folded his arms on its surface. "Thirty percent of gross yield on your next ten harvests. Ten percent after that."

"Steep."

"Seventy percent of something is more than one hundred percent of nothing."

"What if I miss a payment?"

He sniffed and leaned back in his chair. "Don't."

"That's too vague," Ellie said. "I can't enter a deal in good faith when I don't know the exact consequences for failing to uphold it."

"We take back what's ours," said the thin man.

"And enough to make up the difference," the burly man finished.

She nodded. "How's that calculated?"

"By some pinhead in Albany."

"Is that where you're based?"

The man scratched his ear. His forearm was covered in thick black hair and he wore a plaid shirt under his overalls. "You don't have to worry about that. Anything crops up, the buck stops here."

Ellie nodded more, as if mulling this over. The room was chilly and smelled like manure and dusty fur. "Do you have a contract?"

"Too good for a handshake?"

"If the consequences for nonpayment are 'Don't ask,' I prefer to be very clear about what does and doesn't satisfy payment."

The burly man drummed the desk, then gestured at the thin man, who slid open a cabinet with a metal rumble, paged through the documents inside, and handed Ellie three stapled pages. The letterhead was handwritten calligraphy. Including an Albany address. She wanted to laugh.

"I'll take these home and look them over." She stood, chair scraping. "Thank you for your time."

The man at the desk leaned on his forearms. "Thought you were in a hurry."

"I am. So excuse the brusqueness of my goodbye."

She exited. The thin man watched her from the doorway, face shaded by his hat. She biked back home. Her legs were sore; her body was used to hardships, but she'd put a lot of miles on herself that day.

George and Dee had been keeping watch on the grounds. They converged on her on the path through the field.

"They give you any trouble?" George said.

"I don't think they recognized me." Ellie got off the bike, sniffling against the runny nose she'd picked up riding through the cold air. "I think they might have him."

"What? Where?"

"Albany."

George turned to the torn-up field of yellow straw and brown dirt. "They haven't said a word to me. Why would they take my son?"

"Doesn't matter," she said.

"It matters like hell! What if their intention is to work him to death?"

"I don't like to assume motive unless I don't have any other leads. If you're chasing a motive, you tend to discard any facts that don't fit it." She watched the clouds march across the sky. "Maybe this is nothing. But I'm going to Albany to rule it out."

"I'll start packing," Dee said. "What will we need?"

"We?"

"He's my fiancé. I'm going with you."

Ellie stared at her. Dee wasn't her flesh and blood—like George and Quinn and so many other survivors, theirs was a makeshift family, bound by circumstance rather than birth—but Ellie knew the look on Dee's face. If a stranger had walked in on them, no one would have ever guessed they were anything but mother and daughter.

11

After that day by the ditch when Lucy had almost stuck Tilly with the knife, they became fast friends. Lucy taught her to throw the knife and a baseball without looking like she might fall down. Tilly taught her which jeans to buy from the Goodwill that wouldn't get her laughed at by the other girls. Lucy'd never had a real friend before and, with the benefit of hindsight, she knew she hadn't always treated Tilly right, but despite all Lucy's flaws, the same quality that led Tilly to befriend her kept Tilly coming back, too.

Middle school was even worse for Lucy. In the classroom and at home. It got to the point where she wished everyone in the world would up and die—a wish that soon came true, incredibly enough—but through it all, Tilly was there for her, though she didn't always acknowledge Lucy when the other girls were around to see. But when they walked home together, or Tilly found her down at the ditch, that's when Tilly put her arm around Lucy and told her how much fun they'd have when they were grown up.

Or the day Lucy had been behind the gym with Jordan Brewster. Lucy hadn't intended for much to come of it. Maybe let him grab a feel above her shirt. Nothing any heavier than that. Lucy's sister Sara was just three years older and was about to have a baby girl. Lucy would swallow a whole bottle of her mother's pain pills before she'd get knocked up.

Anyway, it was fifteen minutes to the end of lunch, they wouldn't have time for more. They lay in the grass behind the gym. Jordan smiled at Lucy like he was the slyest dog on the farm. He leaned in and kissed her. He smelled like Axe body spray and shampoo. His breath was minty, like he'd been expecting this, and his tongue moved in and out of her mouth. Within moments, his hand was on her chest.

"Enjoy it," she said. "That's as far as it goes."

He pulled back and gave her that canine smile. "Don't put limits on yourself, Lucy."

They kissed some more. It felt good and she was getting kind of hot. He tried to go under her shirt, and to reach between her legs, but she grabbed his wrist and he backed off. Then more kissing for a while. Lucy could see herself doing this again.

"Jordan?" Tilly stood over them, mouth agape. "What the hell?"

Jordan scrabbled back. At some point he had unzipped his pants and his penis stuck from his fly, fleshy and thumblike. He went as red as coals and tucked himself back in, struggling to zip up.

"What are you doing here?" he said.

"What are you doing with Lucy?" Tilly said. "Did you have your thing out?"

"Shut up!"

The bell rang from the other side of the building. Jordan glared at Lucy, then turned and ran. Lucy got up and brushed the grass off her seat.

"What were you thinking?" Tilly said. "With Jordan?"

"What's the matter with Jordan?"

Tilly grabbed her arm. "We're late."

They headed back to class. Right then, Lucy was mad, but when she thought about it that night, she'd been glad Tilly had pulled Jordan away. Because when she'd seen his thing, she hadn't been upset by it. Maybe she would have just touched it a little, but maybe she would have ended up like her sister. Pregnant. No husband. Life every bit as done and gone as their mother always told Lucy she'd wind up.

A few days after, Lucy found Tilly in front of her locker. Tilly was struggling to wedge a textbook into a wrinkled mess of papers.

"Don't you listen to the rumors," Lucy said.

Tilly jerked her chin toward Lucy. "What rumors?"

"The ones Jordan spread. About you two having sex in his older brother's car."

Tilly's face went red. She shoved her book into her locker with all her weight. "That never happened. Bring it up a second time and I'll never talk to you again."

Lucy knew it hadn't happened and she didn't know what Tilly was on about, but Tilly was her only friend, and she'd saved Lucy from what might have been something terrible. She didn't mention it again. Neither did Tilly. Because true friends knew when to back off and give a girl her space.

These acts of loyalty and protection, among other reasons, were why Lucy had come to the city to repay her debts—and now stood in the round upper floor of a former restaurant with a strangled body at her feet.

Nerve folded his arms and considered the silent skyscrapers. "This is the hardest the Kono have ever pushed us. I want you to push back."

Lucy looked up from Zoe's body. "How hard?"

"Hard enough to convince them it's a bad idea to keep this up."

"What about the Feds?"

"They don't have the strength to get in the middle. Don't let the collateral damage spill to the civilians and they'll turn a blind eye."

"Gotcha." Zoe's dead eyes stared up at her. She stretched her foot and nudged the lady's head to the side. "What kind of a name is 'Kono,' anyway? They Hawaiian?"

Nerve spun from the window. It was the first time she'd seen him anything but calm. "They think they're gangsters. I imagine it's short for Cosa Nostra."

"For real? You'd think they'd take the opportunity to start with a clean slate. What kind of resources I got at my disposal?"

"Distro's a meritocracy. The better your results, the more you'll be given to work with."

"Is that another way of saying I'm by my lonesome?"

"Bootstraps, Lucy. Pull yourself up."

"You got it, boss."

She knew the score. Nerve wasn't treating her any different from when he'd used her to get to the mole. If she threw a wrench in the Konos' gears, great. If she died in the street, the crows could throw a feast. She was expendable. Replaceable. A cog in the machine.

"It's wonderful to be wanted," she said, "but I didn't show up here out of the kindness of my heart. A friend of mine is working for y'all.

I'd like to see her."

"What makes you think she works for us?" Nerve said.

"Word on the street."

"Do you find the street to be a reliable source of information?"

"That depends on how much it fears you." Lucy brushed imaginary dust from her shoulder. "Look, you all think you're some end-times Walmart, right? A proud member of the Fortune 1? Then let's talk salary. Benefits."

Nerve smiled the way you would at a snake that's slithered out of a cage you thought you'd locked. "Make your proposal."

"First off, I want a place to stay. Feds got me in this place with no heat and I got to walk up a whole mess of stairs. It's awful."

"We have room and board for anyone who's worth it."

"Second, I want to see my friend. Tilly Loman."

Nerve folded his arms and tapped his fingers on his elbow. "I oversee this pier. I can't make promises about the rest of the organization."

Lucy snorted. "Is she a secret agent or something? You afraid to ask your boss?"

He nudged the dead woman with his toe. "Speak with more respect or you'll share her grave."

"Sorry, I ain't used to having a job."

Lucy smiled some but didn't try to bat her lashes or anything that gross. She got the idea Nerve was the type who could see right through a person. There was something hidden to him. He wasn't a large man; he didn't do much yelling; he hadn't gotten excited even when Kerry was choking the woman to death. Even his threats were businesslike, impersonal. There was a sniper's watchful patience to him. Like he knew he had all day to take his shot. And most likely, you'd never see it coming.

"Get used to it," he said. "I'll see about your friend."

"Last, I want a salary. Something I can sock away for my golden years."

"Management gets salary." He gestured toward the piers. "Workforce gets food and shelter."

"You gave me three days to uncover your mole. I didn't know a damn thing about you or your people, but I did it. How much you bet I can get done in three months? Three years? You got to pay for talent, son."

"That's the last time I remind you about respect."

Lucy shuffled her feet. "Sorry, boss."

"Your thinking, though? That's correct. Talent is scarce. If you want to keep it, you have to pay for it. Since you're new, we'll start incentive-based." He beckoned to Kerry, who had taken up position against the wall to the left. "Tea. Half ounce."

"No shit?" Lucy said.

Kerry opened the second drawer of a metal file cabinet and brought her a thick baggie of dried brown curls. Lucy frowned at it and sniffed.

"Oh," she said. "Tea."

"It's lightweight, doesn't go bad, and everyone wants it," Nerve said. "If you prefer ammunition, leave an order with our gunsmith."

She bounced the baggie in her hand. "Know what, tea's not so bad. You know if this stuff grows down south?"

"It prefers warm, stable weather," he stated rotely. "Which makes the South a candidate, but one hurricane could destroy everything."

"Right," she said slowly, surprised he'd known that offhand. "So what's next on my agenda?"

He turned to gaze out the window. "You're new in town. That's an asset. Did the raiders get a look at you when you spotted them before the strike?"

"Nope. They would have planted me in that courtyard."

"I need to know whether this raid was a one-time move or if it's the start of a new campaign."

"And how do you intend to do that?"

"By stealing a page from their playbook: I'll plant a mole."

"I got no problem pretending," Lucy said. "Just so long as I don't go so deep I can't see my friend."

"The Kono work out of a bar uptown. Where they can peel off disaffected Central Park farmers from the Feds. Head up there, hear what you can hear, and see if you can't ingratiate yourself with the natives."

"I'll start tomorrow." She nodded at Zoe's body. "Been a long day."

Nerve didn't argue. While Kerry hauled the body into a side room, Nerve brought her downstairs to speak to the woman who oversaw the pier's records. He informed the woman that Lucy was to be housed in the Bracket Building and fed conventional dailies. The woman nodded, taking notes. Nerve departed. The woman summoned a young man from the enjoining office and informed Lucy he would see her to her new lodging.

"Wow, the Bracket Building," the young man said as he led her across the street into the tangle of towers. "You must be special, huh?"

"Why's that?" Lucy said.

He turned and grinned against the hard autumn light. "Electricity!"

"You don't say. Know where it comes from?"

"Nope. It is budgeted, however. But don't run your TV and your blow dryer at the same time and you ought to be fine."

The tower was a glass and steel structure a few blocks from the piers. The boy jangled a key into Lucy's palm and accompanied her through the airy lobby to the stairwell. Inside it, yellow lights buzzed steadily, echoing from the concrete walls. Her room was on the third floor.

Nice place. Not much bigger than her Fed apartment across the island, but the windows let in lots of light and most of the overheads worked too, including those in the bathroom. Best of all, it was warm—she had a thermostat.

"Just don't push it above 64," the kid warned. "Whoever runs this place is worse than my old man ever was."

He let her know to come by the pier office if she needed anything, then left, the door clicking hollowly behind him. Lucy went to the balcony, which was hardly deep enough to stand on, and looked down on the vacant street.

Assigned to go double-agent against the Kono struck her as a load of shit. A good way to get got. So she'd apply a light touch, dawdle a bit. No sense getting in too deep. All she had to do was play along until Nerve got her in front of Tilly. Then it was goodbye, Manhattan.

With that in mind, and with it being early afternoon and much too soon for sleep, she fired up one of her joints, headed downstairs, and wandered around the canyon-like streets. It was a spectacle, she'd give it that, and there was so much habitable space she had no doubt a person could dig up all kinds of useful leftovers from the smorgasbord of civilization that had so abruptly ended. But in the end, it was just a bunch of stuff. Every town had stuff. She didn't see why people gathered in New York when it would be a hundred times easier to make it in a place where you didn't have to farm the sidewalk planters.

Yet as she walked down the filthy avenues, an image of the city's post-plague history took shape in her mind's eye. Place this size must have had thousands of survivors. Plenty of those split in favor of less chaotic pastures. But enough had stayed that, after the aliens seemed gone for good and people began to crawl out of the woodwork—both native New Yorkers and fools drawn to the dried-out core of the Big Apple—they were able to put together a patchwork society.

No sooner had people started swapping wares and jury rigging electrical lines than the Feds had put on their dead daddy's hat and pretended they ran the place. Some sharp cookie with travel connections set up Distro, bringing foreign goods to sell to the locals, some of whom—those without farmland or the inclination to tend it—wound up driving Distro wagons or humping barrels off the docks. Others like them, but less interested in working for others and more interested in violence, established Kono. Who nobody was real impressed by, but were apparently feeling their oats enough to begin launching attacks on the dominant non-government power: Distro.

Just as clearly, she saw Manhattan's future. There wasn't enough farmland here to feed the population. Distro and maybe those Kono jokers had more shipped in from outside, but what were they trading for it? Goods and scrap scavenged from the stores? Well, most of that stuff was useless now, and what wasn't would rust, rot, and run out. You wouldn't think it, but some objects seemed to decay faster when they weren't used. Clothes, for instance, yellowed and grew stiff and brittle; bugs dug into the cloth. Chemical products separated into sickly layers of differing color and viscosity. Durable objects like chairs and tables were more or less oblivious to time on a human scale, but that meant everywhere had chairs and tables. Manhattan's were nothing special.

Now, could be that by the time the city's supplies of interesting goods ran short, Distro would be making enough from trading other people's goods to stay afloat. That the Feds would pull enough tolls and taxes to sustain their personnel and infrastructure. That Kono would continue...whatever it was they did.

But Lucy doubted. When Manhattan's output dwindled, times would get leaner all around. Those at the top would tighten their belts—and those at the bottom would get squeezed. Hungry people tended to riot. To loot from those who had wealth and food. To burn down the towers that had once held them in their place.

When that happened, the only person in Manhattan who'd be having a good time would be the Reaper.

Golly, she was stoned.

She walked back to the docks to grab some dinner and to requisition the rest of her gear. Belly full of fish stew, umbrella in hand and .22 pistol velcroed to her ankle, she biked back to her apartment and slept straight through to morning.

Her apartment was a northern exposure and the light was fine but she turned the electrics on anyway. Even better, it had running water. The temperature never climbed above lukewarm, but the shower was the first time she'd felt water pressure in over five years.

After, she lounged around a while, unconcerned about whether anyone was watching from the apartments across the street or about the chill of the 64-degree air on her bare skin. Because it felt good.

Because life was for enjoying. Easy to forget that when you're a big important person with big important things to do. She herself needed to extricate Tilly from this island before the dummy was snatched up for some bozo's harem or caught in the crossfire of warring clans. After that, she'd have to get them to the car, drive back to Florida, and convince Tilly this whole thing had been a big mistake. She had a lot of work ahead of her.

But she'd just had a shower. Not with a sun-warmed camp bag with zero pressure, but with heated plumbing. And once she left here, she wasn't likely to have one like that again for a very long time.

So once she was good and ready, dried and relaxed, she got some clothes on, her umbrella and pistol, lugged her bike downstairs, and hit the road. A cold wind blew off the harbor, carving down the barren streets. As she rode north, the towers got higher and higher, proud old things with fancy stonework next to modern monuments of dust-dulled glass. Had to wonder how much longer that shit would last. Glass, the material proverbial for its tendency to shatter and break, and they'd gone and built a whole city out of it.

She stopped her bike in Times Square. It was gray and quiet and the sidewalks wore a patina of dirt and gum. She spat in the street and continued on. Past the lower edge of the park, the buildings calmed down a bit. She took Amsterdam to 93rd and leaned her bike in the doorway of a Thai restaurant to finish to the Kono bar on foot.

Its sign called it Sicily, a brick place on the ground floor of an apartment tower. It had a sandwich board out front declaring "BEER" and "LIQUOR." Past the windows, the inside was well-lit and people sat at red vinyl booths and a long wooden bar. The door was padded red faux leather studded with brass buttons. As she approached, a tall, stout man opened it, filling the frame.

"You armed?"

".22 pistol on my ankle," she said. "Couple of knives around my belt. You want 'em?"

"You can pick them up on your way out."

She nodded, unstrapped the pistol, slipped the knives from their sheathes, and handed them over. The man eyeballed them, set them on a table inside the door, and passed her a receipt.

"You sure you're of age?"

She rested the tip of her umbrella on the toe of her shoe. "Don't tell me the Feds care."

"If you'd bought it, I would have declared you too naive to enter." He stepped aside. "You'll be fine."

The inside smelled like beer and sweat, both stale. Blue wildflowers thrust from a box lining the front window, but it didn't much help. Faces turned Lucy's way. Two women, fourteen men.

She didn't much like when grown men sat around public places in the middle of the day. It typically meant one of two things. First, that they were unreliable or otherwise unemployable, which did bad things to the male self-esteem and worse things to its judgment. Or second, they did specialized work that was infrequent yet important enough for them to have all kinds of down time. Such as the work she was doing right now.

Keeping one eye on these characters, she made her way to the bar. Her rear hadn't fully made contact with her prospective bar stool when a man approached from her left. He was in his early thirties and his eyes glimmered behind his long black hair. He said his name was Duke and Lucy almost laughed at him, but she was on a mission. She introduced herself.

"Bourbon," Duke said to the bartender. He grinned at Lucy. "They make the real thing here."

"That right?" she said. "You got a limestone cavern in the cellar?"

He looked confused but quickly shook it off. "What brings you to Sicily?"

"Looking for work."

"You don't say."

"Get that grin off your face. If I wanted that kind of work, I'd go into business for myself."

"We offer a safe, clean environment," he said. "You'd be great for it."

"I know. I got two of everything I'm supposed to have two of and one of everything I'm supposed to have one of. Pretty incredible to be so blessed, and maybe I'm a fool to not take advantage of my God-given talent to be fucked, but you know what, Duke? I got other plans in life."

His self-satisfied glee froze dumbly to his face. The bartender rescued him, setting down two glasses a third full of thick brown liquor. Lucy took a smell and then a sip.

"I think you been had, Duke," she said. "This isn't bourbon. Where's the charred oak?"

The way his grin looked ready to topple, she expected him to thank her and retreat to a dark corner of the bar, but he recovered enough to laugh.

"I'm sorry for insulting you, Lucy," he said. "A lot of girls are happy to spend some time in the sheets if that's all it takes to put a roof over their head and a meal on the table. But it takes all kinds to make the world go 'round, doesn't it?"

"I like a man who's not afraid to admit when he's wrong," she said. "So how about other lines of work?"

"What are you looking to do?"

"I get the impression y'all are fixing to run this island. I'd like to help make that happen. Hop on board for the big win."

"I might have some sway." He watched her a minute. "Want

another drink?"

"Little early for that," she said. "I don't like to start unless I can finish."

"Let me close my tab."

He walked to the far end of the bar and spoke to the bartender. The bartender shook his head, as if they were haggling, then poked his head through a side door, returning a moment later. He and Duke talked some more. Duke slid him a small cardboard box, like the kind you might keep a ring inside, then thunked back across the hardwood toward Lucy.

"Let's find someplace we can talk."

Lucy got up and followed him to the back of the bar. The bartender glanced up at her, then down at the bar, which he scrubbed with a soiled rag.

Duke held a door open to a narrow brick hall. "Tell me more about what you'd like to do. We're always on the lookout for skilled people who can establish new business leads, but there's a big need for people who can enforce our existing contracts, too."

Lucy's laugh echoed down the hall. "Enforcement? Sign me up."

"Think you got the muscle for it?" He smiled and opened a dented metal door, beckoning her through. Lucy mock-curtseyed and stepped into a shadowed cobblestone courtyard enclosed on all sides by high walls.

Even before the men moved from the shadows, she knew she'd made a mistake. The door slammed behind her. Two men emerged from behind the planter trees. Duke tapped a knife against his thigh and smiled.

12

"You're staying right here." Ellie pointed at the ground. "There's every chance this is just a wild goose chase. Except the goose can shoot back."

"It's too dangerous for me?" Dee said. "Is that the problem?"

"The problem is I don't have any idea."

Dee rolled her eyes. "So it makes a lot of sense for you to run off to find out all by yourself."

Ellie bit back a reply. She turned to George. "What do you think?"

He pushed his lips together. "Do you think this is a real lead?"

"It's a lead. I have no idea how 'real' it is."

"It's still possible he's out here hurt in a field. If you think we ought to play to our strengths, that would argue that I should continue the search here. I know these lands better than anyone."

"Agreed," Ellie said. "This lead doesn't make a whole lot of sense. It could be a complete red herring. But if it's real, and we don't run it down, the consequences could be unpleasant."

"Why would they take him?" George blurted.

"That route leads to nothing but stress and speculation."

Ellie felt self-conscious about all the aphorisms she'd been spouting lately. Not because her advice wasn't meaningful, but because she didn't like making such blatant displays of expertise.

Matters like this, however, were best approached with a certain mindset. One that rarely if ever came up in the quiet, patient life of lakeland farming. George and Dee needed a crash course. And maybe Ellie needed to remind herself.

"Focus on the goal," she went on. "Not what might happen if we don't reach it."

Dee huffed. "How am I supposed to 'focus on the goal' when you won't let me help achieve it?"

"You can help here. We haven't even begun to search the mountains."

"I'm going crazy here. I want to get out. To move."

Ellie smiled in anger. "Do you remember what happened in New York? It wasn't an adventure. It wasn't a game. We barely made it out alive."

"But you did," Dee said. "Because you had Dad."

"And what did it cost?" Ellie regretted the words at once. Dee's eyes went bright. Ellie's stung, too. "Do you need to go? Or do you just want to go?"

"I love him."

"That's a terrible reason!"

"It's why you came for Dad, isn't it?" Dee laughed, spilling tears. "It sure wasn't for me. But you did it. For the same terrible reason. How dare you say I can't do the same?"

The gears of Ellie's head circled wildly. Most of this churning was emotional. Irrelevant, for the time being, though she knew she'd have to sort through it eventually. Once she'd gotten the messy feelings shut down for later maintenance, two factors remained. First, finding Quinn without getting anyone else she cared about hurt. And second, continuing to shape Dee into the kind of person who would someday be capable of navigating situations like these without any help from Ellie.

The understanding made her queasy. But you had to start somewhere.

"You follow my lead," she said. "You don't get to argue. You don't get to run off on your own. If I say it's too dangerous, you turn around at once. Do you understand?" She waited. Dee nodded. Ellie folded her arms. "I need to hear you say it."

"I understand," Dee said.

"Then come on. We've got a lot to pack."

They headed down the path through the woods to their house. Dee didn't talk, but her face was etched with the spinning of a worried mind. That was something she'd need to learn to cope with. Anyway, Ellie had her own concerns.

At the home, she saw to the chickens, then got out a road map. Albany was roughly 150 miles dead south, most of it along I-87. It was a good road, as far as she knew. Should be able to bike there in two days. Give it another two days to investigate, and one more in case of detours or difficulties, and they'd be back within a week.

She got out one of her checklists—Winter, Intermediate Duration—and copied it to a fresh sheet of paper, adapting it for two people. It was her most hated list. You could almost convince yourself you could carry it on your back and/or a bike basket. Especially with two people, who in many ways required no more equipment than a lone traveler. You had to double up food and water, but you didn't have to double your cooking supplies. Just one extra cup/bowl, one more fork, one more spoon. Same situation with the bedding: extra blankets, but no need for a second tent.

But no matter how hard she tweaked the numbers in her favor, they always wound up supporting the need for a trailer. It would slow them down. On the other hand, if you rode out under-supplied and had to stop to forage or scavenge, that usually wound up hurting more.

It wasn't the trailer itself that was the problem. It was that, as close as the non-trailer solution felt, she could never get it to add up.

In the garage, she pulled the tarp off the bike trailer and started packing. Jugs of water. A tent, blankets. Spare socks and shoes. Sweaters and jackets for layering. A couple boxes of ammo. And, since they were visiting a human settlement, the goods of trade.

This was a dilemma in itself. There was no single currency. Some still favored gold, silver, and jewelry, but that stuff was no longer scarce. Humans were scarce. Spend enough time picking through the old homes and safe deposit boxes, and anyone could become "rich" with metals and gems, devaluing all of it. Ammo was better, because much of it had been hoarded during the collapse, and was now hidden or lost, but ammo was heavy. And some of the more survival-oriented crowd were drowning in it.

The true coin of the realm was anything consumable or semi-perishable—meaning people often ran out—that couldn't be easily replaced. Coffee. Tea. Chocolate. Antibiotics. Herbs. Spices (which, she had discovered, were often more useful as preservatives than for their flavor). Recreational drugs were favored by some, and she'd toyed with the idea of growing marijuana, but Chip would have frowned on that. Although, now that Dee was an adult...

Focus. She settled on a diversified portfolio. A few gemstone necklaces and small bars of silver. A couple boxes of ammo she didn't use herself, .357 and .223. Half a box of chocolate bars, stale but delicious enough to anyone who hasn't tasted chocolate in years. A fat baggie of coriander seeds and tiny Tupperwares of oregano, turmeric, and chili powder. Packs of disposable lighters.

The camping and cooking gear was already sorted and boxed on the garage shelves, ready to be used. Ellie loaded it into the trailer. Dee came in with a couple of bags and added them to the load.

"How much of that is clothes?" Ellie said.

"You said we'd be gone for a week."

"That means two pairs of jeans. Max."

"That's gross. We're going to be biking all day."

Ellie set down the fishing net she'd been considering adding to the hunting/foraging supplies. "If this is how it's going to be—"

Dee grabbed a bag from the trailer and rolled her eyes. "Fine. Two pairs of jeans. When we're sharing a tent and I smell like a football team at halftime, you'll know who to thank."

Ellie continued packing, then went to the larder and bagged up all their bread. Over the short term, you didn't need much more, though she tubbed some dried apples and venison, too. The garage door was open and it smelled like cold and the fresh scent of the lake. As she finalized the trailer and triple-checked her list, Sheriff Hobson appeared in the entry and doffed his hat.

"I hear you're on your way to our fair former capital."

"Ruling out a lead," Ellie said.

"I hope it's a strong one." He leaned on his cane. "A trip to Albany will require, say, a week? Forgive my indelicate words, but if Quinn Tolbert is still missing by the time you return, he may not ever be found."

"A lot of people will be looking for him in the normal places. I want to cover the un-normal."

"And I would like to offer my assistance."

Ellie glanced up from the bike chain she'd been inspecting for weak links. "Don't you want to lead the main investigation?"

"Like you said, the main investigation is the exhaustion of the normal. So let it be handled by the normal. Additionally, George would appreciate my inclusion."

"This is a very speculative trip, sheriff. I'm not sure it's worth your time."

He smiled, self-effacing. "Thank you for the attempt to spare my feelings. Now, shall we discuss your true objections? You were a professional, were you not?"

"Police detective? No. Intelligence analyst? Yes."

"Whereas I was no such thing. My background is entirely amateur."

"I hadn't known that," Ellie said.

"Then I'm disappointed in myself. I perceive you to be dedicated. Thorough. The type to reach her own conclusions rather than trusting the common knowledge. I suspect that, the moment I nominated myself to uphold the law, you delved into my background to assess my fitness for the position. How am I doing?"

Ellie laughed. "Strong start. Let's see how you finish."

He spun his bowler on his finger. "You discovered a CV that is light on experience, to put it generously. Having no interest in the position yourself, or believing it was a harmless show, you did nothing to object. But now that we have a real case in front of us—one that involves your family—you wouldn't trust me to handle its subtler edges any more than you'd tackle a wasp's nest with a wiffle bat."

"You're right. On all counts. Including the fact this isn't a dispute over a farmer's broken fence—this is my family."

"It's bigger than that, though. I'm pledged to protect the lakelands. If an unknown group is poaching our citizens, I am duty-bound to uncover it—and to root it out."

"All I care about is finding Quinn. I can handle that on my own. If it turns out he's been snared by this shadow org, they're all yours."

"George tells me you belonged to the Department of Advance Analysis. I've never heard of such a group. The only reason I know of it, and your involvement in it, is because you've let it be known." He narrowed one eye at her. "You take me for an amateur. What if I find myself most effective at my job when everyone else assumes I'm as incompetent as you do?"

Ellie rocked back on her heels. "Or that's bullshit to talk your way into a trip you have no business taking."

"The world is full of possibility."

She flexed her hands, which were stiff from taking notes regarding the status of their supplies. She was quick to judgment. She knew that. Most people would consider that a fault, and she couldn't argue with them (except to point out that quick judgment, if accurate, could save your ass when you come under fire). But at least she was quick to reassess those judgments when presented with new evidence. She would rather be right from now on than to stubbornly insist she'd never been wrong in the first place.

"We leave in thirty minutes," she said. "With our without you. And I lead."

He nodded thoughtfully. "Do you happen to have an extra bicycle? Turns out I ran here."

Between setting him up with a pack and Dee's last-minute fussing, it took closer to an hour. Ellie felt uncharacteristically sedate about the delay. Once their wheels hit the road, and the cold air rushed past their faces with the smell of pines and motion, all that mattered was the next mile.

She bore the trailer. To hedge against disaster, Dee and Hobson also carried a fraction of the essentials in their bike baskets—a gallon of water each, some bread, a couple blankets. At the first highway, Hobson got out his pocket watch.

"Got an appointment you didn't tell me about?" Ellie said.

"Measuring our mileage," he said. "May be useful if we need to determine whether we can reach shelter before dark."

"How fastidious."

"With my life? Yes, it's a rather eccentric trait." He checked his watch at the next marker, as well as the three after that. "About eight miles per. Hills aren't helping. Assuming we use every ounce of daylight, we might squeak into town by sunset Friday."

"That's my plan." She filled him in on what little there was to know about the men in the black fedoras. "Has anyone else gone missing from town lately?"

"Not that I'm aware of. It may be possible, however, they have deliberately targeted those whose vanishments would go unnoticed."

"Or there are no 'vanishments' at all."

"A skeptical approach. I approve."

"But why would they take him?" Dee said. "What are they doing?"

Hobson glanced at his pocket watch. "Between loss of machines and population, labor is in short supply. I have heard rumors of rampant slave-taking in more chaotic portions of the nation."

"But they can't do that."

"What's to stop them? Men like me?"

"Don't you?"

"I'd like to. But evil breeds in darkness, and these days, almost every corner of the map is black." He sniffed against the cold. "I never used to be a believer in big government, but our brave new world makes a convincing case."

"Let's not get ahead of ourselves," Ellie said. "The first goal is to determine whether he's there. In the meantime, stay focused. If he was taken, they may be just ahead of us."

With the sunlight down to its last legs, she pointed out a rutted dirt path through the pines. They turned off. The dirt road snaked so far into the forest she feared the faux cabin at its end was remote enough to be occupied, but there were no candles in the windows and the pane beside the front door was broken with no sign of repair. The inside smelled of the dust that layered the floor. They opened the garage, brought in the bikes, closed it, and set up the tent in the back room to enclose as much heat as possible.

After a dinner of bread and venison jerky, it wasn't yet seven o'clock, but Ellie was sore and exhausted from a day of biking. She slept until an owl hooted her awake hours later. It was still dark, but Hobson's pocket watch ticked along; by the flame of a lighter, she saw it was five in the morning. Hobson woke, hair askew, and their furtive shuffling to go out back to pee and then to share some water from a canteen woke Dee. The moon was high and ringed by a vast white halo.

"Ice crystals in the sky." Hobson's face was pressed against the window and his breath fogged the glass and slid down in droplets. "Suppose we should pray to Notus, the south wind?"

"We need modern gods." Ellie's voice was hoarse and scratchy. "Me, I'm asking for the blessings of Starbucks."

The moon-ring wasn't a good sign for the weather, but it helped light the way. They got to an early start, taking an easy pace down the highway through the black woods. They crossed through a town so dark and silent it could have been a cave. Ellie imagined the whole continent to the west, equally vacant and primeval. The void could drive a person crazy. The stars twinkled, delivering her a vision of the creatures that had unleashed the plague on Earth. What if, when they left their homeworld, they hadn't been bent on extinction? What if their minds had been warped by billions and billions of miles of darkness? By the time they found us, eliminating mankind might seem like a mercy.

The sun rose, vaporizing her black thoughts. They stopped for breakfast, biked on, rested, ate, and continued, slowing to scout the scattered forest towns for signs of hostile strangers. They had reached the main highway early on and it sloped steadily downward from the retreating mountains, but that seemed to make the climbing sun feel all the more distant and cold, an aimless yellow pebble that might never come back.

They passed the night in a stern-windowed home overlooking a former campground south of Lake George. They set up the tent in a back room on the ground floor so they could use candles without being spotted from the road. A shuffling noise woke Ellie in the deep part of the night. She lay in her down sleeping bag, waiting for each gentle scraping step beyond the window. It was surely just an animal, and much smaller than it sounded, but she took a long time to fall back asleep.

The morning came too early. They were down from the mountains and the highway threaded through town after town. Ellie kept her pistol on her hip and her rifle velcroed to the bike's wire basket. Columns of smoke were rare, isolated to the woods beyond the grassy meadows, protected from the unwanted traffic on the highway. They neither passed nor saw another traveler. A breeze fluttered from the north, but as they rode, their velocity matched it perfectly, leaving them in a moving bubble of perfect stillness.

A mile north of Albany, with the smell of a river drifting through the trees, torched cars all but blocked the highway. Ellie stopped and scanned the overgrown parkland. A bird rustled the branches. Hobson dismounted his bike, bent his knees and hitched his pants, and used the curve of his cane to hook a sign downed in front of the cars. He held it up and blinked owlishly, as if uncovering lost Nordic runes.

"'PROPERTY OF THE CLAVAN BROTHERS,'" he read. He peered past the highway to the shops and homes poking through the trees. "I assume they mean the town. If they're referring to these cars, I would say the Clavans suffer from a marked lack of ambition."

"What does it mean?" Dee said.

"Who knows?" Ellie said. "Could be the Clavans died years ago. Or it could be they're the ones we're looking for."

"That's like so helpful. I see why the government put you in charge of figuring stuff out."

Ellie's annoyance flared. "When you're young, a wrong answer sounds better than no answer. Experience is the process of learning when you know nothing."

"Is that a quote?" Hobson said.

"Not to my knowledge."

"Then I won't feel poorly for not recognizing it."

"Here's another one: open eyes, open mind."

Dee sighed. "What's that mean, Confucius?"

"It means you let what's in front of you shape what's in your head. Not the other way around."

She recentered her weight on her bike and pedaled down the road, trailer dragging behind her. A Walgreens slumped apologetically at the edge of town. The windows were bashed in and it had been heavily looted, but there was a phone book behind the front desk. She tore out the page and ran down the address on the contract from the men with the black fedoras. Couple miles in from the river, right off I-90.

It was 3 PM and the sun waned to the west. A winding road snaked past the trees on the other side of the highway and the three of them cut across the rough field to intercept it. The address was a glossy, six-sided oblong beside a two-level parking garage. A wood axe tonked from the distance. The crick of a socket wrench echoed past the pillars of the garage.

Ellie left her bike in the grass by the road and walked to the glass doors, carrying nothing but her pistol and her lightweight day-pack. The doors were automatic sliders. Nonfunctioning, of course. Hobson pushed one open. The lobby was dimly lit by the fading sun and two electric bulbs. A machine thrummed from somewhere beneath the floor. The front desk was empty. Ellie walked up, cleared her throat, and rang the bell.

After her third ring, a man emerged from the side door. He wore glasses and clean jeans but his fingernails were crescents of black. He smelled like motor oil. "May I help you?"

"We're looking for someone," Ellie said.

"Does he work here?"

"We think he may have been brought here."

The man wrinkled his forehead. "Brought?"

"I represent an interested client," Ellie tried. "Discreet. Wealthy."

The man reached for a sheaf of papers. "I'm not sure I take your meaning."

"Light-skinned African-American, twenty years old. Farmboy build. If you've seen him, I have an offer."

The man looked up from his papers. "Young black male?"

"His name is Quinn," she said.

"I don't think I can help you."

"Bullshit. You know him. I saw it in your face."

The man's gaze rested on hers. Unknown gears clicked behind his eyes. "Who did you say you represent?"

"I didn't."

"Hang on a minute." He left the desk and exited through the same door he'd come in.

"What's happening?" Dee said.

Ellie glanced around for cameras. "Stay quiet."

"Suppose he's bringing someone back?" Hobson said.

She touched the butt of her gun. "Dee, if something happens, you run. Meet us on the highway at the Clavans' sign."

Dee stuck out her jaw, lips parted. "You want me to leave you? What kind of plan is that?"

"The one that saves your life. I made this very clear: do as I say or go home now."

Dee tipped back her head and shook it, as if concluding a conversation with the ceiling about how stupid Ellie was. The door opened. Ellie tensed. A woman with white curly hair walked inside and smiled. Her back was bent, but she moved smoothly enough.

"James told me why you're here." The woman's eyes moved

between the three of them. "What's the nature of your relationship to the boy?"

"Like I told James," Ellie said, "we're agents of an interested party."

"No need to get testy. I ask so I know how to break the news." The old woman showed a fragile expression that could have been a smile or a frown. "Yesterday, a body was found in the woods. Young black male."

"What?" Dee screeched. She swayed into Ellie's shoulder.

Ellie found Dee's hand and squeezed. "I'd like to see it."

The woman folded her hands in front of her stomach. "Ma'am, it's a body."

"And right now, it could be anyone's."

"It's been in the woods. The animals. There won't be much left to see."

Beside her, Dee's shoulders shook. Ellie leaned over the counter. "She needs to know."

The old woman sighed through her nose. "Excuse me."

She went back through the door. Ellie expected to have to console Dee, but except for her shallow breathing, the girl seemed to calm down. The old woman returned less than a minute later.

"State park west of town. About ten miles. Take Thacher Park Road in, then follow the trail where it meets Beaver Dam. James said it's a couple hundred yards from there. On the left."

Hobson scribbled notes. Ellie nodded. "Thank you."

"Be careful," the woman said. "Bears. Dogs. Night's coming. Might be best to wait till tomorrow."

Ellie nodded. Dee stared at nothing. Ellie took her arm and led her toward the doors. Outside, the cold hit them like it had been sprayed from a hose.

Ellie got out her map from the phone book and traced a route. "Need to ride hard if we're going to beat the sunset."

Dee got on her bike, keeping pace without complaint. To Ellie's right, Hobson watched the trees fronting the highway, keeping his thoughts to himself. His cheeks and nose were red with cold.

The highway crossed a downtown of sedate brick storefronts. A few towers rose from the trees near the river. They exited the highway to a long two-lane road that stretched through wooded subdivisions, then fallow farms. The sun arced to the west and they chased it up into the hills. Clouds overtook them, and then the sun, too. The air grew as sharp as sheared metal.

The road was swallowed by pines and rough-cut trunks. Twilight swept over the woods. Where the roads met, Ellie dismounted, lit two lanterns, passed one to Hobson, and found the trail. The lanterns flickered. It smelled like spent oil and pine needles. Ellie spaced them twenty feet apart and walked parallel to the trail, with Dee closest to it, Hobson in the middle, and herself at the outer edge.

Fine white dust sifted through the pine needles. It had begun to snow.

The powder fell with the sound of hushed surf. At once it was as dark as midnight. Hobson veered toward Dee to share his light. Leaves crackled underfoot. Beyond that, there was no sound or sight of life. After a quarter mile of walking, Ellie stopped and turned around for another pass back toward the roads, putting some distance between herself and the trail. The ground froze and the snow began to stick, frosting the grass and leaves, gleaming white in the light of the lanterns. Ellie tried to keep her eyes open and her mind quiet, but the silence of the forest invaded her with visions of Quinn's upturned face, gawking and blind, sight stolen first by death, and then by crows.

"Ellie," Hobson pointed.

The body lay in the leaves, shirtless, shoeless. Little was left of its face. Dee fell to her knees and screamed.

13

"I must warn you," Lucy said to Duke, "I have an umbrella."

Duke lifted his brows. The knife remained near his hip. "You do! What do you intend to do with it?"

"If I hit you too low, I might make you wish you'd never been born. But I'm probably just going to kill you."

He laughed with little humor. Lucy faced a couple of problems. First off, Duke and his boys added up to three, and she only had two shells in the umbrella. Beau had tried and tried to rig up more, but she knew she was lucky to pack more than one while retaining the illusion that it wasn't in fact an operational firearm. If she was clever, she might maneuver to wing two of them with one blast, but whatever she did, she was going to have to take at least one hand to hand. And they were bigger than her. Surprise and resolve were great equalizers, but they'd only take you so far.

And second, she was supposed to be getting in bed with the Kono. If she started planting them in graves instead, that threw Nerve's whole use for her out the window. Not a great way to convince him to fast-track her request to see Tilly.

"Don't make this any worse for yourself," Duke said.

"God was kind to men like you," she said. "For his most venomous creations, he stamped them with a bright red hourglass, or gave them a rattling tail so you'd know better than to poke at them. Well, he forgot to give me a stamp or a rattle, so you need to listen to my words instead: put down that blade and walk away."

He titled his head. "I know you from somewhere, don't I?"

"I doubt that."

"Brian, how do I know her? This whole time I'm trying to put my finger on it but it keeps slipping away."

One of the two men across from Lucy—Brian, presumably—rocked on his heels. He had a buzzcut and looked like he ate a lot of sausage. "I don't know. Maybe she's got one of those faces of the world."

Duke glared at her, as if his misfiring memory were her fault, and took a step forward, tapping the tip of his knife against the side of his jeans. "Whatever. I'll have all the time I need to figure it out when you're working for me. Times are tight, you can't turn down a good job like that."

Lucy had the impression most people used it as a figure of speech, but when she got mad, it was like a red sheer curtain dropped from the sky and shaded the whole world. Later, she could say exactly why she did it—people using their power to take it from others drove her ten kinds of crazy—but at that moment, the "why" wasn't exactly foremost on her mind.

She leveled the umbrella and pulled the pin that functioned as its trigger.

The shot crashed across the courtyard. Duke didn't have time to look shocked or scared or sorry. The blast pounded him in the chest and he dropped in the kind of heap that doesn't get back up.

She whirled on the other two. They were more experienced than the boys she'd taken the car from; the third man already had a pistol rising toward her chest. She fired at the same time he did. Her arm went hot; his bullet whined off the brick wall. Her shot took him in the middle of the body and he fell with a high-pitched moan. She sprinted at him and aimed her now-empty shotgun at Brian.

He hesitated with his hand in his armpit. The man on the ground was fumbling with his pistol. Lucy flipped her grip on the umbrella and bashed his wrist with its reinforced handle. The gun skidded away. She cocked back golf-style and smashed the handle into his head. As soon as she felt it connect into his skull, she dropped and snatched up his pistol.

"You aren't too fast, Brian," she said.

"You shot them!"

"I did. And I'll shoot you, too. But I got a deal for you."

"I got friends in there." He jerked his chin toward the bar. "They won't think that was a firecracker."

"Could be, but they disarmed me when I came in. Anyone who heard the shots would guess they were Duke's way of taking care of me."

Sweat popped across his pale face. "What do you want?"

"Duke saw me at the docks, didn't he? Your little raid on the Chelsea Piers. Were you there with him?"

"I'm dead as soon as I tell you what you want to hear."

She shook her head. "I get good vibes off you, man. If you play it straight with me, I'll return the favor."

His eyes tick-tocked between hers. "It wasn't just a raid. It was a scouting mission."

"To do what?"

"To see how much we could take from you."

"And Distro gave it away without a fight." Lucy perched a grin on her mouth the way you'd set a pair of glasses on the end of your nose. "You're coming back, aren't you? To take a lot more than coffee."

Brian shook his head so hard his chin wobbled. "I don't know. I'm a grunt. Duke keeps me around because I helped him through the plague, but he doesn't exactly invite me to tribal council."

"Think you better get used to talking about ol' Duke in the past tense." She took a look at the door, which remained closed. "He never let slip anything more juicy?"

He slicked sweat from his beefy face, then froze again and looked at her with pure horror, terrified that he'd dared to move. When she made no move to plug him, he let out a shaky sigh. "Duke's been popping off about Distro ever since you started undercutting us on imports. No one understands how you bring them in so cheap."

Lucy was starting to get a bad feeling that "Duke" was more than a nickname. "And when exactly did this start?"

"This summer was when we noticed. July 4th, when you brought in the ice. Who has ice on July 4?"

"One more question," she said. "Any last words?"

The sweat sprouted from Brian's face anew.

"Just messing with you," Lucy laughed. "Seriously though, is there another way out of here?"

Arm quivering, he pointed past the planters at the end of the courtyard, which were overgrown with trees and grass. "Follow the hallway to the other side of the building. I don't know if it's locked."

"Thank you." She lowered her pistol. "Your friends are dead. There's nothing to do for them. If you're an honorable man, you'll give me a couple minutes' head start."

Defiance cracked the fear in his face. "And if I'm not?"

"Then think long and hard whether you want me for an enemy."

She grinned and backpedaled toward the other side of the courtyard, keeping an eye on him the whole way. He pivoted to watch. The metal door opened on a dark hallway. As the door closed, it stole the courtyard's sunshine with it, leaving her in a world of outlines and silhouettes.

Lucy jogged for the far end. She pocketed the looted pistol and touched her arm where the unnamed man had shot her. It was the slightest bit damp. A graze. She'd gotten lucky. Maybe the man with the scythe had been too busy licking his chops at Duke's blood to cast his white gaze on her.

Light glowed from the other end of the hall, which opened to another restaurant, dusty and cobwebbed. A skeleton was scattered across the floor. Despite the disuse, the front door worked fine.

If she'd circled back the way she'd come in, she might have been able to retrieve her bike without being noticed, but she didn't feel like rolling the dice on that. The Feds would just have to bill her for it. She ran west, then swung south at the next intersection. Her shoes pounded the asphalt. After a couple blocks, she eased up and pulled the spent red plastic cartridges from her umbrella, dropping them on the road with the tongue-clucking sound so particular to empty shotgun shells.

After a mile of flat-out running, it was pretty clear they weren't going to find her. She had zigged close to the shore and caught glimpses of river at each intersection. She saw a few bike chains and horseshoe locks discarded next to planters, but the bikes had been claimed long ago. The Feds must have wanted a monopoly.

That meant she had to cross the five-odd miles to the piers on foot. She was well-callused but earned some new blisters on her toes by the time she jogged in sight of the piers. She headed to the restaurant and climbed the stairs to the rotunda. Nerve looked up from the paperwork on his desk.

"Did you speak to the Kono?"

"You know, I think it went pretty well." Lucy threw herself in a padded leather chair and pulled off her shoes. "One of their people even offered me a job. As a prostitute, mind, which I wasn't too keen on. He seemed insulted when I turned him down. Long story short, I killed him and one of his friends, but here I am."

"You're joking."

"Want to smell my umbrella?"

"Are you fucking crazy?" Nerve's voice was unsettlingly level. "The Kono are violent. I don't need to launch a study to know that. What I do need to learn is whether this raid is the first spark of a brushfire. And you think the best way to embed yourself in their ranks is to gun them down on their home turf?"

"They made me. Recognized me from the raid. A person of lesser integrity might try to hide that from you, but I figure a leader is only as good as his intelligence."

He moved his hands to a drawer of the desk. "You're pretty calm for someone reporting a disaster."

"I may have made a spectacle, but I doubt I made anything worse." She peeled off her socks, smelled her foot, and made a face. "I grilled one of their men. The raid was a dry run. They can't compete with your prices, so they're looking to muscle you out instead."

Until then, Nerve's face had been a taut mask. Now, it came to life. He walked around his desk for a better look at her. His hands were empty. "He said that? How'd you get him to talk?"

"I guess I got a face men want to confess to. How do you import so cheap?"

"Efficiency. We measure and analyze every dimension of our business. Streamline every link of your chain of trade by 2%, and you wind up 20% ahead of the competition. Kono tries to cut costs by using slave labor, but slaves are inefficient. You have to devote a whole new infrastructure to capturing, buying, and guarding them. Hiring doctors to keep your investment healthy. Not to mention the motivation problem."

Lucy scuffed her feet around on the carpet to wipe off the sweat. "And the whole 'slave' part."

"That's the Konos' philosophical problem." Nerve pulled a chair across from her and seated himself, crossing his legs at the knee. "Say they try to conquer us. The risk is off the charts. They could wind up wiped out themselves. The only guarantee is that both sides' operating costs will rise—you have to hire troops, equip and feed them, deal with attrition. If they invested that money into their business instead, they're building a much safer long-term projection. To put it another way, would you rather invest in the market? Or in the lottery?"

"Man, it is a bad move to assume you're the only dude in town with both halves of his brain. What if their boss is just as smart as your boss? He's put his eyeball to the figures and seen he can't keep up if he plays by your rules. So he makes his own. Instead of coming after your bottom line, he comes for your throat."

"I don't think Hector Udall is that smart. I know Ash isn't. But you make a point."

"They're desperate. They just can't keep up with you." Lucy laughed. "They said you got ice in July. How'd you do that?"

"Ice isn't as fragile as you think. It insulates itself." Nerve pointed to the wall where a map of the United States and Caribbean was studded with pushpins. "Our trade network runs all the way to Venezuela and beyond to the tropics. We have access to goods no one else has. And ours never go out of season."

"Yeah, but unless you stashed UPS away in a bunker during the Panhandler, your shipping costs got to be crazy."

"Do they? What does it cost to ship goods?"

"I dunno, what about fuel?"

He shook his head. "Wind is free."

"Labor costs," Lucy said.

"We don't employ most of these people. They profit from the trade itself. Additionally, what is the real cost of employing a person to steer a ship from there to here?"

"Food and water."

"That's right. And before you object that no one would work for food and water, let me inform you that most former Americans now in their twenties and thirties spent the pre-collapse as students, receptionists, and customer service reps. Their entire lives played out in small rooms while older people told them what to do."

"After that, a life on the open sea sounds pretty sweet," Lucy followed. "And you're all too happy to exploit their thirst for adventure."

Nerve raised one brow. "They get a cut of the goods, which we're happy to exchange for liquor or bullets or anything else they think they need. The larger point is that it costs much, much less to sustain one life today than it did six years ago. Distro was the first to figure that out and build a network around it. Our lead is too big for the others to close."

"I'm sure Rome thought the same thing about the barbarians."

"Yet parts of it lasted a thousand years." Nerve leaned back and tugged a loose thread on the seam of his pocket. "Back to business. Considering your results, I don't know whether I should be rewarding you, but I checked in with my people. Your friend's with us."

Lucy swung up her head. "Tilly? Where is she?"

"Safe. You can see her in three days."

"You got a deal."

"Unfortunately, you've destroyed most of your value to me. I'm transferring you to security. If the Kono are on the warpath, we need to ramp up our scouting. Report to Major Deunsling two piers down."

It sounded exciting. It wasn't. Major Deunsling was a major pain in the ass, a humorless bitch who could stand to cut down on the fried fish. Lucy's new duties, such as they were, consisted of sitting on a rooftop overlooking Twelfth Avenue. In addition to binoculars, she was decked out with an analog bullhorn and a red lantern. If she spotted anything resembling an approaching war party, she was to light the latter and scream into the former.

Boring as hell, but she did her duty. Couldn't risk screwing the pooch when she was three days out from Tilly. She did some pushups to prevent herself from going crazy, and spent much time contemplating the tower that dominated Midtown, but mostly she watched the streets and waited for the Kono.

It was a good thing she'd made the trip. She'd figured Tilly would be in over her head, and she was right. Distro was too slick for the Kono to handle with anything but gunplay. The island was about to be drenched in blood. If the underpowered Feds jumped in to try to calm things down, it could wind up a three-way war.

Not exactly where Lucy had expected to end up. But she owed it to Tilly—and to Tilly's dad. Freshman year, Lucy's mom got worse than ever. She'd go missing for two, three days at a time. Seemed like she had a new boyfriend every month. Once when she left to get the groceries—a rare event, after she'd sold her car—Lucy went into her room and found the pipe and the baggie of crushed-up white crystals. Lucy thought about busting the pipe and flushing the meth, but left them intact. They would only help kill her mother faster.

You had the screaming matches. A few times, she and her mom scratched and punched each other and Lucy stayed home from school until the bruises faded. She made a few friends from similar circumstances; they liked drugs and older boys, who bought them beer and cigarettes and condoms. Even the 22-year-olds didn't quite know what to make of Lucy, keeping one eye on her, wary in the same way a man walking his dog after dark watches a skunk. But she knew it was only a matter of time.

Because she was on a Path. Same one her older sister, already pregnant again, had taken. Same one her mom had taken. It didn't necessarily lead straight to the Reaper, but it wound through his world. A world of lowness and predation not all that different from the one they'd all come to live in after the plague.

Before the end times, still in freshman year, she began to run away. First time, she slept in a park; on her third night, a man pulled a knife and who knew where it would have gone if Lucy hadn't screamed and a good man hadn't come sprinting in to run the other man off. Second time, she went to stay with one of the older boys, but he only wanted her to pay rent in one way, and he tried to get it through vodka and blunts. One night, drunk on shots, he'd taken it out and tried to make her touch it and when she wouldn't he yelled at her and stomped to his room to take care of it himself. After, he passed out in bed with his shirt on and pants off. Lucy had a wicked buzz, but she'd scooped up her clothes and laced up her shoes and ran. Left the front door open, too. With any luck, someone would stab him.

When she got home, her mom was sitting in the dark on the couch, pipe clutched in her hand, wreathed in the smell of burnt cleaning spray. "Who says I want you back?"

"Who says I want to be here?" Lucy said.

"How much longer before you go out and don't come home? He sniffs you out and he finds you. The police find you in a ditch with eyes so round they'll never close."

"You're crazy."

"I'm crazy?" The woman stood, unleashing an odor of sweat and a semi-sweet chemical stink like the disinfectant wipes she used to use on the counters. "I know why you're out there. You want to wind up like your sister? You that mad for children? Or do you just love the taste of sperm?"

The red curtain fell over the window of Lucy's eyes and her hands shook like branches in a winter wind but she went to her room and locked the door. When her mom pounded on it, Lucy put in her headphones and turned it up until she could hear nothing but the music. In the morning, her mom was gone. Lucy stole the change from her drawer and jogged out the front door.

She didn't want to go to school where her mom might find her so she hung around the library instead, surfing around the internet, then walked across town to the Burger King and ate a double cheeseburger and then sat there until an employee not much older than herself asked her if something was wrong.

She didn't head back to the park until after dark. No one saw her. She got through three nights that way. On the fourth, as she bundled up beneath a metal slide, shoes scuffed through the chips of red wood bedding the grounds. The slide blocked the man from the thighs up. His shoes were hard-worn brown boots with black laces so new the aglets hadn't yet begun to fray.

Silent as an owl on the wing, Lucy drew the knife she'd stolen from one of the older boys. The blade was five inches long and the pommel was the head of a dragon.

"Hey," the man called softly. "You in there, Lucy?"

She blinked. "Who is it?"

"Vic Loman. Tilly's dad."

"I know you. What do you want?"

He swung his head below the slide to get a look at her. His gaze moved over her blanket, her pack, her knife. "You all right there?"

"Why, you looking to move into the neighborhood? Rent's cheap, but the schools ain't shit."

Mr. Loman continued to hang there, head sideways. "Tilly told me where you were. Come on out."

"I ain't going home."

"Who said anything about going home? You can come stay with us. What you can't do is live under a slide like a lost Yorkie."

She combed her greasy hair back with her nails. "If my mom finds out, she'll cut your nuts off."

"Let me worry about my nuts," he said. "What do you say?"

She said yes. And her life changed. Not to say it got perfect. She was still too different from the other kids, and she'd missed so much school she had to talk to both principals and the cop they kept around for security, and getting that sorted out was such a to-do she didn't see why she should bother at all. Also, after the first three days, Mrs. Loman made Vic spruce up the garage so Lucy could sleep there instead. Not that Lucy minded the space itself; it was clean of spiders and she had her own TV. But the fact Mrs. Loman didn't want Lucy in the house made Lucy want to piss in her closet.

But it got better. Stable. It set her on a new path, one that ran away from the man with the scythe. Lucy never forgot who to thank for that. And when the plague came, and Vic got sick, and he asked Lucy to look after Tilly, Lucy had sworn on her life that she would.

Tilly hadn't always made it easy on her, but so far, she had honored her promise.

Two crisp fall days dribbled past. After her shift, she climbed down from the roof and walked to the pier to check in with Nerve, but Kerry brushed her off. Lucy was miffed, but decided to give them one more day before raising any hell.

Next morning, she reported to the security building as usual. Kerry stood on the pier, arms folded. "What do you think you're doing?"

"Work. You heard of it?"

He scratched the back of his shaved head. "Thought you wanted to see your friend."

Lucy grinned. "Quit teasing and show me the way."

He grabbed his bike and headed toward the tower at the island's heart. The last few days had been cold and dreary, but the morning light was as sharp as chipped glass and as amber as honey dripping from a spoon. Often the Empire State Building was hidden behind the cliff-like apartments and offices, but at intersections its spire pierced the sky.

It felt even taller up close. So big that going near it felt wrong, like it could wake at any moment and squash you as flat as the tarry gum cemented to the sidewalks. Lucy tipped her head to take in its vertical lines and nearly toppled backwards.

She quit gawping and focused. If Distro restricted its residents' movements, she and Tilly might have to leave in a hurry. The inside was a palace of marble floors and plentiful sunlight. Armed men loitered around the lobby, rifles hanging from their shoulders and leaning on their chairs. The troops eyed Kerry and nodded him through. His footfalls echoed along the patterns zigzagged on the stone floors.

"She know I'm coming?" Lucy said. She had her day-pack and umbrella and the pistol she'd taken from Duke's dead friend.

"Don't think so," Kerry said. "She was across the river until an hour ago. Dragging firewood up from Jersey. She drives one of our wagons."

He opened the door to the stairwell. Dim electric lights gave it the look of a movie theater before the lights went all the way down.

"How are you gonna have power in a building like this and not run the elevators?" Lucy said.

"If you want, we can go home."

"What floor?"

"Eighth."

Lucy brushed past him and clopped up the stairs. All she'd need to do was convince Kerry to let her have a private moment with Tilly. Imply a lesbian angle, if that's what it took. Because if she could explain the score, by all appearances, she and Tilly would be able to walk right out the glass revolving doors.

Worse came to worst, she'd pop Kerry in the head, grab Tilly by the hand, and run downstairs before anyone was the wiser.

They reached the eighth story. The floor was cool granite that seemed to suck out all the light from the few lit bulbs. Kerry got out a piece of paper, glanced at it, walked down to 822, and rapped the door with the back of his knuckles.

Muffled steps from inside. Lucy couldn't help her grin. The door opened and there, at last, was Tilly.

"Lucy?" A funny look flooded Tilly's face. Some of it was surprise, which Lucy had expected. But most of it was something different. Something that made Lucy expect to look over her shoulder and see that Kerry had shed his skin and emerged as a six-foot spider.

Because nothing else would explain the commingled horror and disgust awash on her friend's face.

Tilly slammed the door and snapped the bolt shut.

II:

BLIZZARD

14

In the pines and the snow, Ellie froze mid-step. It wasn't the body or its gnawed-up state that stilled her. Everyone born before the Panhandler had seen enough bodies to grow tolerant of them, if not exactly inured.

It was the fact there was a body at all. She should know better, but she couldn't accept the fact that as recently as four days ago, she'd seen Quinn walking around, hugging Dee, pledging to help his dad recover their grain from the Franklins. This piece of meat on the forest floor—half buried in leaves, features lost in the attack or to hungry carrion-eaters—she couldn't reconcile it with the Quinn Tolbert who would soon become a permanent part of her own family.

So while Dee's shrieks faded to hitching, jittery sobs, Ellie stared.

Sheriff Hobson knelt down beside the corpse, hitching up the leg of his pants. He wore thin leather gloves against the cold, but he pulled these off, finger by finger, then reached into his pack for a pair of thin latex. He touched the remains of the young man's face, turning it side to side. As Ellie's mind regrouped, he got out an honest-to-god magnifying glass and inspected an exposed cheekbone.

"Light, please?" he beckoned.

Ellie walked close and raised her lantern. "Do you see something?"

"Bit of a scrape on the bone."

"Given the condition of the body..."

"I'm aware the skin wasn't borne away on the wings of angels," the sheriff said, unusually testy. He rocked out of the way, crablike, and held out his magnifying glass. "It's the manifestation of the scrape that has me nonplussed."

Ellie glanced at Dee, who had balled herself up in the leaves and snow, then took the glass and moved close to the body. The blood was frozen, and with the eyes and nose and mouth missing, she was better able to pretend this was an object and not a dead human.

Hobson pointed to a thin line across the pink-stained bone. "You see?"

She looked closer. It was an inch long and needle-thin. "And?"

"Unless we're dealing with a species of landfaring pike, I don't know many animals with teeth that fine."

"A knife? So he was killed by people, not animals or weather."

The sheriff steepled his hands in front of his chin. "At the risk of indelicacy, can we take a step back? What I see is a body that fits the general description and our timeline. But we still haven't confirmed it's ours."

Ellie nodded, absorbed this, then nodded harder. "You're right. I shouldn't be jumping ahead."

Hobson closed his eyes and shook his head lightly. "A natural process. When stress increases, rational faculties diminish. I expect that, when our ancestors were ambushed during a cave-calculus lesson, they discovered the solution could wait until they'd finished fleeing from the tiger."

Still, she was embarrassed. So obvious in hindsight. But this wasn't the time to indulge in self-laceration. "Dee, what was Quinn wearing the night he disappeared? Dee?"

"I don't know," the girl whispered.

Hobson gestured to the body. "Well, surely he wasn't wearing a jumpsuit, was he?"

"Almost looks like a prison uniform," Ellie said. Snow fell on the body and didn't melt. "Back at their office, did you smell the oil?"

"The lights were electric."

"Automotive oil. When they came in from the side door, the smell came with them. I think they were working on machines."

"Could be a mechanic's garb." Hobson raised his latex-gloved finger to his mouth, perhaps to tap it against his teeth, then arrested it a few inches away and stared at it guiltily. He lowered it and leaned close to Ellie. "Were the two of them...intimate?"

Ellie glanced up sharply. "What the fuck does that matter? She loves him."

"I was wondering," he explained, with admirable patience, "if she might recognize any distinguishing physical characteristics."

"Dee," she said. "I know this is awful. You hurt worse than the world. But Sheriff Hobson wonders— "

"I heard him." Dee lay on her side, eyes wide open. She rolled to her knees. Leaves stuck to her hair; her face was damp with tears and melted snow. "Quinn has three moles in a line below his left hip. I used to call it the Belt of Orion."

"Cursed jumpsuits," the sheriff muttered. Ellie reached for its snaps. The sheriff waved her off. "I've got it."

"I'm not a shrinking violet, sheriff. I froze for a moment. I'm fine now."

She opened the man's shirt. The body was stiff with rigor or cold or both and it took the two of them to roll it on its side. The sheriff braced it while Ellie tugged down the jumpsuit top and exposed the man's hip.

"Light," she said. The sheriff stretched for the lantern and held it up. She touched the brown skin. It was eerily cold. "Dee, can you come look?"

Wordless, Dee walked on her knees through the leaves and bent over the body. "I don't see them." She glanced at its belly and moved his underclothes aside. "Doesn't shave right." Her eyes went brighter than the lantern. "Holy shit!"

Ellie grinned and embraced her. "Oh sweetie."

"I'll assume the verdict is good?" The sheriff eased the body to rest on its back. "That raises new questions, doesn't it?"

Ellie nodded. "Was the woman at the office just passing along a rumor? Or actively trying to throw us off?"

"Wounds are awfully rough." He pointed to the gashes in the neck, which had become more and more obvious as they'd wrestled with the body.

Ellie sat back and lifted her lantern. "No obvious sign of struggle."

"Rules out animals?"

"Right. But a person could have killed him elsewhere and

dumped him here."

Hobson's eyes glittered in the lanterns. "Or taken the lad by surprise."

Dee laughed hoarsely. "Get married already."

They both gave her a look. Ellie tried to move the body's left arm, but it wouldn't budge. She set its brown fingers against the light contrast of her gloved palm. The nails were grimed black. She leaned in and sniffed.

"What are you doing?" Dee said.

"Smells like grease." Ellie let the hand go. "Add the jumpsuit, and I'd say he's one of their own."

"Explains rather neatly how the old woman knew about him," Hobson said. "And if she knew it wasn't Quinn, then it stands to reason she intended to mislead us—perhaps to obscure his trail."

"Let's take it as fact that she knows about the kidnappings. She doesn't necessarily know about Quinn." Ellie sniffed. Her nose was running and her knees were soaked through. "Let's find shelter. If the snow gets much deeper, the bikes won't be any good."

Ellie walked away from the body without a second thought for burying it. The ground was too hard. Anyway, it was extraneous to the mission.

A half inch of snow lay on the road. On flat stretches, the bikes could handle it without skidding, but at the tops of hills, they had to coast to a stop and walk their bicycles down to the bottom. Ellie's heavy trailer fought her the whole way; at the steeper points, Hobson helped her wrangle it while Dee walked the other two bikes along.

The first house they stopped at had broken windows and a dusting of snow across the front room. The second house came to them like a present: intact windows, unlocked door, a package of Presto logs shrink-wrapped beside the fireplace. They cleared the home for animals and people, then Ellie opened the flue and broke up the crumbling sawdust logs and banked them into a fire. A needle-thin draft pierced one of the windows, but the house soon grew warm enough that they stopped being able to see their own breath.

"What now?" Dee said, wrapped in a down sleeping bag in the middle of the room, smooth face lit by the flapping fire. "Where is he?"

"We're on track," Ellie said. "We'll find him."

But it was a thing she said, not a thing she believed. The world had grown too big and too dark to be certain of anything. Snow hit the window, glinted in the firelight, and melted away into nothing.

She woke in the middle of the night and quietly revived the fire from its embers. She woke again, uncertain of the time except that it was hours later, but she knew her body well enough to know she wouldn't be able to get back to sleep. She went outside to pee. The snow had stopped. Four inches lay on the ground, muffling everything to perfect silence.

She unwrapped the last of the artificial logs. The crinkling of the package woke the others. Dawn touched the snow, too hesitant to melt it. The bread had grown as tough as the jerky. Finished eating, Ellie unhitched the trailer from her bike and rode circles through the unpaved snow. Turning was difficult, and she skidded every time she braked, but she thought they'd be okay.

The five-mile ride was an hour-long slog. Snow squeaked beneath their tires and draped the roofs. It had come early in the year, but the clouds were high and gray, suggesting more. Ellie had always liked snow—it slowed things down, seemed to clarify them; within that homogenous white world, each sound and movement stood out like blood on a porcelain floor—but in this age, it meant something more. The end of growth. Of easy days. You lived on what you'd gathered during the green months, and if you had to leave your home for unknown lands, the margins of survival were an act of threadlike fineness.

At the hexagonal office, an engine grumbled from the garage. Hobson got out his pocket watch and clicked it open. "I'm going to take a constitutional. I shall return in twenty minutes."

Ellie pushed open the door and rang the desk bell. After her third try, the man with the glasses and dirty fingernails came in from the side door.

"Nan's not in," he said. "Try back this afternoon."

"We found the body," Ellie said. "What was left of it."

"Was it him?" the man said. Ellie nodded. He lowered his eyes. "I'm sorry."

"People pushed death to the horizon for a couple of centuries.

Now it's close again." She gazed at the side door. "My employer will want the body."

He frowned. "Have at it."

"We can't bear it on these bikes. Not through six inches of snow. I heard you might have some machines here?"

Until now, the man had maintained a look of awkward consolation. Now, professional interest emerged in his eyes. "Could be. What are you looking for?"

"We're from the mountains. Got any snowmobiles?"

"Sure," he said. "We've got everything."

He held the door open to a frigid underground garage. Parking spots were occupied by cars, trucks, tractors, combines, four-wheelers, ATVs. Many were partly or wholly dismantled, but others sat complete and ready, dust-free.

"Nice collection," Ellie said.

He glanced over his shoulder, smiling proudly. "This is our main business. We sell across the whole state—Buffalo, Rochester, the city."

"People buy these?" Dee said. "You can get cars anywhere."

"Sure. But ours run." His shoes echoed past the concrete pillars. He led them to the far corner and pulled a blue tarp from a bright red snowmobile. "Not much demand for these, but if you ask me, there ought to be. When the snow gets deep, the roads might as well not be there at all."

"We didn't bring much in trade," Ellie said.

"We have a credit program."

"What kind of terms?"

"Flexible for your needs."

"And in case of nonpayment?"

The man peered through his glasses. "Do you expect that to be a problem?"

"My employer would whip me skinless if I entered a contract without knowing the terms."

He blew into his hands and rubbed them vigorously. "That's Nan's business. I'm just the fixer-man."

"Looks well taken care of." Ellie walked around the snowmobile, examining it. "Do you deal in more organic forms of labor?"

The man tugged a single hair from his head, puzzled, then jerked his chin to the side. "That's not our trade. We didn't take your boy."

"Any idea who did?"

"This highway leads straight to the city. People come through here all the time."

"My employer's looking for some extra hands." She touched the handlebars of the machine, waiting, but the man offered nothing more. "We'll be back to see Nan about these."

He accompanied them through the garage to the lobby, then watched them walk outside. Ellie zipped up her coat. "Notice anything?"

Dee shrugged her shoulders high. "Should I have?"

"This isn't a test."

"I didn't trust him. He didn't feel right."

"How so?"

"Like he molests his cars' tailpipes." Dee walked toward the sidewalk where they'd left their bikes. "Plus, when you asked about Quinn, he got all weird."

"They slipped up when they told us about the body. Should have denied everything and let us twist in the wind. They got too clever."

"So what do we do now?"

"We take a run at Nan. If that fails, we tail them. Stake out the town. Stay all winter if we have to."

"In the meantime, what happens to Quinn?"

Ellie rubbed her nose. Footsteps crunched in the snow, saving her from an answer. Hobson walked up, cane in hand, a self-satisfied smile on his face.

"Learn anything, ladies?"

Ellie shook her head. "You?"

"Indeed." He tapped his cane against the soles of his feet, knocking off the snow. "Someone here drives a truck."

"Wonderful. We should find them and congratulate them."

"Let me drop one more detail: the owner of the truck is in the habit of carrying as many as six other men in it with him."

She met his eyes. "What did you find?"

"Follow me." He swept his cane north. Past the windowless garage attached to the office, he hooked left to a field between the garage and the highway. Tire tracks cut through the snow, half-blurred by fresh powder. Twenty yards from a blank door in the garage face, Hobson stopped and nodded at the ground. "What do you see?"

The snow was heavily churned. Plenty of footprints, but parts of it seemed to have been dredged away, too, swept smooth. Ten feet away, parallel tracks led to four yellow stains in the snow.

Hobson pointed with his cane. "Notice the way it trails off?"

"Male," Ellie said. "Could be soldiers. Mechanics."

"Odd of them to walk here and pee shoulder to shoulder. For that matter, why did they all have to go at once? Synchronized bladders? Or are we looking at the first documented case of tetraphallia?"

"They don't go to the bathroom on their own schedule." Ellie gazed at the tire tracks leading back to the road. "Captives. Tied together. Allowed to pee before being forced onto the truck."

Hobson flicked moisture from the brim of his bowler. "Perhaps our arrival precipitated the move to more obscure grounds."

"We need to follow these before it snows again." She crunched back toward the road and the bikes without glancing at the office or garage. "Let's get any eyes off us."

They rode east for a couple blocks, putting a row of strip mall dentist offices and veterinary clinics between them and the hexagonal building, then turned north and paralleled the other road. The snow ground beneath their tires. Ellie's calves quickly grew fatigued. After a quarter mile, she cut west and intercepted the road. The truck's tracks continued north past more shopping sprawl and into an older neighborhood of brick storefronts with local names. Near the corner, the dormer windows of a three-story manor peeped over the vacant lanes. The tracks fed into a cobbled alley between it and its neighbor, another stately home that had been converted into a Mediterranean restaurant.

Ellie paused at the alley's edge. From blocks away, a truck engine grumbled over the muffle of the snow. "We're close."

They parked their bikes just inside the alley. Ellie walked in the truck's tracks to minimize her own, snow creaking beneath her shoes. She thought the alley fed straight through, but it hit an unruly hedge and made a right turn behind the restaurant. The dunder of the engine rose sharply. Ellie glanced back at the mouth of the alley, then hurried around the corner. She ran smack into Nan.

Ellie fell back. The old woman gaped. Behind them, a truck

lumbered into the alley and slid to a stop. With its engine idling, two men popped their doors and moved to the front of the truck, pistols on their hips, and waited.

15

Lucy grabbed the door handle and rattled it hard. "Tilly! Open this door!"

"What are you doing here?" Tilly said.

"What do you think? I came here to find you."

Inside, Tilly laughed, a sick, wretched lurching. "Why do you think I left, you fucking idiot?"

"To see the big city?"

"That was just the cream in the coffee. I left to get away from you."

Lucy's jaw went tight. She hammered her fist against the door. "You don't know what you're saying. Open this door and look me in the eye."

"Fuck off, Lucy. Turn around, tuck your tail, and go on home."

Lucy crouched and pulled the .22 from her ankle holster. Kerry grabbed her wrist. "What do you think you're doing?"

"Get your hands off me so I can shoot this door down, you brute." She yanked her arm, but he held firm.

"Tilly?" he said. "It's Kerry Malone. Can I come inside? No funny stuff."

Tilly laughed. "I already said all I got to say!"

"She came a long way to see you. I don't think she's going to go away without an explanation."

The hallway went quiet except the buzz of the lights. "Make her get away from the door."

Kerry pointed down the hall. "Why don't you stand over there a minute, Lucy?"

Lucy tried to pull away again, but the guy's grip was like an iron bear. "She's my friend. Why don't I go in and talk to her?"

"How about you let me find that out?"

"This is goddamn childish." She swore and relaxed her arms. Kerry raised his eyebrows, then let her go. She put away the gun and walked down the hall and sat down on the cool stone floor.

The door opened. Kerry held up his hands and went inside. Tilly shut and locked the door, leaving Lucy with herself.

She had figured Tilly might do some whining and crying. The typical Tilly pleading. But it had never crossed Lucy's mind that Tilly wouldn't walk out the door with her. This was such an unexpected turn that Lucy spent the next five minutes sitting on the floor in a kind of awed silence.

Kerry exited the room, smiled back inside, and gently closed the door. He flicked his fingers in a "come here" gesture and walked to the stairwell. Lucy followed him down to the lobby like a trained dog. They exited under the watchful eyes of the guards. After the cavernous dimness of the foyer, the brittle yellow daylight felt harsh and revealing.

Kerry stood on the sidewalk and watched the empty street as if waiting on a date. "Got a smoke?"

She dug into her bag and passed him one. "Winters are hard here, huh? Nothing but wind."

He lit it and inhaled and scowled at it, as if expecting something different, something better. "Did you come all this way just to see her?"

"It was my idea to come up here," she lied. "Then Tilly did first. She does that, acts before she's had the chance to think it through. I just wanted to make sure she was all right."

"She won't talk to you."

"Figured that much."

"You okay?"

"Why wouldn't I be?"

He shrugged and exhaled into the cold morning. "Probably for the best."

"How's that?"

"Nerve's had his eye on her ever since you brought her up. His girlfriends don't tend to last."

Her nerves thrummed. "He murders them?"

"No, he doesn't murder them, what does he look like, the Dating Game Killer?" Kerry gave her a disgusted look, like she'd been proposing to start a serial killing partnership themselves, then took a drag and made a rolling motion with his hand. "He's a big believer in utility. A thing has it or it doesn't. When it doesn't, you throw it out and move on."

"So he'd throw her out of Distro."

"Just hope he waits for spring. Winters are rough here." He tugged the collar of his leather jacket. "Coming up, I had this friend we thought we'd play baseball together—this was years ago, before your time. Some day we'd turn double plays for the Mets. The Orioles, if we had to. Every day, we'd head to the park, throw a ball around, hit batting practice. Every day for three years.

"Then one day he isn't there, it's just me and my glove. Next day at school I ask him what happened and he gives me the shrug. Well, it doesn't take a genius. I ask around and sure enough, he's got into drugs. Every day for two months I'm bugging him about baseball, hey, I think we make the team this year, and it's always the same: Yeah, sure, I'll see you on the field. Then I go out for tryouts and he isn't there."

"What happened?" Lucy said.

"I made the team." Kerry stared down the street, the buildings squeezing the space between them into a narrow path, the world beyond them lost. "I didn't see much of Mike after that. Ran into him at a party two years later. He didn't recognize me. Wouldn't have recognized his own mother. But what can you do? What, I drag him by his ankles to the baseball diamond? Tape the bat to his hands? When a person walks away from you, you can't force them to come back. They have to want to come home for themselves."

Lucy tipped back her head at the Empire State Building, which was so close she couldn't see its top. "Probably died in the plague anyway."

Kerry got a funny look on his face. "Probably."

Together, they rode back to the pier. Lucy pulled more scout duty. She biked uptown and climbed her building and sat on the roof. Wind riffled the river. She picked pebbles off the tar-papered surface and chucked them to the street. It was too far away to hear them land.

He was right, of course. Lucy had done plenty of running away and the only times she'd come back was when the place she'd run to had wound up even worse than the one she'd left. Could be her mom knew that's how it would go and that's why she'd never come looking for Lucy. Then again, more likely the woman had been too strung out to notice.

Tilly had told her to go to hell and Lucy's first instinct was to tell her to go to hell right back. To stomp out of the city and leave Tilly to be caught in the grinders of war or tossed in the street by Nerve after he'd had his fun. If she came out of it alive, maybe that would teach the girl a thing or two.

Except Lucy had made a promise to Mr. Loman. Granted, he was dead now and would never be the wiser if she broke it. Lucy didn't believe in ghosts. Or, for that matter, God or the Devil or even Death, at least not the robed skeleton her mother had been ranting about since Lucy was born. People liked to personify these things to pretend they could be beaten. If the Devil is some red dude with a pointy tail, well, one good right cross ought to knock him on his ass. But if the Devil isn't a person, but a force—hurricanes and earthquakes; greed and starvation; that voice inside you that insists there is nothing more important than getting those crystals into your lungs—well, you're just fucked, now aren't you?

And she did believe in evil. The virus had made sure of that. No God and no Devil meant there were no commandments from on high, but everyone was born with a set of commandments within. If you broke your inner rules, your heart's own code, that opened holes in you that evil surged to fill. It'd tear you up like cancer. Shred your brain worse than syph. Call it guilt if you like, but the way she saw it, guilt was something imposed on you by other people. The corrosion she was talking about came from within. Impossible to heal.

She didn't have a choice, then. She would bring Tilly home. She was just going to have to get creative.

She went about her job, spending as much time gazing at the Empire State Building as she did the streets. Two days later, she was daydreaming about rappelling in through Tilly's window when the clatter of hooves rang down the street.

She lit her red lantern, swung it south, and ululated into her bullhorn. Ten blocks south, at the observation deck of a blue glass office, a matching red lantern flared to life.

Lucy ran to the north edge of the roof. Some twenty horses pranced down Twelfth Avenue, each bearing an armed man. She ran to the stairwell and lit her personal lantern and raced down the steps. By the time she hit the ground, the troop was already two blocks down the street, horses' tails swishing back and forth.

But they weren't in any special hurry. That was curious. Lucy detoured a block east, then sprinted dead south toward the piers. There, men and women heaved barrels, sandbags, and sawhorses into a barricade. Rifles took aim on her chest.

She threw up her hands. "Do I look like Sherman's March? It's Lucy, you idiots."

The guns lowered. She ran down the pier. Around the back of the clothing store, Nerve spat orders to armed stevedores, pointing them into position along the docks. At his right hand, Kerry saw her and nodded.

Nerve glanced at her and his face creased with irritation. "Grab a rifle and get on the lines."

She took one from the woman with glasses who ran the records department and also apparently served as emergency quartermaster. Most of the good guns had been taken; Lucy's didn't even have a scope. She found an empty spot near the middle of the lines and rested her rifle over a sawhorse.

"This ain't my job," the man next to her muttered.

"Think you'll get overtime?" Lucy said.

He wrinkled his nose as if she'd joked about his dead mother and turned his attention to the entry to the piers. Up the block, hooves tocked on the asphalt. The Kono approached ten abreast, a second line on the heels of the first. Each rider bore a personal armory: several had assault rifles slung over their chests; some carried scoped rifles crooked in their arms; others wore a pistol on each hip.

"Hold your fire," Nerve said from behind the lines.

The riders stopped a hundred feet from the barricade. A lone figure ambled forward, separating from the host. Bearing and size looked female, but when they spoke, Lucy was no longer sure.

"You in there, Nerve?" the warlord called. "Or did you hire

someone to take the bullet for you?"

Nerve stood and walked toward the lines, shrugging off the aid of Kerry and two other security members who tried to fall in beside him. Lucy hadn't heard him raise his voice before and his words thrust across the damp, cold air.

"You're not here to shoot, Ash," he said. "If you are, your tactics are decidedly Civil War."

Ash—who Lucy had tentatively decided was male—flipped up his sunglasses and laughed. "If I were here to fight, you'd already have three of my bullets in your ass. I'm here to cut you a deal."

"Bring it to the main office. I don't run Distro."

"I'm not wasting my breath on that old son of a bitch. You're the arm of this place same way I am for mine. Arms are the ones that move things."

Exasperation stole into Nerve's voice. "Then quit talking and talk."

Ash laughed and glanced back at his troops, inviting them to share the fine wordplay. "I know you don't want a fight, Nerve. Let me guess, it's 'inefficient.' Good news: Kono's willing to collude. You get everything south of 49th, we get everything north."

"Including Central Park."

"Plenty of other parks down here. The best water access, too. The Brooklyn and Williamsburg Bridge. Holland Tunnel. If you wanted, you could even take City Hall. Shit, I'm starting to think I screwed myself on this one."

"The most important resource on this island isn't the parkland or the infrastructure." Nerve walked past the barricade, hands clasped behind him, lecturing. "It's the population. Most of whom have aggregated around the water and farmland of Central Park. If Distro gives up that market, we may as well relocate to Jersey."

"Hey, if that's your choice, I'm happy to send some of my boys to help you move. Promise they won't break nothin'."

"Splitting up the city makes sense. Neither of us can take full advantage of its potential by ourselves. But we can't forfeit Central Park."

Ash leaned over his horse's neck and glared at Nerve in disgust. "Man, I can take it from you whenever I want. Hey, I'm the mayor of Central Park! What are you going to do? You going to fight me for it?"

Nerve rolled his eyes at the sky. "We'll offer the farmers more goods for lower prices. What's your plan then? Chain them in the park? Plead with them to buy local?"

The man's high voice took on a pronounced edge. "We'll see how eager they are to bargain-shop after we break a few of their kneecaps."

"So then when we do ride in, they join us and rise against you too."

Ash spit on the pier, scolded his horse, and wheeled around. A couple other riders spat, too. The dock workers eased down their rifles but waited behind the barricade until the rattle of the hooves faded to the north.

"Security team, take alert position," Nerve said. "Rest of you, let's get back to work."

The man beside Lucy shouldered his gun and stood. "We get paid extra for this?"

Nerve stared him down. "The next time they ride in, would you prefer to remain unarmed?"

He strode toward his restaurant headquarters. Lucy supposed he'd just ordered her back to the rooftop with the lantern, but she jogged after him.

"Who was that?" she said.

Nerve glanced back. "I'm not paying you to ask me questions."

"A well-informed workforce is an effective workforce, right? You really think that dude is going to sit on his thumb while you squeeze him out of business?"

"I made him doubt. Winter's coming. He won't want to fight. He'll wait until spring. And discover it's too late."

"Does he run the Kono?"

"Like he said, he makes it move. If he digs in his heels, the old man won't be able to push forward."

Nerve entered the restaurant. Kerry barred the way for Lucy. She gave him the eye and walked uptown and climbed back up her tower.

She saw nothing there but birds, clouds, and the bucket-like water towers on top of nearly every old apartment and office. There was no sign of the Kono the next day, either. Maybe they were huddled uptown, arguing their next step, burning time while Distro undercut them one string at a time. Nerve had done a convincing job. Lucy wasn't privy to the ins and outs of Manhattan politics, but messing with Distro sounded like a bad idea.

The day after, she had a rare day off, so instead of crouching on top of an apartment block watching for the Kono, she spent it crouching on top of an office block watching the Empire State Building.

Traffic was at its relative heaviest in the morning. Men and women dribbled out on bikes and on foot. Two heavy-hitters emerged from the parking garage with horse-drawn carriages. A few of the non-VIPs pulled enough weight to warrant bodyguards, or at least boyfriends whose overprotectiveness extended to the carrying of automatic weapons. Including chauffeurs and armed guards, the day's total departures numbered less than fifty people. Manhattan wasn't quite the metropolis it used to be.

An hour before noon, she descended and crossed the street and entered the Empire State Building's revolving doors. Inside the regal stone halls, a thick-set man blocked her way.

"Pass?"

"That's my plan," Lucy said.

"You don't got a pass, or a face I know, you swing right back out that door."

"And what if I make it worth your while to take a long look at the ceiling?"

The man didn't hesitate. "You want to bribe me? Sure. Did you know the Empire State Building now features a prison?"

"I don't see how it's a crime to want to see my friend. She lives upstairs."

"You want me to ring her up?"

Lucy gritted her teeth. "You know, I just remembered she's at work. Maybe I'll try back tonight."

The man smiled wanly. "See you then."

She went back to the rooftop across the street. She liked the feeling of looking down on people. She did just that for several hours more until, in the middle of the afternoon, Nerve rode down the street on a horse, tied it to the iron railing of a sidewalk planter, and removed a bouquet from its saddlebags. He adjusted the collar of his snappy powder blue suit and walked inside the tower.

Lucy hissed between her teeth and descended to the ground floor to watch through the lobby windows. After ten minutes of waiting, she sat crosslegged on the cool tile floor, umbrella across her knees. A fat man walked outside and brushed Nerve's horse. The horse defecated. An hour and a half after he'd gone inside, Nerve walked out the front door, glanced over his shoulder, and spoke to someone in the lobby.

Lucy popped up and stalked across the street. She didn't trust horses, not at all, but she walked up beside Nerve's and patted its neck and stroked its mane.

Nerve finished his conversation and turned toward his mount. He registered Lucy but didn't break stride.

"What were you doing in there?" Lucy said.

"Careful," he said. "My horse bites."

"Business? Or pleasure?"

He shook his head and reached to untie the reins but she moved in front of him. He glanced back toward the doors, then advanced until their faces were just inches apart. "You've fucked up your own business too much to think you can inject yourself into mine."

She didn't pull back. "You stay away from her. Plenty of other girls in this city who aren't my friend."

"You think she's your friend?" He laughed and shuffled around her to unloop the reins. "You live in a different world, don't you? If it hurts to bump into reality, maybe it's time to go back home."

He slung himself into the saddle and clipped down the street, bouncing rhythmically. She watched him go, then glared through the clean glass windows on the ground floor of the Empire State Building. She envisioned stomping inside, shotgunning the guards, clocking Tilly on the head, slinging the girl over her shoulder, and jogging across the bridge to her car.

But she knew that was a fantasy. A way for her brain to soothe the piercing sting of powerlessness. The truth was that she was alone in a strange place surrounded by tribes of violent men. Tilly was lost and didn't want to be found. Lucy could no more wrestle her off Manhattan than she could swing Nerve around by his feet and fling him into the next borough. This whole trip was a farce. A delusion of her vanity.

As soon as she had the thought, she backed away from it, the way you'd back away when you turned a bend in the stream and saw a bear fishing the other side. Once she was at a safe distance, she started down a new path.

You didn't always have to crash through the front door gun in hand. Not unless you wanted to shake hands with Death. Lucy had that much to thank her mother for: the old bitch had taught her to walk in darkness.

She watched the Empire State Building until twilight, but didn't see Tilly come out once. In the morning, she dropped by the piers before sentry duty and ran down Kerry.

"Hey, you know how the main office has all those carriages and things?" she said. "Where do they keep the horses?"

He shrugged. "In the garage."

"Right there in the building?"

"Sure. I dunno, not my area. What makes you ask?"

"Seems wrong, that's all." She scowled at the flat gray river. "A horse should run around in the sun."

Atop the tower overlooking Twelfth Avenue, she had plenty of time to think, but didn't get far. Theoretically, Tilly might never have to leave the building. Surely she left for walks and things now and then, maybe even on a schedule, but Lucy wasn't exactly swimming in the free time necessary to observe these things.

Two days later, there was a fight up at the park. A Distro soldier had been stabbed. Might not make it. Everyone at the pier was surprised the brawl hadn't been much worse. There was talk of reprisals. Assassinations. Rolando Quiroz, one of the men she'd suspected of being the mole, went so far as to suggest exactly how Nerve should do it.

"Forget about a gunfight," he said to the circle of stevedores on the pier exchanging opinions on how best to do Nerve's job. "None of that Rambo bullshit. Konos drink coffee too, right? Buy vodka from the dude downtown? You find their shipment and you put some arsenic in it. Bam. Half their crew's dead before they know it."

"No way," croaked a woman named Kara. She had that apple-headed look of someone who'd spent a couple years on the meth, but Lucy had heard her speak before and knew she'd been to college. "How you going to get them all to drink it at once? Throw them a party, then go all Red Wedding on their asses?"

Rolando didn't let it go. "Then you do like the aliens did. Infect them and let the disease do the work."

"You got any spare smallpox, smart guy? What's the plan, invite somebody with cholera to drop a deuce in their well?"

It was pretty much moronic, but it gave Lucy an idea. Early that afternoon, with no sign of anything more threatening than a few skinny pigeons, she left her post and rode to the coffee house on the other side of the island. She asked around for Reese, the dirty-faced dude who'd tipped her off to Tilly's involvement with the Kono, but he wasn't in. She left a message with the cowboy behind the bar and biked back to her post.

That night, as she readied for bed, she heard a faint voice calling her name. For a split second, she went stiff, imagining it was her mom. The voice called again. She went to the window and cranked it open. A man waved from the street.

"Hey Lucy! It's Reese!"

"I see you," she said. "Quit hollering and I'll be right down."

She put her pistol in the back of her waistband, tromped down the steps, and let him inside the foyer.

He grinned wide enough to show his dead molar. "Heard you were looking for me."

"I'm looking for drugs. Roofies would be best, but I'll take anything strong enough to throw a person for a loop."

"What are you offering in trade?"

"I still got some tobacco. Bud too, if you prefer."

He looked her up and down. "I was thinking something we might both enjoy."

She gave him the eye. Scrub the dirt off his face and he might be halfway handsome. And it might do her well to zap her mind with a good orgasm. But if all she wanted was sex, she could get that from one of the men at the dock any time she liked. Swapping it for a couple of pills wasn't her idea of a great trade.

"Not this time. But if this works, then we might have something to celebrate about."

He nodded at the gritty entryway. "Should I ask what it's for?"

"This city traffic is just so loud at night," she said. "A girl needs her sleep."

Reese smirked and waved. It was three days before he returned with the pills. In the meantime, she kept watch for the Kono by day and for Tilly after hours, posting up outside the thousand-foot tower with binoculars at hand. She didn't see Tilly leave once, but one day at dusk, Nerve trotted up on his horse and didn't leave for two hours.

Reese arrived with her pills, let her know she could use them on him any time, and departed with six hand-rolled cigarettes. Lucy had been hoping for a less circuitous way to get to Tilly, but the girl was too much of a homebody. Or it could be Nerve no longer allowed her out. Either way, Lucy was going to have to get stupid.

The following morning, she lingered on the pier, waiting for Nerve to leave, but a surprise showed up instead. In the parking circle fronting the docks, a black limousine squeaked to a stop. Tiny American flags fluttered on its hood. Six men in black suits and mirrored sunglasses piled out like the world's soberest clowns and jogged toward the docks, clearing away the laborers. They returned to the car and escorted an old bald white man to the restaurant. Lucy sighed and headed uptown to her post.

After her shift, she headed back, but Kerry stood in front of the restaurant doors and shook his head. "Nobody sees him. Not today."

"This about the old bastard in the limo?" Lucy said. "Who was that?"

Kerry laughed. "You mean to say you don't recognize the President of Manhattan?"

"I guess I missed his last State of the Union. Nerve must feel honored."

"Not exactly. Feds caught wind of our little disagreement with the Kono. President warned us to knock it off or face sanctions."

"Sanctions?" she snorted. "Like what? You got to pay them an extra dollar to walk across the bridge to New Jersey? My God, by this time next year, you could be out five dollars."

"They could raise tariffs on our imports. If they press hard enough to cut profits, someone's got to eat the loss: the men on the docks, or the ones in the tower."

"It ain't never the ones in the tower."

"You ever read Machiavelli? That sort of thing? When your people are starting to turn on you, you redirect them against an outside enemy. Maybe Distro decides to take a short-term hit from the Feds and wipe out the Kono. Or maybe they buddy up with the Kono and take down the Feds instead. Either way, it's enough to make a guy like me reconsider his career."

Lucy crossed her arms. "Sounds like you should be running this place."

"I used to be a campaign manager." He glanced up at the rotunda. "Nowadays, you take what you can get, you know?"

For a moment she was sad, but she didn't have time to spare on Kerry's wasted potential. Things were headed for a blowup. One way or the other, Distro was going to war. By hook or by roofie, she had to get Tilly out of Dodge before the cannons began to roar.

That meant getting inside Nerve's office. While he wasn't there.

It was another three days before she got her chance. She had a day off and was hanging around the piers watching the river and chatting with the workers, who were expecting a shipment of goods late that morning. Noon came without sign of the boat. Around two, a red-faced woman ran down the dock and into the converted restaurant. Five minutes later, Nerve walked out the front door and hustled toward the street.

Lucy beelined inside the building. From somewhere around back, the furious voice of the woman who kept the records berated whomever had wronged her, but the stairs were clear. Both eyes out for Kerry, she headed up to the rotunda.

It was vacant. She made a quick pass at the file cabinets, looking for older stuff, something he wouldn't miss any time soon. Within two minutes, she had her piece: a lengthy report, dated three years ago, detailing the failure of the someone to accomplish the something. Didn't matter. All that mattered was it had enough of Nerve's handwriting for Lucy to learn and forge.

She pocketed it and crossed to his desk to search for personalized stationery, which would be the cherry on top. As she slid open the drawer, feet thumped on the stairs.

She eased it closed and hurried toward the stairwell. The steps neared.

"Hey, you seen Nerve?" Lucy called.

As if summoned by black magic, he appeared on the stairs below. "What are you doing in my office?"

Her hand moved toward her pocket. She stopped it cold. "Well, I was looking for you."

He stared at her with unsettling resolve. "Get downstairs. Stay there."

"What's up?"

"I'm sending you out of the city." Nerve walked up the steps, brushing past her on the landing.

"Sure thing," she said, but inside she was buzzing, mind collapsing, plans burning up like a pile of autumn leaves.

16

"Ah," Ellie said. "Just who we were looking for."

"What are you doing here?" Nan said.

"Like I just said. Looking for you."

Nan looked past her to the men in front of the truck. "You shouldn't be here."

The two men crunched through the snow. They hadn't yet drawn guns, but their hands hung close to their holsters.

Ellie still didn't have a plan. "We found the body. It was him. We wanted to thank you."

"You're welcome." The old woman stood her ground. "But this here is private property."

The men stopped six feet behind her. Ellie nodded placatingly. "I understand. But that's not why we're here. We spoke to your mechanic. At first, we were interested in purchasing snowmobiles from you, but then I saw all that equipment and I realized I was thinking small."

Hobson carefully kept his gaze away from Ellie. Nan's eyes flicked over Ellie's shoulder; she nodded at the pair of men. Ellie didn't look back, but she could feel the tension thaw from the air.

"You want to talk business," Nan said.

"Our employer's a big believer in kismet. While he won't be happy to learn what happened to our man, he would see the circumstances arising from it—our meeting—as meaningful. Particularly when he's looking to expand his operations."

The old woman pursed her mouth. "Why don't we step inside?"

Nan led them to a back door. Ellie made a small scene of

stomping and scraping the snow off her shoes. The others followed suit. Nan watched with quiet approval, then brought them to a sitting room with dark wood panels and deep-seated couches.

Nan tasked one of the men to heat tea, then turned to Ellie. "First things first. Why don't you explain who you're speaking for?"

"Forgive me for having to play coy," Ellie said. "You know how these things are. Let's say he runs a settlement north of the border."

"Sounds cold."

"And isolated. Which is how he likes it. But that means extra work, too."

"Same story everywhere." Nan's blue gaze lingered on Dee. "Who's she?"

"She works with us," Ellie shrugged.

"Right. You're the ambassador. Your man with the hat is the muscle—former lawman, maybe. But why the girl?"

Ellie blanked. Dee got a small smile on her face and inclined her head. "Because some men are best convinced with things besides words or force."

Nan chuckled throatily. "Interesting team, I'll give you that."

"Our employer's tactically flexible," Ellie said. She stopped herself from sighing in relief. She'd managed to convince Nan this meeting was intentional. Time to pivot and see whether she could come out of it with something useful. "You represent the Clavans?"

"You've heard of them?"

"I saw the signs."

"And you'd like to know whether I'm authorized to speak for them." Nan leaned back and tucked her glasses into her shirt pocket. "That won't be a problem."

"You deal in machinery," Ellie said. A kettle whistled from the kitchen, startling her. "Anything else? There are some chores a machine is no good for."

Nan pressed her palms together. "What would your people have to offer in trade?"

"Vegetables. Grain. Meat."

"Food is cheap. The Clavans are interested in more exotic goods."

"Such as?"

The old woman smiled. "We're open to proposals."

"Some of our citizens make fuel," Ellie tried.

"You think I'd put together a fleet like this and not produce my own gas?" Nan smiled with half her mouth. "Here's how it works. We establish a franchise in your settlement. Run by our people. In exchange for access to your market, your employer will receive a cut of each sale. We'll start simple—a couple trucks, a tractor. If your people can pay with something more interesting than wheat, then we'll see about expanding our offerings."

Hobson thrust out his lower lip. "Would you consider operating on a wholesale model?"

Nan laughed. "We don't want distributors. We want markets. We bring the goods, we make the sales, you get a piece. Where's the downside?"

A man walked in with a tea tray, keeping his steps low and level, porcelain cups rattling on the silver platter. That was the end of business. They left with tea in their bellies and a sheet of listed goods. Ellie examined this as they walked their bikes south from the manor, fighting the snow. The goods were all mechanical, mostly automobiles and farming equipment with a smattering of less obvious vehicles like snowmobiles and golf carts. The equipment's list price was given in several currencies—grain, bullets, penicillin, a whole series of painkillers (hydrocodone, oxycodone, oxycontin, morphine), and "Surprise Me!"—with a second column breaking out the prospective partner's commission of each sale.

"I got the impression there are no Clavan Brothers." Hobson cackled. "She uses them as a front for herself!"

"No doubt." Ellie waved the list. "No mention of human goods here."

"I expect she's as sly about that as she is with her front. Selling people is a dark business. Wouldn't trust us with that knowledge until she knows we're operating in good faith."

"Which we have no way to prove. Even if we tried to bluff her about our 'employer,' the back-and-forth could take weeks."

"If Quinn's still here, they could move him at any time," Dee said.

"I know. We'll have to try to find where they're keeping the captives."

"Doubt it's the house," Hobson said. "She let us in as if she had nothing to hide."

"But the captives were in the truck," Ellie said. "Its tracks led straight to the house."

Dee gestured ahead of them. "What about the other tracks?"

Both Hobson and Ellie turned. Ellie got the words out first. "Which others?"

"Down here a ways. They split off to the east. I don't know how you missed them."

Dee led the way. Ellie glanced back toward Nan's house. She and her people were predators. Specifically, they were pack hunters. Attracted by herds of prey. When Ellie got back to the lakes, she'd have to think long and hard about relocating herself, Dee, and the Tolberts. It would be a hassle and a half, but if it kept them away from trouble, it would be well worth the work.

Backtracking their way down the street, the divergence of tire tracks was obvious. They must have been riding too fast. Assuming there was only one set to follow. If not for Dee's sharp eyes, they might never have known different.

The intersection was roughly halfway between the manor and the main office. They followed the tracks east past a slew of local businesses, riding down the center of the road where the snow was thinnest. After just two blocks, the path turned into the parking lot of Clavan Dry Cleaning.

Ellie rode on past. Hobson cleared his throat. She shook her head. Three blocks later, she turned north and pulled her bike behind a Taco Bell.

"We'll wait till night," she said. "I don't want to risk bumping into anyone else. And we're close enough to hear if they try to relocate again."

Hobson nodded. "Did you note the bumper of the delivery truck sticking out from the back?"

"Yeah. What do you think?"

"Feels right. Much more so than Nan stashing them at her own house."

"Agreed," Ellie said. "Should have brought the bike trailer. If Quinn's here, I don't want to stick around town once we've got him."

"Shall I go back for it?"

"We don't have much else to do until nightfall."

He saluted and rode north. Ellie tried the door of the Taco Bell. Unlocked. Dee held it open while she wheeled the bikes inside. They stomped off the snow on the rug in the entry, then went to the drive-thru window to keep an ear on the street.

It was no warmer inside than out. A few times an hour, Ellie got up to walk around and stir her blood. Dee, typically talkative, gazed out the window at the motionless snow. Hobson returned with the trailer a couple hours later, coming in from the north, having looped clear of Nan's office/garage as well as the dry cleaner.

"Brisk out there, isn't it?" He was red-faced and bright-eyed. "Any movement?"

Ellie shook her head. She napped, then killed more time studying the map of town she'd taken from the phone book. With the sun hidden by the clouds, she had little sense of time until the light began to fade. As soon as it went, snow sifted from the sky.

With no electric lights, and the moon concealed by thick clouds, the streets were all but pitch black. Ellie went outside to pack snow into their empty gallon jugs and bring it inside to melt. Food would be a problem on the return trip. If the roads were snowy all the way to the lakes, the ride could take three times as long as it had on the way down.

At eleven o'clock, they slipped from the Taco Bell on foot, heading east before doubling back to approach the dry cleaners from the back access alley. Another inch of snow had fallen and more was coming down fast. Good. It might hide their tracks.

Ellie hunkered down at the corner of the neighboring building. She saw no movement except the snow. The back wall was blank concrete with two loading bays, both shut with metal doors, and a plain exit. Gun at her hip, she hurried to the exit door. Footprints marred the snow. They'd just begun to fill.

She glanced at the others, then tried the door. It didn't budge. She opened her mouth to ask Dee whether she had a hairpin when a voice spoke from beside them.

"God, it's cold."

Her skin prickled. She pulled her gun, glancing to all sides, but saw nothing more than snow.

"It's senseless," the voice went on, tinny but distinct. "You figure they mean to stick us in a field somewhere, right? How am I supposed to pull a plow when I lose my foot to frostbite?"

"Shut up," a second voice moaned.

Hobson pointed to a vent in the wall. It had, in all likelihood, once carried steam outside, but now it carried the voices of prisoners. Ellie walked up to it. Tiny icicles hung from its slats.

"Hello?" she whispered. The men on the other side went dead silent. "Can you hear me?"

"Who's that?" The man dropped to a whisper, but his voice was clearer than a moment before.

"Are you being held against your will?"

"No, I'm just too lazy to find a blanket. Or to untie myself from this bed. You outside?"

"I'm looking for someone," she said. "Quinn Tolbert. Twenty years —"

"I know him."

"Is he in there?"

"Truck took him and the others away two days ago. Headed south."

Ellie's heart quickened. "What did the truck look like?"

"White van. Like the one they brought us here in," the man said. "Hey. I've told you all I know. There's five of us in here still. You got to get us out."

"Are you under guard?"

"Couple dudes. Think they're up front. Asleep."

"Armed?"

The man laughed. "If they weren't, I would have bitten my way out."

"You hang tight and be quiet," Ellie said. "We'll see what we can do."

"My name's Nelson," he said. "Now you know my name, you got to come get me."

"See you soon, Nelson."

She turned to the others and gestured toward the neighboring building. Together, they ran to it in silence. Ellie continued past and didn't stop until they were back to the Taco Bell. Fat flakes of snow swept into her face with stinging cold.

"Mom," Dee said.

"We have to go now," she said. "If the snow stops, the guards will see our tracks. If it doesn't stop, it may be too thick for the bikes."

"You told them you'd save them."

In the darkness of the restaurant, Ellie moved to pack up the blankets they'd used during the day. "So what?"

"He said the guards were asleep."

"You think they'll stay that way once we break in? What if we take down two and a third comes in from the back room?" She grabbed a Ziploc bag of bread and shoved it in the trailer. "No matter how good your odds, once the bullets start flying, you can't be certain one won't take you down. That's why violence is the last tool in the box."

She knew she was babbling, but it was something Dee needed to know. She found the jugs of snow and added them to the trailer. "While I was training for the DAA, I took some karate classes. I once saw a girl tear her ACL without being touched. She stepped wrong and boom, down she went. Crutches for months. The sensei had a running joke about such things. Said he'd hurt himself worse training to handle himself in a fight than he ever would have if he'd never learned. If that's the risk of training, can you imagine the risk of a real fight?"

"So we leave them?" Dee said. "They're all Quinn to someone."

"You can't save the world. You'll die trying. But if you stay focused, sometimes you can save the piece that matters most." She put her rifle in the trailer. "You ready?"

"Not until we do something for those people."

They glared at each other. They might have gone on this way until the sun rose and glared down on them both, but Hobson cleared his throat.

"Dee, I reluctantly agree with your mother. We can't intervene directly without exposing ourselves to undo risk."

"Oh yeah?" Dee said. "And what about intervening indirectly?"

He smiled, extremely satisfied about something. "You're a sharp one. Which segues neatly into my plan: we pass the prisoners knives through the vent."

"That is so stupid," Ellie said.

"Is it? From the acoustics, I'd say the vent has clear passage into the room. They're tied up, but if they're capable of reaching the vent, the knives will take care of that. From there, it's five of them and the element of surprise versus two guards. Voila! We've discharged our moral duty without exposing ourselves to harm."

"Except if the guards see us. Or Nelson decides we're being punks and sounds the alarm to punish us."

But now that the idea was out there—and it was such a simple plan, the sort of thing the DAA had termed a "walkaway": something you set in motion, then stroll away—Ellie couldn't turn her back on it. By herself, she would have had no problem leaving innocents behind. Most of the world was innocent, and she, like just about everyone else, was only concerned with her corner of it. But there at the Taco Bell, Dee was staring at her with such intense judgment it could have carved commandments into stone.

"At the first sign of trouble, we split up and run," she said. "Rally at the Clavans' sign on the highway. Got it?"

Dee smiled. "Got it."

Hobson nodded, expression calculated but ultimately unreadable. Ellie led them back to the laundromat, sneaking around from the side the same way as before. She gestured Hobson and Dee to stay in the shadow of the neighboring building, then crossed to the vent.

"Nelson," she whispered. "What's on your side of this?"

"Nothing," he said. "Just some torn-up duct tape. Feeds right into the room."

"Good," she said with little enthusiasm. "Can you reach it?"

Soft scraping and shuffling drifted through the vent. "With my foot."

"Here's the deal. We can't come inside. My daughter's with me. I can't put her life at risk."

"Hey, hold on a minute," he said, voice climbing. "You can't leave us in here. We haven't done anything!"

"Be quiet," she commanded. "I'm going to pass you some knives. Use them to free yourselves. In the event you're recaptured, you tell them nothing. Understood?"

He was quiet a moment. "What if I yell to the guards?"

"I came back for you, Nelson. I didn't have to."

His sigh echoed down the duct. "Give me the god damn knives."

She grabbed two of the vent's slats and bent in opposite directions. They yielded, providing a hole large enough to pass a knife through. She tossed in a jackknife. It clattered down the metal vent, terribly loud, and bounced on an unseen stone floor. Ellie winced and glanced around the quiet lot.

"Too far," Nelson whispered.

She tried again with a paring knife she was quite fond of. It skittered over the metal and clacked on the concrete. Shuffling sounds followed.

"Got it."

Ellie set three more knives just inside the slats. All told, the five blades made up half of what they carried, but knives, at least, were easy enough to replace. "The others are inside the vent. Good luck."

"Thanks?"

She watched the parking lot a moment, then jogged back to Dee and Hobson. They mounted up and rode down the street. Several blocks away, Ellie stopped and got her bearings.

"We ready to leave?" she said. "Or do we have some kittens to rescue?"

"Where are we going?" Dee said. "We still don't know where Quinn is."

Except Ellie did. The mechanic had hinted that way, but worse, her gut knew it. She rarely trusted her gut's guidance, and recognizing this, it had more or less learned to stop providing advice at all, but every now and then it piped up with a certainty as cold as the constellations of snow falling to the white-carpeted streets.

"We're going to New York."

She hated the words. The place she hadn't been to since the end of the world—and the death of the only man she'd wanted to save.

17

The boat swept through the waves, sails taut with the frigid northern wind. The towers of the city thrust from the south of the island like giant's teeth. To the ship's right, the green lady held up her torch like anyone gave a damn.

Lucy sighed and dug her chin into her collar to protect her nose from the wind. It wasn't much of a boat, really, but she'd never been out in anything bigger than Beau's itty bitty sloop he was always trying and failing to catch marlin with, and by comparison this one, with its cabin and deck, felt pretty grand.

Their mission, however, felt like a fool's errand.

"I don't see what y'all are so worried about," Lucy said. "So what if it's a few hours late? Where's it coming from, Brazil?"

"Caribbean," Kerry said. He stood at the railing with his back to her, surveying the gray waves like a French admiral. Four other troopers sat on padded benches around the cabin.

"That's a thousand miles from here. Maybe the captain hit some bad winds. Or got the runs."

"She didn't."

"Oh, you were there with her and saw it all. Mission accomplished!"

Kerry turned to stare at her. "You don't need to know the ins and outs. You're here to follow orders and shoot anything I tell you to shoot."

He'd taken on a real superior attitude since they'd shoved off from the pier. Lucy, by contrast, was feeling good. Much better than a couple hours earlier when she'd thought Nerve was about to banish her. His summons, as it turned out, wasn't about her at all. Rather, he was concerned about Distro's little shipping depot. Situated on the New Jersey coast, it was the final waystation the Distro vessels dropped by before chugging in to port; when a boat reached the depot, they radioed in to the city, allowing Nerve advance notice to schedule his laborers to offload its cargo.

Or something like that. All Lucy knew was that a boat hadn't arrived when it was supposed to. Suspecting Kono interference, Nerve had dispatched them to find out what had gone wrong.

That was just fine with Lucy. She still had his papers in his pocket. In a day or two, they'd return to the city, and she'd lure Tilly into her trap.

The boat cut through a channel between two big chunks of land, crossed a broad bay, and entered the open Atlantic. The eastern horizon was a straight gray line. The captain wheeled the boat south, keeping the boat within a quarter mile of the Jersey coast.

Gulls flapped around. An hour after hitting the sea proper, Lucy spotted a white lump further out to sea. Another vessel.

"What if it was pirates?" she said.

"Don't think so," Kerry said.

"Why not? If it's worth shipping, it's got to be worth stealing."

"This attack would be the first." Despite his skepticism, he got out his binoculars and stared at the other boat for a long time.

Yellow sand striped the shore. Houses sat shoulder to shoulder. Smoke rose from a couple chimneys. If Lucy cared, she would have suggested docking and grilling the locals for witnesses, but Kerry seemed hell-bent on getting to the port. She wasn't about to fly ideas that would only slow them down.

Round about dusk, with gulls heading inland and the sails still snapping, the captain angled closer to shore. He slowed. His mate hung a lantern from the prow. They drifted into a green channel a couple hundred yards across, bracketed by beaches. The north was vacant and pristine. The south front of the channel was overseen by a towering lighthouse, red on its top half, white on its bottom.

At the end of the strait, the captain swung south into a narrow bay. The lantern glimmered on the placid water. Up front, the mate leaned forward, peering into the gloom for obstacles or snags. The air smelled salty and fishy but in a clean way. With the world reduced to shadows and outlines, the captain guided the vessel into a marina and tied off.

Kerry hopped down to the dock, furtive, and knelt there, gazing at the stately building at the foot of the piers. "Do not shoot on sight. We have people here. You see someone, call 'Elephant.' Their response should be 'Ivory.' Anything else, treat them as hostile."

He ordered a man and a woman to set up as snipers on the dock. Once they were positioned, he gestured the others forward. Lucy crept along beside him. Wavelets washed against the moorings. Dull, cloud-filtered starlight shined on the barnacled hulls of weather-scarred ships. Less healthy vessels projected from the water or lay tangled on the docks, broken by storms. Tens of millions of dollars busted up and lost. Lucy grinned. She hoped the yachts' owners had had a good time, because their money sure as shit hadn't saved them from the scythe.

The clubhouse looked like an Atlantic mansion: three floors, white trim, a big round window high on one side. Deck out front, complete with chairs. Lucy's ears and nose stung from cold. The windows were silent and dark.

Kerry opened the front door and stalked inside with his gun out SWAT-style. Lucy and the other two followed him in. Inside, it was as dark as a cave. They went room to room, edging past furniture and through doorways, and then upstairs, where Kerry flicked a Zippo so no one would fall from the landing. The floors were well-swept. In an upstairs office, the desks were arranged with charts, ledgers, and hand-cranked radios, but the building didn't hold a single soul.

Outside on the deck, Kerry waved his hands over his head at the boat to call in the snipers. "This is fucked."

"You'd rather we got shot at?" Lucy said.

"We had people here. Where'd they go?"

"Croatoan?"

"It's too dark for this shit. Secure the grounds. We'll resume the search in the morning."

While the snipers watched from the upper windows of the clubhouse, Kerry led the rest of his people in a sweep around the building. The road on the other side held a few rusty cars, nothing more. Kerry circled back to the deck and went inside and fired up lanterns. A minute later, the captain and his mate walked in from the docks and locked the door behind them.

They got a fire going, ate smoked fish and potatoes baked before they left. Kerry established a watch and called lights out. Lucy's shift was in the middle of the night. She watched from the round upstairs window, the black bay, the dead town.

Kerry woke them early. By the time the sun streamed in over the Atlantic, they were fed and ready to search. Nothing appeared out of place: no blood stains, no overturned furniture, no broken windows or locks.

Lucy got bored pretty quick. While the others thumped through the yacht club for the third time, searching for secret doors or subtle clues, she headed into the freezing morning. A semi-circle of fancy shops and restaurants—windows broken, roofs ripped by past winds—faced a brownish field pocked by standing water. Footprints led away from the marina.

Much of the field was brackish marsh, but there were patches of solid ground. On one, two furrows lined the earth, fifteen feet long and spaced ten apart, like wagon ruts to nowhere. She walked up close. Beside one, rabbit turds scattered the turf. Looked funny, though. Little creases down their middle. She crouched down and picked one up. It was hard. She brought it to her nose. Coffee bean.

She stood and walked back to the club. As she climbed the front steps, Kerry walked outside.

"Where were you?" he said.

"Had to take a leak," she said. "If this was the Kono, your people went out easy. What was on the boat?"

"What's it matter?"

"Maybe your own people got greedy. Hijacked it and sailed off for warmer waters."

"That would be a bad idea."

"How would you ever find them?"

He smiled a bit, goaded toward a secret, then caught himself and shrugged. "Our reach is longer than you think."

The west half of the little peninsula had been dredged to form saltwater canals; each and every home sat on a waterfront and sported its own dock. Kerry sent them to knock on doors and call inside. When they all came back empty-handed, Lucy swore, certain they'd spend another day on this frozen little spit, but Kerry detached two troops to stay at the yacht club, then set sail for Manhattan.

"Could the Kono know about this place?" she said once they were underway. The wind still streamed out of the north and the captain had to zigzag his way up the coast.

"I don't see how," Kerry said.

A light flared in her mind. "Maybe Zoe told them."

He turned from the sea. "How would she know? She never worked anywhere but the docks."

"You mean the place every one of your boats comes in? Yeah, she'd never have a chance to learn anything there."

Kerry rolled his lip between his teeth. "Bribe the crew. Or simply chat them up. In a careless moment, they slip a detail. She passes it to the Kono."

"And they sit on it until Nerve rebuffs their offer to divvy up the city."

The big man nodded slowly. Lucy coughed to hide her smile. That ought to stir things up.

Between the headwind and their late start, they didn't reach Manhattan until hours after dark. Lucy wasn't about to go to bed, though. She flipped on the lights in her apartment, got out Nerve's report, and practiced copying his handwriting.

She had learned forgery from an early age. Writing as her mom, initially; first school attendance notes, later checks. In middle school, after Tilly had made it okay for the other kids to talk to her, Lucy branched out and established a side business writing notes for them, too. That's when she'd gotten downright artsy with it. Copying individual letters wasn't hard. Any fool could trace them if they lacked freehand talent. But when you traced, or focused on letters one at a time, it gave the finished writing a jangled, messy look that raised the suspicions of even the most naive mind.

You had to make it flow. Stitch the letters into a seamless whole the recipient would never think to look up from. In a sense, you made the handwriting itself invisible, communicating the ideas inside it directly to the reader's brain.

Not that she expected Tilly to be an expert on Nerve's handwriting. It was possible the girl had never seen it—though of all people, new lovers were most likely to send each other little notes. Still, she wasn't about to let her whole scheme collapse because she didn't know Nerve put a tail on his d's.

So she spent a few days getting it right. She had plenty of free time on watch on the tower roof. Her second day at it, snow powdered down from the skies, but it wasn't enough to stick. Day after that, gunshots crackled from up north. She stopped her pen and listened. Some back and forth to it, stretches of silence busted by flurries of bangs. She wasn't hearing a crime of passion or some drive-by thing. This was a proper street battle.

Soon as her shift ended, she raced to the coffee house. Reese was in. She placed a new order with him and headed back to the piers to pick up the gossip.

There had been a fight, all right. It was after dark and the stevedores had returned to their apartments, but most of the security team was gathered in the ground floor of the restaurant. Waiting on orders, they had little else to do but talk.

In response to the missing men in New Jersey, the Tower—versatile Distro slang for the Empire State Building as well as the bigwigs who lived inside it—had sent a patrol up to the southern edge of the park. Which had immediately run into the Kono. According to her fellow security officers, the Kono had fired first. Couple casualties on both sides. One of the Tower's troops was in bad shape.

After a couple hours with no new news, Lucy headed home. The next day, she wrote her note. Nothing too saucy; Tilly thought of herself as proper. Instead, she went heavy on mystery.

The timing came together better than she could have hoped. At the piers, she heard a presidential envoy had swung by that morning to request the presence of Nerve and some Tower folk at City Hall the following evening. When Lucy biked to her apartment after a long day on watch, a silhouette waited for her on the front stoop. Reese hopped down the steps and grinned.

"Got the stuff?" Lucy said.

He lifted a canvas Gristedes bag. "If whoever this is for stands you up, you know where I am."

"Persistent son of a bitch," she laughed. She pulled the folded note from her pocket. "Need you to deliver this to the Empire State

Building, 3 PM tomorrow. Do not be late."

"No problem."

She took the canvas bag from him. "So what do you want this time? More cigs?"

He tipped back his head. A couple other people lived in her building and one of them had the lights on. "You have electricity? A TV?"

"Damn right. My services don't come cheap."

Reese shuffled his feet around and ducked his eyes. "Can we watch a movie?"

Lucy drew back her head. "Man, you're an all right guy. Don't make me shoot you down again."

"It isn't like that. I haven't seen a movie in four years."

"You're serious?"

"Is it that weird?"

She laughed and walked up the steps. "Come on."

Upstairs, Reese turned in a circle and whistled. "Nice digs."

"I know. I almost hate to leave." She checked the contents of the bag, then stashed it in her closet. "Well, choose wisely."

The living room was furnished with several shelves of DVDs. Reese took his time, inspecting each title, winnowing it down to a stack of ten, then five, then three. At last, he held up a single case: The Terminator. Lucy popped it in and flipped off the lights and sat on one end of the couch. The flatscreen threw the room in shades of blue and black. Lucy hit play and lit a joint and passed it to Reese. He took it without looking, grin so big his teeth were even brighter than the screen.

Lucy kept an eye on him until the bit where Arnold blasted his way through a nightclub. She wasn't much for nonsense like time travel, but you had to admire the way the big man handled a shotgun.

In the quiet after the scene wrapped up, Reese spoke for the first time since the movie started. "What's all this about?"

"Robots and shit."

He shook his head. "The wine. The note. What's it for?"

"Friend of mine."

"Boyfriend?"

"Girl I know from way back before the plague," Lucy said. "She's in over her head with Distro."

He gazed at her, puffy-eyed and suspicious. "So what are the drugs for?"

She had a glib one for that, but something stopped her—maybe it was the old comfort of being in a dark room with a story on the TV, but maybe it was that she hadn't had anyone to talk to in a very long time.

"I don't expect her to skip away with me hand in hand," Lucy said. "She doesn't much like me anymore."

"Why's that?"

"How should I know? She won't even talk to me. Probably mad about her boyfriend, but they'd been broken up for months, and anyway it wasn't my fault. Tell the truth, she's been acting hinky for a couple years. Which is a bushel of bullshit. I been keeping her out of trouble since the world went to hell."

Reese slumped deeper into the couch and gazed at the blue light on the screen. "Maybe that's the problem. She resents you for acting more like a parent than a friend."

"I promised her daddy I would look after her. She was born for shopping malls and Starbucks. Instead, we're wearing dead women's shoes and trapping possum for meat. She wouldn't last a week without me."

"Well, I bet she loves the hell out of that attitude."

Lucy sat up straight. "Are you gonna watch your movie or what?"

"I'm just sayin'."

"And if you want to keep sayin', then you can get the hell out of my apartment."

He glared at her. Onscreen, guns went off. The two of them didn't talk again until the movie ended and Reese got ready to leave.

"Three o'clock," Lucy said. "I can count on you?"

"'Please. I'm a pro." He zipped his jacket high and snapped the collar closed around his neck. "Good luck with your friend."

He left her alone and she felt bad for spoiling it when all he'd wanted was to watch a movie. Should never have gotten personal with him. Was his fault for asking. He probably only wanted to watch the stupid thing because he had the hero's name.

She got up early and went to her post on the roof as usual. Around three, she snuck downstairs and ran home. Reese had left a note under the door: "DONE." She hiked upstairs, grabbed her bags, and ran to a twelve-story apartment a couple blocks from the Empire State Building.

She'd seen it while spying on Nerve. It was short enough to walk up, but more important, it had a full-fledged garden on the roof. One half of which was dead flowers, with the other half an urban jungle of weeds, but it would be romantic enough for her purposes.

The wine was Riesling, a sweet white Tilly drank like soda. The wintry air would keep it cold. Lucy popped the cork, then replaced it and settled in for a long wait. Hidden by the clouds, the sun headed for the hills. She did some pushups to keep warm. Plucked some of the flowers that weren't dead and set them in a water glass on the wooden table in the middle of the roof. After the darkness was complete, she got out a baggie of white powder, dumped it in a wine glass, poured it tall with Riesling, and swirled it around until the powder dissolved. She set it on the table, along with a folded note in Nerve's handwriting bearing Tilly's name, which she weighted down with a smooth ruddy stone she'd picked up from the street on the way here.

Heels clicked down the pavement. Lucy peeked over the gut-high wall on the edge of the roof. Too dark to make out the figure below, but she knew the walk. She hid behind a dense wall of shrubs.

A couple minutes later, the rooftop door opened. Footsteps approached with hesitant taps. As Lucy watched from behind the screen of brush, Tilly walked into the courtyard, wearing a coat over a pretty black dress.

"Nerve?" Tilly's eyes caught the glint of light on the dew on the wine glass. She frowned, looked around, picked up the note, and smiled. She took the glass to the edge of the roof and leaned her elbows on the wall and watched the dead city lie at peace.

Tilly didn't look so happy ten minutes later when her glass was empty and Nerve hadn't shown. Nor five minutes after that, when she blinked heavily and staggered into the table with a scrape of wood on stone.

"It's all right, Tilly." Lucy walked out from the shrubs and winked. "When you wake up, you'll be in a better place."

18

Flakes of snow lurched from the sky. Ellie stood her full weight on the pedals, but her back tire spun on the ice they'd compacted with their footsteps. The trailer refused to budge. Hobson got around back and pushed until she found purchase. Snow creaked beneath her wheels.

Snow crusted the brim of his bowler. "Shall we take the highway?"

"I'll never make the onramp," Ellie laughed. "We'll hook up with it at the edge of town."

They rode northwest, away from the makeshift prison, then hooked back around to cut through the suburban lanes leading south. Twice, Ellie got stuck mid-turn and had to get off and haul her bike out of its ruts. The snow piled five or six inches deep and grew thicker by the moment. When the path was straight and level Ellie was able to keep the bike moving, but she had to lean into the pedals and was soon panting, breath steaming from her mouth.

An hour later, at the south end of town, they curled up a gentle onramp. Ellie stalled on the steep curve. She swore and hopped off and kicked at the heavy trailer.

"Like me to spell you?" Hobson said.

She planted her hands on her hips and breathed in and out. "We need to get as far as we can. If the snow stops, they can track us all the way here."

"What happens if they catch us?" Dee said.

Hobson unhatted himself and flicked the brim to pop off the snow. "They profit from the trade of humans. Safest to assume maximum barbarism from them at all times."

"Pretty much," Ellie said. "Time's wasting."

Hobson took over, but he couldn't get the trailer moving, either. Ellie leaned against it, feet skidding in the snow. Her shoes were soaked through. They'd need a fire. It was going to be a long night.

The highway ran dead south, the Hudson river glinting across the white plains. Another mile and Hobson was puffing like an antique train. Dee offered to take over and managed a half mile, stalling repeatedly in the drifts. Ellie couldn't feel much in her toes. The snow continued to swirl. Three hours from leaving Albany, with her feet half numb and her legs burning from strain, she exited the highway—onto yet another street named Beaver Dam, making her feel as if they were still stuck in Albany in some horrendous post-apocalyptic Groundhog Day—and turned into the drive of a stately two-story home tucked into the woods. She barely had the energy to open the garage and help lug the trailer inside. Snow lined the creases of its tarp.

There were no logs beside the fireplace. The pile outside was buried under deep drifts. Hobson found a rust-pitted axe, turned the coffee table on its side, and smashed it apart right there in the room. Dee watched from the couch, glaze-eyed. Ellie got a couple books from the shelves in the master bedroom and crumpled up the pages in the fireplace, then arranged the table splinters in a pyre above the shredded paper. She flicked her lighter, but no sparks emerged. It had gotten wet. Dee crawled over on her knees and set the pages aflame.

They stoked up the fire, wordless, as if human speech might scare the ancient heat away. Ellie closed every door she could, minimizing the space. The room smelled like woodsmoke and the chemical tang of varnish. Oh well. After six years of eating organic, she expected her body could handle it.

She pulled off her shoes, peeled off her damp socks, and changed her jeans, which were wet halfway up the shins. She laid out her socks and shoes in front of the fire. Steam rose from the fabric. She thought they ought to keep watch, but it was nearly four in the morning and she was so exhausted she fell asleep sitting in front of the fire.

She slept until mid-morning. The snow had stopped, but the

clouds remained. The snow on the railings of the back deck looked eight inches deep. When Ellie went outside to pee, she sank to the calf, with drifts that touched her knee.

Inside, she stomped off the snow and brought her shoes back to the fire; they'd already gotten wet again. "There's no way we get the bikes through that."

"What do you propose?" Hobson said.

"Walk. Or wait for it to melt."

"We can't just sit around," Dee said. "If they had a truck, Quinn's already in the city."

"Which is 140 miles from here. How long do you think it takes us to walk that in this weather? Ten days? Two weeks? It isn't even December. The snow could start melting tomorrow."

"Or it could last until spring. If we stay here, what are we going to eat? Our shoes?"

"Yet another argument for wearing leather," Hobson said.

Ellie sighed. Her legs were stiff and sore. "Food's going to be a problem no matter what we do."

Dee picked at a loose fiber on the carpet. "What if we went back and stole the snowmobiles?"

"By now, Nelson's led a slave rebellion. They've escaped or been killed. Either way, Nan and her people will be on high alert."

"Then what's your solution? Complain about all the things that could go wrong until our mouths freeze shut?"

"Maybe then I'll have the peace of mind to figure out what to do."

Hobson cleared his throat. "I have a suggestion that may clarify our path. It's a single word. Two words? Or, if you're a proponent of hyphenation, perhaps somewhere in between—"

"Spit it out," Ellie said.

"Snowshoes."

"Snowshoes?"

"Indeed," he said. "People have crafted them for thousands of years. The wicker baskets in the laundry room should do nicely."

Ellie hunched forward. "We're going to need to search for food. We might find skis."

"I don't know how to ski," Dee said.

"You can learn on the job," Hobson said. "What do you say?"

"I like it," Ellie said. "Come on, Dee. Let's have a look around."

The sheriff clapped his hands. "I'll get to work on the shoes."

They went door to door through the neighborhood. They were just a quarter mile from the highway and years of travelers had picked most of the homes clean, but they found thick wool socks and balaclavas and a jar three-quarters full of white rice. Many of the houses had been broken into, windows shattered or front doors hanging open, locks broken; snow rested on stained carpets and foyers. Birds and squirrels had made nests on cabinets and entertainment centers. Bones lay in beds, victims of the plague.

Ellie didn't find any skis and she berated herself for not thinking to search back in Albany. Then again, she'd never been stupid enough to trek across the state during a blizzard. Learning experience. She did find a set of wicker chairs which she and Dee dragged back to the house, chair legs leaving trails through the snow.

In the front yard, Hobson walked awkwardly across the surface of the drifts, round wicker shoes flapping on his feet. He lifted one foot and rapped its rim with his cane. "Stylish, wouldn't you agree? I daresay we'll be the talk of Fleet Street."

Dee laughed. Ellie asked to see the design. It was a rough job, but effective: he'd framed the rims with thick wicker and tied it to the main body of the shoe with shoelaces and fishing line looted from one of the rods in the garage. From there, he'd braced the wicker with broken-off pieces of yardstick, and finalized the design by threading the wicker through with belts, which they could strap firmly over their normal shoes.

While he set to work on the next pair, Ellie ran triage on the bike trailer. They'd have to cut back to bare essentials. She ditched the tent. Along the Hudson down to the city, there would be little space between towns, and many of them would be outright contiguous. Finding a roof shouldn't be a problem. She set aside all but one jug of water, too. Between the snow and the river, they'd be fine until they entered the city.

Piece by piece, she winnowed their supplies to the marrow. Food. Blankets. Spare clothes and shoes. Two knives apiece. Their trading goods. Some cordage and spare chair slats for snowshoe repair. The emergency kits. A single pot, and one bowl per person, which would also function as a cup.

Between their late wakeup and Hobson's work on the shoes, it was clear they wouldn't be leaving that day. As she sorted gear, she assigned Dee to chop wood and pile it at the back of the house. When Ellie finished setting up their packs, she swept the snow from the back patio, lit a fire, and boiled the entire jar of rice. The carbs would be good for the trek and as cold as it was, there was no chance the leftovers would go bad before they finished them. Anyway, they might not be in position to do much cooking for a while.

Hobson finished the third set of shoes by dusk, then spent the evening tweaking them, reinforcing the frames and straps. As the light vanished, the snowfall resumed, but it was spotty and small, bright silver motes that added no depth to the white coat enfolding the world.

"I'm hoping it'll take a week," Ellie said. The fireplace was bright and the room smelled like smoke and the mildewy water drying from their socks. "Keep your eyes out for game. We'll need it."

Dee rested her chin on her knee. "In school they told us people can go weeks without food."

"Not when they're burning four thousand calories a day pretending to be Arctic hares."

"Leather is edible," Hobson said. "Provided it's sufficiently boiled."

Ellie left it at that. They'd made their decision. At this point, they were closer to the city than the lakes. Either they'd make it or they wouldn't.

They went to bed early enough to be up and ready by dawn. They ate rice warmed over the fire and the last of the venison jerky. Ellie's pack was heavy but bearable. They strapped on their snowshoes and walked toward the highway.

The shoes helped immensely, but Ellie soon learned they'd be lucky to make it to the city inside a week. The snow was fluffy and the snowshoes sank several inches. They soon shifted to a single-column formation, but the person at the head had to break a trail, smoothing and compacting the snow for the followers. Her calves lost strength rapidly. They cycled the lead position every thirty to sixty minutes.

Once, they saw a brown rabbit watching from the side of the

road, but Ellie missed her shot and it bounded into the snow. At twilight, a mallard and his mate squawked toward the river, wings pumping like mad, but their bullets sailed harmlessly wide.

Ellie threw her rifle over her shoulder. It smelled like spent powder. "Would help if I could hit more than atmosphere."

"A bird on the wing with a rifle?" Hobson said. "You're a farmer, not John Wayne."

"It doesn't matter. I need to be better than this."

She was still angry when they went to bed in a farmhouse. The next afternoon, the sun poked out for the first time in days, but its weak rays did nothing to diminish the snow. They made fewer miles than the first day. Dee complained about her calves and they rested four different times. Ellie's hurt just as bad, but she forced herself to press on. They sheltered the night in a home just off the road. It was small, but that was better. Easier to heat. She plucked pine cones from the yard and they dug out the seeds with their knives.

On the third day, the rice ran out. Ellie was hungry from the moment she got up till the minute she went to bed. They needed more food than they'd been eating; they were only advancing about fifteen miles a day, but each one was grueling. The best pine cones yielded just a dime-sized pile of seeds and extracting them was laborious. But with such sparse game, and snow covering anything green, that was how they spent their nights, prying seeds lose with the tips of their knives while the fire crackled and their socks steamed. Ellie passed around the chocolate she'd meant to barter. She hadn't eaten chocolate in two years and it tasted so sweet it hurt her mouth.

She watched the horizons for smoke and the towns for signs of life: anywhere she could trade her tea and silver for bread and meat. Near Kingston, a column of smoke climbed to meet the gray clouds, but it was in the western foothills a half day's walk through the woods. Any survivors from these lands had moved away from the road or learned to hide the evidence of their lives.

No sooner had the sun come up than Dee shot a squirrel from the tree. As Ellie dressed it, forcing Dee to observe and learn, Hobson blasted a rabbit across the road. He cleaned it and they built a fire and spitted the meat and ate right there. It was greasy and gamey, but after a day of nothing but pine nuts, it tasted like fresh honey.

After that, they didn't eat for two days.

They soon grew silent, focused on the snow ahead, on smoothing a trail for the two behind them, on the grumbling of their guts and the aches in their legs and heads. With an hour of daylight left, they quit marching to scour the homes of a subdivision, but the canned corn they turned up was bulging with botulism.

Ellie stood on the front porch and stared at the snow-clogged street. At the corner, a yellow lab bounded from behind a home, snow spraying with each jerky leap. Ellie raised her rifle and set her eye behind the scope.

"What are you doing?" Dee said behind her.

Ellie lowered the gun. "Thought it was chasing a rabbit."

That night, she ate more pine nuts. She could feel the hollowness in her belly but it no longer hurt. She dreamt she swept the snow away from the back garden and revealed a potato casserole, still warm. Ellie knew it wasn't a sign—it couldn't be—but when she woke, she went out back with a snow shovel and dug down to the grass.

At best, they were halfway to New York. The snow was an inch or two shallower than it had been outside Albany but still deep enough to snarl bicycles. She figured it would be another five days on foot. With their stomachs empty and their muscles flagging, they wouldn't make it.

While Dee was out using the bathroom and brushing her teeth, Hobson walked up beside Ellie. "Well?"

"Well what?" she said.

"As to the matter of our impending starvation."

"We'll find something."

"Perhaps we could hasten that process by dedicating half a day to a deer hunt."

She scowled into the glare of the snow. "Seen any tracks?"

"A few," he said, voice pitched high with the concession that he might be generous with his estimate. "And I doubt the game warden will fine us if we happen to bag a doe."

She laughed dryly. "How can there be so much land and so little to eat?"

"There's plenty to eat. The problem is nature has helpfully preserved it beneath a foot of goddamn snow."

"My fear is we go out to hunt and come back with nothing. Meanwhile, there could be a populated settlement two miles down the road, or wasteland all the way to New York. What's the right move?"

He rubbed his hand across his salt and pepper stubble. "That's the conundrum, isn't it? All we can do is guess."

"I'm not much for guessing."

"So I gathered." The back door slammed. Dee scuffed her boots. Hobson raised his eyebrows. "So?"

"We'll see what the road brings today." Ellie wasn't certain she was making the right call, but the act of deciding brought strength back to her nerves. "If it's more nothing, we'll hunt tomorrow. Wait any longer and we might not have the energy."

"Fortunately for us, it doesn't take much get up and go to sit behind a tree and wait for a buck to snort." He clapped her shoulder. "We'll make it, Ellie."

"What are you guys talking about?" Dee said.

"Think we'll try hunting tomorrow," Ellie said. Maybe it was just the tan she'd earned from the sun on the snow, but Dee's cheeks looked sharper. "Some venison would be pretty good about now, right?"

"Right now, a pig's asshole would taste pretty good."

"Jesus!"

"Wouldn't it? Some butter and pepper? Sweet potatoes on the side?"

Ellie refused to dignify that. Especially since denying it would be a lie. They strapped on their snowshoes and hefted their packs and continued into the white.

The cars on the shoulder of the highway were suggestions of steel under snowy drapes. Ellie's knees didn't want to lift, but she forced herself to smooth the trail, one step after another, using the rote repetition of her feet to prevent her head from dwelling on the emptiness of her stomach. She had never been without food for so long. Not even after the collapse. If anything, it had been easier then. Such a swift and total end that kitchens and pantries were full of cans and jars and sealed bags. Every house you visited yielded a new buffet.

But those days were gone. The leftovers had spoiled or been

devoured. The old world was now as bereft as the blank plains of the Hudson Valley. You coaxed your life from that, or you starved.

They had done that, the people of the lakes. Even George, troubled as his farm became, had built a lasting corner for himself. He and Quinn hadn't wanted, not truly; Ellie's farm produced enough for the lot of them. Self-sufficient, independent, they would have been immune to the tricks and temptations of outsiders.

But George's shortcuts doomed him. His pride ate holes in that armor of self-sufficiency. He couldn't bring himself to rely on Ellie—whether because she was a woman, or simply a person who wasn't himself—no matter how temporarily, no matter how close their two families were to becoming one. So the offer of the men in the black fedoras had penetrated that armor like a crossbow bolt: take on our line of credit, and everything you deserve can become yours.

It was a hook like any other, attached to a transparent line of terrible strength. And the mouth at the end was always hungry.

A fat flake of snow struck her face. She blinked, then laughed. Gone delirious with hunger. She breathed, bringing herself back. And saw a column of smoke not long to the west.

She stopped and pointed. "Smoke."

Tired and hungry, the others had been paying all their attention to their feet. They looked up, wary, as if language could no longer be trusted.

Hobson's whole face brightened. "How interesting."

"People?" Dee said.

"Has to be." Ellie brought her binoculars to her face and saw black. She'd left the lens cap on. She pulled it off and tried again. The woods were much too dense, but she didn't need to see the house to know it was there. The smoke of a forest fire would form a plane. This was a single rising line.

"Shall we approach?" Hobson said. "Or do you deem it too risky?"

"Everything we do now is a risk." She capped her binoculars, oriented herself to the hills, and stepped off the road.

Scattered snowflakes sieved through the trees. A squirrel chided them from the branches and Ellie reached for her gun, then thought perhaps it wouldn't do to be shooting at things on their way to a stranger's home. It smelled of snow, like always, but within ten minutes, she smelled smoke, too. Somehow, it reminded her of bacon. Her stomach sprang to life with a fierce ache.

The home waited in a clearing of tree trunks and drifted snow. Its lower windows were boarded over and the side of the yard was filled with trucks in various states of dismantling. A pillar of gray smoke unfurled from the chimney. The home was painted dull brown with irregular black zebra stripes—woodland camouflage.

"Careful," Ellie said. "But try not to look like you're being too careful."

"What?" Dee said.

Ellie opened her mouth to holler a greeting. The front door parted before she got out a single word. A man stood in the doorway, bearded, rifle in hand. "Keep your hands where I can see them."

"We're out of food," Ellie said.

"Eat each other. Problem solved."

"I've got trade. Gold, silver—"

He snorted, breath misting in the cold. "I'm a man, not a crow. I don't give a shit about shiny rocks."

"Coffee," she tried. "Tea. Some medicine, maybe."

"'Maybe' like St. John's nonsense? Or the good stuff?"

"Pharmaceutical. And 'maybe' as in I don't want to give it up."

"There's a reason 'pain' starts with 'pay.'" He glanced between them. "Where you from?"

"Up north."

The man smiled. "You ask inside our home, but all you'll trust us with is 'up north'?"

"Albany," she said. The lie was instinctive, and she knew at once it was a bad one. Her mind had seized the first name that wandered through it. It was the kind of mistake she could only have made after days of nonstop effort without food.

"Albany," he said, before she could backtrack, rolling the word around his mouth like a piece of hard candy. He was early middle-aged and had an upstate accent whose stretched vowels sounded tailor-made for bellowing across the wooded valleys of New York. "What brings you down here?"

"Looking for someone."

"Bet you are," he mused. He tipped his head toward the house. "Come on in."

They filed up the steps, Hobson taking up the rear. As he entered, the man scanned the yard, face somber, and closed the door. With the windows boarded, the front rooms rested in twilight; in the back of the house, the kitchen was bright with snow-reflected sun.

Ellie more or less stopped functioning as soon as they got inside. The whole house smelled like roasting chicken.

"Let me grab my wife," the man said.

He left them alone in the kitchen where a round-topped wood-fired oven crisped the skin of a bird that had been born for Ellie to eat. Her mouth flooded with saliva. Between the smoke, the smell, and the sudden warmth after hours of cold marching, Ellie was mesmerized. The few non-food thoughts she was capable of fielding were directed toward restructuring the remainder of their trip. If they bartered for enough food that they wouldn't have to forage, they could make the city in five days. Four, if they pressed hard. Meanwhile, the odds of dying in an emaciated huddle in the middle of the road receded beyond the horizon.

"God damn slavers," a woman said behind them.

Ellie whirled. A young woman faced them, eyes wide-set and furious. She pointed a double-barreled shotgun at Ellie's chest. Behind her, the bearded man walked across the linoleum, steel handcuffs glinting in his hands.

19

"Lucy?" Tilly clung hard to the wall at the edge of the roof, listing like the tower had tilted twenty degrees. "What did you do to me?"

"I drugged you, idiot." Lucy strolled across the rooftop. "Now be a good girl and go to sleep."

Tilly's eyes were as wild as a newborn foal's and her knees were just as weak; when she tried to bolt, her leg wobbled and she sat down hard. "Ow."

"Hold still before you hurt yourself."

Tilly blinked and slapped at the ground, dragging herself toward the doorway. Lucy sighed and stepped in front of her. Tilly smacked at her shins, limp-handed, then slumped to her back and tried to roll through Lucy like a log on a slope. She banged into Lucy's legs and rocked to a stop.

"He'll come for me," the girl slurred. Her eyes were outlined with kohl like an Egyptian queen. "He'll rescue me. You'll rue it."

Lucy laughed. "Rue what, precisely?"

"All that which is rueful." Tilly gazed up at the clouds and stars, breathing shallowly. Lucy folded her arms and waited. Tilly's eyes closed. She snored softly.

Lucy went to the edge of the roof for a look at the street, then picked Tilly up and slung her halfway over her shoulder, smelling peach perfume. At the door, Lucy shifted her weight to free her hand and open it, then trudged onto the landing.

She had a problem. The stairs were pitch black. And there were a lot of them. Tilly weighed on her like a sack of oats; no way she could carry a candle and her friend's fat ass.

After a moment's thought, she plunked Tilly on the landing, fired up a candle, set it on the landing below, then went back up for Tilly. Bracing herself against the wall, she plodded down the steps, bearing Tilly to the landing below the candle, where it was now too dark to proceed. She lowered Tilly, caught her breath, went up for the candle, and brought it to the landing below the unconscious girl, who she then picked up again and bore another flight lower until the light got too wimpy to go on.

It was a hell of a lot of work. Especially heaving Tilly up off the cement each time. But it beat the tar out of stumbling in the dark and breaking both their necks. The stairwell was nearly as cold as the night, but by the time she got downstairs, she was damp with sweat, tremble-legged, and utterly out of breath.

She rested on the lobby's cool tile, Tilly sprawled beside her. Among her other preparations, she'd gone to a gardening supply store for a wheelbarrow, which she'd left in the front corner of the lobby where Tilly would be unlikely to see it. Or to care, even if she did notice. All kinds of junk was abandoned at odd places around the city. The cause was obvious: with all this free shit lying around, scavengers gathered it up by the packload, only to swiftly decide that it was too heavy, bulky, or outright useless to carry after all. As a result, debris was scattered hither and yon, and tended to pile up at places where transportation was difficult (such as stairs; Lucy had had to clean this building's stairwell top to bottom before enacting her plan) or where a sudden case of reality set in (like outside doorways, where people remembered just how long of a walk they had ahead of them, or at curbs, where they tried to hop on bikes and discovered they were too top-heavy to continue). After a while, you got to where you hardly noticed, but every now and then, when you stumbled over a speaker on a staircase or a herd of Beanie Babies on the sidewalk, you'd swear that, now all the humans were gone, the objects had decided to get up and walk around like the tiger in Calvin and Hobbes.

As soon as Lucy had the strength to stand again, she hoisted Tilly inside the wheelbarrow, careful not to whack the girl's lolling head on the metal rim, shouldered her pack, and pushed her way out the front door, rubber wheel bouncing down the steps.

She grinned at the night. The next few miles would be a bitch, but they were all that stood between her and getting out of this wretched place.

She got less than a block before footsteps pounded down the street.

Lucy swerved into the nearest storefront and leaned around the corner. Five men ran down the street and headed straight for the apartment she'd just extracted Tilly from. One of the runners kept his back so straight it didn't look like he was moving at all. Dark as it was, Lucy knew that stillness anywhere. Nerve.

He headed into the apartment building with two of the men. The other pair stayed outside, eyes on the street. Tilly made a choking noise, like she was gagging on her own spit. Lucy grabbed her chin and turned it sideways and the noise stopped.

Five minutes later, Nerve walked out the front door and spoke to his people. While two remained streetside, the other three went door to door. Lucy wheeled Tilly inside the store. It smelled heavily of leather. Coats hung from racks, but others had been cast to the floor, snarling the lanes. She powered through them and located a staircase that fed into the upstairs apartments. Quietly as she could, she ran up to the third floor, found an unlocked door, stashed her bag, and came back for Tilly, whose white shins dangled from the edges of the wheelbarrow, legs spread most unladylike. Outside, men called back and forth, growing nearer.

Lucy picked Tilly up. Her back twinged. Halfway up the third floor, she slipped on a step and crashed down on the side of her foot. Her ankle collapsed. Pain rifled up her ligaments. Somehow, she hung tight to Tilly, mashing the girl into the wall to prevent them both from falling. Someone shouted, muffled. Using the wall for support, Lucy slid upright. White heat shot directly from her leg to her brain, but the initial pain had already begun to fade, and she forced herself to climb on. Tilly's warm body dragged her down like a thousand pounds of sun-baked sidewalk. She got to the third floor landing, gasped for breath, then limped her way to the apartment and locked the door.

She threw Tilly down on the bed, generating a cloud of dust, and slumped her back against the door. Tears of pain slid down her cheeks. Things had gone from swell to fucked in a hurry. Tilly must have left the forged note in her apartment. Nerve found it, saw his faked handwriting, gathered his people, and ran straight for the address. That was some garbage luck right there. Ten more minutes and she'd have been half a mile away. Another hour and she could have been up into Kono territory. Ghosted, gone.

She went to the window and parted the blinds. Two men had run off to have a scout around, but the others continued their methodical sweep of the street. They weren't in much hurry. But she'd left a time on the note, too. Nerve would know she couldn't have gotten far.

"Tilly?" he called, voice echoing down the channels between the buildings. "Are you there?"

Lucy smiled harshly. He would delay her, that's all. Soon as they moved on, she'd wheel Tilly across the river, load her in the trunk, and drive on back home.

Something thumped heavily to the floor. Beside the bed, Tilly swayed on her hands and knees, head hanging, drooling on the carpet.

"Where are we?" she said, spit gleaming on the corner of her mouth.

"What kind of bum drugs did that boy sell me?" Lucy said. "I just sent you under not thirty minutes ago!"

"Tilly!" Nerve called.

"Is that him?" Tilly tried to stand and fell to her knees. She looked up at Lucy, hair dangling down her eyes, and laughed like such a Hollywood imbecile it made Lucy want to cry. "I told you he'd come for me. He loves me."

"You're drugged," Lucy said.

She laughed some more. "He's gonna be so mad at you."

"He won't have the chance."

"Think so? I think when I scream my little lungs out, he'll come running like the wind."

Lucy clenched her teeth. "You keep your mouth shut."

"Or what?" Tilly grinned. "You'll shoot me?"

"I'll shoot him." She grabbed her umbrella from beside the door. "Moment he steps in the door, I'll sponge-paint the walls with his guts."

Tilly's face grew somber. "You can't do that. I'll warn him."

"Then maybe I'll bash your teeth in. I never made no promises about saving those."

The other girl blinked heavily, mouth hanging half open. "What are you talking about?"

"Quit talking or you'll find out."

Miraculously, Tilly obeyed. On the street, men went in and out of fast food joints and dress shops and discount shoe outlets, giving each store no more than a minute or two before moving to the next. Weren't going door to door, then. About time she caught a break.

"What do you think happens next?" Tilly said, more quiet and lucid than before.

"Once they get tired of hunting for your replaceable ass, we walk on out of here."

"I'm not leaving the city."

Lucy braced her umbrella across her knees and put on a special-big grin. "I'm afraid you don't have a choice."

Tilly rolled her eyes. "And then what, genius?"

"We take a walk across the river. I got a car parked over there. Town's got the most ridiculous name you ever heard."

"After that. Back home. You think I'll be grateful? That I'll learn my lesson? Jesus, do you think we're friends?"

Lucy looked from the window. "How do you mean?"

"We barely spoke the last year!"

"Friends don't need to see each other every day. We were off doing our own things, that's all."

Tilly laughed sickly, then touched her temple. "My head hurts, you dumb bitch."

Lucy rooted around in her pack and flipped Tilly a white pill. "Here."

"What's this?"

"You think I'm gonna drug you again?"

"Don't try to play innocent with me. I know you far too well."

"It's Advil." Anger welled up inside Lucy. "What's your problem?"

The girl shook her head and dry-swallowed the pill. "Don't even start."

"Is this about Lloyd?"

"My boyfriend? Why would you think that?"

From the window, Lucy thrust her finger at Tilly's chest. "Ex."

"You think that makes it better? What kind of fool doesn't know you don't go after a girl's ex?"

"There aren't exactly many dudes around town these days. You expect me to cross state lines every time I want some dick?"

Tilly snorted and looked to the ceiling in disbelief. "Do you have any idea how selfish you are?"

"You should talk," Lucy said. "You're the one who fucked Jordan Brewster."

Her eyes snapped to Lucy's. "I did not!"

"That's what I told him when he was bragging around school. Then he told me about the scar on your butt. The one you got from the nail on the dock."

Tilly squeezed her temples, eyes shut, voice gone weary. "We didn't have sex. I went down on him. Didn't even take my bra off."

"And even though he was gonna be my first boyfriend, I forgave you. Boys are just boys. There's always a new one. They're nothing to wreck a friendship over."

"This isn't about Jordan or Lloyd or any other boy, Lucy. Sometimes the past just adds up. For me, that town is nothing but bad memories."

"Well, I don't believe that at all," Lucy said. "That's where you grew up."

"Exactly!" Tilly laughed. "You should know all about it. The way the other kids treated you? That's where you want to stay your whole life?"

"We had fun, too. What about the Sunday we went down to the river and we fished and swam around and dried off on the rocks? And while we were lying there, you said what if we just never left? So we stayed the night, even though we had school the next day and your parents would be worried sick."

"They cussed me blue. Surprised they didn't slap me red, too."

"Or when Myra Lowe got that Mercedes for her birthday. Remember? It wasn't even new, but she was so snotty about it. Gunning it out of the parking lot. Swearing at us when we were walking home. But I knew she kept her keys in her locker, so you said we should teacher her a lesson about—what was it, 'the temporal nature of material things'?—and we stole them, and you drove that Mercedes right out of the school lot. Drove around town until it was running on fumes, then you crashed it into the ditch!"

Tilly frowned. "Lucy, that's not how it happened."

Lucy quit cackling. "They had to winch it out. Whole front end was as busted as Myra. Remember?"

"I said we should park it in the lot behind the school to give her a scare. You're the one who was driving. When you drove it into the ditch, I swear to God I thought I was going to die."

"I don't think so. I think you were driving."

Tilly shook her head. "You cut your eyebrow on the steering wheel. You probably still got the scar."

Lucy thumbed a small ridge on her eyebrow. Down in the street, two men approached their building and disappeared inside. "Well, I know this much. You were there with me, and you were enjoying yourself."

"Whatever. I don't care about what happened then. That's the whole point."

"You can't do that!" Lucy bolted upright. Something clunked down on the street. Her survival instincts squeezed her wrath dead; it evaporated, leaving her pain crystallized and inert. Her voice, a shout just seconds before, was steady and low. "You were my friend. The only one I ever had besides my cat, and he didn't have a choice. Then one day you quit on me without a word. Well, you can't do that. You owe me."

"What kind of ass-backwards logic is that?" Tilly said. "I never had to be your friend in the first place."

"But you did. So that means you got to stick with me. It was like all of a sudden you got too pretty to be seen with me."

"Oh please. You had nothing to worry about, Black Swan."

"Then what? Was I too low-down?" Motion in the street. Lucy waited for the men to go inside the next building before she continued. "How were you supposed to get invited to their parties when you hung around with a girl whose momma was a meth head?"

Tilly crossed her arms tight and jutted her jaw. "You make me sick, throwing all this on me. You duck blame like it's thrown at your head."

"What did I do?"

The girl laughed, harsh and righteous. "My dad the saint brings you into our house. Six months later, my mom moves out. You think I can't add two and two?"

Lucy understood at once, but it was a long moment before she could find the words. "You think me and your dad?"

"Quit it! God, the way you lie, it makes me want to vomit."

"Nothing happened!"

"That's not what my mom said. You do nothing but take with no regard for anyone else. First you take my dad from me, and when that isn't enough, you take him as a man. It so happens this takes my mom from me, but do you care? Not one whit. You just stuck around, eating up our food, stinking up our garage. And then—and this is the biggest joke of them all—you were the one with him when he died."

"Is that what you think?" Lucy got quiet as church. "What's the matter with you? Why didn't you say something?"

"Like you'd listen?" Tilly's eyes got as bright and red as embers when you blew off the ash. "What was I supposed to say? 'Hey buddy, you mind keeping your panties on around my dad'?"

"Once he took me in, your dad was my dad. I could never have done a thing like that."

Tears blipped down her cheeks. "Then why did my mom think you did?"

Lucy sighed shakily. "The way he talked, she wasn't happy with him even before I moved in. Then he's got a teen girl around—and a troubled on at that—and her middle-aged mind starts going crazy. No wonder she made me sleep in the garage."

"I told her you could share my room. She said it would only encourage you to keep taking things that weren't yours to have."

Lucy pressed her knuckles against her brow. "I'm mean when I don't have to be and I get mad too easy and I'll shoot a man who looks at me cross. But when a person treats me right and doesn't want a thing in return, I won't never betray them or let them down."

Tilly's voice was dreamy. "I know all that. Why do you think we made friends in the first place? You were the toughest girl I ever saw."

"You believe me?" Relief washed across her heart. "Then how about we walk out of here?"

"Walk out? I got a new life here. A job and a boyfriend and everything that makes life life. Do I got a new perspective on the past? Well, maybe so. Goody-gumdrops for me. But I can't pick up on the past like all the years between were nothing but a bad dream."

"You can't stay here, Tilly. A fight's coming. And Nerve and Distro are right in the middle."

Tilly swatted her hand through the air. "Little boys trying on their daddy's pants. Once they calm down, everything will be peaches and schnapps." She'd quit crying, but a tendril of drool spooled from the corner of her mouth. She touched it and blinked at her glistening fingers. "You bitch. That was no Advil."

"I'm sorry," Lucy said. "But I made a promise to keep you safe."

Tilly tried to stand, but her legs were no good. She sprawled on the rug and glared at Lucy. "Why does everything always got to be your way?"

"'Cause I'm the only one who ain't blind," she murmured.

Tilly fought to stay awake, propping herself on an elbow and pinching the skin above her hip, but after a minute, her head sagged to the rug. Lucy made sure she was breathing okay, then returned to the window to watch the men work their way down the street.

She felt as clean as a spring rain. And, against all odds, grateful toward Tilly. The girl must have hated her with the heat of a stove. That's why she distanced herself that year before the plague. But afterward, she came back. Lucy couldn't delude herself about the why—Tilly had known that if anyone was to make it through the aftermath, it would be Lucy—but she liked to think that, as they'd begun their new life together, Tilly had been making an effort to reconcile, too.

For a while, they'd gotten back to normal. Between themselves, anyway; meanwhile, the rest of the world had gotten fucked up like you wouldn't believe. But Tilly had tried to put the past behind them. Lucy could see that now. They'd set up a couple of homes right down the block from each other, sowed gardens, gone fishing in the sea, shot possums and squirrels in the woods. If Lucy hadn't had that drunken tumble with Lloyd, could be they'd still be neighbors in sunny, quiet Florida.

The sex hadn't meant a thing to Lucy, but it had meant the world to Tilly. Once more, her best friend was coming after the only man she cared for. But rather than beating Lucy's face in, or slitting her throat in her sleep, Tilly had run off to New York without one hurt word. Because she wasn't like Lucy. She was a good person. Heart as gold as a field of corn.

A drop of water hit the windowsill. Her eyes stung. She couldn't remember crying since she'd been the smallest little girl. Another droplet hit the outside of the window and slid down the pane. It was snowing.

Lucy pressed her face to the window. It was frigid on her cheek and her nose fogged the glass. A block away, Nerve pointed at the sky. The men gathered, shaking their heads, gesturing this way and that. They pulled their collars up to their chins and walked away.

She gave them ten minutes to clear out. Would have preferred longer, but she didn't trust the second dose to last any longer than the first. She brought her bag downstairs to the clothing store, then climbed back up for Tilly. Her legs weren't too happy about this repeat performance, and her tweaked ankle had a few complaints as well (though it was in far better shape than she'd initially feared), but at least it was only two flights of stairs. She took them without a candle, feeling each step forward, gruelingly slow. At the bottom, she lowered Tilly to the wheelbarrow, covered her with a puffy black winter coat off the racks, and wheeled her outside.

Snow sifted darkly to the streets and melted there. Wind swirled between the buildings in irregular gusts, twirling the flakes, driving them sidelong at Lucy's face. She put on wool gloves and headed northwest.

She'd spent enough time on the Twelfth Avenue rooftops to know the stone arches of Lincoln Tunnel were less than half a mile away. She drove the wheelbarrow steadily along, its rubber wheel whispering over the pavement. Snow stuck to Tilly's hair and melted on her face. It was going to be a long roll to the car, particularly if Tilly woke again, but Lucy had some nice thin rope and it was easy enough to make a gag. One way or another, they'd soon be gone. Who the hell wanted to live a place where it snowed?

As she entered the looping, spaghetti-strand snarl of the roads leading to the tunnels, an analog bullhorn boomed from the rooftops.

Lucy stared up in disbelief. The man's voice repeated, calling out her location. Lucy leaned into the wheelbarrow and made a break for the tunnels. Footsteps pounded from two directions, ricocheting between the shops and offices. She curved along the road and entered the high-walled culvert feeding to the dark mouth of the tunnel.

Hampered by the wheelbarrow, she couldn't manage more than jogging speed. Shoes slapped toward her. "Lucy!"

She slowed, reaching for her umbrella.

"One more inch and I shoot you in the back."

She stopped and sighed, too weary and too close to her goal to muster more than exasperation. Nerve strode up to her, pistol extended from his body.

"What's the big deal?" Lucy said. "I'm just doing my laundry."

"You are kidnapping a Distro employee." He stopped five feet away, strands of slick black hair blowing in his eyes. "One who means very much to me."

"She was never supposed to be here. It was all a misunderstanding. Why don't you go back to your big-city business and let us country gals get on with ours?"

"Because she's mine. You should pray that her sense of loyalty is stronger than yours. You know what I do to traitors?"

"Bring them a car so you never have to see them again?"

He pulled the trigger. The bang roared between the culvert walls. The bullet struck Lucy square in the chest like a mustang's kick.

She dropped to her seat. Snow battered her face, but she felt warmly numb and giddy, as if her body were about to laugh at the silly thing that had just been done to it. Nerve took her umbrella from the wheelbarrow, pocketed the shells, and tossed it to the street with a clatter. One of his troops jogged up and took her bag.

Nerve lifted Tilly's head and spoke her name. She slept on. He scooped her from the wheelbarrow, threw her over his shoulder, patted her butt, and spat on Lucy. She wanted to stand, but she had never felt weaker in all her life.

20

"Hang on," Ellie said. "There's been a mistake."

The woman kept the gun trained on her chest. The man approached and motioned Ellie to turn around. "The mistake was letting you people live the first time you came around."

He took away her gun and slid it across the floor to his wife. Ellie tried to catch Hobson's gaze. "Our people? I haven't been through here since the Panhandler."

Sheriff Hobson smiled tightly. "I believe the good man thinks we're associated with the Albany Clavans. Ironic, given that we oppose—"

"Quiet down, you old fart." The bearded man pulled Ellie's wrists behind her back and closed the handcuffs on her with a click of steel teeth.

"We're from Saranac Lake," Ellie said quickly. "The Clavans—"

The man grabbed the chain of her cuffs and twisted. Metal bit into her skin. Her arm bent against her side, pain flaring in her elbow. She inhaled with a hiss.

"Last warning," the man said. "One more word and my wife repaints the kitchen with you."

The cold wrath in his voice made Ellie a believer. He disarmed and cuffed Hobson and Dee. With the woman's shotgun trained on their backs, he marched them down steep stairs to an unfinished cellar. Tubs and bins lined the walls. Sunlight fought through the snow muffling two narrow windows high on the back wall.

"Sit down," he said.

"Sir," Hobson said gently. "We are hunting down the very people who hurt you. I am a sheriff. Tell me the crimes against you and I vow to do my utmost to bring you justice."

The man seemed to consider this, then slammed a right hook into Hobson's jaw. Unsuspecting, hands bound, Hobson dropped straight to the dusty concrete. The man turned on Ellie and Dee. The woman held the shotgun steady. Ellie knelt, gaze locked on the woman's trigger finger. Dee lowered herself and sat on her heels.

The man turned and clumped up the stairs. The woman followed. He closed the door. Metal scraped from the other side. A heavy padlock clunked shut.

"What are they doing?" Dee whispered.

"Getting friends or equipment. Neither option's good."

"Sheriff Hobson?" Dee shook the old man's shoulder, but he remained lost to the world. His slack face and the egg-white skin beneath his eyes looked much older, as if the spark in his eyes were all that kept the decades at bay.

Ellie cast around the dim room. Dee had her dark hair in a ponytail, her ragged bangs clipped tight to her temple.

"Your bobby pin," Ellie said.

"I think he's hurt," Dee said.

"We don't have time. Lean down and close your eyes."

Dee cocked her head, but did as she was told. Ellie turned her back so her cuffed hands could reach Dee. She owled her head over her shoulder and groped the side of the girl's head, working her fingernail under the pin. She slid it loose and sat down.

"Do you know what you're doing?" Dee said.

"They trained us for extreme situations," Ellie said. She didn't mention that training had been fifteen years ago and she hadn't messed with handcuffs ever since.

But she remembered the basics. She was cuffed so tight she couldn't get a good angle on her own keyholes, so she had Dee turn her back and extend her wrists. She worked the tip of the pin into the keyhole of Dee's cuffs and bent it to a sharp angle. She brought it out, inspected it over her shoulder, then worked it back inside and added a second bend so the end of the pin resembled a hard-angled S.

Tool in hand, she went to work. With her back to Dee, she couldn't see a thing, but she was working by feel anyway. And after a minute of poking and prying, what she felt was a double lock.

"Son of a bitch," she muttered.

"You got it?" Dee said.

"It's a double. Tricky." She talked it out to help see it in her mind's eye. "You have to work a bar out of the way, then engage the lock."

She explored the lock, twisting the pin, prodding around for the bar, which wasn't easy, given that she didn't know what it felt like. She pushed this way and that, trying to find a piece that would give.

Upstairs, feet thumped across the floors. A door opened and shut. The house fell silent except for the tiny metal clicks of the pin in the cuffs. Five minutes later, Ellie was sweating and frustrated to the point of tears. The pin caught. She pushed, trying to spring the bar, but the bobby pin bent under the pressure and popped free. Ellie cried out and slung it down between them.

"You okay?" Dee said.

"Think I had it. Pin bent on me. I just need a minute to calm down."

"Can I try?"

"Dee, this isn't how it looks in the movies. You have to practice like crazy to get a feel for it."

There was a sudden pause. "I have."

"What, when you were raising hell with Chip? That was ages ago."

"Quinn likes to be...restrained," Dee said. "One time I lost the keys. It took me three hours to get them off him. Would have been much faster, but he kept getting h—"

"La la la!" Ellie said. "I am absolutely not hearing about the sex life of my daughter who damn well better be using condoms!"

"They're all expired." Dee's fingers brushed hers, searching for the pin. "After that, I started practicing. Just in case, and because it was fun. Now hold still."

The tone of her voice made it perfectly clear this was not the first time she'd spoken those words. Ellie forced herself to think about Colorado Rockies games and the cold Snapple she used to drink after a long run. The cuffs twitched against her wrists. With a metal click, the pressure disappeared from her right wrist. Dee moved to the left bracelet and got it off in half the time.

"You have to wiggle the tip past the housing," Dee said. "Push the bar the opposite direction that the cuffs close. Once it pops, spring the main lock like normal."

"Is that all," Ellie said, but when she set to work on Dee's cuffs, they yielded quickly.

Dee shook out her wrists and then gave Hobson's shoulder a nudge. "Sheriff? Mom, do you think he's hurt?"

"Could be concussed." Ellie went to the wall and dragged a heavy plastic bin below the window. It was completely snowed in and so narrow she wasn't sure her head would fit, let alone her butt.

"What are you doing?"

"Oh, I don't know. I was thinking about getting out of here before Mr. Manson and bride return to torture us to death."

Dee sat back next to the sheriff. "What about Mr. Hobson?"

"He won't fit through the window." Ellie heaved another tub atop the first and gave the structure a shake. Wobbled a bit, but it was weighty enough to hold her.

"You want to leave him."

"Pick his locks. If he wakes up, at least he'll have a fighting chance."

"What are you talking about?" Dee's voice was as high as the window. "We can't leave him to die! He's the one who knew that body wasn't Quinn."

"I would have figured that out," Ellie said. "The upstairs door is padlocked. He's not our family. If you want to see Quinn again, we have to get out now."

"That's the result I want." Dee glared across the vacant cellar. "But I don't want a damn thing to do with the process. That's what you're always talking about, right? It's not the results, it's the process. Well, in my book, any process that leaves a man who's helped us behind to die is a big fat pile of shit."

Ellie gaped. "It's a better process than the one that gets us all killed!"

"Run on outside. The sheriff and I will catch up in a minute." She shook the man's shoulder. He groaned, eyes closed.

Ellie climbed the tubs to the window, measuring its width with her palm. It was single-paned and frosted with ice. She hopped down and put her palm to Hobson's hip.

"Get his cuffs off," she said. "I'll wake him up."

Dee grinned and got the pin from her pocket. While she clicked away, Ellie snapped her fingers in front of the sheriff's eyes, slapped his cheek. The upstairs creaked. Ellie glanced up, then pinched the tender skin right beneath the sheriff's lip. He snorted and smacked her hand, eyes blinking.

"I am on the ground," he said. "Who put me here and for what purpose?"

"To shut you up," Ellie said. "So I doubt this is a new experience for you. Feel okay? What's your name?"

"Oliver Marion Hobson, and I don't know what day it is because we've been traipsing through this dratted snow for so long I've lost count." He sat up, hair askew, and rubbed the back of his head; Dee had only picked one of the locks and the handcuffs dangled from his wrist, smacking the back of his neck.

Dee scowled and bent to pick up the bobby pin. "I'm still working."

"My apologies, young lady." He put his palm on the ground with a clack of steel, waggled his jaw back and forth, then looked surprised. "You're the one who's lubricating our escape?"

Dee snickered and pried at the lock. Hobson turned to Ellie. "Did I say something funny?"

Ellie stood. "No. You said something horrible. And unless you want me to knock you right back out, you'll never mention this again."

Hobson looked baffled. "I missed something. But I'm old enough to understand that my ignorance grows by the day and it's best to befriend it. So: where are we and what are we doing?"

"Cellar. Thinking of a way out." Ellie crept up the stairs and pressed her ear to the peeling paint on the door. She tried the door and it jarred against the padlock on the other side.

"Are those windows as small as they look from here?"

"Out of the question. Unless you're willing to cut off half your ass."

He laughed dourly. "I'm far too fond of sitting to part with half of my favorite cushion."

"Door's padlocked." Ellie moved down the steps. "Could try to kick it down, but I expect them back any minute."

Dee sprung the bracelet from Hobson's right hand. He smiled

warmly and rubbed his wrists. "A pretty girl who can pick a lock. If you were ten years older, I might be in love."

"Sheriff."

"Old fashioned ambush?" he transitioned. "They'll never expect it. She'll be lucky to get off a shot."

"With that shotgun, one shot might be all she needs." Ellie scanned the basement. The stairs were open underneath. The main drain pipe descended from the ceiling and out the wall. A couple of sinks collected dust against the front wall. Besides that and the tubs of goods, there was no cover. "If he comes down first, we can't get to her. She'll murder us."

"So we set up atop the stairs. Rush them the instant they pull the lock."

"Only room for one of us."

"I volunteer." He waved a hand through the air, dismissing any objections. "Do you know the natural span of the human life? Without modern drugs, treatment, and surgery, it is roughly 64 years. I have lived a full 90% of my allotted span. If it ends now, I won't feel cheated."

Ellie gestured at the bins. "Try to find weapons. We don't have much time."

They popped the lids and pawed through the contents. Many were filled with dried fruit, meat, and grain. The three of them stuffed handfuls into their mouths and chewed as they searched. Many of the others contained enough toiletries to last three generations. Including two dozen cans of hairspray.

Ellie held up her lighter. "What do you think?"

"Crude," Hobson said, "but crude methods are often the most terrifying."

"I'll be right behind you on the stairs. Dee, I want you next to the window. If we don't make it, you run. Find Quinn. Live your lives."

Dee's expression curled in on itself. "You're not going to get shot."

"All we know is we're about to bum rush an armed woman," Ellie said. "Once the door opens, anything can happen."

The look on Dee's face said she was tired of Ellie's ongoing argument that they didn't and couldn't know jack about shit, but Dee showed no interest in poking it further. The girl climbed up the tubs under the window and thumbed open the rusty catch. The window held firm, then opened with a squeak that probably sounded much louder than it actually was. Powdered snow tumbled through the gap.

Hobson flicked the lighter, testing it, then spritzed the hairspray. "If this explodes, at least I'll be blessed with the dramatic exit I've always deserved."

He climbed the stairs and set up an inch from the door. Ellie crouched on the steps behind him. The couple had already been gone longer than she could have hoped. When five more minutes went by, she began to think they might be able to kick open the door without being heard—had the two gone to the neighbors? Fallen off a cliff?—but before she could convince herself to dry, the back door creaked open. Boots stomped repeatedly, knocking off the snow. A key scrabbled into the padlock. The door opened.

Hobson bowled through it. Ellie leapt in behind him. The bearded man stared in shock, a metal toolbox in hand. Behind him, his wife's shotgun dangled from the crook of her arm. Hobson streamed hairspray and flicked his lighter.

It burst with a whoomp of light and heat. The bearded man screamed. The stench of burnt hair filled the small landing. The man fell back, legs kicking, knocking into his wife. Thrown off balance, her shot blasted into the side of the kitchen sink. Ellie knifed past the man and grabbed the gun. The barrel was smoking hot; she slid her grip down, grabbed the stock with her other hand, and twisted. Fingerbones snapped and popped. The woman shrieked. Ellie yanked the gun away and butted the stock into her head.

The man bowled into her knees. She shot him in the back. He slapped to the white linoleum and didn't move. The woman pushed her back against the door, blood gushing from a gash on her forehead down the left half of her face.

Ellie swung the gun's barrel at her chest. "We're not with the Clavans."

"You shot him!"

"You should have listened!"

The woman sneered up at her, unflinching. "I know this land. I'll run you down and gut you in your sleep."

Ellie bulged her lower lip with her tongue. "I believe you."

She fired. The woman's body jerked against the door. Ellie turned away, ears ringing. Downstairs, Dee poked her head out to see, eyes gone wide.

"Start packing food," Ellie said. Dee disappeared. Ellie reached past the body and pushed open the door. "Help me get these outside."

"Are we burying them?" Hobson said.

"I don't want her to see."

He nodded sagely and helped pull the wife and husband into the snow. They rolled the pair into the dead flowerbed beneath the back window, then wiped the blood off in the drifts, streaking it red. Inside, Ellie found dish towels in a drawer to dry their cold hands. She supposed she should feel guilt, but the clatter of Dee from downstairs kept any such feelings far away.

Dee came up one step at a time, bearing a bulky transparent tub with a blue lid. "What happened?"

Ellie shook her head. "They're gone. But they could have neighbors. Let's get that in our packs and move."

Hobson rounded up their snowshoes from the front porch and found their guns while Ellie and Dee transferred plastic bags and jars of canned fruit to their packs. They ate as they worked. Ellie tossed Hobson a bag of venison jerky. He chuckled happily and dug in, a brown twist of meat jutting from his jaws as he strapped on his shoes. And then they were back outside in the bitter cold with the snow gleaming like an exploded star and Ellie quit eating before she'd have to throw up.

It was early afternoon. Ellie thought they could make five or six miles before they'd need to find a house. Night was the time for questions, when everyone could stare at the fire and avoid each other's eyes, but Dee surprised her by speaking up less than a mile down the highway.

"Why did you shoot her?"

"Did you hear what she said?" Ellie said. "Do you think I shouldn't have?"

Behind her on the packed trail, Dee watched her sidelong, squinting against the glare. "I think you have a reason for everything you do."

"I'd just shot her husband," Ellie said. "She meant to hunt us down."

"Which she might have. Or might not. But we couldn't know. That's what you mean when you talk about violence."

"That's what I believe."

Dee shuffled through the snow. "That's pretty bad, isn't it? Doesn't it mean you shoot first and ask questions later? Anyone who bluffs gets shot."

"When someone pulls a gun on me, I tend to take them at their word." Ellie followed the trail Hobson smoothed through the snow. "Maybe that's why I don't like to leave Saranac."

Dee gazed at the powder glittering around their snowshoes, working this over. Ellie believed what she'd just espoused very strongly—though when didn't she—but while she typically pushed hard enough to ensure her words would leave an impression on Dee's young, dense skull, this time, she felt no need. The events of the last hour spoke much louder.

"It's an odd thing," Hobson said. "They must have had a recent run-in with the Clavan gang. Almost certainly lost someone. It left them so alert for the return of the kidnappers that they ensured the cycle continued. Violence is an infection, isn't it? A perverse strain where the more you're exposed to it, the less you're able to fight it off."

"They should have moved after the first time the Clavans came," Dee said. "They were so vulnerable by themselves."

They slept the night in another house. Mechanically, Ellie helped break up chairs to build the fire. She ate but couldn't remember what she'd eaten. She checked the kitchen cabinets. This, too, was mechanical, but when she saw a half-empty bottle of cooking sherry, she poured herself a glass and sat at the dining room table and watched the starry darkness.

"I would have done the same," Hobson said from the doorway, jolting her. "But I suppose the only thing that matters is you're the one who did."

He waited there a moment. When she said nothing, he left. She drank a while and went to sleep and had dreams she couldn't remember. She didn't think she'd had that much, but when morning came, her stomach hurt and there was a thickness to her head like melted sugar. She ate some trail mix from their looted food and walked on.

It snowed two days later. Nothing major. Just enough to layer fresh powder on the sun-crusted snows.

"You said they taught you some hand-to-hand stuff back in the day," Dee said. "How much do you remember?"

Ellie laughed, possibly for the first time since the house. "Do you want to learn?"

"It seems like I ought to."

It had been some time since Ellie had practiced anything more advanced than her stretches, let alone imparted those techniques to an amateur, and she worried she had lost them among the dissolving memories of her twenties. But once upon a time, she'd practiced rigorously. That evening, when they took off their shoes and socks and went to work in a dead stranger's living room, she found her skills dusty, eroded, but present.

She worked up a light sweat showing Dee a few basics. Starting with punching. Dee had worked on the farm long enough that none of her motions was utterly hopeless, but she had a bad habit of letting the tip of her thumb drift past her knuckles. Didn't always keep her wrist straight, either, which was a great way to break it. She showed the girl a straight kick which Dee got right away.

Dee had problems with her grabs and holds, however. As with her punch, she tended to lose track of her thumb. Anyone with the presence of mind to grab it and twist would put Dee down on the spot. Ellie opened her mouth to criticize, but Dee saw the error herself and shifted her thumb from the underside of Ellie's wrist.

Quite suddenly, Ellie knew that if she'd harangued Dee for it, she would have quit for the night. Perhaps for good. But she had a feel for it. Her flaws were technique issues, surmountable with practice and concentration. And though they weren't related, she shared a few things with Ellie. She was quick to frustration. Particularly when it involved a challenge to her knowledge or expertise. A good teacher would see this, and use a light touch.

"Keep an eye on that thumb," Ellie said. "If it's hard to remember, a good way to practice is to try to maintain technique during day-to-day activities."

"Like when I'm brushing my teeth?"

"Exactly."

They continued their practice.

"What style is this?" Dee said when at last they stopped.

"Standard-issue US government hodgepodge." Ellie dampened a kitchen towel and ran it around her neck and armpits. "A few things that are reasonably effective and take almost no time to learn. It's not what you'd call an art. Those take six to twelve months of daily practice to learn and years to master."

"Maybe I should just learn to shoot."

Ellie laughed. "I reached the same conclusion myself."

She didn't think it was a great idea to try full-fledged target practice, but when they took breaks from their march, she showed Dee a few things about guns, too. Dee was familiar enough with basic safety and use—again, farm life, not to mention the end of the world—but wasn't so skilled at the near-basics. Leading a target. Finding cover and using it as a support platform for her shots. Failing that, to form triangular braces of her limbs. Aiming for center of mass. And being ready, once that mass had been hit, to finish the job.

"Which means," Hobson said, "once you get very good at this, you should aim for the spine."

Dee looked dubious. "The spine?"

"The head moves around a lot, you know. The spine is rather static. More important, it turns out the organs are rather more resistant to damage than the nerves that control those organs."

He walked away whistling.

The land and the Hudson sloped gradually downhill. The snow grew shallow enough that they might have been able to use bikes, if they'd burned the time to find them, but their packs were so bulky it would be hard to keep steady without a trailer. Anyway, their legs and pace were used to the snowshoes. They walked on.

The tenth afternoon after they left Albany, they trudged up a gentle rise. At its top, towns and valleys spread for miles. Beyond, Ellie saw the thing she'd hoped to never see again: the Manhattan skyline, windows sparkling yellow, the towers so high and proud they were like insults from a world lost for good.

III:

HARVEST

21

And then she was alone in the snow.

She sat in the road, the sloped concrete walls boxing her in a barren canyon. It hurt some and she bled some but neither was as bad as she had always imagined getting shot would be.

But she appeared to be paralyzed. Not in the busted-spine sense, though she waggled her fingers and toes just to be sure. Instead, she had no will to move. It was like the breakers in her head had been tripped and she wasn't sure when or if they'd come back online. Was she about to die? She couldn't say. Would she ever see Tilly again? That, too, was a mystery. Had she made poor choices with her life? Well, the fact she'd been shot in or around the heart could be a sign, but due to just that, she might never know for sure.

Snow twirled from black clouds, first fine and crystalline, then in pea-sized drops, then in fat globby lumps that looked like the molecule chains from her sophomore chemistry textbook. Melted flakes stained the pavement a deeper black, then formed a coating so much like a clean white bedsheet that Lucy felt she could give the whole ground a shake and fold it up for later.

If only she could stand up.

She unwound her scarf and pressed it to her wound. The pain lurched forward but soon retreated to its former distance. The men had left a long time ago and she heard nothing but the whisper of snow on hard ground.

High on the white tower that faced her, a shadow unfurled, long and curved like a Muslim's sword. She was no longer alone. His head followed, massive but without features. A dark absence: the

Reaper, the father she never had. At last he had found her, yet he waited with cosmic patience, knowing that, in the end, it was not he who had to move.

She wanted to run to him. To be embraced. To be swept away from this life that, since birth, had been nothing but misery and pain. Unloved and so became unlovable. It was a joke, to be brought to exist and to have that existence be so mean, so far from virtue, like a crippled wasp or a rattler with a broken back. She wanted to run to him and cry like a child and be taken back to that place before life that was so like a world muffled and smothered by snow.

But the joke ran deeper than that. She had been hammered by one thing after another until her core was as sharp and steely as the blade of his scythe. She couldn't let him take her any more than an avalanche could turn and flee back up the hill. She laughed and it hurt and with each pulse of pain the shadow retreated from the tower's face. Her blood was hot on her hand, the most vivid red she'd ever seen. It was hers to keep.

And she was alone again, sitting with her legs sprawled in the snow. Her knee jerked. Her chest felt tight and pink bubbles oozed from her wound. She pressed her scarf to it and stood.

Nerve had taken its shells, but left her umbrella, the way you might throw a man's balls at his feet after castrating him. She crouched to pick it up and used it as a cane as she walked away from the tunnel mouth. Its metal tip tapped and scraped the pavement beneath the bedsheet of snow.

She had properly burned all her bridges with Distro. The Feds might blow smoke up her ass about treating her wound, but she'd seen how little they actually provided their people. Reese would help her, she was positive of that, but even if she found him at the coffee house, she was equally certain he didn't know a damn thing about prying a bullet from a body. She needed people with the skill and the motive to help her.

The Kono were warrior-gangsters. They would have surgeons. After what she'd done to Duke, they'd also have plenty of reason to hasten her short march to the grave. But she had something to make them reconsider.

She walked on, block by block, watched by the buildings' vacant eyes. Her numb shock ebbed away and waves of pain surfed in to take its place. Her eyes stung. Snow whacked her in the face, melting on her cheeks and dribbling from her brows to her eyes. At 42nd Street, she stopped in front of a theater. When she hung her head, a bushel of flakes fell to the sidewalk. She was having a hell of a time catching her breath. Her chest felt so tight she could hardly pull in air. She'd figured this was all part of the fun of getting shot point blank, but in a moment of clarity, she understood something more was wrong. Yes, she'd been shot in the chest, and her lung was likely all fucked up, but for the last few blocks, it had been getting worse.

Once upon a time, Tilly had been in love with those sexy doctor shows. Lucy'd found them dumb as hell, but had suffered through them, at first so she'd have more excuse to stay at Tilly's house and avoid returning to her own, and later, when she'd moved into the Loman household, because it seemed rude (even by her lax standards) to demand Tilly change the channel in her own home.

All that suffering might be about to save her life.

She cast about the street. The equipment she needed was worthless enough that any hospital was likely to still have it despite years of looting, but she was in Times Square. That real estate was about a thousand times too valuable for something as stupid as a hospital. It was all theaters, Hard Rock Cafes, and watch/t-shirt/souvenir stands. She moved to one of these, pawing through the wallets and hoodies, chest feeling tighter by the second. No tubing, but the search turned up a single Zippo engraved with the words "BROOKLYN ZOO." After a couple flicks, the flame caught.

She was a bit dizzy, fluttery. Her fingertips were clumsy and tingly and felt strangely warm. Figuring they might have an aquarium, she lurched through the door of the Hard Rock, the light of her Zippo flickering over shredded booths and the stomped-up debris left behind by people who'd come for its food in the early days of the plague. Broken glass was everywhere, raising her hopes that it might lead to a fish tank, but it was merely the byproduct of smashed display cases. Someone had actually bothered to steal Clapton's guitar.

She fought for air. With mounting desperation, confusion, and fear that she'd be found dead in a Hard Rock Cafe, she stumbled deeper into the restaurant. Big swinging doors led to a kitchen. The floor was crusted with rotten food. Her lighter played over dust-dulled stovetops, pans, ladles, and lids. The cooking stations were much tighter than she expected, and even after all these years it smelled like frying oil.

Culinary tools dangled from hooks and scattered the floor. Lucy whipped her gaze across the tongs and skewers and fondue forks. She'd been looking for a turkey baster, but what she found was even better: a fat-nosed flavor injector, complete with syringe-like handle.

She tore open her shirt, inserted the tip of the flavor injector into her wound, and pulled up on the plunger.

Her brain must have ordered her chest to shut up about its problems, because this didn't hurt at all. A lot of air and a bit of frothy, pink blood filled the chamber of the injector. The pain and pressure in her chest decreased. Sweat popped out across her entire body in such a thick sheen that she could have used the sidewalk as a Slip 'N Slide. Then she got very dizzy and had to sit down.

She pushed the plunger of the injector, squirting a flatulent blast of air and froth, then returned it to her wound and sucked more air. Already, her chest felt leagues better. That seemed to do it, and so she sat there for a good while, breathing the cold air, letting her senses return. After a while, she gathered herself and walked outside.

The makeshift cane of her umbrella tapped along the street. She continued north. Sometimes she smelled the smoke of heating oil, soon replaced by the crisp scent of fresh snow. At other times she had to stop and draw more air from her wound. The walk uptown took approximately several forevers. At least the north-south blocks were the short ones. That helped her sense of progress when her limbs got heavy and the throbbing in her chest got so bad she wanted to curl up on the elegant steps of Fordham University.

After another mile, the walk was just a thing she did because there was nothing else to do. An inch of snow clung to the streets. Back when the city had lights, it must have been the prettiest sight in the world.

Down the blocks to the west, smoke rose in orderly plumes from Central Park. She supposed if you lived in Manhattan and you didn't have electricity, that's where you set up shop. Not a lot of wood stoves in the apartments, she'd wager. Must have built themselves new houses right there in the park. Feds might have parceled out the land to reduce disputes. Then again, it sounded like the Kono held sway over much of it and Distro had their finger in the pie as well. Too many chefs. With guns. Shootout right there in the Hard Rock kitchen.

She laughed some, already forgetting why, and then she didn't think much at all.

She came back to it on the street she'd fled down after shooting Duke. The snowfall had slowed. Around the block, light spilled from the front of Sicily. She walked up to the red padded door, cane clicking.

The stout bouncer emerged into the cold. "You armed?"

"Only bullet I got is right here." She opened her jacket, exposing pale skin. A hungry look came over his face. He got a gander at the blood washing down her chest and looked like he might puke instead.

He looked up to her face. "You're that girl. The one who capped Duke."

She zipped up her jacket. "I need to see Ash."

"He needs to see you, too." He opened the door and leaned inside, keeping an eye on her. "Brian! Ludrow! Get out here!"

Two men emerged: Brian, and another who was the kind of idiot who wore short sleeves in a snowstorm because he'd be damned if he wasn't going to show off the veins on his biceps.

"Yo Brian," the bouncer said. "This the girl who exed Duke?"

"Shark eyes," Brian said. Snow caught in the stubble on his scalp. "That's her."

"I want to see Ash," she said flatly.

"Why didn't you pull the trigger on me?" Brian said.

Lucy shook her head. A bad idea. The world shook with it. "You weren't a bastard. Come on, guys. Most cultures consider it rude to leave a lady in the snow when she's been shot."

Ludrow, the man in the short sleeves, walked up close enough that she could smell his sweat. "I don't think you're a lady. Anybody who shoots Duke and then comes back for more must be packing eight pairs of balls."

Faces appeared in the bar windows. The white ones looked as pale as Lucy felt. Smelling a fight, men and women stepped outside, zipping leather jackets and heavy padded coats.

Ludrow jerked a thumb at her. "This is the girl who shot Duke. What do you think he'd like us to do to her?"

"I vote we don't do a thing," the bouncer said. "Let that chest wound do its work. Hours of fun."

Lucy's knees quivered, but she knew if she fell, the Kono would kick her until the rest of her guts were in worse shape than her lung. She found Brian's eye. "Will you get Ash for me?

"I think she needs more hurt," Ludrow said. "Get me an icepick. We can put out her eyes without killing her any faster."

Someone shoved her in the back. She winced and cast around for Brian but he was gone. All that remained was a sea of angry faces. She turned to snarl at the woman who'd pushed her and Ludrow cocked back his arm and slapped her across the cheek. Her face was half numb and the pain tingled and burned like hot needles. A man kicked at her stomach. She turned her hip into it. The kick was clumsy and half-committed, but it nearly knocked her down. Lucy staggered, braced herself with her cane. She couldn't fall.

A woman kicked at her umbrella. Lucy yanked it away, her ribs spiking with pain. Warm spit struck her face. Something hit her in the side.

"Get her!" Ludrow shouted. "Take away her face!"

A fist cracked her in the nose and blood popped down her lips. She had thought herself too tired to fight, but she swung her umbrella like a bat, raking its end across Ludrow's leering face. He shrieked and clutched the blood gleaming in the furrow in his cheek.

Someone hit her in the back of the head and she reeled forward. A woman danced up and socked her in the jaw. Lucy's knees gave out. She fell to her hands, umbrella skidding, fingers splayed in the harsh snow. A boot stomped toward her right hand. Dimly, she had the presence of mind to pull it back. The boot crashed into the snow, spattering her face with slush. A toe banged into her ribs, rocking her and sending white heat shooting up her spine. Blood dribbled down her stomach. She closed her eyes.

"You fucking idiots." A high and pretty voice knifed across the grunts and babble. "How about you let me hear the crazy idea that brought her back here? Then you finish beating her to death."

Ash glared his way through the circle of assailants. He was trim and short and the bones of his face were as pleasant as Tilly's, but his expression could have eaten holes in a battleship. He crouched next to Lucy and lifted her chin. He smelled like his red leather coat and the musk of aftershave.

"What brings you uptown, you cuckoo clock?"

"The hospitality." Lucy tasted blood. She swiped the back of her hand across her mouth. Her nose was swollen and possibly broken. "So hey, as long as I'm here, want to know how to destroy Distro?"

"I was thinking about shooting them. Got a better idea?"

"I know where their trade comes from. Cut that and you bleed them to death."

"Where, the sea? I'm not the East India Company. I don't have a fleet."

Lucy swung her head side to side. "A few armed men should do it."

Ash squatted back, snow glimmering on his long hair. He rested his wrists on his knees. "My attention? It's yours."

"Nuh uh. You don't get any more. Not until you patch me up. Once I'm good enough to travel, I'll take you there."

"That's a convenient bargain! And when you're well enough to walk around, what's to stop you from running out?"

She lifted her head and met her eyes. "Nerve's the man who put the bullet in me. I aim to return it."

"He's an asshole like that, isn't he?" Ash rubbed his smooth jaw. "So what do I get if you don't make it?"

"My death."

"Sold." He stood and snapped his fingers three times. "Get her to surgery. And somebody go wake Doc."

"He's drunk," Brian said.

"He was about nine sheets to the wind when he took my tooth out. I lived. You know who won't if he doesn't get that bullet out of her? This girl."

Ash rolled his eyes and strolled inside. Hands reached for Lucy, but this time, they helped her to her feet. The world shrank to a dime, then a pinhole, then decided to go away altogether.

When she woke, she was lying on a table. A masked man leaned over her with a blade.

"Shit." He straightened and tugged down his mask; an uncombed beard seemed to burst from his face. "Nurse! My whiskey!"

"I think you've had enough," Brian said from behind Lucy.

"For my patient."

"What?" Lucy slurred.

The bearded man sat next to her on the table and put his hand on her shoulder. Which was bare.

"I'm a doctor," he said. "You've been shot."

"Oh."

"Things are all Civil War around here. I can't put you under, but I need you to stay very still. To help you be brave, I'm about to get you extremely drunk. Can you do that for me, Lucy?"

She tried to sit up for a look at her chest but her whole body cried out the moment she moved. "Please."

He smiled and patted her shoulder. "There's my girl."

Brian returned, donned in scrubs and a blue surgical mask, and handed the doctor a tumbler of brown-yellow liquor. Brian helped her sit up. The doc brought the glass to her lips. It smelled like oak beams and old forests and it burned her throat so bad she choked, snorting it out her nose. The doctor smiled patiently and dabbed it away.

"Tell me once the medicine's kicked in," he said.

She nodded. She was already breathing easier. Five minutes later, she told him she was ready.

"Excellent." He twisted around, then held a narrow, leather-wrapped tube above her mouth. "You might want to bite down on Mr. Stick. Don't worry, he's used to it."

She clenched it between her teeth. Her breath whistled from her nose. A line of fire sliced across her chest. Her body went stiff and she bit down on Mr. Stick until it creaked.

"I know you can be brave!" Doc said. "Know how I know? This bullet's in your chest, not your back."

She tried for him, but she was done. She went black and she stayed there.

Lucy woke to daylight and a bed. The apartment was narrow and the curtains were so musty she could smell them from where she lay. A scrabble at the door had woken her; the doctor entered and walked to the side of her bed. He set down a black satchel and peeled the bandage from her wound.

She sucked air through her teeth until the hurt quieted down enough to let her talk. "How do I look, Doc?"

Doc wore the aggrieved patience of a man with stones in his bladder. "Like something I scraped off my shoe with a stick. I can't believe you walked all that way. I've got a special bandage on you that should prevent more air from getting into your chest cavity, but if you feel any pressure, additional pain, or shortness of breath, you have to let me know."

"Am I gonna make it?"

"Every word you speak decreases your chances."

She slitted her eyes. "I question the soundness of your medical opinion."

He poked her chest, flooding her with pain. "I'm sorry, does that hurt?"

She gasped at the ceiling. "You son of a bitch."

"How do you feel?"

"Like I got to pee."

"Good news is your room has plumbing," he said. "Bad news is that when you stand up, you're going to wish you could pass out."

She eased up on her elbows. "You got running water?"

"The Feds charge a president's ransom for it. We're in the wrong racket."

"Which racket's that, extorting protection money from farmers?"

"Question the ethics as you please. All I know is I've had to treat a lot fewer clubbed, stabbed, and shot farmers since the Kono brought order to the park." His brows pushed together. "You need a hand? Or were you planning to wet the bed?"

With his help and a lot of sweating and pain, she made it to the bathroom, then tottered back to bed, legs quivering. "What now?"

"Think of it like a hospital. Where you're under house arrest." He tapped her shoulder with his fist. "Cocktail hour."

"Are you sure you're a doctor?"

"That's what my degree says. That reminds me." He dug into his pocket and held up a coin-sized lump of gnarled metal. Its base was largely intact, cylindrical and copperish, but its tip was mushroomed and leaden. "I imagine you're the type of girl who'd like to keep this."

He deposited it in her palm, walked out, and locked the door from the outside. She slept again. When she woke, a sandwich and a glass of water waited on the nightstand. She ate ravenously.

She didn't see another person until the day after that, when Ash swept open the door. "Lucy, I'm home!"

She eyed him. "Like I ain't heard that a hundred times."

"Doc said you're recovering like a champ." He clicked across the room and scootched his rear into the windowsill. "Our deal stands, right?"

"Sure."

"How about a hint?"

She laughed. It hurt. "Not until I feel good enough to fight back."

He sighed and flicked at a cobweb on the curtains. "I don't like this deal anymore."

He'd no sooner left than Brian entered with scrambled eggs and toast that even bore a faint smear of butter.

"They got you as my nursemaid?" Lucy wriggled upright. "How you feel about that?"

He set down the plate. "I haven't had much of a role at all since you shot Duke."

"I'd say I was sorry, but he tried to turn me out."

"I know."

He walked out. Her room didn't have electricity, so when he came back with lunch, she asked him for some books.

"What kind?"

"I don't know," she said. "Got anything with pirates? Or dinosaurs?"

"They don't write many books about dinosaurs."

"Then what good are they?"

He left again. That night, all he brought was dinner. Onions, potatoes, and bread (all of which she would eat a lot of in the next couple weeks). She figured he'd forgotten about the books, or didn't give a shit, but the following morning, he walked in with a cardboard box of paperbacks and set it on the foot of her bed.

"Enjoy." He wiped the dust on his hands and locked the door behind him.

She spread them out. He'd found a few with pirates—though most of them were the kind with bare chests, curly locks, and a woman draped over their arm in a posture so traumatic to the human spine you could almost hear the vertebrae cracking—but one of the books had the silhouette of a T. rex skeleton on the cover. While snow fluttered past the window, she read it from front to back. It was the first book she could remember finishing.

A couple days later, Brian walked in with a chess set. "Do you play?"

She shook her head. The light in his expression went out. She rolled onto an elbow. "Got checkers?"

He did. She could tell he found the game mechanical and predictable, but he seemed to enjoy himself anyway. Lucy chatted him up about life outside the apartment, but between the snow and the Kono saving their juice for the intel Lucy was sitting on, hostilities between them and Distro had simmered down to mutually nonviolent disdain.

The Doc came for her stitches. With her special bandage affixed to her chest this whole while, it was the first time she'd gotten a good look at them. She was horrified. The black threading looked like a mummy's mouth.

Doc offered to let her keep those, too. She declined.

She rolled the bullet around her palm and watched the snowy streets. This part of town showed much more life than down around the piers. At the bar, people came and went, glad for the chance to grab a meal they didn't have to cook themselves. Every morning, a horse-drawn wagon clopped west toward New Jersey, returning in the afternoon full of split wood. The woman who drove it dickered with one of the Kono over the woods' price every single time. Initially, Lucy resented the yammery back-and-forth—Christ on a cracker, choose a rate and stick with it—but the daily bargaining session soon became just another thread in the weave of uptown life.

Between her injury and the bed rest, Lucy had lost a lot of strength. Once the stitches were out, she paced around the room. Pushups were out of the question, but she discovered that so long as she was careful, she could get away with sit-ups, lunges, and jogging in place. When she wore out, which was much too damn fast, she read the other books in the box, but none were half as good as Jurassic Park.

Three weeks after she'd walked up to their front door, Doc came in with a stethoscope and some rubber tubes and pumps Lucy didn't like the look of at all.

"You get that out of a museum?" she said.

"Some of it." He listened to her pulse and her breathing and had a look at her incision, which had closed right up without redness or much in the way of discharge. "You heal like the devil."

"Am I ready to once more face the world?"

"I wonder if it's ready to face you." He frowned distractedly at her boob, which under any other context would have been disconcerting and might well have earned him two black eyes. "I'm a little concerned about the lung. It sounds good, but these things can take a couple months to heal. Go easy on it." He looked up at her; if he'd been wearing glasses, he'd be gazing over the top of them. "If you're capable of such a thing."

He left, locking the door as always. Hours later, Ash walked in for the first time since his initial visit where he'd asked her for a hint.

"Doc says you're cleared for active duty," he said. "Time to pay your bill."

Lucy walked to the window. The first snow had melted a few days after she'd been shot. More had replaced it the week after that, but there hadn't been a fresh fall in days and the slush in the streets was grimy and black.

"You got a boat?"

Ash arched one brow. "You said I wouldn't need one."

"I said you wouldn't need a fleet. We can walk there if you like, but two days from now, when your shoes are soaked, your ears are numb, and you're tramping around in the pine barrens wearing fifty pounds of guns, ammo, tents, and—"

"I have a boat," Ash cut her off. "I've got shitloads of boats. If you need a submarine, I'll get you a submarine. Just get me to their source."

Lucy primly laced her fingers together. "Anything with a sail should do fine."

He grabbed her wrist and pulled her to the door. "Real battle plans are drawn up over beer."

She got her shoes and the hoodie Brian had brought her when she'd mentioned the room had a draft. After three weeks in the musty apartment, she stepped into the dingy hall with the zeal of a conqueror. Downstairs in Sicily, Ash grabbed them a booth and the two of them drank beer from bottles that had lost their labels long ago. Men and women glanced over each time Ash gestured or raised his piercing, androgynous voice, which was often. Lucy got the idea he was something of a live wire. His unpredictability could throw a wrench into her plans, but it was easy to stir such people up and unleash them in the general direction of whatever you wanted destroyed.

The plan didn't take long to hash out. She didn't tell him where they were going or what they'd see. Just that it would require a boat and some troopers and that it might devolve into a shootout.

"You are intransigent," he said over his bottle. "If you're withholding details because you're lying about the whole enterprise, I'm going to send you to sleep with the fishes. Starting with your toes. I will personally slice you into chunks and put your chunks in a bucket and chum you across the Upper Bay."

He swilled down the rest of his beer and smacked it on the table. He had everything ready by the following afternoon, but they hung around Sicily until dusk, meaning to sail past Distro's Chelsea holdings under cover of night. The boat was several feet longer than the one Kerry had led down to the New Jersey coast. Possibly to make room for all the guns, which included a rocket launcher, and the bevy of passengers, which included Ash, Lucy, Brian, four men, and three women. Lucy didn't have so much as a knife. If they turned on her, she'd either have to loot the cabin's armory, or jump overboard and see how long she could hold her breath.

They pushed off. A modest wind blew from the land. A few lights pricked the skyline, evidence of the sporadic power the Feds provided those who could afford it, but that just made the city's black towers all the bleaker. The crew passed Chelsea Piers in perfect silence.

Once they were out of hearing range, Ash grinned and spat into the river. "Bozos. We'll clean their clocks."

Lucy let the captain know to head out to sea and swing south along the coast. They scooted out the channel and hooked to the right. The Jersey shore was nothing but a bunch of dark lumps. After a few miles, Lucy told the captain to make way for High Bar Harbor.

The boat pitched on worse waves than she'd faced on the trip down with Kerry. She went down the steps to catch a nap. She woke as the captain wrangled his way through the channel to the bay. The man's expression was as tight as his knuckles.

"Pay no mind to Captain About-to-Shit-His-Pants," Ash told her. He waved his hands down in a swimmy motion. "He's scared it might be dangerous to sail into an unfamiliar harbor at night."

"It hasn't been dredged in years," the man muttered, glancing between the shores bracketing them to right and left.

"What's the worst that happens? We run into some sand? If the Bedouins aren't afraid of sand, why should we be?"

"The Bedouins never had to swim the Atlantic in December."

They were operating silent and without lights. At one point the captain got in a hushed yet heated argument with Ash about dropping a pole into the water, but Ash made a series of obscene threats and the captain relented, though not before promising that, should they run aground, he would leave the Kono to start a new life in the Rocky Mountains, as far from the sea as he could climb.

After some more grumbling, he sailed around the long spit extending north from the yacht club, then maneuvered into the artificial residential canals on the western side of the small blob of land. They tied up parallel to shore. The captain slumped in his chair, mopped his brow, and fetched a pint bottle from the pocket of his pea coat.

"Land ho," Ash said quietly, voice hanging in the cold, damp air. He clapped Lucy on the shoulder. "Ready to spill the beans?"

"Funny you should say that," Lucy said. "Follow me."

He climbed down from the boat, then offered her a hand, which she declined. He was armed with a pistol and he brought along a silent man with a black assault rifle. The others remained onboard. Lucy led the two men through the decaying houses and into the salt marsh. A dusting of snow lay on the solid parcels of ground, helping Lucy to pick her way through the darkness. Between the snow and the gloom, she had to circle around a couple times before she found the parallel ruts in the soil.

She eased herself to one knee and pointed along the lines. "You see?"

"Incredible. You've discovered dirt."

"Right. Now check out the tracks in the dirt. Now imagine the helicopter that made those tracks."

Ash's frown deepened like the approach of twilight. "You think Distro is bringing their goods in via helicopter, then shipping them from here to the city?"

"That's how they bring in so much exotic wares. And why they always know exactly when it's supposed to arrive. They don't have to worry about storms and winds and shit. They're flying it in as close as they can get without exposing their system to you guys."

"And they're using this patch of ground—which you could slip through a regulation-sized mail slot—instead of the streets right over there." Ash gestured across the field toward the houses standing between them and the yacht club. "How many can an average boat carry? Would you call it a boatload? Now imagine your helicopter. How much weight do you think it can carry?"

"Maybe they make multiple trips." Lucy brushed away the snow and bent close to the ground. "I found coffee beans. Right here beside the tracks. If they're not offloading the goods right here, how the hell did those beans get spilled? Did a Colombian albatross stop to take a dump?"

Ash turned to his soldier. "What do you think?"

The man sniffed. "I think they're using boats."

"Interesting you should say that. Because if they're using boats, and we knock out this harbor, they'll just set up another somewhere else." He brought his face inches from Lucy's. "You told me you knew how to destroy them."

"You see a lot of functioning air power these days? If you knock out their whirlybirds, the city's yours." Lucy's mind raced. "Today's Thursday. New shipments came in every Saturday morning. If I'm right, the shipment will land here tomorrow."

"If it doesn't?"

"Then you can take back my life that you saved. But you remember one thing: I want Nerve dead just as bad as you."

"Oh, I doubt that." Ash bounced to his feet. "Back to the ship."

They sloshed through the marsh to the boat. Ash ordered two of the soldiers to scout the marina, then told Lucy to get downstairs. The man with the assault rifle came down and watched her from a padded bench.

Some time later, boots thumped around above deck. Voices murmured. Lucy couldn't make out their words. She wasn't too happy with herself. The street would make a much better landing pad than some soggy old field. And if you ruled out the field, that meant the coffee beans were a red herring. Her whole theory collapsed.

Troops took turns watching her. She managed to sleep some. Right before dawn, she woke to the sound of boots on the steps. The soldiers and crew were all piling below, getting out of sight. Ash and one of his men stayed up in the cabin, presumably to watch the skies. When Brian came downstairs, he gave her a long look, but said nothing.

The Kono stayed belowdecks the whole day. Pissed in a bucket and left it by the steps. Every few minutes, Lucy was sure she heard the whop of a chopper, but it was her ears being tricked by the wash of the tide, the stirrings of the two men above. The soldiers murmured to each other as if she wasn't there.

It was one of those days that lasted forever yet was over in a blink. After nightfall, Ash called the crew upstairs. Ropes and feet thumped around. The boat swayed away from the dock.

"Sorry," Brian told her.

"If you're that sorry, go talk to him. Tell him we got to stay another day."

"We did talk. His mind's made up."

She stared at the plain white ceiling. "He's making a mistake."

"He's not afraid of making mistakes," Brian said. "He's afraid of standing still."

The boat pulled away from the dock. It leaned to the right, swinging around the spit, then leveled out, cruising toward the open sea. Waves knocked against the hull. And then she heard the sound of the surf, except instead of waxing and waning, it climbed and climbed until she could feel its thunder in the healing wound in her chest.

"It's not a helicopter." Lucy's jaw was somewhere around her ankles. "It's a jet."

22

"Get down," Ellie said. "We're not alone."

She ducked behind a sedan angled on the shoulder. Dee and Hobson moved in beside her. She got out her binocs and gazed down the lanes spanning the river. Past the latticed steel tower near the far end, concrete barriers choked the road. Behind these, a man turned his back to her. She could just make out the black line of a rifle spiking from his shoulder.

"Two of them," she said. "Armed."

"Can we use another bridge?" Dee said. "Holland Tunnel?"

Hobson took off his bowler and inspected the brim. "Logically speaking, if they're guarding one of them, they're guarding all of them."

Dee peeped around the side window. "If they wanted to kill us, wouldn't they ambush us? And not stand right there in the open?"

"Listen to that," Hobson chuckled. "How does Deputy Dee sound?"

"Absolutely not." Ellie put away her binoculars. "Well, come on."

She led the way onto the bridge. They had spent the night in a neighboring township and the morning light was flat and gray. Snow plastered the rooftops across the Hudson, but the wind had swept most of it from the bridge's surface, leaving slicks of black ice that left Ellie's snowshoes skidding. She tottered forward, glancing between the guards at the other end and her unsteady footing.

The guards noticed them within seconds. One produced binoculars. They left their rifles on their shoulders as Ellie and crew moved within hailing distance.

"Hello, ma'am," one of them said. He had the spontaneous patter of a salesman. "And sir. And other ma'am. Could you stop right there? I'd love to let a couple pretty girls inside, but unfortunately, the nation of Manhattan's tourist season is now closed."

"We're not tourists," Ellie said.

"We're also closed to business, pleasure, passage, and to anyone who isn't a documented citizen of the island."

"You're with the government?"

He grinned. "What tipped you off? The uniforms, or the refusal to let you get anything done?"

"Then I would like to file a formal complaint against the human traffickers operating in your city."

"Human traffickers?" The soldier exchanged a look with his partner. "I don't think we got any of that going on here."

Ellie stepped forward. "Several weeks ago, my daughter's fiancé was kidnapped from Saranac Lake. We've tracked him to the city. I don't care if it's tourist season, flu season, or C.H.U.D. season. I'm coming inside."

His partner leaned in. "Could be those uptown shitheads, man."

"Zip it," the first soldier said. He scrunched up his face as if enduring great pain. "I take you seriously, ma'am. Seriously enough that, even though we're not really closed for tourist season but because we got a lot of people in here who seem bent on shooting each other, I doubt that information is going to turn you away. Am I right?"

"Utterly," Ellie said.

"Here's what I'm going to do for you. I'm going to take down your names and give you temporary passports. Then you're going to go straight to City Hall, explain your situation, and do whatever they tell you to do. Is that a deal?"

"If they tell me to leave, I'm going to tell them the same thing I told you."

He brayed laughter, mist drifting from his mouth. "Listen, will you pretend to agree with me so I can swear up and down to my prick of a superior officer that you solemnly swore to abide by the adjudications of the sovereign nation of Manhattan?"

Despite herself, Ellie laughed. "I so swear."

"Boom! I'll grab the paperwork and we can get you on your way."

He walked to the shack behind the barricade and returned with three clipboards and pens. Ellie set to work filling in her name, residence, and reason of visit.

As she passed it back, the second soldier frowned at Ellie's rifle. "What about their guns?"

The first man rolled his eyes. "Jesus, Ezra, do you want to send someone into the island unarmed right now?"

"Then you get to answer to Valentine."

"No problem. I'll just tell her you were asleep at your post." He laughed some more, collected Ellie's paperwork, and passed them each a laminated badge. "You know where City Hall is?"

"I used to live here," Ellie said.

"Why didn't you say so? Welcome home!" He stepped aside with a flourish. As they passed, he winked at Dee.

Past the bridge, they descended to street level. Hobson lifted his gray brows. "Well."

"Did you know they had a government?" Ellie said.

"I'd heard rumblings. I'd always assumed it was a tin-pot setup."

"Unless they're a complete farce, they'll know about the slave trade. We'll pry the intel out of them and go straight to the source. Could be out of here in a couple days."

The wicker frame of Hobson's right snowshoe snapped. He cursed, but the shoe held together. "Let's pray they're corrupt."

Dee raised one eyebrow. "Why would we want that?"

"Easier to bribe."

They walked past miles of brownstones and tall project towers. An hour later, they paralleled the park, walking along a stone fence that had been topped with barbed wire. Log cabins and shacks dotted the fields and hid in the trees. The grass had been plowed under; most of the land was brown dirt and churned-up stalks of the fall harvest. Axes thunked wood. Here and there, people strolled down the paths, dogs clicking along beside them. Watching them, Ellie could almost pretend the plague had never happened—except each man and woman carried a rifle on their shoulder or a pistol on their hip.

"This is so weird," Dee said.

Ellie took in the skyline of Midtown. "Remember it?"

"It smells even worse than it used to."

Hobson chuckled. "Makes you wish you had an off switch for your nose."

Once the park was behind them, the city grew quiet. Every few blocks, Ellie glimpsed a drape stirring or a figure watching them from an apartment, but virtually all the windows were dark or broken or thick with dust.

The steel mountains of Midtown sloped down to the foothills of Chelsea and a Village that had just managed to become completely gentrified before the Panhandler wiped the slate clean. Ellie felt like she was trespassing over a grave. Nonsense, of course. More people had died in New York in the centuries before the plague than during the collapse. Cities like this had always been cemeteries. The only reason you didn't notice was because people had been so good at replacing the corpses with live bodies.

She kept both eyes out for trouble, but the turrets of City Hall soon climbed from the downtown highrises. As they crossed its plaza, a wary soldier exited the front doors, stopped them, examined their laminated passports, and allowed them inside. They unbuckled their snowshoes and left them by the door. After the last two weeks, walking without them made Ellie's feet feel lighter than air, as if her legs faded into nothing somewhere around the shins.

"Dude," Dee said, voice echoing across the stone chambers. "They have lights."

"So do we," Ellie said. "They're called candles."

"Yeah, and they smell like sheep fat."

An expansive walnut desk commanded the back of the room. It was abandoned, but the click of their heels summoned a woman from the chambers beyond.

"May I help you?" she said.

"We're looking for someone," Ellie said. "We're— "

She held out her hand. "IDs?"

Ellie handed over their passports. "We just got here."

The woman looked up sharply. "The island is currently closed to visitors. Were you invited by one of our citizens?"

"Not exactly, but— "

"Then I'm going to have to ask you to leave."

Ellie braced her forearms on the desk. "We don't want to be here any more than you do. Unfortunately, neither of us has a choice. You want us gone? Then give us a hand."

The woman sighed and looked past Ellie's shoulder. "Garza! Bollings!"

Boots echoed from the front and sides. Four soldiers in urban camo converged on the desk.

Hobson thumbed back his hat and planted his feet. "Are you on orders not to listen to a single word we have to say? I am Sheriff Oliver Hobson, chief lawman of the Lakeland Territories. We are here on the official investigation of the kidnapping of one of our citizens. I will speak to a representative of your law enforcement or make it known to all that Manhattan has no law."

Colloquially, Ellie was used to thinking of their homeland as the "lakelands," but as Hobson spoke, she heard them in a new light, capitalized and proper. Not just a vague patch of mountains spotted with big pools of freshwater, but a unique place: the Lakeland Territories. A village—or perhaps a loose-knit clan—of farmers, shoemakers, fishermen, and shopkeepers. They weren't all in tune, but even Mort Franklin's religious fanatics had recognized, in the end, that they were responsible to something greater than themselves. Not just their god, but their people.

As the receptionist hemmed and hawed, processing Hobson's proclamation, Ellie saw the power in that. The Lakelands didn't have to be a herd of prey animals, where it was a matter of course to lose a few of their own to outsiders every now and then. There was power in numbers. Especially when those who were good at keeping the predators at bay—and in turning the hunters into the hunted—put their talents to use.

"Federal agent Ellie Colson, DAA," she said. "I'm working in conjunction with the Sheriff of the Lakelands. I've got no interest in being forced to pursue a charge for obstruction of justice."

The receptionist went very still. "Do you have identification?"

Hobson tented his fingers on top of the high desk. "Do you think it's wise to try the patience of a man stupid enough to wear a badge in this day and age?"

She pressed her lips together. "I'll speak to the Sheriff of Manhattan. I can't guarantee he'll see you."

"If he won't, I'd like to see his badge."

The woman glared at Hobson, then clicked away from the

counter and entered the back rooms. The soldiers watched them from across the lobby. While they waited, two women and a suited man emerged from a frosted side door and murmured to each other, eyes on Ellie.

"Suppose they'll go for that?" she said.

Hobson shrugged mildly. "Depends on whether their sheriff wears the tin for its shine, or what it represents."

"This is a joke," Dee said. "They can't guard the whole island. We could row across the river any time we want."

Ellie smiled, put a finger to her lips, and glanced at the soldiers, who were busy pretending they hadn't heard and that the island was indeed under their complete control.

It was some time before the heels clacked from the back office. The receptionist returned, accompanied by a young man who followed so close behind her that he appeared to be tied to her elbow.

"The sheriff will see you," she said.

The young man smiled and detached from his host, showing Hobson and his "deputies" up the marble stairs to the second floor. The sheriff's chambers were expansive and draped with thick rugs. After the echoing vastness of the stonework, the carpets seemed to swallow all sound.

The sheriff wasn't as old as Ellie expected. Late forties, though thickets of gray had taken root in his temples. He sat in a plain wooden chair with scuffed arms and scratched varnish.

"Reba tells me you're from upstate," he said. "You got a car?"

Hobson shook his head. "We used our feet. Primitive, but rather more reliable."

"Through all that snow?" The sheriff puffed his cheeks. "Hope I've got good news for you."

Ellie laid out the situation, starting with George Tolbert's loan and following the line through Quinn's kidnapping, transport to Albany, and the van that had taken him away right before the blizzard. As she spoke, the sheriff's face grew more and more pinched.

"That's a thread I wouldn't hang much weight from," he said. "You said the van headed south. How do you know it came here?"

Ellie leaned forward in her chair. "The Clavans' employees

specifically mentioned doing business with the city. The captives we spoke with reinforced the idea they were making a delivery here."

"Don't know about the rest of the continent, but in Manhattan, slavery's illegal."

"So what?" Dee said. "The real government used to make drugs illegal, and I could get them any time I wanted." She glanced at Ellie. "If I'd wanted."

The sheriff nodded distantly. "That was a different time. We got fewer rules now, but we take the ones we've got more seriously. For me, I see little difference between slavery and murder."

"How many men do you have under your command?" Ellie said.

"Enough I can't always keep track of their names."

"They patrol the whole island? We crossed most of it on the way here and I didn't see a single man in uniform."

He narrowed his eyes, as if trying to spot a trout below the surface of a river. "No doubt there's corners of the room that escape our broom. But it's tough to hide an operation like a slave ring. If there were such a group operating in Manhattan, this office would know about it."

Ellie wrapped her hand around her fist. "When I find it anyway, I'll try not to rub it in your face."

"I'm not sure how you got into the city, but you might have heard there's a brouhaha brewing between our two biggest gangs. Think about the kind of people who might be dealing in human slaves. The timing's no good to be asking hard questions of bad people."

"Is it ever?" Ellie laughed. "People like this trade in fear. These people took my daughter's fiancé. Pushed her past the point of fear. As for the sheriff, he fears lawlessness more than gangsters. And me? I get the best of both worlds."

The man was silent for three seconds. The skin around his right eye twitched. He made an upward gesture that might have been a salute or a signal that, if she were so intent on making a mistake, he wouldn't stand in her way.

"Good luck to you," he said. "If you find your boy, bring me the details. I'll have work to do."

Ellie got up. The others followed her into the hall. The young man was waiting for them. "How did it go?"

"Regretfully, the sheriff had no useful information."

"Are you going to keep looking?"

She met his eager gaze. "Until we find him."

"Then I'm supposed to give you this." He passed her a folded note. Ellie read its contents at a glance: "THE TEMPLE. MET. 5 PM."

She held it up between her first two fingers. "Who gave this to you?"

He shook his head. "I don't know."

"Did someone stuff it in your ear while you were tying your shoes? How can you not know?"

"They left it here with a note for me while I was in the bathroom. I'm sorry."

Ellie bit down her frustration and jogged down the stone staircase. In the lobby, Reba called after her. "If you're staying in Manhattan, you're required to register your residence."

Ellie didn't slow down. Reba repeated her order, but no one tried to stop them. Ellie had figured as much. Their government was theater. They put on their titles and costumes and badges, but when it was time to enforce their power in the real world, the light came up and exposed them for the actors they were.

At the doors, the three of them grabbed their snowshoes. One of the soldiers followed them out and watched them cross the plaza. Hobson wore a funny smile.

"Care to share your note with the rest of the class?" he asked once they were out of easy earshot.

"Someone wants to meet us at the Met."

"The Met?"

"Metropolitan Museum of Art. Uptown, other side of Central Park."

"That's it?" he said. She handed him the note. He glanced at it, turned it over. "I'd assume it's regarding a tip."

"Or someone who wants us to think they have a tip."

Dee glanced between them. "What else are we going to do, wander around looking for the van? Put Quinn's face on milk cartons? I'm going."

Ellie sighed and checked the sky. "If we're going to get there in time, we'd better leave now."

"One question," Hobson said, crunching through the snow behind her. "What's 'the temple'?"

"Exactly what it sounds like."

They took Broadway uptown. At 14th Street, Ellie stopped in Union Square to eat lunch on one of the park benches. A mounted statue of George Washington watched them eat their dried fruit and meat. The supplies they'd taken from the house in the woods were running down, but Ellie thought they had enough for at least four more days before things got tight. They finished and moved on.

"That used to be in all the movies," she said, pointing to the wedge of the Flatiron Building. "Think it was in Spider-Man."

"Cool," Dee said in that particular teenage tone that always made Ellie feel like the oldest and stupidest person on earth. She quit playing tour guide and headed straight to Fifth Avenue, following it all the way north.

The Met stood beside Central Park like something teleported from the glory days of Louis XIV. Pairs of columns supported a scalloped roof. A mountain of steps funneled patrons to the front doors. Behind dingy plastic cases, giant posters advertised the upcoming Giacometti exhibit. The dates were six years behind.

"I remember this," Dee said. "We came here for class sometimes. I always got lost."

"Me too. Stick together." Ellie tugged off her snowshoes, jogged up the steps, and set them beside the front doors.

Inside, sunlight streamed through the windows, lighting up amoeboid swirls of dust. The collection bin by the front doors had been shattered and a constellation of coin-sized blue entrance badges scattered the creamy stone floor. One statue had been toppled face-down, chips of marble astered around it. The others looked untouched.

Hobson turned in a slow circle. "With a place this fine, it's a wonder some roving band of assholes hasn't been by to smash it."

Ellie nodded, not paying particular attention. "What time is it?"

He clicked out his pocket watch. "4:07. Assuming I've been remembering to wind it."

"Then we might actually have time to find the temple."

She wandered past the cobwebbed admission booths to the broad left-side doorway. Marble statues beyond, blank-eyed Greeks. Memory jogged, she pulled a 180 and crossed the lobby to the opposite wing that housed the Egyptian collection. Dee slowed to look at the jackal-headed statues and sarcophagi. Some had been stolen, others toppled and abandoned as too heavy, but most of it was still in place.

The vacancy of the place was one more sign of how much sway the "government" really had here. Ellie wasn't the sentimental type, but these treasures—including some actual bodies—had been taken from their homeland and brought here to display. The remains, both physical and cultural, deserved to be honored. Stored away safely, at the very least. If the government couldn't take care of that much, she had no illusions they could do better for their people.

The lengthy passage fed them into a high and open chamber. Slanted windows covered one whole wall, overlooking leafless trees and piebald grass.

"Ah," Hobson said. "The temple."

Waning light displayed the two pieces dominating the room. On one end of a low platform, a stone gateway stood fifteen feet high. On the other, separated by a vast flat space, a small temple fronted by two stone pillars squatted under the high modern ceiling. Statues perched here and there. A shallow moat had once isolated the temple platform, but the water had dried up long ago, leaving nothing but a greenish stain on the channel floor and several dollars in spare change. Ellie walked around to the flat bridge and peeked inside the temple, but it was empty.

"Guess we're early," she said.

The room was clearly vacant, but she checked its nooks and corners anyway. Dee found the placard for the exhibit and read it raptly.

"This thing is like a million years old," she said. "Who just buys an ancient temple? What kind of country sells one?"

"In their defense," Hobson said, "they had an awful lot of the things."

Ellie tried the door leading out to the park. It was locked or stuck. That left two points of egress: the passage they'd come through, and another leading back into the heart of the museum. Besides the two pieces of the temple, there was little cover. As Dee fooled around behind the stone chamber, Ellie conferred with Hobson.

"Take cover behind the temples?" she said. "Or post one of us to the side of each entrance?"

"I'm not exactly a latter-day Clausewitz," he said. "But if our blind date is bearing bad intentions, I'd rather start with some space between us."

"Right. Sticking near the temple will make it easier to regroup, too."

"Boo!" Dee said from above them. She'd climbed onto the temple roof and popped her head over the ledge.

"Jesus, Dee!" Ellie flinched, throwing her hands up around her face. "Get down from there before you break something."

"Think the guards used to climb around on this after hours?" she said. "They probably did cannonballs into the moat. Forget about paying admission to see a bunch of old rocks, they should have—"

A shot roared through the cavernous chamber. Above, Dee's head disappeared from sight.

23

"I fucking told you so," Lucy said. "Now how about you let me upstairs so I can do some proper gloating?"

Brian glanced up at the boat's ceiling. "Hang tight."

He hurried up the steps. A discussion ensued abovedeck. Brian thumped down the top of the steps and beckoned her upstairs.

It had been halfway warm down there and the sea wind clawed at Lucy's ears and nose. Ash and his troops stood with their heads tipped back and turning in slow arcs, trying to match a point of light to the rumble of engines. The sound seemed to approach from the east, but in the hollow vastness, there was no way to be sure.

"Like I just told Brian, I told you so," Lucy said.

Ash shook his head. "That's a jet. Jets land on strips. If jets try to land on swamps, they transform into fireballs instead."

"Whatever. If they're using planes, you can bet they don't have many of them. Pilots, neither."

"Captain, swing around. Let's go back for a closer look."

The harried captain grimaced and strained his eyes into the darkness, as if they were navigating sandbars rather than sailing down the middle of a half-mile channel. The boat leaned. Lucy grabbed the slick metal railing. The turning boat slashed gouts of foam from the waters, filling the air with the smell of salt.

"There," a woman pointed.

To the south beyond the bi-color lighthouse, a dark vessel skimmed a couple hundred feet above the sea. It drew in over the land and Lucy lost it for a moment before picking it back up on its way toward the yacht club.

Ash extended his hand. "Binoculars."

Someone slapped a pair into his palm. The vessel bled speed. Even the captain watched as it slowed and slowed until, like a bullet fired straight into the air, it came to a complete stop. It hovered gently to the ground, disappearing behind the buildings on the northeast side of the peninsula.

"How about that?" Lucy said.

"That," Ash said, "is fucked up. Time for stealth mode. No talk, no lights, no nothing."

The captain guided the boat through its turn. Two crewmen yutzed around with the sails to make them quit flapping. The sea washed against the hull. The ship made the arduous pivot around the mile-long spit jutting north of the not-quite island that housed the yacht club, then hung dead south toward the street they'd berthed on earlier that day. All the while, Ash watched the homes and fields through his binoculars.

A tiny cone of light appeared from the buildings fringing the marsh field. It moved forward, waggling side to side. Lights blared from the middle of the field, revealing a black lozenge the size of a fattened semi. Semi-circular wings extended from each side, finlike.

Nobody had been talking, but Lucy got the idea that even if they'd been arguing over abortion laws, the sight would have knocked them dead silent.

A ramp unfurled from beside the cockpit. What could only be described as a thing climbed out of the hatch, propelled by whippy limbs and spiked feet. The ship's hard light showed a compact, pill-shaped body and a head as bulbous as a watermelon. The man with the flashlight toddled forward undeterred.

"Well, shit in my mouth," Ash said, so soft Lucy could hardly hear him over the slop of the waves. "I knew Distro was sleazy, but I never imagined they'd get in bed with the crabs."

"How can they do that?" Brian said.

"The market follows no ideology but its own," Ash said, bending his high voice into an eerily accurate mockery of Nerve's. "When the exchange of resources is beneficial to both parties, trade occurs despite artificial barriers like borders. Or the fact you're from two different fucking species who want each other extinct."

Brian waited a moment before plowing ahead. "What do we do

now?"

"Duh," Ash said. "We're going to blow it up."

"Don't you think we should report to Udall?"

"Udall's not here. That means who's in charge? The captain, technically, but does he understand I'll use his balls for bait if he disobeys my command?"

"Abundantly," the captain murmured; like the others, he watched the salt marsh with a look somewhere between disgust and horror.

"So. Executive decision. We blow it up." Ash glanced back and got a look at Brian's face. "What? They're not going to punish us. Breaking our thumbs won't undo what we've done. If Udall comes after anyone, it'll be me, yeah?"

"I suppose," Brian said.

"So buck up! We're about to blow something up!"

He looked around, as if he might have spoken too loudly, then grinned some more. His mirth was short-lived. A flap opened on the back of the ship. Two other aliens deplaned and transferred goods onto the ground. The first approached the man with the flashlight, who stopped twenty feet from the vessel. In the light shed by the ship, the two species gestured back and forth.

It made Lucy's skin crawl. She had never actually seen a live one before. She'd only ever seen direct evidence of the invaders on two occasions. Once up in South Carolina, where a friend of a friend had cured one of their exoskeletons and mounted it in his garage and was still fighting with his wife about it two years later. And the second time in Jacksonville, where the wreckage of one of their fighter jets cratered Highway 1.

Along with eight metric shitloads of stories, rumors, and whoppers, that was her entire exposure to the aliens. Her patch of Florida coast certainly hadn't been important enough to invade. They hadn't exactly stuck around, either. Six months after their arrival, the aliens were toast. She'd heard an international team of mercs had distracted the mothership with a fleet of small boats, helicopters, and light aircraft while one man rammed it with a nuke-bearing F-22 Raptor. Blown the whole thing straight to tentaclemonster hell. Now and then you heard stories of alien survivors cropping up and raiding a city or eating everyone in a settlement, but that's all they were: stories.

And here she was looking at them in the flesh. If you could call whatever they wrapped their guts with "flesh."

Ash ordered the boat closer. Everyone on board got all churchmouse. Lucy kept expecting the beings to look up, point a snakelike tentacle at the ship, and gurgle-screech like a body that's been snatched, but the Kono sailed around the marsh to the homes on the canal without a peep from the creatures in the field.

The crew tied up. Ash went downstairs and reemerged with the rocket launcher and two assault rifles, one of which he handed to Lucy.

"Could be this feels sudden or frightening or unjust," he whispered to his people. "You just remember those things are the motherfuckers that made us live like this. They're the ones who killed your friends, your husbands, your daughters. And now Distro's making money with them."

He smiled. In the darkness, his elfin features became as twisted and awful as a goblin's. "Me personally? I can't wait to put a bullet in every last one of them."

The doubt that had fostered on his soldiers' faces vanished. As memories of past wrongs and wounds were dredged from the mud of time, their eyes filled with angry resolve. Ash split them into two groups. Lucy's wing would circle through the marsh and set up a couple hundred yards from the ship. Ash's division would hang back, then head straight in once the first group was near position.

He assigned a woman named Gen to head Lucy's team. A canal separated the subdivision from the swath of marshland. Gen crouched down and jogged down the street, the four others following her single-file, and swung into the field. The jet rested on the ground some three hundred yards away. Shrubs and trees broke up their line of sight, but at times they moved over open ground, exposed, shoes squelching in the brackish water. A topcoat of snow stuck to the dirt wherever it was solid and Gen used this to navigate her way over land interrupted by shallow channels of saltwater.

After a hundred yards, she stopped and got down for a look behind them. The silhouettes of Ash's team entered the field. Gen got up and moved on, circling to the right to cut off the direct line between the jet and the yacht club a quarter mile to its southeast.

The aliens set down bins with plastic clunks. Their pointy feet thumped into the dirt. Otherwise, they moved in silence. Gen slowed and crouched so low she could have trailed her fingers along the grass. Placid surf lapped against the shore beyond the alien vessel. When they got within a hundred yards, the shrubs gave out, leaving nothing but low grass between them and the ship. Gen got down and motioned the others to do the same.

A blue beam licked past her, painting a sizzle of steam through the humid air. One of the men shrieked and stood up. The beam reappeared and sliced straight through his neck.

Guns opened up beside Lucy. She flung herself in the muck and pelted the wildly gesticulating monsters. The Distro soldier beelined for the subdivision bordering the field. Lucy swung her gun on him and fired. The first shots were behind him; she swung past, leading him, and knocked him into a canal.

The air smelled like burnt powder and seared flesh. Behind and to the left, Ash's team tromped toward the battle. One of the aliens raced to the other side of the ship, tentacles twirling. Another lashed its laser through the brush, kicking up the scent of hot salt and burning twigs.

Lucy sighted in on the creature. Beside her, Gen emptied her clip at it; it jolted repeatedly, but held its ground, spiked feet planted in the dirt like posts, its tentacles tangled in the shrubs. Lucy shot until her rifle clicked dry.

A man got up and ran behind Lucy. A beam punched through the brush, dropping him with a wet pop. Lucy swapped her empty clip for her single spare. Ash's team knelt in a line and opened up on the alien. It juddered and dropped.

The jet's engines flared. A high whine droned across the field. Bullets plinked uselessly from its sides. It lifted from the dirt with a slurp.

"Clear!" Ash shouted in his crystalline, androgynous voice.

Flame gouted behind him. The jet rose, swaying. The rocket streaked over the marsh, a red meteor, and plowed straight into the vessel's side.

Lucy had sense enough to bury her face in her arms. Somehow, she still saw the flash. The heat washed over her first, then a jolt of pressure, then the bang. A cloud of fire fell to the marsh and disintegrated in a second explosion. Debris arced in all directions, spinning smoke behind it.

Ash stood and thrust his middle finger at the flaming wreckage. "You like that, you slimy shits? How does it feel to die on a world that isn't yours?"

"Man down!" Gen said.

"And about eight inches shorter than I recall," Ash said, gazing at the headless body. Meanwhile, the man who'd been shot behind Lucy whimpered and gasped. Ash snapped his fingers. "Stewart, see if you can do something for that SOB. The rest of you follow me."

He loped toward the yacht club. Lucy followed. "They got a radio."

"Good. We can always use more radios."

The man in the control room took a couple shots at them as they ran across the street, but Lucy led the Kono straight to the unlocked front door and pointed them up the stairs. The radio room was locked, but Ash shot out the knob. Gen and Lucy laid down covering fire as Ash threw himself through the door and gunned down the lone defender before he could get off a round.

After the ruckus of the gunplay, the club was as silent as a snowy wood. Ash took a quick look around and ordered his people to grab up the radio and the ledgers. Finished, they returned to the field, where the downed ship continued to burn. The flames had spread to the cargo and the whole marsh smelled like roasted coffee.

"Don't know my own strength," Ash said. "I was hoping to loot that thing."

"I'd say you just knocked out their main pipeline," Lucy said. "Time to go for the jugular."

"You ever shot a tiger? I have. Fucking thing must've escaped the Brooklyn zoo. I got it in the lung and knocked it down, but it was lying in the street staring at me. If I'd gotten close, it would have lunged and torn out my throat with desperate-tiger strength.

"So what did I do? I let it bleed out. Because I'd shot it and there was nothing it could do." Ash grinned. "We'll do the same to Distro. In a couple of months, after they can't pay their workers and soldiers, we'll walk in and cut their throats." He slung his gun over his shoulder. "Grab the bodies. No reason to let them know it was us."

His people gathered up their dead and bore them back to the

ship. As soon as the last man was aboard, the captain shoved off. It was near midnight but Lucy was far too amped to think about sleep. The ship lugged its way up the coast, fighting the winds, which felt cold enough to convince Jack Frost to pull up the covers and stay in bed.

"I feel like solid gold," Ash said to her once they were properly underway. They stood on the railing together, wind chapping their faces. "How did you know about this?"

"Distro's people disappeared from it about a month back," Lucy said. "We went down to take a look. They figured it was you."

"What do you know, they predicted the future."

"Still don't know who took them out. Maybe Distro's got more enemies than we know. Good time to press the advantage."

Ash shrugged and spat into the churning sea. "They were dead either way. We're about to unleash our mandatory labor program. Will we have the luxuries, the coffee and sugar? No. But we'll undercut them on everything else. And after tonight, I doubt they'll be shipping in any more Jamaican Blue Mountain, either."

"Mandatory labor?" Moonlight shimmered on the crests of the waves. "You're talking about slaves."

"Don't get high and mighty on me, little girl. Distro pays their people room and board and a pinch of tea. If you're really lucky, you might get to run the lights an hour per day. Does that really sound different from what we're doing?"

"Least their people are free to leave."

"Free to starve. Or get murdered by bandits. If they're really desperate, they can throw themselves on the mercy of the Feds and go mine coal instead. Where do you think the power comes from?"

"Assholes, generally," Lucy said.

Ash laughed. "At least with us, you know where you stand. You screw up, you catch a beating and get back to work as soon as you've recovered. Distro will grin something about your next performance review, then slit your throat in your sleep and replace you with someone cheaper."

She went belowdecks and curled up on a bench. The sleep she got wasn't too good, but she was glad for what she got. As soon as they tied up in port, Ash ordered Brian to deal with the bodies, then marched straight in to Sicily.

"Drinks!" he commanded squeakily, a dim figure after the hard morning light outside. "Drinks for all. Keep them coming until I start telling you what a sad childhood I had."

He piled into a booth and demanded the rest of the party join him, including the haggard captain, whose exhausted face looked ready to puddle around his shoes. The bartender conscripted a server from one of the three people who'd been sitting around Sicily before Ash rolled in. Ash called for three rounds of tequila, which the returned soldiers consumed dutifully. Lucy decided to enjoy herself. It had been a couple years since she'd tasted pre-war tequila.

Ash rehashed the previous night with the troops and crew, laughing garrulously, standing on the padded red seat and waving his arms around like the writhing of tentacles. It wasn't yet eleven in the morning, but word got around. People filtered into the bar in ones and twos: official Kono members; hangers-on and wannabes; neighborhood locals who were happy to rub shoulders with gangsters so long as it meant a fresh beer in front of them. Some stuck to their booths, absorbing the scene from the fringes. Others walked up to Ash to make jokes about his close encounter. The way they asked—half-teasing, little bunny smiles on their mouths—you could tell they feared it was a put-on and they'd walk away as fools. But by the time Ash finished his tale, they left as believers.

Things got loud. Lucy couldn't say she was surprised when Ash climbed up on the table, knocking shot glasses to the floor, and clapped his hands for silence.

"Does everyone here know Lucy?" he said. Several faces turned her way, few of them friendly. Ash grinned. "I know, I know. She shot Duke. And with him passed a life of such class and grace the whole world is poorer for it. That is, unless you're a black man, a female anything, or a person who can't help the fact they were born with the voice of an angel."

He glared down from the table, words ringing in the air, daring them to defy him. "Duke never did anything but ride his uncle's coattails. You liked him because he was here, not because he deserved it. Tonight, Lucy Two held the stake while we drove it into Distro's heart. She's done more for the Kono in one month than Duke did in his sad little life.

"So ask yourself this. Do you care about the Kono? Do you

believe in our destiny as the rulers of this city? Or do you care about the loss of one mean little son of a bitch?" Without looking, he stretched out his hand and flapped his fingers. Someone slapped a bottle into it. He hoisted it, sloshing liquor over those below him. "To Lucy!"

"To Lucy!" the room roared.

Electricity shot up her spine. She had never been recognized publicly before—for anything good, at least—and the thrill was so potent it scared her.

But it sure was nice to be appreciated for once. She could see herself becoming the person these people were cheering for. Joining the Kono and meaning it. The Distro were dead in the water. If she wasn't already Ash's lieutenant, she soon would be. Play her cards right, and in a couple years, she might supplant him. Or become the unseen boss all these men paid homage to.

She let herself dance with these thoughts. Anointed by Ash, she spent the next couple hours being approached by gangsters. They made good-natured jokes about her name. Asked about the aliens. Flirted. Sure, some stuck to their booths and studiously avoided eye contact, but most had changed their tune. She was in.

They drank and laughed through the afternoon. Some staggered off but were replaced by others. All of a sudden, Lucy thought it would be a great idea to bike downtown through the snow and see Tilly's building. As she rode south, skidding on hidden ice, she couldn't say why she needed to go see the Tower—she was more than a little drunk; she didn't even remember how she'd gotten the bike—but it thundered in her mind, imperative.

By the time she stood across the street from it, the concrete stacked nearly a quarter mile into the sky, winter's swift night had fallen on the city. She breathed in and out, fog whirling from her mouth. She'd burned off a bit of the tequila during the ride and now realized she'd have to make the same trip back through the slush and the cold. What did she think would happen—Tilly would rush outside and ask to be whisked uptown with her? A deep feeling of stupidity flash-flooded her veins.

Then, as if her thoughts had caused it to manifest, a woman walked out the revolving door of the Empire State Building. She was bundled in a scarf and thick coat, but Lucy knew Tilly's walking-across-coals step anywhere.

And though it was perfectly dark, the girl wore a pair of dark sunglasses big enough to cover her whole eye sockets.

Lucy had seen her make that fashion statement before. Right before the plague, while she was still living in the Lomans' garage, Tilly had started going around with a boy named Jude. Jude was a drinker, and when he indulged, he became a beater. Between her makeup and sunglasses, Tilly hid it from her mom and dad, who were so busy bitching at each other about their separation they wouldn't have looked up had Godzilla stomped across their living room, but Lucy noticed.

Lucy stood in the shadows of a recessed doorway and watched Tilly glance up and down the street. Just as Lucy decided to cross over, hooves clocked. Nerve rode up to Tilly, horse steaming. Without a word from either one of them, Nerve got down to help Tilly climb up. The pair trotted away.

Once the hooves faded, Lucy got on her bike, twice as sober as five minutes before. She made one stop at a Staples along the way, then continued to the toasty Village coffee shop. Inside, the cowboy gave her the evil eye, but she ignored him and headed straight for Reese.

"I'm surprised they don't charge you rent," she said.

He sat at a booth with a couple friends who made no bones about looking her up and down. "Can I help you with something?"

"Come on outside."

He looked ready to protest, then raised his eyebrows at his friends and scooted from the booth.

Out on the dark street, Lucy passed him a sealed envelope. "Can you deliver this to Chelsea Pier? Guy named Kerry. Big old bald dude."

"I've seen him. What's in it for me?"

Lucy reached for her bag, but drunk as she was, she hadn't brought anything but herself. She grimaced at the blank pavement. "I'm sorry about the movie. I was a dick to you when you were just trying to help me out."

"I don't want an apology. I want something I can use."

"I don't have anything, man. I'm trying to do someone a good turn. Will you please get this to Kerry?"

"Never thought I'd see you beg." Reese sniffed against the cold. "What's it say?"

"Nothing they'll enjoy hearing about," Lucy sighed. "You'll want to lie low for a while."

"A deal like that? How could I say no?"

She kissed him on the cheek. "Don't get any ideas. But you're a good dude."

She hopped on her bike. He was still standing on the sidewalk watching her go when she turned the corner and was swallowed once more by the canyon of skyscrapers.

Back at Sicily, she climbed the steps to her floor and flung herself into bed. When she finally woke, light sliced through the blinds. It was several minutes before she remembered what she'd done. She regretted it, but she knew that was the hangover talking.

She headed downstairs for some chow. The bartender greeted her by name. Ash wasn't around. Sleeping it off, no doubt. Either that or reporting to his superiors about the game-changing success of his mission. She hung around, picking at her eggs and sipping brown liquid the bartender swore was coffee, then went back to her room to clean up. She was freezing her tits off in the shower when she heard the first screams.

Lucy ran from the stall without turning off the faucet. She stood at the window, water dripping from her hair. Below, fire bloomed from Sicily, whooming like a sheet flung over a bed. In the middle of the street, a member of Distro security reared back and hurled another flaming cocktail at the bar's face.

24

A second shot crashed through the room. The bullet smacked into the top of the temple, spitting flecks of stone onto the smooth floor. Ellie bolted for cover behind its wall, the sheriff right behind her.

"Dee!" she yelled.

Three shots blasted past Hobson, shattering panes of the slanted wall behind him. He pulled in tight against the temple and stuck his rifle around the corner.

"Mom?" Dee called from up top.

"Come down the back side," Ellie said, running to the structure's rear. "He won't have a shot."

Hobson's rifle discharged. From the entrance through the Egyptian wing, the shooter fired back. Dee's shoes dangled off the lip of the roof. She squirmed her lower half off the edge, keeping low, then dropped to the ground in a deep crouch.

"It's a trap?"

Ellie pointed across the dry moat to the exit deeper into the Met. "Cover that door. Shoot anything that moves." She rolled around the other corner. The sheriff was glued to the temple's side, eye trained on his scope. "How many?"

"One that I saw," the man murmured. "He's pulled back. I think my last shot was too close for comfort."

She glanced out the bank of windows, which were broad enough for any of them to squeeze through, and her skin prickled. Branches shivered across the black grass. "I think someone's outside. Only thing saving us is the darkness. We've got to move."

The sheriff swore. "How's Dee's aim?"

"Unpolished."

He didn't take his eye from his scope. "Post her on the corner to cover the shooter. You make a break for the other door. If you make it, you can return the favor."

Ellie laughed wryly, keeping both eyes on the park beyond the windows for the glint of metal. "Try not to let him get a shot off. You don't want me bleeding all over that fine suit of yours."

Hobson smiled faintly. "It wouldn't be the first time I've scrubbed blood from a suit."

To her surprise, she found she trusted him. She went around back to Dee, who sat with her rifle braced across her raised knee, watching the other door. Ellie explained their next move.

"You're just going to run?" Dee said.

Ellie gazed at the empty moat. She could run along its bottom, hidden from view, but climbing out would leave her exposed and essentially motionless for several seconds. "Unless you know how to fly."

"Well, don't get shot!"

"Don't let me get shot."

Dee gave her a look of twisted fright that Ellie read as clearly as the placard on the tomb: how could you ask this of me?

Ellie dropped down beside her, keeping one eye on the dark mouth of the passage to the heart of the museum. "I was scared to be your mom, you know. I was so afraid I'd screw it up. But after the job Chip did with you, I had nothing to worry about. There's no one I'd rather have covering me."

Dee blinked, then edged forward to the stone corner and swung her gun around the other side, taking aim at the doorway they'd used to enter the chamber. There hadn't been another shot since the sheriff's last exchange. She returned to him.

"At the count of ten," she said.

He nodded. Ellie unshouldered her rifle and clicked off the safety. Counting in her head, she moved beside Dee. "Three. Two. One."

She sprinted onto the open platform. The bridge was set back toward the door they'd come in through and she locked her eyes on the dark tunnel. At the steps down to the bridge, she stumbled, arm thrown in front of her. A rifle boomed behind her, followed by a second. She caught her balance and sprinted headlong into the second tunnel feeding from the temple chambers.

Heart hammering, she jogged past glass cases, the light fading as she got further from the windows overlooking the temple. At the T-intersection ahead, with no sign or sound of strangers, she turned around and returned to the tunnel mouth.

"Clear!" she shouted. She installed herself at the corner, took a look at the windows, and sighted down her rifle at the first doorway across the room.

Back at the temple, Dee held up three fingers, counting down. When her index finger fell, she broke cover, eyes so wide they looked painted on. Her run was the longest four seconds of Ellie's life.

Dee fell in beside her at the wall, smelling like the ammonia-laced sweat of sheer panic.

"Come up here and cover the windows," Ellie said.

"Right," Dee said vaguely. Ellie stood and Dee crouched beneath her to help watch the dark tunnel to the Egyptian wing.

Hobson signaled, counted down, and ran. He was older and he ran with a shuffling, low-kneed style that felt like it took forever to cross the room. Then he was beside them, too, breathing hard, his bowler lost at some point during the run.

"I have never resented one hundred feet of space more thoroughly than I do now," he whispered breathily.

"It's pitch black ahead," Ellie said.

"If our assailant has doubled back, or has an accomplice outside, a light will paint a target on our chests." Hobson risked a look around the corner.

A bullet crackled past his ear and whined off the far wall. Ellie opened fire on the light that had flared from the other tunnel. Glass shattered.

"I'll light the lantern," Hobson said. He rattled it from his pack. Within seconds, he had the oiled wick aflame. He hurried down the tunnel past cases of curved swords and lacquered armor. Ellie sent Dee first, then waited for the pair to reach the T-intersection before racing to catch up.

"Which way?" the sheriff said.

"Right," Ellie said. Not that she had any idea how to get to the entrance or the nearest emergency exit. But left would run them back toward the Egyptian wing.

Hobson trundled forward. Ellie walked after him, rifle in hand. Dee held hers tight to her chest. The lantern flashed past portraits of colonial Americans, presidents and preachers and masted ships at war. The next door opened to a cavernous room of furniture and antique household goods. Ellie was too focused on putting space between them and the attacker to pay much mind.

"Left," she said.

Hobson veered through the door. Broken glass crunched under their feet. Rusted knives rested in the few displays that hadn't been looted. Ellie took the lead into another expansive room. The torchlight shined on full suits of armor, lances soaring above the empty figures' heads. By her count, they'd made three left turns and should be headed back to the main entrance, but the far wall of the next room was blank. Doorways led left and right.

"God damn it," Ellie said.

Dee gazed at lacquered red Japanese armor. "Are we lost?"

"Keep your voice down." She tried to picture the museum's layout in her head, but the grounds were massive, with scores of rooms on each floor. Something scuffed behind them. She whirled, but the room they'd just left was utterly dark. She dropped her voice to a whisper. "Blow out the lantern."

Hobson frowned. "Did you hear something?"

"Blow it out!"

He snuffed the lamp. The room went so dark she thought her eyes might pop from the strain. The scuffing noise repeated, nearer. She could no longer see Dee or Hobson, but she felt them freeze in place, eyes arrested on the doorway beyond. The feet swished over the tile, in the doorway now, not twenty feet away. Ellie's thighs quivered. The figure began humming: Brahms. He chuckled softly, then moved past, continuing toward the center of the museum.

"Look," Dee said once the scuffling faded to nothing. Ellie wanted to laugh, but she could see the outline of Dee's arm pointing in the darkness. Reoriented toward the way they'd come in, the room to their left was lit by the faintest hint of silver.

Ellie made her voice so soft she could hardly hear it herself. "Not a word."

She edged forward, step by step, leading the way with one hand.

She passed into the next room. Skylights allowed the pale glimmer of stars to touch the white statues and wood furniture arrayed around the walls. Ellie paused to listen. High above, wind scraped the leaves against the windows.

From the center of the museum, a man screamed, first in terror, and then in an octave-climbing shriek of pain.

Dee sucked in air, the precursor of a scream of her own, and clapped her hand to her mouth. "What was that?"

"Guardian of the museum?" Hobson said, inappropriately amused.

"Doesn't matter," Ellie said. "Time to go."

She walked briskly, commanding herself not to run—too noisy—and squeezed past a staircase to the left. Down a long hall, she saw more silver light. The front doors.

"Cover me," she whispered.

The two knelt and trained their guns across the expansive room. Ellie bent low and jogged to the doors. There, she got down and braced her gun over one knee while first Dee and then Hobson crossed. Outside, they grabbed their snowshoes and ran without pausing to buckle them on. Their feet sank to the ankles in the snow. Ellie zagged east, then north, then east another block.

"Do we have a destination in mind?" Hobson said. "Or is it 'away'?"

"The attack tells us we're on to something. We need to follow up at City Hall, but the sheriff's office will be closed by the time we get downtown." Ellie cast about the street. Her shoes were soaked. "Let's get as far south as we can. Try to find an apartment. Basement will be warmest. We'll return to City Hall in the morning."

"And what if the trap was set by the sheriff?"

"Then he'll be right there in arm's reach."

He looked unconvinced, but didn't argue further. They put on their snowshoes and trudged south down Park Avenue, passing stately hotels and office towers that looked ready to blast into space.

"Okay, so I'll ask what we're all thinking," Dee said. "Who do you think that was?"

"The attacker?" Hobson said. "Or the attacker of the attacker?"

"Either one!"

"Much as I'd like to imagine it's a vengeful mummy, it was more likely your run-of-the-mill lunatic."

Ellie's mind kicked out an answer. "The shooter's someone who knows about the slave trade."

The sheriff crooked a brow. "What if it's the government themselves?"

"Then why go for a botched ambush five miles away from your base of operations? If they thought we were that much of a threat, they could have marched us inside a courtroom and executed us."

Hobson tipped his head to the side. "Though the incompetence of the plan would fit your typical federal modus operandi."

They made it a couple miles before Dee mentioned that her toes were numb. Ellie was about to chide her for not speaking up sooner —the inconvenience of stopping a half hour sooner than Ellie would like would be nothing compared to the inconvenience of being hobbled or disabled by frostbite—but understood, for once, that such lectures by the Mom-Sergeant were likely the exact reason Dee felt compelled to soldier on despite unhealthy levels of discomfort.

"Please speak up if you ever need a break," she said, in what she hoped was her most non-critical tone. "Or if you see me pushing myself too hard. Quinn needs us healthy."

"I know." Dee's two words could have been intoned a hundred different ways and Ellie was relieved beyond measure that they weren't defensive, but were instead spoken in soft agreement.

This parenting shit was hard. Kids bristled at the power imbalance while adults grew frustrated with the knowledge they were even less perfect than their kids believed. Negative vibes all over the place. Hard not to get petty about it. But remembering Quinn helped her stay focused. Forget counseling, what parents of teens really needed to hone their communication skills was the occasional statewide rescue mission.

They found a Midtown apartment with basement rooms that presumably once housed the super and staff. Ellie got off Dee's shoes and rubbed her feet until the feeling came back. Once her toes were dry and halfway warm, Dee pulled on three pairs of socks. With no heat source, they shut themselves in a single bedroom to trap what body heat they could and slept in layers of pants and socks and long-sleeved shirts.

It wasn't a fun night, but nobody froze. Ellie woke stiff and tired.

Another cold breakfast. Microwaves had made things so easy that hot foods eaten cold had become something of a treat—cold pizza, iced coffee—but away from her home and stove, food had lost its joy, repetitive and bland, one more small task to take care of to keep yourself going, no more pleasurable than drying out your socks or packing clean snow into your water bottle.

Maybe it was the lack of accomplishment, too. She didn't have to catch this food or even cook it for herself. Back in the old days, there had been a certain hunter-gatherer satisfaction in grabbing takeout Chinese and returning home, victorious, to eat your bounty in front of the TV. Of course, they had captured the food they now ate. Violently. Yet it didn't make her feel proud or victorious at all.

They got off to an early start and arrived at City Hall shortly after nine. The government continued to keep its old hours; a soldier was already out front. He examined their passports and showed them inside. A different receptionist held down the desk today and he tried to bumrush Ellie with the same BS about the island being closed to tourists. As she prepared to pull him across the desk by his tie and lay down the law, he relented and let them upstairs to see the sheriff.

"You're back," he said mildly.

Ellie planted herself in front of his desk. "Does that surprise you?"

"These days, the only thing that would surprise me is if I got to go home early."

"I'm about to add to your workload. Since you last saw us, someone tried to kill us."

"Now that's the city I grew up in."

"Is that why you brought it to City Hall?" she said. "Before we left, an anonymous note requested a meet at the Met. It was an ambush."

The twinkle faded from the sheriff's eyes. "Who gave you the note?"

"The gopher who brought us upstairs yesterday. Wasn't him."

"What about the shooter? Got a name? Description?"

Ellie shook her head. "By now, there's probably nothing left but bones. But his motive was clear enough: to stop us from tracking down the slavers."

"I don't know if you realize this, ma'am, but you got an air around you that might rub some the wrong way. Could this attack be personal?"

"After they shot at my daughter?" Ellie said. "You're god damn right it's personal."

"We may be from the sticks," Hobson said, "but it's a mistake—and an insult—to assume we're rubes. This woman is a former federal agent. Until the digital era turned the industry into a tedious game of Google, I was a private investigator. Yesterday, in the course of pursuing a criminal, another crime was perpetrated upon us. You sit here trying to throw a cloud of dust on the matter. Is that because you're lying? Or because you're so witlessly incompetent that you're not aware of the slave trade that exists in the city you're sworn to protect?"

The sheriff clenched his hands on his desk, face going as hard as the butt of a gun. But there was a crack in the flint of his eyes. The guilt poured through and he swiveled his chair to face the bright window.

"It's not a good time to be a person with beliefs," he said. "Even ones we used to hold self-evident."

"You mean equality?" Ellie said. "Freedom?"

"I do protect this city. I'm its servant. But I got other masters, too. The ones who provide the weight to my words. If they tell me there's no such thing as slaves in Manhattan—and that even if there were, that my duty is to the citizens, not outsiders who couldn't keep themselves from trouble—what's a man do? This is a desirable job. I try to buck, or resign in protest, and this time tomorrow they'll have a new face smiling from behind this desk. One who's more interested in playing ball than doing right."

Hobson smiled ruefully. "This precise philosophical conundrum is why I left the force to open my own business."

"I don't care who's right and who's wrong," Ellie said. "I want my family back."

The sheriff of Manhattan leaned forward and clasped his hands over his paperwork. "Indulge a brief lecture in economics. Used to be we had too many people and too little work to keep them busy and fed. Since the big die-off, that's reversed. The computers are gone. Most all the machines, too. Most people are too busy trying to pry potatoes out of the ground to care about working some idiot job.

For those few who are interested, what do you have to pay them with now that there's no money?"

"Luxuries," Ellie said. "Anything that's so wanted yet so hard to come by that most everyone will accept it in lieu of cash."

"Sure, and for some, there's a real thrill in negotiating to be paid in chocolate because you speculate it will only be worth more one year to the next." The man laughed and shook his head. "A salary in Hershey's. Unbelievable."

"And having things to trade is only valuable if there are other people to trade with."

"There's no currency in a pond, so to speak. I'll cut to the chase. When anyone with two legs can find themselves a subsistence farm, nobody wants to be paid with something as blasé as food. So you pay laborers in luxuries. Power, heat, coffee and the like. But these laborers still need to eat. That means you need to make sure the farmers are productive enough not just to subsist, but to provide."

Ellie's blood cooled. "Your government's running plantations."

He scrunched up his face like he was heading into a sunrise after a long walk through the night. "Here's where things get gray. Say a third party takes it upon themselves to make sure the farmers produce more than they can eat. They provide machines. Field hands. The third party takes their cut; the farmers sell the surplus; the government is kept stable. Everyone wins."

"Except the slaves!" Dee said.

The sheriff bent his eyebrows. "I'm the messenger, not the man who ordered the chains."

"The soldiers on the bridges," Hobson said. "Are they to keep people out? Or to make sure they stay in?"

"It's a double-duty gig. Anyway, if one of your people got snared in the net, there's no way to know where he's been sent. But I'd have a pretty good guess."

"Central Park," Ellie said.

The man nodded. "A woman named Nora Ryan lives in the boathouse on the east side of the Lake. Know it?"

"The reservoir?"

"No, the Lake. By Strawberry Fields." He got a look at her puzzled expression and sighed. "Come in East 72nd and follow the path straight to the big red terrace. It overlooks the Lake. Nora runs a clean farm. She used to work for me. Let her know the score and that I sent you." He slid open his drawer for fresh paper. "Now, about the man who ambushed you at the Met."

"I told you, we didn't get a look at him. Look at your people for connections to the 'third party' bringing captives into the city. That's your mark." Ellie stood. "Thank you for your help."

He stopped them halfway to the door. "How do you do it, sheriff? Do more good than harm?"

Hobson put his fists on his hips and looked down to the carpet for answers. "Your worry is you'll be replaced by someone worse. I believe that if my life is lost in the pursuit of my duties, the people who replace me will be inspired to improve on my work."

The sheriff of Manhattan squinted, silent. Hobson tried to tip his bowler, then remembered it was missing. They headed downstairs and exited into the overcast morning.

"From here on out, we need to think about every move we make," Ellie said. "Someone has already tried to kill us to keep this quiet. Once we're rubbing shoulders with the captives, one wrong word could bring the hammer down on our heads."

"Why do I get the idea you're only talking to me?" Dee said.

"Because you're still young enough to think the world revolves around you."

Hobson chuckled. "Whereas I am old enough to think that Ellie was talking to herself most of all."

"It's for all of us." Ellie hiked her pack up her shoulders and walked through the trail they'd flattened in the snow on their way down. "Let's move."

They faced a five-mile walk back to the Upper East Side. Their snowshoes chuffed through the snow, which was largely free of tracks. By the time the park's trees sprouted darkly behind its concrete walls, it was early afternoon and Ellie had resolved that, if and when they got back home, she would stay seated in her chair by the fire until next July.

She led them down the sidewalk, keeping the street between them and the park's barbed wire-topped walls. Many of the lawns were clearer than they'd been before the Panhandler. Trees had been cut down for cabins and farmland. Some old growth had been replaced by young trees—apples, cherries, and other fruiting varieties, presumably. Post-apocalypse, the New Yorkers had made Central Park every bit as space-efficient as the gridded skyscrapers had once been.

But many trees had been left in place to block the wind, delineate borders, and break up the chimney smoke of the cabins dotting the fields. She could smell the smoke as soon as they'd gotten within a block of the park, but rather than rising in many separate fingers, it hung over the greenery in a dispersed gray pall. Clever stuff. You'd never guess you were looking at the city's breadbasket.

They followed 72nd into the park. The lanes were bordered by snowed-in grass and leafless trees. As with every settlement Ellie had seen, there were no homes directly fronting the road. Instead, log cabins peeked from copses of trees, hidden by shrubs and ivy. After a quarter mile, the road went past a red terrace overlooking a lake. They climbed down the steps, passed a fountain, and followed the trail to the northeast. Ducks honked from the water. A couple of men sat on the banks with fishing poles and fingerless gloves. Each watched until Ellie and the others disappeared behind the trees.

The boathouse was hard to miss. A long structure with an expansive patio, roof held up by columns. Banks of windows looked over the lake. Ellie walked around front and knocked.

The door opened six inches. Through the gap, a young man stared back. "No room for strangers."

"Is your mom Nora Ryan?" Ellie said. "We're friends of a friend. It's important to speak to her."

He closed the door. The glass panels had been boarded over. Ellie heard his bare feet thump off. A minute later, steps advanced with adult weight.

The woman who reopened the front door had short dark hair and the build of a person who did their own grunt-work. "Sheriff Monroe sent you?"

"We're looking for my daughter's fiancé," Ellie said. "We have reason to believe he was brought to Central Park."

The woman nodded knowingly. "Come on in."

The front of the boathouse was a former restaurant dining room, now partitioned with sheets and tapestries. Nora brought the three of them to a partition hidden from the windows and poured them bitter tea. Shreds of garden weeds floated in the greenish liquid.

Ellie explained the broad strokes. Nora listened patiently until the end. "I'm sympathetic. Just because God's given us hard times doesn't mean He's taken away a person's right to be free." She tapped her nail against her mug. "But times are harder than ever. There's fighting in the city. And one of the fighters runs the trade that brought you here."

Ellie sipped her drink. The taste was awful, but it felt nice to have something warm in her stomach. "You've got kids. You're worried about blowback."

"Not to mention blizzards, ergot, and a rat population that thinks it's got more right to the rye than the person that grew it."

"Ah, but we aren't looking for trouble." Hobson smiled and settled his elbows on the table, leaning in conspiratorially. "To the contrary, we are a family—patriarch, wife, and daughter—looking to begin a new life here in the spring. As we're starting from scratch, we think it's prudent to explore all opportunities to hasten the construction of our homestead."

"You might pass," Nora said. "But I can't vouch for you. The locals know my stance on their not-so-hired help."

"We'll keep you out of it," Ellie said. "We don't need a place to stay. Just information."

"And food," Dee said.

"Dee."

"What? Like I haven't noticed lunch keeps getting smaller?"

Ellie turned back to Nora. "And food, if you can spare it. I've brought trade."

Nora waved her hand. "This is one charity my wallet—and larder—are always open to. The man you want to see is Hank Kroger. He runs the big farm on the north side of the reservoir. Most people here are small-timers who don't find it worth their while to feed and handle slaves they only need come planting and harvest. Kroger owns a few dozen. Rents them out for a cut of the crop. If your boy's here, chances are Kroger's seen him."

"He sounds like quite the entrepreneur," Hobson said.

"His money's stained with blood," the woman said. "And everyone's eager to get their taste."

She provided them with meat pies, baked potatoes, and bread, along with some dried food that would last longer. Ellie insisted on paying with some of her instant coffee and gold, which Nora said a few of her neighbors still valued.

"Stop by if it doesn't pan out," she said. "But be careful. These people deal in stealing lives. You give them trouble, and they won't think twice about taking yours."

Ellie thought about exiting the park and taking Fifth Avenue all the way to Kroger's farm, but there was no guarantee the man would have Quinn. With another long walk ahead of them, it would serve them best to put it to use to get a feel for the park and find other leads should Kroger fall through.

For the most part, the trip was more of the same. Cabins, trees, fields. A few people walked dogs around the paths. One woman even picked up her shiba's excrement in a crinkly blue baggie. Axes thunked monotonously. Winter wheat poked from the sheets of snow. Other fields were blank white patches waiting to be seeded. After a long, winding march, a vast reservoir opened before them. They followed the path around it to a compound of log cabins and tin sheds surrounded by cut crops and metal fences, behind which cows and pigs pawed at the snow.

A man sat on one of the fences. Maybe he was taking a breather, or maybe it was his job to watch the path all day, including during the dead of winter, but as they walked up, he hopped down, discharged a brown gout of chaw-spit into the snow, and blocked the way forward.

"You know where you are?"

"I'm hoping this is the establishment of Mr. Hank Kroger," Hobson said, managing to sound politely affronted.

"On what business?"

"Just that—business. We're looking to move here this spring. Naturally, we'll need a house. I've been told Mr. Kroger can provide enough labor to ensure the timeliness of its completion."

The man just stared. "Come on up, Fancy Dan."

He brought them past the fence to the largest of log buildings, which was more like one of the vacation "cabins" on the Saranacs than something from the frontier. The man told them to wait, then entered the iron-banded front door. It took five minutes before he returned.

"Mr. Kroger will be out to see you shortly." He held out his palm.

"First, your firearms."

Ellie complied. The man set their guns on a table inside a tool shed beside the home. He hooked his thumbs in his belt loops and didn't bother to say a word until the door opened and disgorged a tall blond man, late middle age, with deep, kindly wrinkles around his eyes and teeth so strong and straight they could open a can.

"Hank Kroger." He strode through the snow, hand extended. Hobson met it and shook. The man nodded at Ellie and Dee. "Call me Hank. My man says we might be neighbors some day."

"Indeed," Hobson said. "We're from upstate. Very scenic, but there's very little of what you might call society. My daughter will want to marry someday and my wife and I don't find the mountains especially stimulating, either."

Kroger nodded soberly. "After the plague, people killed themselves to get away from everyone else. Now they're remembering there's nothing more important than family, friends, and neighbors."

"That is precisely our experience. And that is why we've come all this way in the dead of winter—to ensure that, come next winter, we'll be snug inside our new home, enjoying the smell of fresh pine timbers and toasting our foresight."

Kroger maintained a smile through Hobson's speech. "Want a little help, do you? Looking to rent? Or buy?"

Hobson stroked his chin. "If the right candidate were to present itself, I'm inclined to buy. The house is just the beginning of our work."

"Gonna run you a penny or three more than renting, naturally. Let's have a look and see what you think."

He crunched through the snow deeper into the park, shadowed by his man. Ellie, in turn, shadowed Hobson. She hadn't been treated as such a nonentity since her stint as a junior agent and she bristled at Kroger's every word. But there were advantages to being ignored. She couldn't afford to waste her attention on annoyance. It was time to keep her eyes open.

She had expected squalor. Flagrant, foul evidence of man's inhumanity to man. But the barn-like structure where they housed the slaves was clean and whitewashed and even had windows—albeit narrow things that were more like arrow-slits than portals of light. Kroger unlocked the door and smiled at Hobson.

His man stalked inside ahead of them, swinging his arm like a club. "Afternoon, gentlemen!"

"No need for that." Kroger brushed past, giving his man a pat on the shoulder. "Howdy, people. Got some folks who'd like a look at you. Mind lining up for me?"

The inside was a single high-raftered room. Single beds were set perpendicular to the walls. It was on the cool side but habitable. At the other end of the room, twelve men got up from the tables where they'd been playing cards and dominoes and stood abreast in the center of the room. Quinn wasn't among them.

"Nice digs, huh?" Kroger grinned, flashing his white teeth. "I like my people to be fit. Healthy. And not for the reasons you'd think. Hey Denver, what do you think of life here?"

A thin man with long brown hair shrugged his broad shoulders. "Before the ranch, I was a highwayman. Not a good one, either." The others laughed huskily. He craned his neck to look between them. "It's true! I was so thin you could have used me to darn your socks. Here, I've got work. I get meals and a roof. I wish I'd been picked up years ago."

"I'm not naive enough to think we're friends," Kroger said. "But I believe that if I offer these men clean beds, a hot meal, and my respect, they'll work not because they have to, but because they want to."

"I see." Hands folded behind his back, Hobson prowled down the line, inspecting. "And for a man like this, your compensation..?"

"Now, these are my professionals. Men I trust to clean my kids' rooms while the youngsters are still in bed. Rental-only. But for the work they'll give you, they're worth triple the cost."

"Hmm," Hobson said. He headed for the doorway.

Kroger moved ahead to show him out. Out in the snow, he smiled knowingly. "I know, it's awkward to talk business in front of them. Trust me, they're used to it."

"Here's the thing," the sheriff said, gazing at the pines beyond the barn. "Do you have anything more...traditional?"

"I'm not catching what you're throwing."

Hobson coughed delicately. "Your setup is quite humane, which is very comforting, but I retain certain...qualms. I wonder if these might be lessened if I owned a slave of a different race."

Kroger gave him a look of puzzled disgust. "First off, they're not slaves. They're assistant labor providers. Second, on the Kroger Ranch, we're an equal opportunity employer. I've seen men and women of all kinds. Age, size, build, and spirit, that's what makes a difference. But if you've got the notion a black man makes a better ALP than a white man—well, let me disabuse you of that idea here and now."

"Progressive," Hobson muttered. "Regardless, they seemed a tad on the old side. For assistant labor providers, I mean; obviously I am not one to cast stones when it comes to age. If I'm going to invest, I'd like to be sure that investment is for the long term."

"Prudent." He smiled at Ellie. "Your husband's got a good head on him. Let me show you something more your style."

He showed them to another barn of mostly younger men, but Quinn wasn't among its residents, either. Nor at the barn after that.

"That's the extent of my male inventory," Kroger said once they were out in the snow again. He was smiling like usual, but his eyes had the impatient look of a salesman who knows the buyer's too skittish to close. "Seen anything that rings your bell?"

"Oh, several," Hobson said seriously, breath wisping from his mouth. "But with a commitment of this magnitude, I want to be perfectly certain of my decision. Do you expect to have more stock soon? Or know others who might be selling? You would, of course, be entitled to a commission."

Kroger shrugged, turning away. "Just got our newest a couple weeks ago. I don't expect more till spring. As for other vendors, selection will be very limited. I'm the only one with a proper lot. At another farm, the only ALPs they'll be looking to part with will be the ones they don't think are good enough for themselves."

"Whereas you possess such abundance it's no matter to part with a piece of it."

"Hit it on the head."

"You've given me much to think about," Hobson said. "May I return after I've had a couple days to process?"

"Take all the time you need."

They shook. Kroger grinned and bobbed his head at Ellie and Dee. His hired man returned with the guns. Ellie donned her snowshoes. The three of them walked east from the park.

"He wasn't there," Dee said.

Gray clouds mounted in the sky. Ellie skidded over a patch of ice. "I know."

"What if he's not here at all? What if he's just getting farther and farther away?"

She turned to look Dee in the eye. "Do you think I'll stop looking?"

Dee's face calmed. "No."

"Then it's not if we find him. It's when."

But she wasn't so confident. Even in the good old days, once you got 48 hours out from the time of kidnapping, it was 50/50 you'd see the victim alive again. These days, with no internet or phones, no FBI or cross-country travel, she had the feeling New York was their last chance to find Quinn before he became lost in the wilderness of the world.

They found an apartment overlooking the park and went to bed early. The next day, they made the rounds, continuing their cover story, going door to door among the farmhouses scattered around the park. Armed with the proper terminology and attitude, Hobson made fewer gaffes than with the unctuous Kroger, but often the doors didn't open to his knock. Twice, they were run off the land by rifle-bearing farmers.

At a log cabin that afternoon, an elderly woman answered the door.

"Good day, madam," Hobson bowed. "My family will soon be moving into the area. I wonder, do you run this farm by yourself?"

She glanced at Ellie and Dee. "I got a couple of boys who pitch in."

"Your sons?" Hobson tried. "Ah, you mean field hands. I was interested in such folk myself."

The woman's eyes flicked past him to Ellie. "This isn't a subject for mixed company."

Hobson turned to Ellie and Dee. "Will you excuse us?"

Ellie smiled and took Dee back up the path. Hobson spoke to the old woman a moment, then jogged awkwardly to join them, snowshoes flapping.

"She is disinclined to speak with me until her husband returns this evening," he said softly. "But get this. She allowed that she'd recently made a new purchase. A 'young buck,' she called him. If I'm up to date on my dog-whistling slang, she might just mean Quinn."

"When can we come back?" Ellie said.

"I, singular, have been invited to dinner. Apparently this is masculine business. Who knew?"

"Do you think that's a good idea?"

"Well, no," he said. "But I think it's a stone worth flipping over."

She didn't like the idea of splitting up. But they were all looking at her: the old woman across the yard in her doorway, disapproving; Hobson, wryly amused by the social niceties surrounding the ownership of other humans; Dee, hopeful and expectant for this new lead. Ellie nodded. Hobson smiled and jogged back to let the old woman know he'd be there.

Around dusk, they returned to the boathouse to check in with Nora.

"The old woman by Turtle Pond," Ellie said. "You know her? House has one of those old fashioned rooster windvanes?"

"Mrs. Talcott?" Nora said. "Why?"

"She's invited the sheriff to dinner. Any reason he should say no?"

The woman tapped her nail against her tea. "She and her husband keep to themselves more than most, but I've never heard a bad word about them. They're getting on in their years, though. I wouldn't be surprised if they've been on the market for a fresh set of hands."

"Which might make the cost to us dear," Hobson said. "Even so, purchasing him cleanly might be less messy than attempting to steal him."

Nora drained her mug. "Got another name for you if that one doesn't pan out. Richard Jimenez. Runs a place just east of Tavern on the Green. He's looking to compete with Kroger and probably gets a look at any new captives."

"Thanks again for your help," Ellie said. "You're the first person we've met who we haven't had to threaten, trick, or shame into talking about this."

She swirled her cup. "My brother made it through the Panhandler with me. I lost him to slavers in Boulder. It just keeps cropping up."

Hobson smiled in sympathy. "To the wrong sort of person, there is nothing cheaper than another man's life."

They waited till dark to leave, and only after Nora's son confirmed the snowy pavement was clear of people. Ellie and Dee walked north with Hobson until their paths diverged.

"I shall see you at the apartment," he said. "With any luck, our next step will be haggling a fair price for Quinn."

He saluted with his cane and headed for the Talcotts' cabin. Ellie had half a mind to drop in on Richard Jimenez—it was barely 5 PM —but the sun was down and she didn't particularly want to expose Dee to another slave-trader until she knew Hobson's lead was a bust. Instead, they walked back to the apartment and dried their feet. Ellie found decks of cards in a closet, but couldn't remember how to play gin rummy, so she and Dee played solitaire next to each other instead.

Hobson had the pocket watch, and with the moon hidden behind a wall of clouds that looked intent to snow, Ellie had no clock but her internal one. By something like eight o'clock, she began to worry. Around a time that might have been ten, she gave up any pretense of playing cards and watched from the window, scanning the park for movement, constantly tricked by the stirring of leaves.

Once she was convinced it was at least midnight—much later than a seventy-year-old couple on winter hours would possibly be awake, much less active enough to entertain the sixty-year-old Hobson—she zipped her coat over her sweater and slung on her gun.

"I'm going, too," Dee said, though they hadn't exchanged a word. "No way I'm letting my mom go in there herself. And if something happened to the sheriff, that means they've got Quinn."

"I was hoping you'd have figured that out," Ellie said. "Now get your gun. We're going to need it."

25

Flames blasted up the face of Sicily. Gunshots popped from the corner, orange strobes that shattered glass and drew screams. Rifles answered from the besieged bar. A machine gun rattled through its entire magazine, hammering the corner of the building across the street into a cloud of stony dust.

Lucy probably ought to go lie down in the tub, but most times there was a shootout, she was in the middle of it. She seldom got the chance to be an impartial observer. With all the lights and noise, it was like watching a fireworks show. One where people were almost certainly bleeding out.

A stray round whacked into the wall two feet from her. She ducked down and waited for the hail of lead to peter out. After the initial outburst of Molotovs and Kalashnikovs, things sputtered down to a halting, sporadic exchange of fire, most of it centered around the bodega across the street Distro was using for a firebase. The Kono tried a charge and two men dropped to the street, motionless. They redoubled their fire, pouring it into the storefront. When they stopped, the night went silent.

A man shouted orders. Troops burst from the bar to overrun the bodega, but Distro was gone.

Lucy opened her window and took a deep breath of spent gunpowder. Men and women ran down the street, giving chase to the raiders. Others knelt by the wounded to check pulses and triage the casualties. Lucy hung around in her room a good long while, ensuring the skirmish was over. She had a rooting interest in the Kono coming out ahead in this dust-up, but if she got her ass shot off in the street, it wouldn't much matter who hoisted the flag over whose corpse.

Fifteen minutes after the last shot had sounded, she grabbed her umbrella, walked downstairs, exited the south side of the building, and circled through the streets to Sicily. The Kono had dragged away the bodies, but red stains seared the snow. Out front, a line of soldiers crouched behind overturned chairs.

A woman burst sideways from the cover, rifle trained on Lucy. "Stay right there!"

"It's just me," Lucy said. "Came running as soon as I heard the shots."

The woman held her aim steady. Lucy strained for a clearer look at her face. Was she one of Duke's friends? One of the people who'd continued to snub her after Ash's little speech? What if she pulled the trigger, said she'd thought Lucy was a stray Distro?

"Is Ash okay?" She slowly lowered her hands until her umbrella rested against the side of her hip. "Y'all need a hand?"

"Did you see Distro on the way here?" the woman said.

Lucy shook her head. "I was over by the river. Missed the whole thing."

"That might have just been the first wave. Get over here and dig in."

Lucy sighed and knelt in the slush behind the makeshift wooden barricade. She spent the next hour freezing her butt off. Finally, Ash walked out of the bar and flicked the end of a cigar into the snow.

"Frank, Allen, keep watch," he said. "Rest of you come off the lines. Fun's over for tonight."

Lucy stood, stiff in the knees, and headed inside. Gangsters sat at booths, weapons propped beside them, glasses gleaming on their tables. What little talk they engaged in was low and cold.

"Take a seat," Ash told her.

She slid into a booth across from three other troopers. Ash set his narrow backside down beside her.

He lifted a glass, but just stared at it. "You worked with Distro. Got a feel for how their minds work. They treat this city like a game of chess where they've captured the enemy queen. All they have to do is play conservative. Outflank us move by move. Wait for us to screw up—and to make no major mistakes of their own."

"In a nutshell," Lucy said. "Nerve figured he has products you can't get and lower prices on the ones you do have. No way to lose unless you launched an all-out war on his ass."

"Right. Which they did tonight. Why did they finally grow some balls?"

Lucy had veered down a path that led to too many questions. Time to get back on course. "We must have hurt them as bad as we hoped. When you knocked down those aliens, you took out their queen. Now they're on tilt."

"That's poker," Ash said.

"Whatever. Point is, they're desperate. And mad. Tonight was just the beginning."

"Then maybe it's time to steal their strategy. Turtle up and wait for them to fuck themselves."

"How'd that work out for them?" Lucy said. "You think you're the only goons in the city? What happens when a squad in Brooklyn sees you were attacked and didn't have the guts to hit back?"

He narrowed his eyes at his glass, then drained it. "That's what I saw when I started watching Distro. Big fish, no teeth. I've been taking bites out of their hide ever since."

She softened her voice. "How many of us died tonight?"

"Three so far. And if Nelson makes it, I'm having that boy buy me a lottery ticket, because his lungs have more lead in them than a Roman pipe." He beckoned over a passing server and ordered two shots of tequila. "Well, as always, your input into our friends is most appreciated. Now be gone from my sight. I've got brooding to do."

For a moment, Lucy didn't understand he was talking to her. She stood and went to her room. The darkness was welcome. She'd dodged a bullet down there. Ash had been rightly suspicious of Distro's attack—it had been so sudden and certain you might wonder whether someone had told them the Kono were to blame for the destruction of their trade route. Such as in the postscript to a note warning a man to get out of town.

She slept soundly that night.

She didn't see much of Ash for a few days. When she asked, Brian told her he was off meeting with the bosses. She was conscripted for sentry duty, standing guard outside Sicily, patrolling the snowy streets. The next time she saw Ash, she let him know where Distro posted their rooftop watchers, but he brushed her off.

With no attacks in days, she was attached to a small troop dispatched to Central Park. While she stood around in the snow, two men went inside the log cabins and metal shacks and came out with bags and small crates they loaded into a horse-drawn wagon. Some of the farmers spoke in raised voices. They didn't like what was going on outside the park's walls. One man wanted to know why he was paying for security when the Kono seemed intent on burning the whole city down. The gangster acting as his customer service representative smiled thinly and told the man he'd pass along his concerns.

After the previous weeks locked up in her apartment, it was a kick to get outside and into the thick of things, but Lucy's restlessness ran too deep. Each day felt wasted. Tilly was still clapped away in the city's tallest tower. Every day they stuck around the city was one more day they might get shot. Or, in Tilly's case, shoved off a balcony by her psycho-robot boyfriend.

When she got a few hours to herself, Lucy hung around 34th Street, hoping to catch Tilly out by her lonesome. But they were either operating on different schedules or Nerve had given her the Rapunzel treatment, because not once did she see Tilly outside.

A week after the attack, she was down in the bar having her first beer of the afternoon when Ash grabbed her by the collar.

"Come along," he said. "Time to have a little fun."

She scooted off her stool. "Where we headed?"

"Oh, a bit of a walk. You got a gun?"

She held up her umbrella. "Don't worry. It's loaded."

He unstrapped a gun belt from his waist and tossed it at her. "Thank me later. Go wait outside."

Lucy pulled on her coat and walked out. Five others stood in the powder-fine snow drifting from the sky. The streets were dark and still. Ash joined them, rubbing his hands together, and headed east, shoes squeaking in the snow.

It was a long walk and low on conversation. Ash led them south beyond the park, then hooked east a few blocks before resuming his southerly course. Candles flickered from a corner bar. The people outside it went quiet and watched the troopers pass, heads swiveling like spooked deer. A while later, an oncoming pedestrian looked up and swerved for the other side of the street without breaking stride.

"Just how far away is this place?" Lucy said after better than an hour of trudging through the snow.

Ash smirked over his shoulder. "There's no such thing as too far to walk. Not when we're going to the last Indian restaurant in the city!"

As they neared the Empire State Building, he veered to keep several blocks between it and their unit. Not long after, he stopped at the corner of 30th and Lexington. After the faded glitz of Midtown, the surrounding towers looked downright diminutive.

"Barry, why don't you walk on by and take a look?" Ash said. "Don't linger."

A bearded man nodded and continued south. Ash walked back around the corner and leaned against a building. When Lucy tried to ask what they were doing, he shushed her.

Within five minutes, footsteps crunched from up the street. Barry raised his arm in greeting; he'd circled around. "He appears to be enjoying his dinner."

"There'd be something wrong with him if he weren't. Those chefs are fucking magicians." Ash turned to the others and smiled sharply. "Here's the score. Basically, Distro is a bunch of fucking idiots who like to follow their routines until the ruts are too deep to climb out of. We're going in. Do not harm the staff. The last thing I want is the Feds to come down on our ass. And one of the cooks is the guy who tipped me off."

"Who's the target?" Lucy said.

"Don't worry about it. You just make sure that anyone who goes for a gun doesn't have time to take a shot."

"How heavy can we get?"

"They're Distro," Ash said. "Hurt them as much as you want."

He backtracked a block to Park Avenue, headed downtown for two more blocks, then swung inside what purported to be a jewelry shop, but the only thing it had on display these days was broken glass and empty cases. Ash used a penlight to maneuver around the worst of it. He entered a back door and strode through a series of back rooms and corridors without so much as a pause for a look around. Lucy brooked no doubt that, as spontaneous as this voyage seemed, it had been a long time in the making.

He exited into a courtyard that smelled like pan-fried onions and slow-roasted cardamom. Light flickered in a window of the adjoining building. Ash walked up to a back door and put his finger to his lips.

"Inside is a no-talking zone. If I hear anything besides 'Hands up,' or 'Put the gun down,' then tomorrow's lunch special will be a hot bowl of You Soup. Got it?"

They all nodded. He opened the door. The scent of spice swirled past on a rush of warm, damp air. Ash drew his pistol and crept down a narrow tiled hallway. On the other side of a swinging door with a porthole window, pans clanked and sizzled.

Ash swept it open and spoke in a conversational tone. "Hello and pardon the interruption. FYI, a group of scary people is about to walk through the door. As long as you stay quiet, go about your business, and for the love of God, don't try anything funny, I promise no one will be hurt. No one you care about, anyway. Agreed?"

He was answered by the hiss of cooking. He beckoned the others through the door. The kitchen was tight and steamy; canary-yellow dishes bubbled on the stove in a heady rush of cumin and onion. Five people stood stock still at their stations. The workers' ages ranged from eight to eighty, but every one of them shared the same expression: icy terror.

"Benson, keep an eye on them," Ash said. "Rest of you, walk this way."

One trooper peeled off to watch the restaurant workers. He had a rifle in his hands but didn't point it at anything in particular. Ash crossed the sweaty room, drew his pistol, and booted open the door.

"Hands up." He swung his gun across the dining room. "You move, you die."

People sat at four different tables. Other than one couple in their thirties, the rest were men in suits, divided evenly between old white wrinklebags and buffed young dudes with pistols on their hips. A craggy-faced old man made eye contact with the bodyguards at the next table. He nodded. Slowly, they lifted their hands.

Ash's people stripped them of their guns, patted them down. Ash strolled up to the craggy-faced man.

"Jim Rimbold?" Ash's jaw dropped in mock surprise. "What are you doing here at the same time and the same place you always come here like a man who doesn't have a city full of enemies?"

The man gazed back steadily. "Supporting local business."

Ash laughed merrily. "Supporting local business! So what do you call trading with the aliens? Adapting to the growing demands of interstellar commerce?"

"Are you here to rob us?" Rimbold said. "You're welcome to anything on my person."

"How kind of you to offer. Know what, it was a long walk and your dinner looks astounding." He dropped into an empty chair and pulled Rimbold's plate across the table with a harsh scrape. He forked up a mound of orange curry and chewed. "What a kingly feast! Want some?"

"What do you want?"

"For you to enjoy your meal. Too rich for my blood." Ash stood, jolting the table. Silverware lurched. Rimbold's guards jerked. Lucy trained her pistol on one man's back. Ash lifted a bite of curry and airplaned it toward Rimbold's face. "Open wide!"

The man pursed his lips like a recalcitrant child. Ash raised his pistol and tick-tocked the barrel back and forth. Rimbold opened up. Ash slid the fork inside and scraped its contents off on the man's teeth. He set down the utensil, put his hand on the man's jaw, and helped him chew.

"What do you think? Delicious, right?"

Rimbold swallowed before replying. "Is there a point to these theatrics?"

"Now that we've shared bread, maybe we can be honest with each other. I don't like you, Jim. I tried to negotiate with your people. I told them you get your half of the city, we get ours. How do they respond? A counteroffer? Gentlemanly negotiations?"

"Is that what you think you're doing right now?"

"Nerve didn't so much as consider my proposal!" Ash went on. "Predictably enough, the fists start to fly. And you—savvy, alien-fucking businessman that you are—decide it's a good idea to send your people to burn my bar and kill my people."

"Hold on a minute," Rimbold said. "That was a message-mission. No one was authorized to kill."

"Used those nonlethal flaming Molotovs, did you?" Ash grinned in fury. "You should have stuck to your business. Because this is how we handle ours."

Rimbold's face paled. "We can neg— "

Ash shot him twice in the chest. Rimbold's partners and bodyguards shouted and began to stand. Ash knocked three of them down as fast as he could pull the trigger. Bodies tumbled back, legs askew. The table uprighted, spilling curries and steaming platters of rice. The fake fruit centerpiece tumbled into the air, bouncing plastic oranges across the floor. A young man in a suit dived at Ash. Lucy blasted him onto the toppled table. Guns roared around her.

The shots stopped as suddenly as if someone had held up a flag. The smell of burnt powder overpowered the spices. The young couple pressed themselves against the far wall. A red string of goo fell slowly from the ceiling. The young man bent double and vomited.

Ash blew smoke from his pistol and jammed it into his holster. "That curry really is good. Wonder if they do takeout?"

One of his soldiers pointed at the vomiting man and his girlfriend. "What about them?"

Ash waved to get the woman's attention. "Hey. You two who don't appreciate a fine meal. You're not associated with Distro, are you?"

The woman shook her head in panicked jerks. "It's our anniversary."

"Probably the most memorable one you ever had! You're welcome." He leaned over Rimbold's fallen body, grabbed the man's face, and shook it back and forth. "That's one dead son of a bitch. Let's get out of here."

He walked back into the kitchen. The employees stared, wide-eyed. Ash collected Benson from guard duty and the group exited into the courtyard and picked their way across the broken glass on the jewelry shop floor.

"Did we just whack Distro's CEO?" Lucy said.

"Would you like to register a complaint?" Ash said.

"No."

"Well, I would. Never, ever use the word 'whack' to describe a killing again."

"Got it," she said. "How do you think they'll retaliate?"

"With any luck, they'll attack us on our home turf." Ash flung open the shop door and took a long breath of the cold night air. "We can end this feud then and there."

They ran uptown through the snow. The streets were quiet, but Lucy had the feeling she wouldn't have to write any notes at this point. As for the massacre, she felt neither guilty nor happy. These people were arrogant. Trading with aliens. Bullying farmers. Taking slaves. They thought all they had to do was get people so scared they'd forget how it ever felt to stand on their own two feet.

But there was a place beyond fear. When you've lived in death's shadow long enough—smelled his breath, felt his knuckles bump down the ridges of your spine—your hatred for whomever put you next to him is the one thing that can become deathless.

The gangs had sown fear for too long. The harvest would be merciless.

As soon as they got back to Sicily, Ash spread the word. All non-essential operations were suspended. Everyone was to be armed at all times. The scouting presence was quadrupled. They were given code words: "Wilson" to challenge the identity of someone unknown to you, "Mookie" to confirm you were Kono.

Three days of fortifications ensued. Men hauled old cars to barricade the ends of the block. Saws rasped and hammers rapped. Ash's sapper planted pipe bombs along the advance to Sicily, concealing the explosives in planters and under piles of trash. Workers affixed hollow wooden panels to the fire escape landings, then packed the panels with dirt and scrap metal, turning the landings into armored firing platforms with access to rooftop snipers' nests.

It was all very impressive. If Distro came straight at it—and after the destruction of their import pipeline and the murder of their leader, they had no choice but to retaliate—they'd die on the ramparts.

While this went on, Lucy helped push Buicks up to the lines. Patrolled the streets with binoculars around her neck, eyes flicking to every flap of a pigeon's wing or swirl of gusted snow. And planned her retreat from the city.

Early in the morning, with a half inch of fresh powder muffling the streets, the call went out. Distro was on the move. Scouts came in one after another updating the army's advance. Times Square. 49th Street. Columbus Circle. Ash sent messengers to muster everyone the Kono could bring to bear. Men and women climbed the armored fire escapes and set up behind the wall of cars. A thicket of rifles grew at both ends of the barricaded block. If things got bad, Lucy would slip into Sicily and out the back side of the building. Pretend she'd been out scouting. After Distro was routed, and the Kono counterattacked the Tower, she'd grab Tilly and be on her way.

But Distro never came. The scouts brought in the news: at 65th Street, the enemy force had swerved into Central Park. They were burning out the farmers. Kono's main source of food, trade, and profit. If the Kono didn't move, the city might be theirs, but there would be nothing left in it worth having.

26

Ellie jogged across the street into the park. It was midnight and the paths were deserted. An unsteady breeze tossed the naked branches. It carried the smell of smoke and snow.

"What could have happened to him?" Dee said. "Wait, nevermind—there's no use speculating, that's what we're here to find out, blah blah blah."

"Add a few more blahs, and you've got it covered," Ellie said. "With any luck, after dinner he was too tired or drunk to walk home."

"Don't bullshit me."

"Don't swear at me." She rubbed her eyes. "But yeah. I don't think he's just drunk. I hope."

"Do you think he parties?" Dee said. "I bet when he's drunk he rides his cane around the room bronco-style. Waving his bowler all 'Yee-ha!'" Dee laughed, but sobered quickly. "We shouldn't have let him go by himself, should we?"

"We had to take the chance. It sounded like he had a real lead."

She scanned the road while they ran, fighting off thoughts of heart attacks. He was far from young and they'd been pushing themselves hard. She had left her snowshoes behind—they were better for long distances, but awkward to run in—and she slipped often. Her feet and knees grew damp. Within ten minutes of leaving the apartment, they turned down the trail to Turtle Pond.

The cabin's windows were blacker than the skies. Ellie stopped, panting, and wiped the wet from her nose. "If I go knock on the door, can you cover me?"

"Got it."

She turned. Dee was already going prone, bracing her gun over a rock beside the path. For a moment, Ellie was saddened, hollowed out that her daughter had so quickly become willing to lie in the midnight snow and open fire on an old woman, but as Dee set her eye behind her scope, the empty sadness became pride. Dee wasn't becoming a monster or sociopath. She was just learning to navigate a landscape after most of the lights had gone out for good. And to protect herself and her family.

Becoming who she needed to be in order to survive.

"Don't be too eager to shoot," Ellie said. "If she's done something to him, she won't be able to answer many questions with a hole in her heart."

Dee nodded. Ellie thought she should impart more wisdom, but there was nothing else to say. She crunched through the snow on the lawn, stopped at the door, and knocked.

After her third try, steps clunked across the floor inside. The window beside the door squeaked open.

"Hands where I can see them," a man said.

Ellie raised them high. "I'm here for Sheriff Hobson."

"About six hours too late."

Heat poured down her skin. "What did you do to him?"

"Not a damn thing," the man said. "They took him. Guess they thought he looked suspicious."

Ellie blinked at the dark window. "Who?"

"Who do you think? The Kono."

"How did they know he'd be here? Did you tell them?"

"I don't like the Kono any more than the next man. They think they own us and everything we grow. But if they gave you the choice between your wife and a man you never even met, you'd make the same decision I did."

"Where did they take him?"

"I had no interest in asking." A gun barrel glinted behind the window. "Now get off my land before they see you here."

She walked from the house. Tracks marred the snow. Some were long and shallow, as if toes had been dragged over the surface. She beckoned Dee over and followed them all the way to the footpath, where they disappeared amid countless other footprints. Ellie knelt, but it was hopeless.

"What happened?" Dee said.

"The Kono got wind of us. They took Hobson."

"Who told them? Kroger?"

"Or Nora."

"Nora?" Dee glanced east through the trees. "But she's supposed to be helping us."

"As far as we know, she's the only one who knows why we're really here." Ellie stood, but she couldn't make her feet move forward. "Or maybe I'm going crazy. We came here to find Quinn and now we've lost Hobson. If our cover's blown, we can't keep poking around the park. We're back to wandering the streets for the Clavans' van. Which probably returned to Albany two weeks ago."

The wind blew the snow across the mingled confusion of tracks. Clouds came and went from the face of the moon. Ahead, the path disappeared into the woods.

"If I told you all that," Dee said, "what would you do next?"

Ellie looked up. "Follow the trail that's still warm. Hobson. If it hits a wall, or wanders afield, return to the original objective."

"So where does Hobson's trail point us?"

"To push back on Nora." She turned and headed back the way they came in. "But first, we need sleep. We're already hours behind. A few more won't hurt us, but chasing after gangsters when we can't think straight is not a winning combination."

With a new course in place, she already felt better. They hiked back to the apartment, peeled off their socks, replaced them with dry ones. Her mind spun, but it was already so late she fell asleep within minutes. Anxiety woke her a half dozen times. Around dawn, she woke Dee. They shared the last of the meat pies and trekked back to Nora's boathouse. The sun was up, but it was hidden behind buildings and clouds, and the early light was foreign and gray.

Nora answered the door in a thick bathrobe. She saw it was Ellie and her lips pulled back from her teeth. "I told you not to come by during daylight."

"Did you tip us off to the Kono?"

"The Kono?" Nora's face bent with anger. "I've risked my family to help yours. If you ever accuse me of helping slavers again, they'll be the last words you speak to me."

"Someone found out who were are," Ellie said. "Last night, they took Sheriff Hobson."

"Get inside." The woman opened the door wide. When Ellie hesitated, Nora rolled her eyes. "Oh, come on. Why would I give up Hobson and not you?"

"I don't know." Ellie exhaled deeply and stepped inside. "Someone at the government has been after us from the moment we went to City Hall. Maybe they heard we came here. Found you. Made threats."

Nora had just closed the door and now looked regretful she'd let them in at all. "I'm sorry your friend's been taken, but I've done all I can. You can't blame me for not wanting to get in any deeper."

Dee snorted. "You're going to just let them get away with it?"

"Dee," Ellie said.

"Don't 'Dee' me. This is ridiculous. The only reason Quinn got taken is because no one in town had the balls to stand up to the men in the black fedoras." She turned on Nora. "You think you're keeping yourself safe by not lifting a finger against the Kono. But as long as they're here, you'll never be safe."

"And if I help you, you're going to scrub them from the city?" Nora said. "Or are you going to find your boyfriend, wave goodbye to New York, and run home to the mountains?"

Dee flushed. "If we show they're not invincible, maybe others will stand up, too."

Nora tightened the belt of her robe. "If they decide not to kill him, they'll probably sell him to one of the farmers."

"Then we're back to square one," Ellie said. "Except now the Kono are looking for us, too."

"I don't know how much I can do. But I'll keep my ears open."

Ellie laughed bitterly. "Or we could turn ourselves in. Who knows, the Kono might reunite us."

Dee frowned at the curtains across the bay windows of the converted dining room. "What if we did?"

"Can't. They might shoot us. Or split us up and sell us to three different people." She rubbed her hand down her face. "We'll keep going door to door. I don't know what else we can do."

She knew it was a deeply stupid idea—one that had already cost them Hobson—but there were only so many farms in the park. If they acted quick and got lucky, they might stumble onto Quinn before the Kono hunted them down.

But it was time to open a new avenue. As they knocked on cabins, asking careful questions of the guarded residents, Ellie inquired not only about whether they'd recently acquired new help, but where she might go to buy it for herself. Most mentioned Kroger. One man recommended checking in at the Kono bar, a place on Amsterdam and 90-something.

"Maybe they haven't had time to sell Quinn yet," Dee said after they'd walked from the farmhouse to a snowed-in bike path along a pond that had partially iced over. "If the Kono are that powerful, I bet they make the Clavans sell exclusively to them."

Ellie nodded. "The Clavans could even be a franchise of the Kono. Or vice versa. Whatever this network is, it's spreading threads through the state like a cancer. When we get home, we'll have to make sure it can't take root in the lakes."

"As long as we're here, why don't we quit sniffing around the park and go straight to the Kono? If we pose as buyers, we could find Quinn and learn more about who they are."

"Won't work. Even if they don't have our exact description—and if the Talcotts gave them Hobson, I'm sure they gave up that, too—there can't be too many young women and their old mothers running around asking about slaves."

"You're not old," Dee said softly. "I think we should get off the road."

For a moment, Ellie thought that was some strange metaphor. Through the trees, she glimpsed four men walking down a path. They were a hundred yards away and following a curve in the trail that would spit them out in direct view of Ellie and Dee. Besides the leafless trees and a couple of scarred benches, there was no cover.

Ellie grabbed Dee's hand and pulled her to the banks of the pond. Reeds grew to unruly height in the riparian spaces. The water at the edges had frozen semi-opaque, layered with thin snow. Ellie led Dee onto the slick surface and crouched behind the thicket of brittle brown reeds. The ice creaked under the tread of her shoes.

Back at the trail, the men slogged through the snow, shoulders swaying. Each carried an assault rifle. They gazed into the trees and didn't speak. At the spot where Ellie and Dee had left the path, one man stopped and stared at the tracks in the snow. He reached into his pocket, removed the half-smoked stub of a cigarette, lit it, and exhaled voluminous smoke into the frigid air.

He jogged to catch up with the others. The men disappeared beyond a low hill. Ellie crawled on her hands and knees toward the bank. The ice popped. A crack traced itself across the surface, as if drawn by a ghost. She lowered herself and spread her limbs to distribute her weight. She was just a couple feet from shore, but the park's ponds were cut deep at the edges. And a brief plunge risked hypothermia.

"Go on," she said to Dee. "Slowly."

Dee's mouth was an O of stress. She army-crawled into the reeds, then rolled into the snow. Ellie followed. The ice creaked but held. On the bank, she stood hesitantly, wary for any sight of the men, then brushed off the snow and shivered.

"Were they looking for us?" Dee said.

"Don't know," Ellie said. "But it might behoove us to call it a day."

It was only another hour till dusk. She was cold and wet, and after hiding on the ice, her palms and knees had gone numb. She headed dead east out of the park and continued to Madison, putting some buildings between them and the Kono-roamed fields, then headed north toward their apartment.

Back "home," they stripped off their wet clothes. Ellie had walked a hole in one of her socks. She wadded it up and flung it in the bin they'd set up in the corner of the front room. She was down to just two decent pairs; the skin on her toes was soggy and white and one of her old blisters had sloughed off, showing tender pink skin. The apartment had socks, but they were white Hanes athletics, thin and flimsy. Should go search the other apartments. She knew that. But the energy wasn't there.

She wrenched apart a loaf of bread and handed half to Dee. They had no way to warm it and no butter. They sprinkled salt and poultry spices on it instead. It took a long time to chew; Ellie had to soften each bite with saliva before swallowing. After the sun went down, they moved to the back room, which was the only one without windows, and lit candles Ellie had taken from a Bed, Bath, & Beyond. They were peach-scented.

"I figure we've searched about half the park," Ellie said. "Could finish it in another couple days."

"If the Kono don't grab us first," Dee said.

"We could back off for now. Let things cool down, then pick up again after New Year's."

Dee's jaw was planted on her knees and when she spoke the rest of her head flapped strangely. "What if we just went home?"

"For the time being?" Ellie said. "Or..?"

"For the winter. If we come back after the snow melts, we can bring a wagon. All the food we need. No more stupid wet socks."

She gazed at the flickering pink-orange candle. "Do you want my opinion as your mother? Or as an investigator?"

"I don't think Quinn and the sheriff need a mother."

"Then here's the deal. If we leave, there's a good chance we'll never come back."

Chin planted on her knee, Dee rocked her head to the side. "Why wouldn't we?"

"Imagine us four months from now, when the weather's not so bad. We'll be three hundred miles away at the lake. Sowing the fields. Planning how we can afford a cow or a pair of goats. It won't be easy to interrupt that for another trip back here."

"I think I'll be more interested in getting my fiancé back than a new goat."

Ellie shrugged one shoulder. "The point is you'll be removed from him in time and space. Psychologically, too. We'll be mired in our regular routines. Pulling ourselves away from that will take motivation and effort."

"I'm not going to give up after four months! I've spent longer than that looking for my favorite pair of jeans."

"Then how long until you do give up?"

Dee's face scrunched in disgust. "Never."

"Really? Next winter, you'll be back down here? What about five years from now? When you turn thirty, and it's been more than ten years since the last time you saw Quinn, you're still going to be interrogating park-farmers who answer the door with a shotgun? You'll never look at another man again? That's how you want to spend your life?"

Dee blinked, knocking tears down her cheeks. "Why are you saying this?"

Ellie lowered her voice. "Because your life will move on. Sooner or later, once the guilt of the idea has faded, everyone stops searching. So when you talk about going home for now, I want you to be very, very clear about the decision you're making. Do you want to keep searching? Or do you want permission to stop?"

"I want to find him," Dee said. "But I don't want to lose anyone else."

"That's the other factor."

"Then it all comes down to the leads, doesn't it? So long as we have a good one, we keep looking. But if they dry up, staying here means risking ourselves with no plausible hope of success."

"That would be my decision-making process." Ellie aimed a small smile at the peach-scented candles. "But there are those who would consider me a cold hard bitch."

"It makes sense." Dee rocked forward and back, chin on her knee, gazing across the dim room. "But if we finish the park and still haven't found them, I'm not sure I'll be ready to leave."

"Not everything you do has to make sense. Just understand when you're not so you can snap back to reality if things get rough."

Dee didn't say more. Ellie went to the windows overlooking the park. She had tried to keep herself focused on the narrow edge of their search, on the actual locating of first Quinn and now the sheriff, but Dee had veered onto ground that had been neglected for too long. A search was only useful so long as it was moving forward. It was never easy to quantify these things, and a personal matter was leagues different than a professional one, but if she'd been handed this case to view through the prism of the DAA, she would be on the verge of calling it off.

She might give her agents the leash to continue a canvass of the park. But with the Kono on their heels, no hard proof the original subject was in the city, and the loss of an agent during the course of the investigation, the leash would end there. She would cut their losses, pull back, and engage more passive, low-risk methods. Hire a local such as Nora Ryan to keep an eye out for Quinn while she and Dee resumed their lives at Saranac Lake. Maybe pay another visit to Kroger and let him know they'd pay handsomely for a very specific ALP.

It was never easy to admit defeat. But Ellie didn't take such things personally. The world was too big and messy to control its every corner. In another day or two, when they wrapped up the park, she would propose they pull back. Dee's thinking was already halfway there. It wouldn't take much to prompt her to the right decision.

She slept through the night. They ate and dressed and hiked into the park. Dee was quiet. Ellie didn't push her. The day before, she'd focused the canvass around Turtle Pond, hoping that someone had witnessed the sheriff being marched away, but that had been a bust. Today, she took them northward, where winter wheat grew under softball backstops and the palatial Met rested on the eastern border.

She heard the first shots while she stood in the dirt in front of a cabin door. Nothing too alarming. They were at least a half mile south, and gunfire wasn't exactly a rarity on the island. She sighed inwardly and knocked again. Half the residents never answered, either because the homes were abandoned or they had no interest in whatever Ellie was peddling. She hadn't been keeping track of which homeowners had actually come to the door. It wasn't impossible that Quinn was being kept in one of the shacks they'd already visited.

After a third try, she walked across the converted softball field to the next cabin over. More shots erupted, still distant and southward. Ellie turned for a look. To the southwest, black smoke boiled from the trees. Six shots counted off one after another.

"Mom?" Dee said.

She hitched her rifle up her shoulder and reversed course for the boathouse. "Better warn Nora."

"What is it?"

"My guess? That war we keep hearing about."

Shots popped a couple times a minute. Locals emerged from their cabins and gazed at the smoke rolling from the other side of the park. Whenever they caught sight of Ellie, they stiffened, heads swiveling to watch her go.

Ellie emerged from a stand of trees and jogged across the grass to the boathouse. The door opened before she got there. Nora beckoned them inside and locked the door behind them.

"What's happening out there?"

"I don't know," Ellie said. "I just wanted to make sure you were aware. We'll leave if you want."

"You can stay." Nora smiled wryly. "Won't hurt to have another couple of guns around."

They gathered at the windows of the back porch to watch the land across the lake. Nora had sent her kids downstairs with strict orders to stay put. She cracked one of the windows to better hear whatever was happening.

"There can't be that many," Dee said. "They're hardly doing any shooting."

Ellie nodded. "Maybe the other side isn't shooting back. Or there is no other side."

Nora took half a step back from the window. "You think they're attacking the farmers? That's crazy. The whole island depends on them."

"Which makes them an especially fat target."

Without warning, the gunfire increased tenfold. Shots rang back and forth, concentrated bursts followed by snipers' measured fire.

Ellie got a bad feeling low in her stomach. "If this keeps up, do you have somewhere you can go?"

Nora shook her head slowly. "All my friends live right here."

"Our apartment is right across the street," Ellie said. "No heat or running water, but at least it's out of the park."

The firefight roared on.

"This is ridiculous," Dee said. "Why doesn't the government stop it?"

Ellie stared at the flat gray water. "For all we know, that is the government."

Movement across the lake. Ellie pushed her nose close to the window. Along the top of the red terrace, a line of people walked eastward. She raised her binoculars. Most of the people carried weapons, but some of the young men appeared to be unarmed. They walked steadily, but without extreme haste.

A heavy hand knocked on the door. The three women whirled. Silently, Nora moved inside the kitchen and grabbed a rifle from a rack inside the door.

The knock repeated. "Open the door! For your own safety!"

"If you want to open it, we'll cover you," Ellie whispered.

Nora nodded. They crept into the front dining room. Ellie and

Dee knelt behind one of the sheets hanging from the ceiling to partition the sprawling eatery. Ellie got out her 9mm and switched off the safety.

The man knocked a third time. Nora moved behind the door. "Excuse me if I'm not eager to open up."

"Ma'am, my name is Brian Devereaux," the man said. "I'm with the Kono. Distro gangsters have attacked the park. We're moving everyone to a safe place until we can secure the grounds."

"What happens if I want to stay?"

"Then we can't be responsible for your safety."

"I've done all right for myself up till now," Nora said. "But thanks for your concern."

The man went silent. After a moment, his footsteps crunched away from the house.

Nora laughed nervously. "Was that the right move? Maybe it's time to head to the apartment."

Ellie pushed aside the hanging sheet. "You're welcome to it. We'll take you there, but Dee and I won't be staying."

"Huh?" Dee said. "Where are we going?"

Ellie raised her eyebrows in mock surprise. "Where do you think? To find Quinn and the sheriff."

27

Ash yanked off his hat and slung it across the street like a frisbee. "Shit and shit some more. We went to the trouble of putting this fort together and now they refuse to play along? They'll be hearing about this at the next UN meeting."

"They were shooting people," the scout said. "Civilians. It's like they've gone crazy."

"When you cut off someone's head, their body tends to spazz out." Ash sighed and climbed onto the hood of a flat-tired Range Rover. "Listen up! Distro just made a big breakthrough: they realized they're a bunch of pussies who can't face us in a fair fight."

Some of the fifty-odd men and women listening laughed. He swept his hair back from his forehead, took a quick look at the sky, and went on in his high and cutting voice.

"Problem is, they know we can't sit back and wait while they execute this completely batshit plan of theirs. Third division, we're keeping you here in reserve and to hold down the fort. Fifth division, your job is to evacuate the park. Save all the farmers you like, but we've got property there that would be a real pain to replace. I want you to escort it to the safehouse. You got me?"

Heads nodded.

"Everyone else? Your job is to shoot Distro's asses like they ran off with your daughter. Let's go!"

He leapt from the hood and landed with a blast of snow. Troops whooped and rushed behind him. Lucy thought about pretending to be part of third division, but the organization was split up by area of residence, and Lucy's division—first—were those who lived directly above the bar. The real members of third would know she was faking. So she fell in with the others, in body if not spirit, jogging east in the snowy gray morning.

Anyway, being in the thick of things wouldn't be all bad. Maybe she would get a shot at Nerve.

The group ran down the street in loose columns. Scouts reported in every few blocks, but Lucy didn't see what information they were in such a hurry to deliver. Distro's gunshots told well enough where they were. And the arms of smoke reaching into the sky told exactly where they'd been.

Ash took them parallel to the park until 81st, where he stopped in the road and sent two men ahead. They came back with the all-clear.

"This is so obviously a lure," Ash said. "That means it's our job to not get hooked. Don't overcommit. We're here to save our land and workers. If you can kill a few Distro, please bring me the heads, but we'll worry about exterminating those rats once we've retaken the high ground. Got it?"

He was met with nods. Didn't sound like a real intricate plan to Lucy. She had the idea Ash was good at two things: the overarching strategy, and small raids. Not so cunning a figure when it came to battlefield tactics involving more than a handful of people on either side. She filed that intel away.

But she had to give him credit for one thing: he was bold. He jogged at the head of the columns, leading the way down the snowy, twisting paths. Shots filtered from the south at irregular intervals. Lucy hung toward the back third of the group. Pigeons fluttered in the trees. People used to jog down these paths for healthier lives and now Ash was using them to go end a whole bunch. Under different circumstances, she would have gotten a kick out of that.

Once they came within a few hundred yards of the gunfire, the fifth division split off to go door to door and get the locals evacuated. Ash stopped beside a road and spread his people out along the treeline, ready to stop any Distro advance from messing with the retreat of the farmers. The troops waited in the trees for some time. The hot, choking smell of smoke drifted across the park. Distro kept shooting. Nothing too crazy, but a fresh shot or two sounded off every minute. Either the farmers were fighting back, or Distro was cowing them—or executing them.

After five minutes of relative silence, with the fifth division away to the north, Ash stood and gestured his people onward. Their feet soughed through the snow. Smoke hazed the air, speared by the sun's faint rays; between the smoke, the clouds, the early hour, and the overhanging branches, it was hard to tell where the daylight came from. The sound of the crackling fires had both an immediate and a hushed quality, as if it might be burning from five miles away or from behind the next tree. The path curved, stretching the divisions' lines across from a series of low hills.

A shot boomed from the other side of the road.

"Contact!" a woman yelled.

Gunfire exploded from both sides. Muzzles flashed from behind trees. The Kono troops clung tight to trunks and fell prone to the snow. Lucy knelt beside a maple. Stray shots shredded the branches, dusting her with splinters of twigs. Up on the hill crosswise to her right, a man stood six feet behind a tree, hidden from those directly across from him, but exposed to Lucy. She took aim with the unfamiliar rifle and pulled the trigger. The stock jarred into her shoulder. Snow plumed and glittered behind her target. She fired again, hitting nothing. Her third pull staggered the man into the snow.

Facing limited return fire, it soon became clear they had the Distro probe outnumbered. Ash ran down the left side of the line. When he reached the end, he screamed a battle cry and his people followed him across the road into the trees at the base of the hills. Lucy joined those who stayed behind in taking potshots at the Distro soldiers as they shifted to fire on Ash's advance.

The outnumbered enemy dropped back, covering each other as they retreated through the trees. Ash turned and waved his hands at his people on the other side of the road. They broke cover and sprinted to join the others. Lucy lagged at the rear. The burnt-fireworks smell of gunpowder mingled with the smoke. One of the Kono had been knocked down in the initial charge and his body lay in the road, arms stretched out before him.

Lucy slowed to gaze at the body. Shots ripped into the snow beside her, ricocheting from the asphalt beneath. To the right, a wave of Distro soldiers poured in to reinforce the beleaguered front line. A machine gun rattled, whacking into the trees in front of Lucy. She threw herself beside the body and propped her rifle over its back. Her shots were wild and defensive. Distro soldiers ducked behind trees and fired back. The body thumped heavily. Blood fanned across Lucy's face.

Her heart thundered. She was pinned down. Separated. She fired at any man who broke cover, but otherwise conserved her ammo. Uphill, Distro and the Kono hammered away at each other in ferocious exchanges that went dead quiet for seconds at a time.

A thrumming force rushed past Lucy's cheek. It was gone before she understood it was a bullet. If she ran, she'd catch one in the back. If she stayed, a couple soldiers could keep her pinned while others circled around to hit her from behind. With the shouts and bangs of the main battle continuing to push south, no one would come to save her. The only people who knew where she was were the people trying to kill her.

Melted snow soaked her elbows. Her gun clicked, dry. She huddled behind the body and swapped out the magazine. She popped up for a glimpse of their movements. Rifles blared, spraying the air with bullets. Her knee slipped and she fell to her side.

And she stayed there.

Playing possum. Real American hero. But her fall had been real and in perfect sync with the shots. She lay perfectly still, snow stinging her face. A couple more rounds whisked past. Footsteps crunched, fading south to join the gunshots and screams.

She held there for several minutes. The clamor of battle grew more distant. Sounded like the Kono were doing just fine without her. With her cheek gone numb and her left leg dampened from ankle to hip, she eased her head up above the still-warm body. The trees stood by themselves. The snow was stirred with fresh footprints, but the grounds were motionless, abandoned to the dead.

She got up and stamped her feet to get her blood flowing. She had half a mind to exit the park and return to the makeshift fortress at Sicily with an explanation she'd been cut off from the group, but her next move depended on how this battle swung. She didn't want to rely on secondhand accounts. Not when she was so close.

On the other side of the road, blood stood from the snow like paint on a fresh canvas. Bodies dotted the hillside, but fewer than she would have guessed—maybe four or five from each side. Weird.

The more people who showed up to kill each other, the less efficient they became at it.

Past the crest of the hills, she hunkered down for a look at the situation. The battle had broken apart into several small skirmishes. The first centered around three cabins, one of which was on fire. At another site, men sniped at each other across a no-man's-land of bare snow, covering in the trees that fringed it. At a third, Kono troops had backed a somewhat larger Distro force against a pond.

Something like 150 men in total. Looking down on them was sobering. This was once the biggest city in the country. Now, the two mightiest armies contending for its soil couldn't field a baseball league.

After a minute, she thought she spied Nerve retreating from the firefight around the cabins. She headed that way, circling through the trees to keep her out of the line of fire until she rejoined the Kono.

As she ran up, a woman swung around on her, rifle trained on her chest. "Wilson!"

Lucy's mind froze. She slid to a stop.

"Wilson!"

"Mookie," Lucy spat out. "Good lord, you want my help, or you want to stand here yelling nonsense back and forth?"

She joined the others at the corner of a cabin. Acrid smoke flumed across the gap between it and the neighboring home. A couple of geezers lay facedown in the snow, blood puddled around their heads. Distro was holed up in the trees behind a wooden fence at the other end of the dead couple's farm. Kono soldiers shot at anything that moved. The two sides traded shots for several minutes without scoring a casualty.

After nearly getting tagged in the head by two different shooters, Lucy swung behind the cabin and pressed her back to the wall. This was some World War I shit. Nobody could enter the open field without getting mown in half. If he'd had more troops to work with, Ash could loop them around to hammer the Distro men from the side, but all his available men were already committed to the field. Didn't help that a fifth of them were off ushering civilians to safety. Smart move by Distro, hitting the park. They had nothing to defend. Meanwhile, the Kono had to commit resources to protect the farmers they extorted all that food from.

Cheers erupted from over by the pond. Lucy jogged past the cabins for a better look. Past the frozen banks, the Distro fled south through the trees. As if someone had thrown up a Bat Signal for cowards, the other groups broke, too, laying down covering fire as their comrades ran away.

"That's the Distro we know and love!" Ash shouted after them, hands cupped to his mouth. "Run home to Mommy. Nerve will kiss it and make it feel better!"

He ordered his men to pursue. Distro retreated orderly, holing up whenever they found cover, forcing the Kono harriers to drop prone and dive behind trunks. Lucy hung around the edges, squeezing off shots that hit nothing more interesting than cabin walls and drifts of snow. After an exhausting running battle, Distro exited the park and sprinted south for the safety of their tower.

Ash called a halt. He turned to his bloody, sodden men and grinned like an ancient chieftain. "We whipped them like a Catholic's ass. Next time, we'll put them down for good."

But it was far from a rout. Both sides had given as good as they'd gotten. Around ten deaths apiece, with the Kono suffering an equal number of non-lethal casualties of varying severity. Distro had managed to flee with nearly all their wounded. The Kono found two survivors among those lying in the fields. A runner went to call in wagons to haul them back to be treated by Doc.

And the farmers, too. Most were all right, and many emerged from hiding as soon as it was clear the fight was over, but others had been shot. Executed. Lucy hid her smile. Distro had gone off the deep end. Even if the Kono backed off, the Feds would take over from here. And when they moved, she would sweep in behind them.

But it was a poor plan to rely on the government to get things done. As Ash coordinated the removal of the wounded, and the continuing evacuation of the park, Lucy hung near him, watching the trees like a good bodyguard. By the afternoon, with the park under wraps and Ash on his way back to Sicily, she finally got the chance to speak to him.

"What's next?" she said. "We can't let them get away with this."

"No shit," Ash said. "I'm thinking a good massacre will fix their wagons. After that, we find us some lances and horse-parade their heads through Central Park. Think that will pick up morale?"

"Public executions would be even better."

"I've always thought doing away with those was one of modern society's biggest mistakes. There's nothing like a public execution to bring people together—and remind them to keep their noses clean."

"Back in my Distro days, I spent some time in the Empire State Building." Lucy stepped over a patch of bloody snow. "I might know something to help us get in."

"I'll see what the bosses have to say."

"Rimbold was a conservative type. But whoever took over—Nerve, I'm guessing—has turned Distro into a rabid dog. You know what you do with rabid dogs, don't you?"

"I hated that manipulative-ass movie," Ash muttered. "Trust me, the bosses won't say nay. They're old school. Distro just came after civilians. They may as well have shot themselves in the head."

Back at Sicily, she went up to her room to clean up, then headed down to the bar to immerse herself in gossip. Distro, as expected, had walled up in their tower. Ash had ridden off to brief his superiors. Wherever they might be. Lucy had the impression they preferred to oversee things from a safe distance. Given the last few weeks, she couldn't say she blamed them.

The mood in the bar was tense. Angry. People were mad about those they'd lost and outraged Distro had come after innocent farmers. A line had been crossed. One you couldn't come back from.

Ash returned that evening. He ducked all specifics, but he couldn't hide his grin. "Drink hard, people. Tomorrow night, Sicily closes at eight sharp. We're gonna need our rest."

The crowd roared. Lucy smirked and stuck around for appearances, but she didn't have time for parties. With people yammering away and moonshine spilled on every surface, she went upstairs to bed, woke before dawn, and was up on the rooftops watching the Empire State Building by first light.

Because Ash's speech wasn't exactly cryptic. He expected to strike the next day. Lucy expected Tilly would still be housed in the Tower—unless the Kono came up with a B-52, it was one of the best fortresses in the city—but things were coming to a head. She couldn't leave anything to chance.

By ten o'clock, Nerve rode up, escorted by two other horsemen.

She might not have thought much of it, except in addition to removing from his horse a couple of rifles and what appeared to be a bulletproof vest, he also got out a shiny gold box. Chocolates.

Lucy rolled her eyes. She climbed down the dark stairs, exited the north side of the building, and jogged uptown.

Sentries stood behind the wall of cars blocking the approach to Sicily, but they recognized her. She went upstairs to pack her bags. Nerve had stolen most of what she owned when he'd shot her. She'd been rebuilding her travel supplies ever since, but the truth was she was a lot of a slob. She gathered up clothes and dry food and first aid kits from counters and corners and stuffed it tight into two backpacks.

She had just finished up when she heard the shouts in the street.

She went for her rifle and threw open the window. Down at the blockade, a gleaming black limousine idled in the snow. Men in sunglasses and dark suits argued with Kono soldiers. After a minute, one of the bodyguards returned to the limo. It switched off its engine. A back door opened and the guards clustered around as the bald old President of Manhattan stepped into the daylight.

She swapped her rifle for her umbrella and ran downstairs. Outside, Ash walked up to the president and saluted sloppily.

"What an unexpected honor!" he said. "What brings you all the way uptown in this weather?"

The old man gave him the eye. "Tell me you're playing dumb."

"Who, me?"

"Would you like to do this someplace private?"

"Step inside my office," Ash said. "My office is a bar."

The president raised his trimmed eyebrows at Ash. "Then you're buying the first round."

Kono members were already drifting toward the bar. Lucy slipped inside and sat primly on a stool. Others piled in behind her. As soon as the president was inside, his men closed the door. Fifteen Kono had made it inside and sat in small groups.

Still donning shades, one of his men scanned the crowd. "We're going to need to search your people."

Ash snorted. "You can have our guns if you hand over yours. No? Didn't think so." He moved to a booth and gestured to the old man. "Finest seat in the house."

The president squinted skeptically and sat down. Ash moved in across from him. The security team took up position around the room, keeping watch on the Kono regulars.

"Let's keep things moving," Ash said. "I've got vengeance to plan."

"Then we're here in the nick of time," the president said dryly. "We're aware of what happened yesterday."

"Oh good. Then I won't have to apologize when I tear out Nerve's heart."

The old man leaned forward, hands clasped on the beer-sticky table. "Passions are running high. I understand. I was fine with you settling things between yourselves—so long as it was kept between yourselves. Now that civilian lives have been lost, this conflict has become a federal matter."

Ash smiled thinly. His high voice went as taut as a bowstring. "What are you telling me, Mr. President?"

"As of this moment, there will be an immediate ceasefire between Kono and the Distribution."

"How marvelous of you to finally pretend like you're fit to govern. Do I need to point out it was Distro who killed civilians?"

"We're headed there straight after we hammer this out," the old man said. "Believe you me, they'll be a lot less happy about this than you."

"You're dropping the hammer? How so?"

The man shifted on his padded seat. "For one, there will be sanctions."

Ash laughed ringingly. "Sanctions? You're going to cut off their trade, is that it? Were you aware they've been dealing with aliens this whole time? And I don't mean Mexicans. I mean anal-probing, plague-bearing space aliens."

The president glared at the table. "Unfortunately, we never passed a law against such a thing—I would never have thought we'd need to—but rest assured the legislation is being rushed through draft."

"What a relief!"

"Additionally, we're launching an investigation of the attack on Central Park. Those found responsible will be tried; if found guilty, they'll be hanged." He lifted one eyebrow. "Better?"

Ash sat back, the disdain on his face replaced by sudden interest. "Getting there."

"As for your involvement, it will be forgiven. So long as it stops now. If not, it's all back on the table. And I think we'll revisit the Thirteenth Amendment."

"Let's say I agree to play ball. What's in it for us?"

The president nodded slowly. "Pledge to keep the park safe, and I'd think that would earn you exclusive rights to negotiate with the farmers. After government taxes, of course."

"Of course. And how about you step up security on the bridges? We had some saboteurs sneak over one just yesterday."

"Security is, as always, our prime concern."

Ash threw back his head and sighed at the ceiling. "I'll tell you, I don't like it. There's nothing I want more than to wear Nerve's face on top of mine. But I think we can do this."

"Are you kidding me?" Lucy jumped off her stool and spread her free hand wide. "You can't just let Distro off the hook!"

The president turned, amused. "Young lady, the guilty parties will answer for their crimes."

"I'm sure. Y'all have done such a fine job policing this nation of yours. Spying on innocent travelers while you give Distro a pass to do business with the monsters who damn near killed us." She cocked her head at the smug bald man. "Say, was that you that murdered Distro's people down at the yacht club?"

The man's face twitched. "We didn't know about that operation until yesterday."

"Bullshit. The Kono didn't know. That leaves you. What, you try to horn in on the action, and when their people didn't bite, you wiped out the evidence? Or were you stirring up trouble between the two groups jockeying for your power, hoping they'd bring each other down? But you didn't expect the bloodbath to spill to the civilians."

"Is this true?" Ash said.

The president pushed himself straight in the booth. "Will you get this girl out of here?"

Lucy laughed. "Don't worry. You'll never have to see my face again."

She leveled her umbrella at his chest and pulled the trigger.

28

"The Kono are clearing out the park," Dee said. "And you think they're evacuating everyone to the same place."

Ellie grinned at her. "Should make our job a little easier."

"Except for the part where we walk right into the hands of the people looking for us."

"And the fact we don't know that either Quinn or Hobson is in the park. But we're not going to get another opportunity like this. I think it's a risk we have to take."

"Did you always talk like this?" Dee said. "How did your mom survive your teen years?"

"I got sent to my room a lot." She turned to Nora. "How soon can you be ready to go?"

Nora waved a hand. "Don't wait for me. We can make it to the apartment on our own."

Ellie gestured south past the lake. "There is an actual war going on. I'm not letting you walk into that by yourself. Now get your shit ready and let's go."

Nora laughed. "Yes ma'am."

The woman jogged downstairs, conscripting her three children to grab their "day bags" and throw together extra food and warm clothes. Within five minutes, they assembled by the front door, bundled in boots and coats, backpacks straining.

"Can you cover the rear?" Ellie said.

Dee moved her rifle from her shoulder to her hands. "Got it."

She was a little too confident for Ellie's tastes, but better that than the opposite. Ellie moved outside, scanned the trees, and beckoned the others out. Rifles popped from the lower third of the park. She walked quickly to the path running past the boathouse and swung north. Nora's children trailed behind her, holding hands. Two looked scared; the third looked excited. Dee walked behind them, head on a swivel. Just before 79th, Ellie turned east, threading through the trees.

They weren't alone. Others fled the park in small groups. Couples, mainly. A few kids. Some of the adults were unarmed. Servants. Ellie eyed each one, but didn't spot the sheriff or Quinn. She jogged from the park into the open street. Smoke smudged the sky, dimming the overcast sun. At the apartment, she looked both ways before letting Nora inside.

"It's not much," Ellie said, "but use anything here. We might not be back."

"Good luck," Nora said, then frowned as Ellie stripped off her coat. "I thought you were leaving?"

"I thought I'd stop for a haircut." She knelt, got her scissors from her bag, and passed them to Dee. "Short. As short as the wheat after we've run the combine."

Dee moved behind her. "You wear it long just so you can do this, don't you?"

"I wear it long because I like it long. But it just so happens that 'long, dark hair' is one of the first descriptors someone—like the Talcotts—would apply to me."

Dee got to work. Hair fell from Ellie's head, draping the carpet in dark strands. Dee worked quickly; within minutes, she stepped back, and Ellie ran her hand over her head. Bit longer than she'd like—more of a Caesar than a buzzcut—but judging by Nora's kids' expressions, it was dramatic enough. She still carried her sunglasses from the long march down from Albany. She put them on along with a plain wool cap.

"What about me?" Dee said, all but dancing back and forth with anxiety.

"Pull up your hood."

Dee let out a breath. "Oh, thank god."

"Thanks for all your help," Ellie told Nora. "Stay safe."

"I'll be praying for you."

Outside, Ellie jogged back to the park. Refugees trudged

northeast, glancing over their shoulders with every gunshot. Ellie followed the loose migration into the street a few blocks up from where they'd dropped off Nora. Four armed men stood around a subway entrance, surrounded by a crowd of some thirty people. The men weren't in soldiers' camo uniforms. Kono.

Another couple arrived thirty seconds after Ellie and Dee. After that, five minutes went by with no new additions. Gunfire banged away. The troopers moved together and conferred.

One of them broke away and approached the crowd. "All right, listen up! We're heading into the tunnels. There's nothing to worry about. It's safe, we'll have lights, and I hear the trains just happen to be working on a six-year delay."

"Where are we going?" an old man said.

"Someplace safe."

"This place got a name?"

"I can't leave my home behind," a woman said.

The trooper rolled his lips together and glanced to the side. "Distro came to the park specifically to hurt you. The farmers. The breadbasket of the city. My friends are fighting them right now to make sure your homes don't get burned. It's my job to make sure you're kept just as safe as your lands. We'll get you back where you belong as soon as we can."

There was some muttering, but when two soldiers lit lanterns and headed downstairs, the crowd followed. Ellie moved to join them. As she descended the snowy stairs, clinging to the bitterly cold railing, chthonic panic rose in her chest. The last time she'd been in the subway—and while the logistics had differed significantly, the goals were eerily similar—she had very nearly died.

Feet echoed through the enclosed concrete space. Her pulse climbed. By the time the crowd reached the turnstiles, the darkness was complete, combated only by the soldiers' two lanterns. A few of the farmers had thought to bring light sources and they paused to fire them up. Ellie had a lantern in her camping gear, but so far, the Kono troops hadn't paid much mind to the individuals under their charge. Ellie didn't care to do anything to draw attention. For her, the darkness was a friend.

Except when it came time to climb onto the tracks.

Light gleamed from the rails and from water dripping from the ceiling. Standing water pooled between the railway ties. It smelled like minerals and laundry. The soldiers jumped down and lifted their arms to help the children to the tracks. Ellie lowered herself, landing with a jolt to her knee. Dee passed down the packs, dangled her legs over the platform, and dropped.

Lantern light swung crazily through the metal pillars dividing the northbound tracks from the southbound. Once the park residents had reassembled on the tracks, the soldiers continued north. Ellie could hear her breathing echoing down the tunnel.

Dee reached for her hand. "You okay?"

"I'll manage."

"Remembering?"

Ellie was about to brush it off, like always, but the words rushed out in a murmur that only Dee could hear. "I dream about it. A walk just like this. The bodies piled just like they were—but sometimes they move. Faces of the dead watch me from the walls. They tell me to go on, and I can't hear it, but I know they're laughing. Because at the end of the tunnel, he's there with the bodies."

"Dad?" Dee whispered. Ellie nodded. Dee's eyes were sunken. "I dream about it, too. But the tunnel's empty, and no matter how long I walk, I'm always alone."

Ellie squeezed her hand. Feet sloshed in puddles. Small things skittered in the darkness. Rats, mostly, but once, a swinging lantern shined on the suspicious eyes of something larger and white. A chihuahua backed away from the travelers. Its muzzle was stained with blood.

Most of the walk was through tight, stale-smelling tunnels; every five or ten minutes, the walls widened to platforms, advancing from 86th to 96th to 103rd. The tracks were free of trains, but somewhere between 110th and 116th, the foremost lanterns illuminated a bed of white across the tracks. Ellie glanced up, puzzled how the snow had gotten in; she didn't feel a draft.

"Shit." The soldier turned back for a look at the refugees. "Why is this still here?"

He'd meant to hiss it to his partner, but the harsh noise carried down the narrow tunnel. The second soldier scowled at him, then stepped back toward the waiting farmers.

"The next bit isn't going to be a lot of fun," he said. "But I've got strict orders to take the tunnels all the way to the river. A minute of unpleasantness is a whole lot better than Distro scouts catching us in the streets."

He made a stoic line of his mouth and continued forward. The farmers followed. Some of them scooped their children into their arms. They all went deathly silent. Their feet clattered as if walking over scrap wood. It wasn't snow that covered the tracks. It was bones.

Back in the plague days, with the virus overwhelming the world, they'd used the tunnels for catacombs. Stacked the dead by the thousands. At first, it was to keep them hidden from those who weren't sick—so naive—but then it had become a practical matter. More than a million dead had been left on the island. Leaving them scattered across their apartments, cars, sidewalks, and workplaces would have wracked the city with secondary infections. So workers had continued to pile away the dead until the workers died, too.

This was what remained.

Bones turned under her soles. She lowered her weight, terrified of the idea she might lose her balance and plunge into the dunes of dead matter. Her toe knocked a skull across a railroad tie. Something dark fluttered behind it; Ellie yelped. The skull pulled free, leaving the scalp draped over the tracks, its blond hair floating on a dark puddle. She stopped and stared.

"Mom?"

"Just a minute." Others picked past them, carefully paying Ellie no mind. The soldiers' lanterns retreated down the tunnel. The plain white bones grew dim. Beside her, Dee became a silhouette.

"Come on," Dee said. "We can't fall out of the light."

"Don't rush me." Her voice was as hard as the femur under her left heel, but the words were lost in the click and rattle of the people moving ahead. Her feet felt locked down by an incredible weight, as if all the gravity of the ceiling and the buildings above it were resting on the crown of her head. Even if she could move, doing so would bring everything toppling down.

"He's the reason I'm alive—and you are, too." Dee reached for her hand. "Just take one step, Mom. I won't let you fall."

Ellie squeezed her eyes shut and forced her breath through her nose. She took Dee's hand. At the touch, her right foot jerked forward. A spree of ribs bounced away.

"Fuck," Ellie said. She made her left foot move too, and she was walking, bones rocking beneath her feet, grinding into the wooden ties. The farmers' passage had cleared the remains from a few patches of the rails and Ellie stepped in these spots whenever she could. Dee shadowed her, stopping when she stopped, pointing out toeholds in the white rubble. She was wordless but the hold of her hand was firm.

After a couple hundred feet, the bones trickled away. Ellie walked across bare ties and musty puddles. Her breathing returned to normal. She let go of Dee's hand and wiped the sweat of her palm on her hip.

At the 125th St. station, rubble blocked the way forward. The soldiers seemed to be expecting this; they set up next to the platform and helped boost farmers and children up to the concrete. Up at street level, brownstones overlooked a thin river. A single bridge crossed to the Bronx. Up and down the river, the other crossings had been smashed, pylons rising naked from the gray water, floes of broken concrete poking from the surface.

The Kono soldiers stood there a minute, listening. Ellie heard no more shots. The soldiers conferred, then looped up an onramp to the lone bridge. In its middle, two men in urban camo watched from behind a barricade set across the lanes.

One of the Kono raised his hand. The government soldiers beckoned him forward. He crossed the bridge alone, stopping before the barricade. Ellie couldn't make out their words. After a minute, the soldier crunched back through the snow to the refugees.

"You all bring your passports?" he said. The people nodded. He shook his head, smiling. "Told you you'd need them. Feds, man."

The group moved forward. Sections of snow had melted and refrozen on the lanes, leaving sheets of ice as thick and hard as the frozen banks of the pond in the park. Progress was slow. Ellie was grateful for the extra time to think.

The Fed soldiers walked from behind the barricade, hands out. The farmers lined up and fed them their passports. Ellie joined the end of the queue.

"What are we doing?" Dee whispered.

Ellie aimed her palm at the ground and gave a short shake of her head. The Feds jotted names on clipboards and let one family through at a time. Ellie shuffled forward until the last family passed through.

The Fed soldier smiled at her and held out his hand. "Passports?"

"We don't have them," Ellie said.

"We can't let anyone in or out without a passport. This is our national border."

Beside her, the Kono trooper's gaze moved across her face. He frowned. She considered trying the truth, but if they'd tortured Hobson, he may have given up their names.

"We're illegals," Ellie said. "The people who attacked the park—Distro—smuggled us in to work for them. It was awful. They barely fed us. We had no heat." She indicated Dee. "One night, my niece nearly froze. I woke up and her lips had gone blue. When I asked for more blankets, the guards told me to tear up my Bible and stuff the pages in my clothes. They said that's what the homeless used to do."

She gazed bleakly at the river. "What would it have cost them to find us another blanket? Five minutes? That's when I knew it was time to go. Two weeks ago, we escaped and went to stay in Central Park with someone the other workers had told us about."

The Fed soldier looked up from his pad. "And that was?"

"Nora Ryan. She lives in the boathouse on the lake."

"Why isn't she here?"

Ellie shook her head and bit her tongue until her eyes went bright with pain and the suggestion of tears. "She was ice fishing with her kids. I went to look for them, but they were gone. When the Kono told us they were evacuating the park..." She put her arm around Dee's shoulders. "My sister didn't make it through the Panhandler. I promised I'd always take care of her daughter."

"It's okay," the watching Kono trooper said. "I'm sure our people got your friend out of harm's way."

The government soldier tapped his pad with his pen. "Entering Manhattan illegally is a federal crime."

"Oh no," Ellie said. "What's the penalty?"

The man's mouth twitched. "Deportation."

"We won't try to come back," Dee said. "We promise. I just want to go home."

The soldier turned to his partner. The Kono trooper put his hands on his hips. "She wants to leave. Are you going to stop her because that's normally the punishment?"

"Get on over." The soldier stepped aside. "And do not let me see you back on this island without documentation."

Ellie nodded. Dee touched the man's arm as they walked past. "Thank you."

The refugees moved slowly across the bridge into the Bronx, helping each other over the slick patches of ice. They gathered in the wide street on the other side. The Kono stopped to confer. The one who'd helped Ellie talk her way past the bridge walked up and pulled her aside.

"You got food? Water?"

"Enough for a couple days," Ellie said.

"Hate to do this, but we can't take you any further. The camp is citizens-only."

"It's already been a long day," Ellie said. "Maybe we could just sleep there tonight."

The man wouldn't meet her eyes. "You said you worked for Distro. I can't compromise the security of our people."

Dee moved beside Ellie, taking her wrist in both hands. "What are we going to do?"

"It's okay," Ellie said. Dee's performance had her on the verge of a smile. She turned it on the soldier. "Thank you for getting us this far."

He smiled back. "Thanks for understanding."

Ellie shifted her pack's straps and walked to the highway crossing Third Avenue. It swept along the shore of the Bronx, hooking north. Within a couple blocks, banks of low apartments cut off line of sight to the evacuated farmers.

"How long until we double back?" Dee said.

"Oh, do you think we should follow them?"

"Unless you're getting bored."

"Of running down deadbeat leads in a hostile, icebound city?" Ellie said. "I don't think 'bored' is the word. But think, Dee. If they catch us following them after telling us to get lost, they'll lock us up."

Dee's shoulders swayed as she ground through the snow. "We'll follow their tracks."

"There's at least one advantage to this ridiculous winter."

After a quarter mile, Ellie left the highway and entered a bodega. The glass refrigerator doors had been smashed long ago and the aisles were plastered with a hard, cement-like layer of flour, sugar, melted ice, and ice cream. Tufts of the bags that had once contained these goods poked from the fossilized spill. Seeing this, Ellie didn't have high hopes they'd find anything useful, but she checked out of habit. After a pass through the store, she sat on a stool behind the counter, glad to be off her feet.

Despite all the fighting, chaos, and travel, it was hardly noon. Ellie let them decompress a while. They nibbled on dried fruit, drank water, repacked their canteens with snow. She wasn't sure if that was hygienic, but nobody had gotten sick so far. Rested, fed, and watered, she left the bodega and they doubled back. As they neared, Ellie cut dead east, keeping a couple blocks between themselves and the government soldiers on the bridge.

The Kono-led farmers were long gone. But their tracks stamped a blazing trail. One that continued to 138th, hung a sharp left, then continued north straight up the boulevard of Grand Concourse.

"Of course," Ellie said.

"What?"

"You'll see."

Back when she'd lived in lower Manhattan with Chip, she'd only been up this way a handful of times, and it was a longer walk than she remembered. The South Bronx looked the same to her as all the outer boroughs: row after row of dull-colored walkups over ground floor sandwich shops and bars and diners. Everything was gray and worn, patinaed by decades of millions of lives. As they walked along a blocks-long park, the subway tracks swooped up from the ground to their left, running brazenly above the middle of the street. Behind the train tracks, the coliseum soared into the sky. At the next intersection, the tracks of the farmers turned to approach it.

"Your dad would have thought this was pretty funny," Ellie said. "He was a Mets fan."

"He never quit talking about the Subway Series. He was so excited when he heard they were going to tear this place down."

Ellie laughed, then cut through the park, using the trees for cover. She stopped behind a wrinkled trunk and gazed down the street. A man with a rifle slung across his chest patrolled the pavement in front of the stadium gates. The off-white walls of the grandstands soared eighty feet or higher, but the top of the outfield bleachers were perhaps half that high, topped by scalloped white arches.

Footsteps scuffled through the snow. Ellie shrunk against the corner of an apartment block. Down the street, another group of refugees marched up to the gates.

Dee waited for them to pass inside before speaking. "What's the plan?"

"We can't be seen. Not unless we want to wind up in chains. If we find a back door, think you can pull your hairpin trick again?"

"I've only tried handcuffs," Dee said. "But how much harder can it be?"

As she waited for darkness to fall, Ellie circled around the back of the stadium, keeping her distance. The few doors set into the back and sides were plain metal. As the sun set, the guards pulled metal grilles across the front gates, sealing the stadium tight.

With darkness settling over the city, Ellie returned to the back walls to get to work. As they crossed the desolate streets, a cough sounded from inside the stadium. Ellie froze, gazing up at the concrete walls, then hurried to stand beneath them.

Their plan hit a wall every bit as solid. The doors were blank. No handles or locks; opened from the inside. Ellie swore and continued around the building.

"Here we go." Dee had found one with a lock. She got her towel from her pack, set it on the snow in front of the door, and knelt. The pin scribbled inside the lock. Dee probed, twisted. A tiny metal snap pinged on the wintry air. Dee went as pale as the snow. "Oh shit."

"Did it break?" Ellie said.

Dee bent the remaining portion of the pin back into shape and poked around in the lock. "I should have used a bigger pin. It's stuck."

"Keep working at it. Unless you want to shoot your way in the front gates, this is our only way in."

"Mom, it's not even moving."

Ellie curled her gloved hand into a fist, fighting to keep the annoyance from her voice. "Should we go find better tools? We've got all night if we need it."

Dee jerked to her feet and threw the broken pin into the snow. She sighed up at the high walls. Her expression went calm. "Who says we have to use a door?"

"Right, we'll just wait for them to open one of those windows they don't have," Ellie said. She looked up sharply. "Oh no."

"Why not? It's not that high."

"Broken necks, that's why. Or good old fashioned broken legs. If one of us snaps an ankle, the search is over."

Dee shrugged. "We've climbed stuff almost as steep as this in the mountains at the lake."

"With the aid of truckloads of climbing gear."

Ellie backed up for a better view of the wall. Most of it was blank, forty-plus feet and fenced with the scalloped frieze they may or may not have been able to climb under. But a small tower hugged the upper decks. A bank of windows striped each floor, recessed enough to provide toeholds. And there was a gap between it and the walls above the outfield bleachers. In that narrow space, the top of the wall was no more than 25 feet above the street.

Dee's was a young person's idea. Deeply stupid—but only if it failed.

Ellie made a face between a grin and a grimace. "If we waste all night on this, we may not get another chance."

"Then we'd better get moving."

They retreated into the brown apartment blocks. Ellie wasn't looking for much—she wasn't expecting to find crampons—but rooting through the stores and apartments, it proved impossible even to find a rope. Which made sense. Unless you were the rigger for a pirate ship, you wouldn't have much call for rope in the old days. With that thought, she considered heading to the river and trying to find a sloop to strip, but when she asked Dee, neither had recalled seeing boats on the way in.

Inside a hardware store, she settled on a garden hose. After testing its weight by slinging it over the sales counter and bracing it while Dee pulled herself up from the floor, Ellie unscrewed the head of a rake and knotted it to the end of the hose. While she worked on that, Dee scraped around with something in the darkness. She emerged dragging an aluminum ladder behind her.

"Why didn't I think of that?" Ellie said.

"You were so into MacGyvering that grappling hook that I didn't want to say anything."

It was still something like 9 PM. A little early to besiege the castle of Yankee Stadium. They ate dinner. Dee napped while Ellie watched the street from the front window. She shook Dee awake around midnight. Ellie coiled the hose over her shoulder and helped carry the ladder back to the outfield wall. At River Avenue, she looked north and south, crossed beneath the shadow of the elevated rails, and set the ladder against the wall.

It wasn't nearly tall enough. About twelve feet short, and the snow beneath its legs left it wobbly. Dee spotted it while Ellie climbed up. It shivered under her weight, threatening to spill her onto snow that wasn't deep enough to save her. She got down and the two of them mounded up snow around the base in case she dropped. Finished, Ellie got back on the ladder. She stopped at the second rung from the top, crouched down, and slung the rake-head over the wall.

It landed with a clank that sounded terribly loud. Ellie waited, motionless. A minute later, with no further noise from inside the wall, she reeled in the hose inch by inch, rake scraping against the other side. Without warning, it snagged tight. She tugged and it held firm. She took a deep breath and swung free from the ladder.

She hit the wall with a soft thump. Heart thudding, she climbed hand after hand, shoes scrabbling the concrete face. She looked down and shouldn't have. Dee's upturned face looked very far away.

Ellie steeled herself and reached for the top of the roof. She'd taken off her gloves for better traction and her fingers scraped painfully over the gritty stone. She found a hold, hauled herself up, and straddled the lip. Seats lined the stands five feet below her.

She beckoned to Dee, who climbed the ladder, grabbed hold of the hose, and monkeyed her way up the wall. They lowered themselves to the seats below.

Crop-stubble poked from the snow carpeting the field. Ellie laughed soundlessly. They'd converted it into a farm. The bleachers had been ripped out and terraced with soil. Thin smoke trickled from each dugout, which had been closed in. Starlight glittered on the snowy grandstands that rose from the park like the Rockies.

Muffled footsteps moved above them. Ellie pulled Dee down

beside her. In the tower overlooking the gap they'd climbed through, a silhouette moved to the fifth-story window and stared out at the silent grounds.

Ellie waited, motionless, until the figure left the window.

"It's too cold out here," she whispered. "They'll have them inside. You ready?"

Dee checked her pistol. "Let's go get our boys."

They rose together and descended into the darkness of Yankee Stadium.

29

Lucy learned that when you kill a president, just about everyone gets mad.

His guards yelped and went for their guns. The Kono went for theirs. A man in sunglasses pulled his pistol on her. Lucy blasted him with the umbrella's second round, then flung herself under the dead president's table. There, Ash's hand scrabbled for the gun on his hip. The president slumped over the padded booth, blood dribbling down the seat.

Guns went off, one after another. Men screamed. Bullets tore into her table, showering her with splinters. Ash's legs thrashed to get him away from the killing. He fired his pistol empty. The thunder in the room was so loud Lucy thought her ears would jerk themselves inside her head like a groundhog that's seen its shadow.

The gunshots stopped cold. A hairy arm reached under the table and grabbed her ankle. She tried to yank free, but it clamped harder, dragging her out. She curled toward it and bit down. The man swore, baritone, and rolled her out into the open. The president's bodyguards sprawled across the bar floor, blood soaking their sharp black suits.

Ash breathed hard, hair askew. "What the fuck was that?"

Lucy's shirt had twisted as the Kono goon hauled her from under the table. She tugged the hem into place. "I was negotiating."

"By murdering the President of Manhattan? Do you know how many federal soldiers are about to swarm this place?"

"None."

Ash ejected his magazine onto the floor with a thump. He

slammed a new one home and whipped the pistol's slide closed. "Know what, I think you're right. Bill! Get me a platter. A silver one."

Hesitantly, a man rose from behind the bar. "Is this for real?"

"If we send the Feds this girl's head, there's a small chance they won't burn us out of the city."

"If that's how you want to play it," Lucy shrugged. "Or you could convince them to burn out Distro instead."

The violence in Ash's eyes went guarded. "You got three seconds to convince me you're not crazy. Then I take a very close and violent look at the exact shape of the madness in your head."

"That old dead bastard told us he was going to see Distro next. Seems to me he ought to complete his itinerary."

"We bring him downtown." Ash started slow, then the words piled out of him. "Dump him in their territory and set them up to take the fall."

"The Feds will be hot for blood," Lucy said. "Maybe you'd just brokered a deal with the prez there. You're just as outraged by his death as they are. Seems to you the Kono would offer your services to participate in a joint raid."

He swept his hair back from his forehead. "I've got a mole in City Hall. He'll feed them the right story."

"You'll need to move fast. Get the bodies in place and your story in the Fed's ear before Distro knows what's happening. I can tell you where they put their rooftop scouts. You could kill them and scatter the bodies around the Feds' to make it more convincing."

"You're crazy." Ash shook his head and laughed long and loud. "Completely out of control. And you know what? I like that a lot more than the President's bullshit deal." He gestured to the man with Lucy's toothprints in his forearm. "Lock her up."

"Huh?" Lucy said. "I thought we had a deal!"

"And until this little dream of ours comes true, I'm keeping you around as a last-ditch bargaining chip." Ash clapped his hands. "Let's move!"

The big man who'd grabbed Lucy motioned to the stairs. She sighed and climbed up to her room. Inside, the man set a chair six feet from hers and held his pistol in his lap. A woman came up to get the location of Distro's scouts from Lucy. She complied agreeably.

The woman left. Downstairs, people thumped around like the

proverbial elephants. Minutes later, the limo engine gunned to life and grumbled down the street.

"What's your name?" Lucy said.

The big man had kept his eyes on her the whole time. "Why?"

"First off, I'm sorry I bit you. That's playground stuff. Second, if you wind up executing me, I want to know how to find you in Hell."

The man chuckled low. "Roger White. Do you really expect this to work?"

"The frame job?" Lucy scrunched up her nose. "I dunno. But I bet the federal crimelab is just a guy and some rubber gloves. If they find their commander-in-chief shot to shit surrounded by dead Distro, you think they're gonna wait to build a DNA tester before they get their vengeance?"

Roger shrugged. "Guess we'll see."

She guessed they would. She sat around a while, then stood. Quick as a jumping spider, Roger pointed his pistol at her head.

"Is it a capital crime to want something to read?" she said.

"I'm guessing this isn't in your nature, but try asking first." He set down his gun.

She grabbed the book about the man who got betrayed by his buddies and imprisoned but came back to stomp all over their asses. She probably ought to be worried, or scheming what to do if Ash failed the frame-up and came for her head, but she couldn't muster up the concern. The dice were thrown.

A couple hours later, a crowd of people thumped around the bar some more. Lucy continued reading. Hours later, with the overcast sky going dark, a tremendous cheer erupted from downstairs.

Lucy grinned. "Sounds like I've been pardoned."

Rhythmic steps climbed the stairs. The door cracked open. A delicate hand emerged and crooked a finger.

"Come on out," Ash said. "I owe you a drink."

Downstairs, Ash explained over his trademark shots of tequila. They'd driven the limo down to 34th, exterminated the nearby Distro lookouts, and tossed the bodies around the car, planting a shotgun on one. After dragging the President and one of his guards out to the pavement, they'd torched the limo, just to confuse things further, installed a couple soldiers in nearby apartments to keep an eye out for unwanted witnesses, and ran off.

According to Ash's mole, word of gunfire had gotten to the Feds within minutes of the frame job. The Feds didn't normally bother to check up on every single instance of gunplay, but given the time and the President's route, they'd dispatched soldiers on the spot.

"I meet with the Veep tomorrow," Ash grinned. "I think our mutual friends are about to get an eviction notice."

"I want in on the fight."

"You've really got it in for Nerve, don't you? If I ever shoot you, remind me to put two in your head."

Before retiring to bed, she asked Bill the bartender for a snack of bread and butter. Upstairs, she wrapped the bread and stuck the butter in some Tupperware and packed it into her bag.

In the morning, Ash had already left to meet with the Feds. Lucy hung around downstairs, ears sharp for news. Plenty of Kono had witnessed the truth—hell, they'd participated in it—but Ash had sworn them to secrecy on pain of death. Those who hadn't been there largely seemed to believe the circulating story: Distro, under the belief the Feds were behind the raids on their coastal supply depot, had ambushed and assassinated the President. Now, they holed up in their tower, confident the government would be as impotent as it always was.

Ash rolled in that afternoon. He kept mum about the meeting, but ordered Bill to collect fresh ice from the courtyard. He drank his margarita with a smile.

Some news must have gotten out. As the afternoon transmuted into evening, Sicily got fuller than Lucy had ever seen it. Men and women packed shoulder to shoulder, drinking and chatting with a hivelike energy. At seven sharp, Ash strode behind the bar and lifted his hands. The crowd went silent.

"Last call's in one hour," he said. "Tomorrow, we go to war."

Inebriated cheers exploded from one end of the room to the other. Lucy grinned fit to split her face.

"Come early and come armed," Ash continued. "In twelve hours, we march. In 24, Distro will be done. And the city will be ours."

He bowed. As his troops hooted and hollered, he took a shot in each hand and downed them one after another. For the next hour, liquor flowed furiously to all corners of the room. At eight, as promised, Ash ordered everyone home. When some of them laughed, he drew his pistol and fired it into the ceiling. Lucy couldn't tell if that was Ash being Ash, or if he was more than average drunk.

Either way, the bar cleared out. Lucy had paced herself well and felt no compunction against chugging the last half of her beer. She waited for the crowd to thin, then climbed up the stairs.

"Hey," Ash said. "You."

She paused, hand on the wooden railing. "What's up, boss?"

He sauntered forward. "What's your deal?"

"How you mean?"

"Are you just in this for revenge? Or because you believe in something?"

She cocked her head. "Both."

He nodded, climbing the stairs until he stood just below her. He wasn't any taller than her and he had to look up. "So I get to have you around for a while."

"Think you're that lucky?"

"I make luck like a cobbler makes shoes." He moved onto her step, standing nose to nose. She was dead certain he was about to put the moves on her—and right after she'd concluded, for the fifth time, that he was gay—and she decided on the spot to go with it. He reached up and patted her on the cheek. "See you at the war."

He turned and jounced down the steps. Lucy wasn't sure if she should feel relieved or frustrated, but she had some fun dreams that night.

She slept patchily. Each time she woke, the window was the same amount of dark and quiet. A knock woke her for the last time. Still dark out, but she could hear people shuffling around in the snowy street. She swung her feet out of bed, went to the bathroom, and put together a light travel pack. She only needed enough food, water, and first aid gear to get her and Tilly to the Knickerbocker Country Club and the car she'd parked there. Felt like a lifetime had passed since she'd taken the camo Charger, but in reality, it had been right around two months.

In the bar, troopers ate breakfast and drank what Bill claimed to be genuine coffee. Some fortified themselves with stronger fluids. Ash didn't show up until the grandfather clock ticking behind the bar read 6:58. His people mustered outside to meet him. He didn't say a word, just took them in with a sweeping and bloodshot gaze, nodded, and headed south.

He'd put together a nice little army. Hard to get a good count while she walked in the middle of the irregular mass, but Lucy figured he had at least a hundred troopers, maybe half again that much. Must have pulled all his people from the park. Made a lot of promises. Distro wasn't long for the world.

Two hours into their relentless march down Broadway, they entered Times Square, and faced a uniformed federal force Lucy was surprised to see was just half as large.

Ash lifted his arm, halting his people, and crossed the broad street alone. From the other side, a man with short white hair and the craggy face of a Roman emperor detached from his soldiers. They met in the middle and shook hands.

Ash turned to his people. "This is General Dalton. He's got a few words. Respect them."

"Let me make this very clear." The general's voice boomed between a movie theater and a glitzy sports pub whose lights had long ago gone dark. "You are a militia operating under government purview. That means you are to follow orders. We will offer Distribution the chance to surrender. If they set down their arms and exit the building willingly, there will be no shots fired. Do you understand?"

The lines of Kono troops looked to Ash, who nodded. They followed suit.

"In the event they do not surrender," Dalton continued, "we will execute the plan. Have your people been briefed?"

"Of course." Ash glanced over his shoulder, mugged a comic whoops-face, and winked at the Kono.

"Very good. Let's move!"

The general jogged back to his men, who jogged in place, then fell in step around him. The Kono circled around Ash. He beckoned his division leaders closer, spoke quickly, and sent them back to the rank and file. The plan dispersed through the troops: the Feds would assemble on the entrances on 34th and 33rd. The Kono would cover the doors on Fifth Avenue and, once the Feds had achieved penetration, would provide the main thrust of the invasion, supported by the professional soldiers. With Distro's defense of the

Empire State Building a "black box situation," that was as far as the strategy extended.

Lucy doubted Nerve and whoever else had taken over would surrender. Too arrogant by half. But if it came to it, she'd take the first shot herself.

The tiered tower threw its shadow over lesser edifices. A couple blocks away, the combined force split into three groups, with most of the Feds circling around to keep a block of buildings between them and the target until the final approach. Joined by General Dalton and a third of his troops, the Kono jogged to Fifth Avenue and slowed to a walk. There had been little chatter after Times Square, but it went dead now.

The Kono split into their divisions; they'd added a sixth to account for the new conscripts. South of 35th, they advanced in parts, with three divisions taking cover behind old cars while the others jogged down the street, took up position for themselves, and trained their rifles on the building while the others caught up. They cycled this way a quarter of a block at a time. The tower reached higher and higher until it seemed to be all that Lucy could see.

They crossed 34th and took up final position behind the cars lodged against the opposite curb. Fed soldiers moved into place along 34th. Powdered snow gusted down the vacant streets. Lucy got down behind a Jetta, swiped the snow from its trunk, and braced her rifle.

Soldiers set up with the shuffle of boots and the sneaky rustle of weapons. Somewhere, a bird twittered. Dalton left his men and walked to the middle of the street.

"I am General Dalton, commander of the Federal Army of Manhattan," he announced to the waiting tower. "We have arrived to accept the complete and unconditional surrender of the organization known as the Distribution, AKA Distro. Emerge at once, unarmed, and by law of the island— "

A single shot cracked from above. The general went silent, tipped back his head, and smacked to the ground like a dropped plank.

The street went so quiet you could hear the snow hissing over itself. Then every gun there ever was opened up on the tower. Feds and Konos hammered the building. Windows burst. Pebbled glass hailed into the streets. Smoke poured from the guns and the tower's walls. A squad of government soldiers broke from the safety of the cars and sprinted toward the brassy front doors. A few shots answered, tufting the snow, knocking one trooper to the ground. The others pulled up along the building's face. Two soldiers swung around the doorframe, lobbed something through the shattered windows, and retreated tight against the walls. A pair of explosions crashed through the ground floor, gouting smoke into the street. Dust stained the snow gray.

Before it cleared, the soldiers flung a second round of grenades inside the lobby. They banged like a string of firecrackers. The Feds charged into the clouded lobby. Ash stood, shrieked like a castrati barbarian, and led the Kono in after them.

Bullets whined past Lucy, whacking into the pavement. She ducked her head and stumbled through the broken doors. Fed rifles flashed in the smoke.

"Clear!" one shouted. Others replied in kind.

Dust sifted to the marble floors. A handful of dead men lay in various states of blown-uppedness, but far fewer than had attacked Central Park. Across the lobby, a uniformed soldier jogged around the corner and beelined toward Ash.

"They've cut the elevators," the man said. "Everything's dead."

"Son of a god damn bitch," Ash said. "The stairs? What do you want to bet they're holed up at the very top of the building like complete assholes?"

"Could be bad. Doesn't take much to defend a staircase."

"We could siege the place. Starve them out." Ash wiped dust from his eyebrows. "But I don't want to have to walk all the way down here again. Let's start climbing and see what they've got."

The soldier nodded and returned down the hall. The mass of troops followed. They set up around the staircase door, rifles trained on it. The soldier moved to it, counted down, then flung it open and leapt to the side.

The door banged against the wall. Soldiers rushed inside. "Clear!"

Their feet rang on the steps. The Kono snaked inside in a thin line. Dozens entered before Lucy stepped through the door. Dark metal stairs zigzagged up beige brick walls. Electric bulbs shed dim light. Footsteps echoed above her. It smelled like sweat and must. Something racketed above them.

"Incoming!"

A fax machine tumbled past Lucy, deflected from a railing, and smashed into the stairs directly below her. People screamed. A tail of debris clattered after it, peppering the troops, who leaned over the railing and shot up at the unseen assailants. In the tight space, the gunfire was so loud it hurt. Coffee mugs sailed from above, exploding in ceramic shards. Keyboards clattered down, spraying plastic keys. Lucy pressed herself against the walls and covered her head.

Feet pounded up the steps above her. Shots crashed back and forth. The gunplay ended quickly. A man's moan drifted down the stairs. The troops climbed on. Three landings later, Lucy walked past a tangle of bodies. A man and a woman pressed bloody cloth to the chest of a Fed soldier whose white-gray camo was stained red.

A few floors up, and a telephone fell from above, the receiver swinging wildly from its wire tether. Binders fluttered from the darkness and landed with heavy whacks. A whole tray of dishes descended in an icy shatter of porcelain. Half a plate sliced past Lucy's cheek, drawing blood. She pressed her palm to the wound. Above, the frontline soldiers charged up the steps but were forced down by gunfire. The defenders retreated a few floors, then resumed throwing debris. The rattle of kipple was too loud to hear the orders Ash shouted from above. At one landing, Lucy stepped over a body, its head mashed beneath a busted TV. The wounded sat against walls and put pressure on the flow of their blood.

A frenzy of shots battered down from the stairwell and ceased abruptly. The climb continued. A couple floors up, six Kono lay dead across from just three defenders. Lucy hadn't fired her assault rifle since the salvo they'd let loose after the general's death. There had been no targets. The stairwell was a grade-A chokepoint. She began to doubt.

But things got quiet for a while, relatively speaking. Feet smacked steps. Hard breathing whooshed from all sides. Spent brass clinked underfoot. Lucy climbed and climbed, thighs burning. Each level was identical to the last, a monotony of white walls and gray steps.

Above, runners sprinted ahead, returning minutes later to report in to Ash and the acting Fed commander, both of whom were too far ahead for Lucy to hear. That was all right by her. She didn't need to know the ins and outs. She just needed to find the civilians—and she had a pretty good idea they'd be hiding behind the defenders. If she turned out wrong, and she had to search the building floor by floor, office by office, she'd probably take a flying leap from the top deck.

Sixty floors up, Ash called a rest. According to the soldiers beside her, the scouts had met no resistance on the staircase ahead, but had heard men shouting behind the door to the 86th floor.

"Top of the main structure," the trooper said. "Observation deck. Suppose Distro's plan is to let us climb ourselves to death?"

Too soon, Ash called down from above, ordering them on. They took the remaining floors in under ten minutes and bunched up on the flights leading to the 86th, Lucy's face pointed at the ass of the man ahead of her. The troops fell quiet. Men whispered above. Hinges creaked. And then the world exploded.

Grenades banged outside the stairwell. Machine guns opened fire with crashing drumbeats. Men yelled in shock and pain.

"The burner!" Ash hollered, his knifelike voice slicing through the ruckus. "Bring up the burner!"

Yellow light flared above. The whoomp of flame was followed by rising screams. Feet thumped away. The gunfire faded, muffled by the walls. The troops above her jogged up the stairs. She followed.

Blood slicked the 86th floor landing. Past the doorway, the ground was snarled by a makeshift, torn-down fence of the extendable, seatbelt-like tape they used to shape lines of people at airport counters and had most likely used to corral the lines to the observation platforms. Bodies sprawled in the toppled poles, belts of fabric tangled around their limbs. The room was a yawning lobby enclosed with windows on all sides. The floor was scorched. Blackened bodies lay twisted on the marble, hands crisped into claws. It smelled like burnt fuel and charred hair and skin.

Lucy swung to the right of the door and scanned the grounds. The main fight was shaping up around the south side of the tower. The enemy had retreated to the observation deck, firing through doorways and windows on the advancing Feds and Kono, turning the lobby into a killing field. Fed soldiers took cover behind a ticket counter and pounded the windows with fire, allowing Kono to rush through the doors on the east side of the lobby to circle around on the Distro resistance.

All of which was very interesting, in a gruesome, terrifying, stenchy sense, but what really caught Lucy's attention was the women and children beyond the north windows. She ran to the northern doors and exited onto the platform. Bitterly cold wind slashed across her face. A bullet crashed into the limestone frieze behind her. She flung herself prone onto the bare deck—the wind had torn the snow away—and snapped off a shot at the old man who'd fired on her. He gasped and staggered into the wall fencing off the deck, which was waist-high stone topped with a tall metal grille that curved inward at the top. Civilians shrieked and fled down the deck.

"Lucy?"

Lucy whirled. Tilly tottered alone across the painted concrete. Her gaunt face had a yellow bruise below the left eye.

Lucy ran to her and grabbed her arm. "It's time to get out of here. I'll roll you down the stairs if I have to."

"I know," Tilly said vaguely.

"I mean the whole damn city. Distro and everyone in it is going down. And if the truth gets out, this won't be the last of the fighting."

Tilly nodded and turned for a last view of the city. For the first time, Lucy saw how high they'd climbed. The city rolled away to the north, mile after mile of sky-climbing towers, a patchwork of gray stone, black glass, and white spires. Streets carved straight rivers between the urban canyons in a lattice of snow. At the horizon, the towers faded into the wintry mists, giving Lucy's eye the idea that it might be endless, stretching forever into the fog, a globe-wrapping sea of buildings. And all those people, lost. It was so beautiful and sad it made her heart hurt.

Shots blared from the south. Lucy guided Tilly to the doorway and peeked inside. Bullets crossed between the Feds holed up behind the counter and the Distro troops beyond the windows, but the Kono were about to pincer them. If it worked, the fight wouldn't last much longer. She took Tilly's hand and crossed the lobby in a dead sprint. Bullets whirred off the concrete floor. She threw herself through the stairwell door.

Inside, the landing had been converted to a triage center. Doc looked up at her, glasses smudged with blood, then returned to his patient, whose neck spurted blood with each pump of his heart. Lucy ran down the stairs, Tilly's feet slapping right behind her.

Lucy didn't talk for a good long while. Isolated in the stairwell, with the gunfire a faint crackle overwhelmed by the sound of their shoes, it was as if she'd been caught up in a dream or a spell, one that might snap if she were to interrupt it with speech.

"I've been waiting for you to come back," Tilly said finally. "He's been beating on me ever since you tried to take me away."

"Why didn't you just run?"

"I wasn't allowed out by myself. I tried to talk to the guards, but he'd scared them too bad. They wouldn't even talk to me."

"He comes off like he's got a level head, but he's a psycho." Lucy shrugged her pack up her shoulders. "Probably have to be to run an organization like this, but he takes it to another level. First time I met him he was happy to execute me. And he did business with aliens. Can you believe that?"

"He said he'd killed you," Tilly said. "But I never believed him. I told him, 'Then show me the body. Because people been wanting Lucy dead for years, self included, and she always gets out fine.' And he wouldn't. So I knew you were alive." She jabbed Lucy in the ribs. "So what took you so long?"

"He shot me, for one. Then it took a couple weeks to convince the rest of the city to burn Distro to the ground. Next time, I'll try to move my ass."

Tilly laughed. It sounded good. "What did I do to deserve a friend like you?"

"Your dad's the only one who ever cared whether I made it to the next day. You want to thank somebody, thank him."

"All these years I thought he wanted you there because you were pretty. That you were trying to take him away from me. Why do we think such dumb things when we're young?"

"We start off thinking the whole world is about us," Lucy said. "Once you learn how little it cares about you, that's when you stop taking things personal."

Bodies littered the next landing. They stepped around them, shoes squicking in the blood. For several flights afterward, the stairs were a mess of broken glass, busted laptops, shattered monitors, and loose paper. Lucy kept her head on a swivel to watch above and below, wary for Distro snipers looking to score a cheap kill, but they were alone together. They reached the ground floor landing without bumping into a living soul.

Tilly was unarmed. Lucy unstrapped her new pistol from her ankle and handed it over. She turned the handle of the door and eased it open, keeping her body back from the gap. At the other end of the corridor, two Kono aimed their rifles at her motion.

"It's Lucy," she said, ducking from sight. "Got someone I need to question."

"Come on out," a man said.

Lucy stepped out, gun at hand, then gestured Tilly after her. She walked down the marbled corridor, ready with a cover story, but the soldiers said nothing. Tilly crunched over the broken glass and held open the front door.

The cold street never smelled so good. From the sidewalk, a smattering of Fed troopers watched them walk away. Lucy headed up Fifth Avenue and made a left on 34th, meaning to get away from the tower as quick as she could. Tilly's grin was as broad as the street. The few Fed soldiers holding down 34th eyeballed them, but offered no challenge. At the intersection, Lucy crossed Sixth and hooked up Broadway past an itty-bitty park separating the diverging boulevards. Trees hung over their heads. Lucy stopped and turned for a last look at the tower. The building thrust above the neighboring structures, head held so high you could hardly see the smoke wisping from its upper deck. Gunshots cracked the sky. Distro must have been putting up a pretty good defense.

Footsteps crunched from the park. Tilly's head snapped back. Nerve's hand clamped her mouth shut. He grinned and put a pistol to the side of her head.

30

The bleacher staircase descended to a deeper darkness than the night. In the concrete cavern of the stadium interior, Ellie stopped to let her eyes adjust to the starlight trickling through the high windows on the outer wall. It was a world of silhouettes and suggested shapes, so dim she could hardly make out her feet against the bare floor. After a minute, she resumed walking, moving so slowly her shoes made no scrape at all.

Concession stands lined the walls. The air was frigid and smelled of dust. Ellie didn't know the stadium or where they were going, but by all indications, the Kono had stashed a few hundred refugees here. It was the heart of winter. Six hours to search before dawn crashed the party. Assuming they weren't caught and killed first.

She crept along the inner wall. Starlight shined on refrozen patches of meltwater. Ahead, dim light glowed from beyond the curve of the wall. She touched Dee's arm, pointed. Dee nodded. They edged closer. Metal buttons on Dee's coat were rubbing together and Ellie had half a mind to stop and cut them off, but the noise was so soft it was often lost in the whine of the wind outside the stadium.

The light grew until she could nearly read the signs above the concessions. Around the bend, it glared from the lantern of a soldier standing in the middle of the floor, back turned.

Ellie shrank into the frame of a closed door, pulling Dee down beside her. Dee's buttons clicked. The guard glanced over his shoulder, lantern shifting. He held position, frowning vaguely, then walked away down the wide corridor, taking the light with him.

Ellie let out her breath and planted her hand on the concrete beside the door. A warm draft moved over her fingers. She bent her face to the sill.

"What are you doing?" Dee whispered.

Ellie lifted her other palm. Dee went quiet. A thin, warm wind touched Ellie's cheek. She got up and pressed her ear to the door, but heard nothing.

"It's warm in there," she said, practically mouthing the words. "Warmth means people."

Dee cocked her head and nodded once. Ellie reached for the handle. It moved. She turned it inch by inch until it disengaged with a click. She paused for any response from inside, then swung the door inward.

It opened to a pitch black tunnel. Lukewarm air washed past her face. Dee moved past her. She guided the door closed, sealing them in blindness. She grabbed the hem of Dee's coat and walked forward, trailing her fingers along the wall, shuffling her feet in case they bonked into something solid.

Her fingernails ticked against a frame. She pulled Dee to a stop and put her ear to the door. Muffled snores sounded from inside. Ellie groped for the handle and entered. To the side of a door, a lantern burned with just enough light to navigate the room, which was filled with single beds. These in turn were filled with bearded men and middle-aged women. Directly to her right, Mr. and Mrs. Talcott slept in neighboring beds.

She exchanged a look with Dee, then began moving row to row. Ellie recognized a few of the faces. Farmers they'd questioned in the park. With no sign of Quinn or the sheriff, they returned to the tunnel, shuffled forward, and encountered another door, which entered to a room identical to the last: bare concrete—former storage, maybe—and crowded with beds. Halfway through the search, Ellie bent over an old man for a better look at his face. He sat straight up.

"Looking for something?" he whispered.

"Our room," Ellie said, adrenaline booming through her veins. "It's so dark we got lost."

"Wrong one."

"Are you sure?" Ellie stalled. She glanced up and was heartened to see Dee continuing to go row by row, but there were still multiple beds to check. "I don't know anyone they housed us with, but we talked to a couple people on the walk in. Quinn, a young man. And Oliver, an older fellow. Are they here?"

"I don't know them," the man said. "Now hush up so I can sleep."

Dee reached the end of the room and gave her a thumbs up. Ellie smiled politely at the old man and left, easing the door closed. They continued down the black tunnel. Ellie's fingernails scraped across another door, but she could feel a wall right ahead of them, too. An exit.

She entered the side room. It was utterly dark. Ellie knelt with her back to the room, got a candle from her bag, and lit it with a Bic. The low orange light showed a room identical to the two others, but half the beds were empty. A woman turned in her sleep, disturbed by the light. Metal clanked. Her wrist was handcuffed to the frame of the bed.

Ellie's heart climbed in her chest. She moved from prisoner to prisoner. They ranged in age from a young man no older than Dee to a bald geriatric with a face like a potato. Strangers, all of them. She gritted her teeth and stepped back.

A cane was propped against the foot of the old man's bed. Ellie blinked, strode up to it, and brought the candle close. The cane was plain dark wood with a curved handle, but instead of a rubber stopper, its tip was tapered. She'd once seen it impale leaves in the woods of Saranac Lake.

They'd shaved his head, his white goatee. In the darkness, she hadn't even recognized him.

"It's the sheriff," she hissed. Dee crossed the room in a blink. Ellie put her hand over his mouth and gently shook his shoulder.

His eyes popped open. Without his beard, the lines in his face stood out starkly, making him look ten years older. But the light in his eyes was as sharp as ever.

"Oh," he said. "There you are."

"Are you okay?" Ellie said. "Have you seen Quinn?"

Hobson rubbed his eyes with his left hand. His right was cuffed to the bed. "These fellows aren't fans of the Geneva Convention, but if your girl can pull her tricks on this bracelet, I ought to be all right. As for Quinn? No. But I have an idea."

The man in the bed next to him stirred. Ellie pressed her finger to her lips. Dee set down her pack and got out a hairpin. She popped the cuffs in seconds. Hobson shook out his wrist, grimacing angrily, then pulled on his shoes and coat. He took up his cane and stood, knee buckling immediately. Ellie swooped in to catch him.

"Thank you," he murmured. "I believe they've outsourced their nutrition program to the Viet Cong."

"Outside," Ellie said.

She moved for the door. He leaned on her for support, but there was no weight to his frame. She'd noticed him shedding pounds on the walk down from the lakes, but in the few days he'd been imprisoned, he'd become downright gaunt. In the hallway, Dee closed the door behind them.

"I'm surprised they didn't kill you," Ellie said.

"They had a mind to," Hobson said. "Until I let slip that I was a former airplane mechanic."

"You were?"

"Heavens, no. But I imagined they'd have a hard time throwing away a resource like that." He blinked at her in the candlelit tunnel. "How'd you get in here?"

"Standard 'hose-rake grappling hook into the outfield bleachers' maneuver. You think you know where Quinn is?"

"My captors brought me straight here. Under less warlike conditions, it's a sort of POW/labor camp; for the first few days, it was pretty quiet. Except when they were shouting at me about you two and our interest in their mandatory labor program. But I was able to take a look around. Then, this morning, they employed me in setting things up for the new arrivals."

Footsteps clumped behind one of the doors. Ellie gestured to the exit. It fed into another tunnel. Gently, she closed the door. Another creaked open in the hallway they'd just left. The steps faded the opposite way.

"As I was saying," Hobson whispered peevishly, "due to my mechanical 'expertise,' I was set to work reversing a lock—so it could only be operated from the outside."

"Bit thin," Ellie said.

"Did I neglect to mention the room was windowless? And that several of the beds were equipped similarly to my own?"

"Now we're talking. Can you get us there?"

"Surely. It was the visiting team's shower."

He led them through a maze of tunnels. Past open doors, she caught glimpses of hoes, rakes, shovels, and other agricultural supplies. Hobson trudged up a flight of stairs, holding Ellie's upper arm for support, then wound down a long, curving corridor of gray cinderblock. It ramped down to a four-way intersection. To the right, Ellie smelled woodsmoke. To the left, a desk stood to the side of a short hallway that made an immediate right turn. Steady lamplight spilled from the turn. So did the echoed conversation of two men. Ellie backed up the hallway.

"The locker room," Hobson whispered. "The showers are just beyond it."

Ellie touched the butt of her gun. "Who's in there?"

"Shall I go ask?"

"We can't go in blind. There could be twenty men in there."

"We could take them by surprise," Dee said.

"Then what?" Ellie said. "Shoot them and tip off the whole stadium? Tie them up? What if Quinn's not in there? Do we cut their throats and stuff them in a locker so their friends won't find them while we're searching the Yankees' side?"

"Jeez. It was just a suggestion." She lifted her nose. "Something's burning down there. Why don't we go stoke it up? Make so much smoke they get scared and run out?"

"Good concept," Hobson said, "but much too complicated. Why don't I run off and make some noise? When they investigate, you two slip inside."

Ellie pulled the knit cap from her head; all this moving around had heated her up. "You can hardly walk, let alone run. What if they catch you?"

"Then please be as resourceful in that rescue as you have been in all else." He pointed up the hall. "Meet me at the service tunnel in five minutes. If you've got Quinn and I'm not there, get out of here."

"You really need to stop trying to sacrifice yourself," Ellie said. "One of these times, it's going to work."

He chuckled lowly. Ellie blew out her candle. They returned to the intersection and she hid behind the desk with Dee. Hobson gave them a little wave and jogged down the tunnel opposite the clubhouse. Dee slid out her pistol. Moments later, glass shattered in Hobson's direction. The men in the locker room went quiet. Wood rattled. Two men ran through the intersection clutching baseball bats.

Ellie waited for the light of their lantern to fade down the hall, then poked her head around the corner to the locker room. A couple candles flickered in the empty space. Dead flatscreens were arranged in a circle in the middle of the ceiling. Rather than metal gym-style lockers, the ones on the walls were like mini-closets made of rich, red-toned wood. Seeing no one, Ellie jogged across the room, startled by a distant bang of metal on cement. A door stood in the back wall. Ellie turned the lock and opened it to a cool, dark room.

She lit two candles and passed one to Dee. The floors were brown travertine, the walls small white tiles. Cots were arranged beneath the showerheads. Men sat up blinking, barring their forearms over their eyes. A few had their ankles chained to the legs of the cots, but most were unshackled. Dee rushed between them, candle whirling as she moved from face to face.

"Who are you?" one of the shackled men said.

"I don't see him," Dee said.

"Quinn Tolbert," Ellie said. "Is he here?"

The shackled man scratched his red beard. "If I can help, what do I get?"

Dee jogged across the room, face strained with panic. Ellie stood over the pale man. "Answers. Now. If they're good, we'll see about getting you out."

The man closed his eyes and shook his head. "I have the strangest condition. When I've got chains around my ankles, I can't remember a darn thing."

Ellie balled her fist. "I don't have time for this."

"Dee?"

Quinn wandered around a tile wall. It had hardly been a month since she'd seen him, but after the combination of time and distance —both physical and emotional—Ellie hardly recognized him. He was thin as a yardstick, ribs protruding from his light brown skin, the bones of his face hard and sharp. His eyes burned like headlights in a fog.

Dee was lean and tough from the last month's hunt, and when

she threw herself at him, he staggered back, arm out for balance. She steadied them against the tile wall and they hugged each other until Ellie thought all four of their feet might lift from the floor.

Chains clanked on tile. The red-haired man shook his ankles at Ellie. "Wonderful moment. Now why don't you share the love and get me out?"

"Sorry," Ellie said. "We're on a tight schedule."

"That's too bad. Because if you walk out that door, I'm going to scream until every one of those Kono bastards comes running."

Ellie turned on him, resting her hand on the butt of her gun. "Not a good idea."

"Bullshit," he laughed. "A gunshot's the one thing that would bring them faster than a scream."

"Want to test that?"

"Go ahead."

He had nothing to lose and she had no doubt he'd yell if she tried to leave. She could try to knock him out, but if you rattled someone's brain hard enough to shut it down, there was a good chance it would stay down for good. And pistol-whipping the skull of a chained-up man was the kind of thing that might prompt the other captives to start screaming on his behalf. She might gag him, but she'd have to bind his hands, too. There'd be a scuffle. He'd shriek his lungs out.

A whack to the head, then. Do it fast and everyone would be too shocked to react. She glanced back at Dee, who stood in front of Quinn, watching.

The door banged open. Two men walked in with bats and lanterns. "What's going on in here? Who's got the light?"

He saw Ellie and Dee, armed and geared, and froze.

Ellie swung her pistol on him. "Get down on the ground with your hands on your head."

He backed away half a step. She cocked the hammer of her pistol, which was entirely unnecessary, but movies had conditioned people to react to this by stopping whatever they were doing to take your orders instead.

"You're fine," the red-headed man laughed. "Back out and get your people. She won't do it."

"I will." Dee stepped beside her, pistol in hand. "Down on the ground or I'll put you down."

The two Kono set down their lanterns and bats and lowered themselves to the cool stone floor. "Don't shoot."

"Where are the keys to these men's cuffs?"

"What are you doing?" Ellie said.

"They're slaves, Mom. I'm not leaving them."

It would make things messy. There were nearly twenty men crammed into the shower and sauna. Released into the stadium, they wouldn't stay quiet for long. Then again, if she left them here, the captives would be guaranteed to throw a fit. And she knew that, if she walked away now, she'd be seeing every one of those twenty faces each night in her dreams.

Ellie walked in front of the prone Kono soldier. "Where are the keys?"

Facedown, he shook his head. "I don't know."

She leaned her knee into the back of his neck and scraped the mouth of the gun into his scalp. "The keys."

"Third locker on the left as you walk in," he blurted. "Behind the brass panel."

She met Dee's eyes. "Go get them. Everyone else, stay still."

Dee exited the shower, Quinn in tow. The redhead considered her from his bunk. "Who are you?"

"Baker, farmer, mother, spy."

"Huh?"

"Here's the deal," she said. "We're cutting you loose. The concourse is guarded and the front gates are locked, but if you're quiet and you're smart, you can make it to a side door."

The man smiled. "Maybe we'll just go with you."

"No," she said. "You won't."

Something in her voice killed his smile dead. Dee returned with keys. Ellie covered the room while Dee unlocked handcuffs and chains, then relocked them around the wrists and ankles of the two Kono. While the unleashed prisoners put on shoes and coats and took up baseball bats, Ellie hurried with Dee and Quinn to the intersection outside the locker room.

Hobson peeped around a corner. "Young master Tolbert!"

"There's a crowd of former slaves about to turn this place into a madhouse," Ellie said. "Which way to the field?"

The sheriff pointed down the opposite tunnel. "Dugout's through there."

Ellie hustled down the tunnel, glancing back to make sure the other three were keeping up. Their candles flickered, gleaming from the monitors of dead flatscreens hanging from the corners. Warm air fluttered down the passage, which soon became sweltering. A sloppy wooden door blocked the dugout. Beyond, they'd turned half the dugout into a fireplace, venting the smoke into the field and piping the heat back into the stadium. Warm as it was, she couldn't imagine it was enough to heat the lukewarm tunnels.

But she didn't have time to examine their infrastructure. She blew out her candle, stepped over sunflower shells frozen to the floor, and climbed past the railing to the snowy field. The looming bleachers were black and silent. Snow glittered on the stubbled ground. She got out her binoculars and homed in on the gap in the outfield wall. The seats around were empty. About four hundred feet to the bleachers.

She nodded to the others. They walked quickly along the third base wall, crunching through the snow beneath the terrace-farmed seats. After the tunnels, the cold was startling. Hobson moved stiffly, but without assistance. Quinn and Dee held hands. With pride both maternal and warrior, Ellie noted that Dee walked on his right side, leaving her right hand free to handle her pistol.

Shouts rang out from inside the concourse. A gun banged. Ellie kept her pace, moving into what had once been the outfield. Another shot echoed across the stadium. Snow spurted from the ground to Ellie's right.

"Run!" She ducked and sprinted through the snow, scanning the grandstands. Light flashed from the stands behind home plate. As the others ran past, Ellie knelt, aimed at the silhouette in the stands, and fired three quick shots. The shooter hit the dirt and disappeared. Ellie waited, sighting a foot above the terrace. Through the scope, a shadow rose, so dark and distant it might have been a trick of her mind. Starlight gleamed on glass. Ellie fired. The shape dropped.

She marked the spot, then ran ten yards toward the outfield wall, where Dee was boosting Quinn up the bullpen fence. Now that she'd put some distance between herself and her last muzzle flash, Ellie got down in the snow and aimed at the stands again. The terrace was motionless. At the bullpen, Hobson scrabbled over the wall, feet kicking. Ellie popped up and ran, zigzagging.

She reached the wall without taking any more fire. She shouldered her rifle and leapt up the wall. Quinn and Dee grabbed her arms. She kicked against the padded fence, got her chest above the edge, and dropped down the other side. They helped each other up the short fence to the bleachers and climbed past the seats to the outer wall. The rake head was gone.

Ellie dropped her gear and handed her rifle to Hobson. "Boost me up."

While Hobson covered, Quinn and Dee lifted her up the wall. She pulled herself up and straddled it. The ladder had fallen. The hose was a dark coil in the snow more than twenty feet below.

"Oh boy," Ellie muttered. She turned and met Dee's upturned face. "I'm about to break my neck. If I survive, watch out for incoming rakes."

Dee nodded. "If you don't, try to land in a way that would make a good cushion."

Ellie scooted along the wall, putting space between herself and the toppled ladder. Snow had drifted against the stadium, but there hadn't been a significant fall in days. If she broke her leg, she might not be able to walk home until it healed. If it healed. And if they found a way to keep themselves sheltered and fed until the snow melted.

Wind gusted over the wall, rocking her. A shot boomed somewhere inside the stadium. She breathed in and out and slid off the wall.

Cold wind rushed past her. A short shriek leapt from her throat. It was so far—and then her feet punched through the snow, and she tried to bounce forward, transferring her momentum into a shoulder roll. Her neck bent hard and she waited for the pop. Her feet flipped over her head and whacked into the snow. She lay on her back, neck and left ankle throbbing, body shot through with pain.

No time for a breather. She forced herself up, dragged the ladder to the wall, wedged its feet into the snow. She looped the rake-topped hose over her shoulders and climbed up. At the top of the ladder, she braced herself, got the hose in hand, and lobbed the rakehead over the wall. It hit with a clank. The hose tautened as the others reeled it in and secured it to the other side.

Quinn appeared atop the wall. He dropped the packs to Ellie and shimmied down the hose to the ground. Hobson climbed the wall and paused at the top to catch his breath. His face was as pale as the snow. He saw Ellie watching, smiled resolutely, then turned his back and climbed hand over hand down the hose. A few feet from the bottom, his hold gave out and he fell heavily into the snow. He gasped in pain. Ellie ran to him.

He waved her off, scowling. "I'm fine. Less meat on my backside than I'm used to, that's all."

He crawled out of the drift and pushed himself upright. Above, Dee hoisted herself up the wall and skedaddled down the hose as if she'd been training in competitive hose-climbing since childhood.

"Everyone good?" Ellie said.

Quinn and Hobson were both breathing hard from the climb, but they nodded. Dee grinned. "Better than I've been in weeks."

Ellie smiled back, turned from the stadium, and headed north. They didn't rest until they'd put an hour and a couple miles behind them. On the edge of a vast park, with Quinn and Hobson sitting on a bench to catch their breath, she gazed south, but Manhattan's skyline was lost in darkness and fog.

They had a long road ahead of them. There was too much snow and too little food. But Dee was still grinning, and so was Ellie. After all that bicycling, snowshoeing, hiking, scavenging, hunting, questioning, and fighting—across weeks of time and hundreds of miles of space—they had their family back.

Home was just a matter of time.

31

Nerve steadied the gun against Tilly's head. His eyes were bloodshot. The nail of his trigger finger had been split. Yellow fluid crusted its tip.

"You've seen better days," Lucy said.

"This one's shaping up better than I hoped," he said, inclining his head in a shrug. "When I saw you marching in, I thought you'd wind up coming back this way."

"You're some kind of coward," Lucy said. "Hiding in the trees while your people die for your crimes?"

"You're so much better?" he said. "Your people are dying, too. And you're running off with the prize."

"Those ain't my people."

"But I doubt they'd be fighting if not for you." He laughed harshly. "Thought so. Now drop your guns. Umbrella, too. That trick's as stale as a bag of prewar Ruffles."

She stared at his seeping fingernail. "Tilly used to have a dog named Max who got an infection just like that in his paw." She let her rifle fall to the ground. "Had to amputate when it went green."

"No more head games, Lucy. Don't forget the one on your ankle."

"He was a great dog. Would do anything for a treat." She unhooked her umbrella from the strap of her pack, knelt, and laid it across her foot to keep it out of the snow. She hiked up the shin of her jeans, revealing the little pistol, and laughed. "Tilly, you remember the trick we taught him for the talent show?"

Tilly nodded slowly. "Yeah."

Lucy ripped open the velcro strap and slung aside the .22.

Empty-handed, she made a gun of her left hand and pointed it at Tilly. "Bang."

Tilly's eyes bulged. She dropped from Nerve's grasp like a stone, playing dead. Lucy rocked back, swinging up the barrel of the umbrella with her foot. Nerve shouted wordlessly and fired his gun through the space Tilly's head had just departed. Lucy grabbed the handle of the umbrella. He jerked the pistol toward her. With Tilly lying flat in the snow, Lucy pulled the trigger.

The recoil knocked her back into the snow. The shot sprayed a layer of Nerve's upper body to the seven winds. He staggered back, gasping, chest a landscape of red. His gun hand shook. Tilly scrambled for the pistol. Lucy chambered her second shell and fired. Nerve's forearm vanished. His hand flopped into the snow.

"Saved you a trip to the doctor." Lucy picked up the assault rifle and sighted in on his head.

"Nope," Tilly said. "This one's mine."

Nerve tried to speak but choked on the word. Tilly aimed the pistol and squeezed. His head jerked to the side. A stream of blood splashed the snow and steamed. The air smelled like burnt powder and flame-touched steel.

"Best move before someone comes to see who's shooting," Lucy said.

Tilly frowned at the body. "Wish there were some dogs around."

"What for?"

"Well, to eat him."

Lucy laughed and hung the rifle from her shoulder. "You're a sick one."

"Learned it from you."

"Anyway, in this city, there's plenty of rats happy to do the job." She started up Broadway. "Long walk ahead of us."

Tilly marched beside her, head craned to stare at Nerve's body, reassuring herself he was well and truly dead. "Where we headed?"

"I got a car stashed outside town. Been sitting in the cold awhile, but with any luck the battery's still good. If not, I guess it's a really long walk."

The girl laughed. "You had this all planned."

"Much as you can plan anything."

The towers looked down on them. There would never be another city like this. Maybe that was a good thing. She gave Central Park a wide berth, angling west to the highway fronting the Hudson. The snow on the wind-blown lanes was thinner than inside the city and it was the easiest walking Lucy had done in some time.

Safely away from the battle, she took stock of their condition. She was pretty tired. Might need a nap before she tried to drive. Meanwhile, Tilly didn't have a pack of any kind. Her feet would be soaked. Would need to find some spare socks and shoes on the way to the car. The snow could make the drive an adventure, too. Well, whatever. They'd deal with it when the time came.

They took a brief rest on 76th and Lucy shared some of the bread and mini-calzones she'd squirreled away from Sicily.

"What do you want to do once we get home?" Tilly said, crumbs stuck to her lips.

"Fall asleep for about a week."

She laughed. "After we've napped, feasted, and drank till we don't know who we are."

"I dunno," Lucy said. "With Distro gone, this city's going to be short on the finer things in life. You ever thought of becoming an entrepreneur?"

"Shit, Nerve never shut up about that stuff. I got a veritable crash course in marketing."

"You handle the business, I handle the grow." Lucy nodded and chewed off a rind of sourdough. "Get us a boat, sail up here two-three times a year. Sounds fun, right?"

They got up and continued on, going silent as they skirted Kono's uptown territory. Beyond the park, as they walked past a ritzy campus, they started telling each other about the last few weeks. Tilly had had a real time of it—soon as he'd learned about her, Nerve had kept her prisoner in the tower—but she didn't seem too shaken up by it. She laughed and marveled at Lucy's stories of getting shot, of seeing the aliens touching down in the marshy field, of battling Distro in the snowy woods of Central Park. Lucy left out a few parts, like when she shot the President of Manhattan, but by the time they reached the steel span of the George Washington Bridge, there was still plenty of story to tell.

Up on the bridge, two Fed soldiers came out from their shack, rifles slung over their chests.

"What's up, Phil?" Lucy said. "How y'all doing?"

Phil cocked his head. "When a pretty girl knows your name, it's always a good day. What can I do for you?"

"Just heading out of town. I found my friend. This here is Tilly."

Tilly smiled and stuck out her hand. "Pleased to meet you."

"Likewise," Phil winked.

His partner moved beside him. "Passports?"

Lucy patted her pocket. "Know what, my bag got stolen."

"I left mine in my room," Tilly said. "I didn't know we'd be leaving."

The second soldier frowned. He had dark brows and lips that never seemed to quit moving. "We can't let anyone through without a passport."

"I respect the law as much as the next man," Lucy said, "but there's been some extenuating circumstances. This morning, I helped your people assault Distro headquarters. My friend here was being held prisoner. We just want to get home to Florida."

"Not without papers."

"Man, you saw me come in here," Lucy said.

"We see lots of people." The man shifted his rifle. "Things have been heavy lately. If we don't do things by the book, we could face a court martial."

Phil gritted his teeth. "Listen, how about we run down to City Hall for the records?"

Lucy snorted. "By the time you get down there, they'll be closed. You're gonna walk all the way back here in the dark? Where are we supposed to sleep?"

Tilly's eyes darted between them. "Maybe we can find an apartment."

"So we get to freeze all night? What if someone catches up with us? Like one of Nerve's buddies who saw us take him down?"

The second soldier's face went guarded. "Were you involved in the commission of an assault?"

"For Pete's sake, he was a war criminal." She huffed, breath hanging in the air. "You want to head down to City Hall and satisfy your curiosity regarding our status, by my guest. Our names are Lucy Two and Tilly Loman. And we're going home."

The man moved around her. "I can't allow you to do that."

"Sure you can," Lucy smiled. "You're a big boy. You can do whatever you want."

She took Tilly's arm and clumped through the snow past the barricade. The day was overcast and the river looked as gray as molten lead. A single flake of snow tumbled past Lucy's face. She looked up and sighed at the clouds. A long day was about to get longer.

"Stop!" Phil screamed.

Something kicked Lucy in the back so hard her legs dropped from under her. At the same time, a gun went off. She slipped into the snow.

"Oh shit," she said.

"Lucy!" Tilly got down beside her, touching her back, her chest. The girl's hands came away bloody.

The second soldier stood in front of the barricade, rifle smoking, drooping from his hands like a spent erection. His eyes shined with the intensity of a mistake that can't be undone. His throat worked.

"I told you no!" He mashed his lips together. He raised the gun again.

To his right, Phil brought up his rifle and shot the man in the back of the head. The soldier toppled facedown into the snow.

"Lucy," Tilly said. "You been shot."

Lucy nodded numbly. "Got my legs."

"No, it's your back. You're bleeding." Tilly turned to Phil. "Come help her!"

Back down the bridge, Phil gaped at the body of his partner. He glanced at the girls, hands hanging from his sides, then ran away toward the city, snow flying from his shoes.

"Hey!" Tilly hollered. "God damn it!" She eased Lucy's pack from her shoulders and got out the spare shirt. "You got any scissors?"

"Left side pocket." Despair fluttered in her chest like a bat trapped in a bedroom. To have come so far and go down like this—trigger-happy psychopath who took her brush-off of the rules as a personal affront—she wanted to pound her fists and kick her heels, but her legs refused to move.

The scissors rasped as Tilly cut the shirt from her back. Tilly pressed the spare shirt against her wound, but the sensation stopped halfway down Lucy's skin. It felt like the one time her mom had taken her to the dentist. On the drive home, her mom had passed her a Coke. The drink was cold on half of Lucy's lip, but on the other half, she felt nothing at all. The Coke had dribbled down her face and beaded on her lap and her mom had laughed.

"Oh Jesus," Tilly said. "We got to get help. You stay right here, okay?"

"There's nobody there," Lucy said. "Just run, Tilly. Car's at the Knickerbocker Country Club. It's a Charger. Assholes painted it camo. I left the keys inside the back bumper."

"No! You listen and you listen good. You came all this way for me. After all you done, ain't no way in the world I'm going to leave you on this bridge." Tilly forced a smile to break across her blood-smudged face. "I know I don't have to tell you to be brave."

Tilly grabbed Lucy's rifle and sprinted back down the bridge into the city. Lucy shouted after her, but the noise came out a croak. She didn't know if she meant to command Tilly to turn around and run to the car or to beg her not to leave her alone.

Tilly's footsteps faded into the distance.

And Lucy understood she wasn't alone. She couldn't feel her legs or her belly, but she felt his breath on her neck, cold as the arctic wind. She had fallen with her back to Manhattan, but she torqued herself around, dropping on one elbow and grabbing her dumb thighs, pulling them around until she faced the city and the man with the scythe.

His cowl gazed down from the ashen clouds. His scythe was the river, a dull gunmetal sweep. His presence killed even the water in the air, hardening it into bone-white bits that swirled around her like slain flies. As cold as it must have been, she felt nothing but a perfect peaceful warmth.

And Lucy got it. His games had not been the thoughtless malice of a cat with a cricket. He had been testing her. Training her. Until she'd become his sweet blond angel. Ready and able to cut his swath across Manhattan and harvest its wicked crop. She had done her deed. Here, at last, was her reward.

As Lucy died, she remembered three things.

First, she remembered Mom laughing about the day she would die, because she always remembered this.

Second, she remembered when Vic Loman had asked her to

always look out for Tilly. Lucy had sworn with such hot vehemence that the life flooded back to his eyes and she thought, for just a moment, that her promise had cured him. The life and light faded from his eyes not sixty seconds later, but the smile twinkling in them lasted past the end. She remembered that look whenever she needed to be strong.

Last, she remembered something from so long ago she couldn't be sure it wasn't a dream. She was young. A grassy field. She'd wandered far from home but knew her mother wouldn't notice. The grass was so green she tried to eat it but it tasted no good. The sun was as warm as a hug. A forest grew from the end of the clearing and Lucy ran to it but stopped in awe.

The forest buzzed and thrummed and pulsed. A sea of sound swept her forward. She ran into the woods and the trees were alive: their skins writhing with wings and legs, each little piece piping its own note, until ten million different tunes became one vast song. She laughed but the forest's noise was so dense she couldn't hear herself. Each step she took stirred a cloud of whirring bugs, but the song played on, too big to ever be broken, vibrating down to the core of her heart. She stayed inside it until the sun went away, then went home to her empty house.

As soon as she woke up the next morning, she ran back to the clearing and stopped on her heels. The woods had gone silent. In the shadow of the canopy, she walked on empty shells—but when she closed her eyes, she could still hear the forest singing. Letting her know that a song, like a life, will always play in the hearts of those who were there to hear it.

She'd been so young, she'd forgotten all about it. Because she hadn't needed to remember until now.

On the bridge to the island, snow touched Lucy's face and melted into streams. You might have thought she was crying, but you would have been wrong.

EPILOGUE

When she saw her house, Ellie stopped so suddenly the sheriff plowed into her back, knocking them both down. They laughed, snow soaking their backsides, and helped each other to their feet.

Hobson grinned down the trail. "Forget you'd put that there, did you?"

She brushed snow from her pants. "I never knew how much a home could mean to me."

The four of them watched it a moment, as if it might jump up and leave, then continued along the trail to the north of the lake.

Three days after leaving New York, a warm wind had blown in from the southwest, stealing the snows from the fields. Puddles riffled shin-deep by the shoulders of the highway. Birds splashed in the melt and pecked at soil they hadn't seen in weeks. After so long slogging around in snowshoes and soggy socks, walking on hard pavement with dry feet felt like flying.

They took advantage of the melt to do some hunting. The deer were out in force, nibbling exposed shoots. Dee knocked one down first try. They took a day to clean and dress it, to salt and smoke as much of the meat as they could and roast a full haunch then and there. The fresh meat tasted like it had been born for them.

The thaw didn't last. Ten miles past Albany, another storm rolled in, dumping four inches of wet, heavy snow onto the woods and fields. Ellie sighed and passed out the snowshoes she'd continued to carry just in case.

But it was nothing like the blizzard that had hit them on the way down. And though Hobson and Quinn tired easily, Ellie had no worries. They had all the time they needed. She and Dee carried the packs and took turns breaking trail through the snow. Ellie intended quite seriously to never make a trip like this again, but if events conspired to break her vow, she'd make sure to drag Dee along with her.

Though she expected Dee would require little if any convincing.

Twelve days after jogging away from Yankee Stadium, they'd reached Ellie and Dee's house and, after taking a long look and brushing off the snow from Hobson's tumble, they continued straight to George's. He stood outside his front door, staring straight at them, as if he'd been waiting there the whole while.

"Quinn!" George scrambled from the porch. Quinn dropped Dee's hand and ran. The two men smacked into each other, clapping backs, laughing like old fools. They parted and George's eyes shined as strong as the lake in July. "Are you okay?"

Quinn shrugged his narrow shoulders. "They didn't feed me too good. I could hardly keep up with this crew."

"Spring planting will fix you right up," George winked. He shook hands with the sheriff, hugged Dee, and moved to face Ellie. "You did it." He smiled, but the lines around his eyes were deep and sad. "I should have gone with you."

Ellie shook her head. "We didn't know he'd been taken. Someone had to stay and search."

"I looked every day." He gazed across his fields and the trees beyond. "Did Old Man Winter take it out on the city as bad as he did the mountains?"

Hobson rolled his eyes. "As if the five boroughs had conspired to commit treason."

George laughed, shoulders bouncing. He covered his face with his hand to hide his tears. Quinn embraced him.

Dee moved beside Ellie and whispered in her ear. "Thank you."

When Tilly ran back to the bridge with the man who claimed to be a surgeon, she found Lucy gazing up at the clouds. Snow frosted the lashes of her eyes. She was smiling like she'd never quit.

The doctor set down his bag. "I'm sorry."

Tilly sank beside her and took Lucy's hand. The fingers were cool but the palm was still warm. "It's not fair. She was tougher than anyone I knew. How come one stupid bullet can erase all that?"

"Most likely because it was traveling at two thousand feet per second." The surgeon sighed and rubbed his face. "Sorry. Long day. Would you like help with the burial?"

"No." Tilly wiped the tears and snot from her face. She probably looked a fright. She felt guilty for having the thought. Lucy would have smacked her. Or more likely lashed her with a phrase that would ring in her ears for weeks. "You can't put her in the ground like some damn rutabaga. This girl burned like a forest fire."

They smashed down the soldiers' shack and laid the timbers in a pyre. She found a lighter in Lucy's bag, lit a candle, then used that to get the fire going.

"My daddy would be so proud of you," Tilly whispered.

And then, knowing it was what Lucy would have done, she turned and walked away.

The car was right where Lucy said it would be. It was reticent to start, dying as soon as Tilly quit turning the key. She didn't know what she'd do if it refused to kick over.

"Walk, shithead." Lucy's voice was so clear in her mind she busted up laughing. After three more tries, the engine caught, grumbling exhaust through the garage.

It wasn't what you'd call a fun drive, but the snow gave out around Washington. From there, she tried to take it in one fell swoop, but pulled over the first time she nodded off. After what Lucy'd been through for her, she didn't dare fall asleep at the wheel.

She rolled into town on fumes, having burnt every last gallon from the jugs in the trunk. Her house was right there where she'd left it. Some possums had broken in and crapped up the place, but after a couple days of sweeping and scrubbing, she had it all back to normal.

In town, the same people as ever were still kicking around. Beau. Lloyd. A few new faces drawn to the rumble of the boys' motors and the easy crops and fishing. Lloyd came around some, but she sent him away. He hadn't tried to bring her back. In a way, this whole fuck-up was his fault. If he'd been able to keep it in his goddamn pants around Tilly's best friend, Tilly would never have felt compelled to run off to the city—and Lucy wouldn't have had to chase her down.

At the same time, she knew she owed it to Lucy to live like the night would never end, but she didn't deserve it. Because it was her own fault, too. After a while, Lloyd and the others quit coming around.

She did what she needed to get by. Farmed the yard and those around her. Fished from the docks. Sleep, work, eat, shit. Didn't seem worth it. Summer came, humid and awful. She had taken the rifle and the umbrella with her from the city and on most nights she sat on the back porch listening to the bugs with the moonlight glinting from the steel.

Would be so easy. But the thought of being found in the grass beside a loaded umbrella was so stupid it made her stomach hurt.

The night she came closest—out of her head on moonshine, katydids screaming from the trees—and found out the barrel of the umbrella tasted like cool blood, she ran to her daddy's grave for answers, tripping in the unkempt grass. And she found that he was as dead as everyone else. She slept there, careless whether she woke again.

The following hangover was the kind you told your grandkids about. Her knees were scraped. Palms muddy. Legs itchy with bug bites. Mouth as dry as Morocco. Lucky she hadn't pitched headfirst into the creek.

There was no magic moment. She didn't think life worked that way. But bit by bit, little by little, the crushing weight eased from her chest. She scared up some paint and redid her house. Started to fence in the neighboring yard. It was there that Lloyd found her, dirt clinging to the sweat on her forearms, hair plastered flat to her temples and neck.

"Ain't seen you in a while," he said. "Heard the work."

"Gonna farm me some pigs."

He got a real dubious look on his long face. "Pigs?"

She stood and arched the small of her back. "Everyone's got to do their part to move the world forward. I mean to bring back bacon."

Lloyd nodded, swiveling his head to take in the dig. "Need a hand?"

She squinted into the sun. He wasn't the brightest of men, and she had historical doubts about his fidelity, but there was an earnestness to him that might flower into a person you could spend time with. "Who doesn't?"

He grinned and walked across the yard.

It was a lovely ceremony—and simple. A few friends from Lake Placid and the farms around Saranac. A table of George's fried chicken, Ellie's bread and cake, Dee's potato salad, and Sam Chase's fresh-caught whitefish curry, the existence of which shocked Ellie on multiple levels. It was held not in a flower-strewn gazebo erected for the occasion, but there in the grass on the island with the tower.

Hobson said he was not only a sheriff, but an ordained minister. Ellie didn't know about that—over the course of their brief acquaintance, he'd also claimed to be a cop, a P.I., a professor, and an airplane mechanic—but no one could prove otherwise, and he acquitted himself with the same cheery aplomb he applied to all things, be it toasting his morning bread or being taken prisoner by New York gangsters. His ceremony was agreeably non-denominational. At the end, Dee and Quinn kissed, then smushed Ellie's cake in each other's faces.

George walked up to her while the kids were still laughing. "It is my life's goal to make you as proud to be a part of my family as I am to be a part of yours."

Ellie hid her smile. "How long did it take you to think that up?"

"Three days," he laughed. "But it's true."

"Look at him." She nodded at Quinn, who scooped Dee up, white dress trailing, and ran with her for the shore. She wrestled from his grip and shoved him back, pointing at her dress. He pressed his palms together in apology, then flung his arms wide and fell back into the lake, tuxedo and all. "You raised the only son here who can keep up with my daughter."

George grinned, surprised, and fetched a handkerchief from his vest pocket to dab at his eye. "You'll have to excuse me. I believe I took a stray piece of cake to the left orbital."

Ellie was about to snort, but with sudden and terrifying clarity, she understood that, within a handful of years—if not months—she would become a grandmother.

Two years later, she walked out to the back porch. The night was so hot you'd think they'd broken nine sins, and Lloyd was enjoying one of the homebrewed beers that had made him the most popular man in town.

She sighed noisily. "One little sip?"

He crooked a brow. "You think?"

"How about you just wave it under my nose?"

He laughed and pushed himself up from the cushioned chair they'd liberated from a neighbor. The beer inside the bottle was room temperature. She missed the way cold bottles used to sweat. Lloyd brought the mouth under her nose and wafted it back and forth.

She inhaled deeply. "God, I can't wait to get this thing out of me."

He laughed some more. "Well, we got to come up with a name first."

"I got that covered. If it's a girl, we'll call her Lucy Three."

"Is that so?" he said. "And if it's a boy?"

"You kidding? Lucas."

He swigged his beer, fortifying himself for an argument, then sighed and laughed and set his fists on his hips. "There's no escaping that girl, is there?"

"We should pray ours is half as tough."

"Mm. Just so long as she ain't too much like her."

"No," Tilly said. She laughed so loud it came out like a honk. "Lord, no. With Lucy, a little went a long way."

But she missed her still, sometimes so fierce it was like pins dragged across the contours of her heart. Lucy had been a lot of things. A friend. A bitch. A force of nature. The most frustrating human Tilly had ever known.

And irreplaceable.

Crickets sang from the yard. They weren't in harmony, but they didn't care who heard. Tilly closed her eyes and smiled.

Late spring wind dragged hot black clouds across the skies of Albany. Ellie used the scope of her rifle to watch the six-sided office burn. A part of her hoped someone would flee it, but they'd been too thorough for that.

"What do you think?" Dee said. "Should we string the bodies above the highway? Change the sign to say 'Property of the Colsons'?"

Ellie pulled away from the scope to stare her down, but Dee couldn't keep a straight face. Ellie scowled. "I'm not sure how I feel about you joking about this."

"Yeah, I'm sorry. These slave-taking assholes deserve a twenty-one-gun salute. Think we can get Robert Frost for the eulogy?"

Out of habit, Ellie shaped a rebuke, but she discovered she didn't believe it. She moved the rifle to the crook of her arm. "We'll catapult them into New York. Kill two birds with one stone."

It was Dee's turn to stare for hints that she was joking.

"Fear not," Hobson said. "Your mother's not that ambitious. Anyway, I heard from Nora. Our departure from the stadium touched off a full-scale riot."

"And we just cut off the supply of replacements," Dee said. She grinned at the sheriff. "High five!"

He held up his hand and awkwardly received her smack. Ellie smiled. This had been the last step; Hobson's posse had dealt with the men in the black fedoras the same day the strike team left for Albany.

The office burned on. Other than the tower of smoke, it was a peaceful summer day. She expected it to stay that way for some time.

But the world had grown large. Dark. She could no longer see beyond the horizon. She doubted it would be the last time the people of the Lakelands would have to take arms to protect each other.

She thought they'd be up for the challenge.

She'd fallen in love as soon as she'd stepped on the island.

The deep blue sea. The haze on the horizon. The wind that took the edge off the warmth. And that warmth—one day after the other, as dependable as the tide, a literal paradise. The only time it came close to cool was the December evenings when the wind blew in from the sea. You could put on pants then, if you felt like it, but you'd feel pretty foolish once the sun was down and the wind left with it.

She and Alden had set up at one of the hotels north of Lahaina. It was a little dry on this side of the island, but the resorts and the town made for easy scavenging, and it was plenty green in the foothills above town. They didn't even have to farm in an organized way. Pop some seeds in the ground and let nature do the rest. Mangos, pineapple, taro root. She had been hesitant, at first, to take the fish—all those stripes and colors made her think poison—but after a little research, she learned which ones were safe to eat. Often, she and Alden flippered into the reefs with spears, as much for the fun as for the catch.

A handful of people lived in town. Others built shacks on the shore, but there was enough space that everyone had their own beach. She heard one of the villages in the jungle on the northeast lump of the island was more or less untouched, but even with bikes, the trip was a bitch—winding roads, bridges collapsed into waterfall-carved ravines, cliffs on all sides.

Anyway, each morning she got to wake up to the sight of Molokai and Lanai warming in the haze like great green whales. She was jealous she hadn't been born here.

But Alden was getting restless. He was well into his teens, and with few girls around, and no video games, go-karts, or wrestling shows, he spent too much of his time kicking down the beach with his hands in his pockets. These days, she could hardly talk him into practicing kung fu.

For his birthday, she came up with a surprise.

"Let's go!" Tristan clapped her hands over his face, yanking him from sleep. "Time to go camping."

He rolled over. "We live in a camp."

She slapped his face. "But it's not a volcano."

He opened one eye. "Volcano?"

"Haleakala," Tristan said, relishing the word. "We'll hike up and spend the night. The sunrise is supposed to be the prettiest thing on earth."

He sat up, sheets bunched around his tan torso. "Will there be lava?"

"I think it's extinct. But I bet the Big Island is still bubbling. If we can handle Haleakala, maybe for your next birthday, we can sail to Kilauea."

"Cool."

He got up without further complaint. She had a bike trailer for hauling fruit down from the hills. She loaded it with gear and they rode across the saddle of the island that connected the western lobe to the larger eastern lands. Haleakala tumbled up from their middle, green and gorgeous in the morning mist. It took most of the day to climb, but as they neared the rim of the crater, the view commanded the seas to all sides. Tristan closed her eyes and shivered. The high wind was the first time she'd felt real cold in years.

But up on the lip, her blood froze solid. In the hidden slopes of the caldera, bushes grew in orderly rings. Crablike monsters stalked among the concentric rows, tentacles waving in the sun of paradise, spiked feet piercing an earth that wasn't theirs.

ABOUT THE AUTHOR

Along with the *Breakers* series, Ed is the author of the fantasy trilogy *The Cycle of Arawn*. Born in the deserts of Eastern Washington, he's since lived in New York, Idaho, and most recently Los Angeles, all of which have been thoroughly destroyed in one of these books.

He lives with his fiancée and spends most of his time writing on the couch and overseeing the uneasy truce between two dogs and two cats.

He blogs at http://www.edwardwrobertson.com

CPSIA information can be obtained at www.ICGtesting.com
Printed in the USA
BVOW06s1845211215

430754BV00024B/321/P

9 781492 184751